CONDITION BLACK

'Gripping, informative and well-paced' – *Independent*

'Gives the many-sided suspense story such a wealth of factual detail, it is in the same class as Frederick Forsyth's best' – *Daily Mail*

'Combines the landscapes and rugged manhunts of Geoffrey Household with the dispassionate sniper's eye of Eric Ambler' – *The Times*

'I would class this book with the first-rate achievements of Graham Greene, Charles McCarry and Le Carré' – *Chicago Tribune*

HAVE YOU READ . . . ?

HARRY'S GAME

A British cabinet minister is gunned down by an IRA assassin. The police trail goes cold, and undercover agent Harry Brown is sent to infiltrate the terrorist organisation and uncover the killer. It's a race against the clock, and one false move will be enough to leave him dead before he reaches his target.

THE FIGHTING MAN

Gord Brown, a former SAS soldier and Gulf War veteran, comes to the aid of Guatemalan resistance fighters caught up in a hopeless war against a brutal military dictatorship. Also pitted against them is another veteran, an American helicopter pilot who owes Gord his life, but, in the depths of the South American jungle, the past is forgotten.

THE UNKNOWN SOLDIER

In the depths of the Arabian Desert, American and British counter-terrorism experts are desperately searching for one man. If they fail to find him, he will re-emerge in a teeming western city, carrying only a suitcase that will wreak havoc and devastation when detonated.

THE WAITING TIME

On a winter's night at the height of the Cold War, in a small East German town, a young man is killed by the secret police. All the witnesses are terrorised into silence. But Tracey Barnes heard the shot that ended her lover's life, and she will wait for as long as it takes until there arises the opportunity for revenge.

ABOUT THE AUTHOR

Gerald Seymour spent fifteen years as an international television news reporter with ITN, covering Vietnam and the Middle East, and specialising in the subject of terrorism across the world. Seymour was on the streets of Londonderry on the afternoon of Bloody Sunday, and was a witness to the massacre of Israeli athletes at the Munich Olympics.

Gerald Seymour is now a full-time writer, and six of his novels have been filmed for television in the UK and US. CONDITION BLACK is his twelfth novel.

For more information about Gerald Seymour and his books, visit his Facebook page at www.facebook.com/GeraldSeymourAuthor

GERALD SEYMOUR

Condition Black

HODDER

First published in Great Britain in 1991 by Harvill

This paperback edition first published in 2013

1

Copyright © Gerald Seymour 1991

The right of Gerald Seymour to be identified as the Author
of the Work has been asserted by him in accordance with
the Copyright, Designs and Patents Act 1988.

A CIP catalogue record for this title is available from the British Library.

Book ISBN 978 1 444 76023 1
eBook ISBN 978 1 444 76024 8

Printed and bound by Clays Ltd, St Ives plc

Hodder & Stoughton policy is to use papers that are natural, renewable
and recyclable products and made from wood grown in sustainable
forests. The logging and manufacturing processes are expected to
conform to the environmental regulations of the country of origin.

Hodder & Stoughton Ltd
338 Euston Road
London NW1 3BH

www.hodder.co.uk

To Gillian, Nicholas and James

Verses quoted in this novel are from 'On Receiving News of the War' by Isaac Rosenberg, 'Futility' by Wilfred Owen, 'The Listeners' by Walter de la Mare (by courtesy of the literary trustees of Walter de la Mare and the Society of Authors as their representative), 'Old Song' by Edward Fitzgerald, 'The Man he Killed' by Thomas Hardy and 'The Owl' by Edward Thomas.

AUTHOR'S NOTE

In August 1990 the storm clouds of war began to gather in the Gulf region of the Middle East.

President Saddam Hussein, Chairman of the Revolutionary Command Council of Iraq, ordered his columns of main battle tanks to blitzkrieg their way through the frail defences of his neighbour, oil-rich Kuwait. The clouds darkened. The risk of full-scale war grew ever closer. President George Bush of the United States of America put in place the biggest overseas military and firepower deployment since the early days of the Vietnam commitment. Prime Minister Margaret Thatcher of the United Kingdom sent that country's largest force abroad since the Royal Navy had sailed to recapture the Falkland Islands in 1982. American and European and Arab forces hurried to the Gulf.

And the question was asked, a whisper first and then a clamour of shouting, could not the threat to the vast oil supplies on which the developed and undeveloped nations of the world alike are so dependent have been foreseen?

There were a few men, a tiny minority, in the grey world of the international intelligence community, who had warned of the gathering storm, and they were not heard. The few spoke out, the many did not listen. A host of excuses were readily at hand to justify the ignoring of the danger. Iraq was the enemy of Iran, and therefore Saddam Hussein was to be coddled. Iraq had billions of oil dollars to spend, and therefore Saddam Hussein was to be humoured. In that region the weight of power politics and money counted, and the cost of those months of inactivity while the war machine of Iraq prepared can now be reckoned.

This is a story of those wasted months, and of the many who closed their ears and shut their eyes and who were governed by stupidity and self-interest and greed, and of the brave few who cried of the danger.

G.S.

PROLOGUE

She walked briskly in front of him, through the swing glass doors into the lobby, and she led him to the front desk, then paused to allow him to collect his key. The night porter, elderly, stained shirt, and the cigarette clinging to the extremes of his lip, leered at the man as he gave up the key for the third-floor room.

There were Americans in the lobby, sitting over maps and guidebooks, discussing the next day's tourism. And the voices of one group of them were loud in their complaint of the filth of the city's streets, even Chicago would not have tolerated such rubbish on the sidewalk, *even* New York. He saw that two of the men eyed the girl with envy and admiration. He saw that one of the women glowered her disapproval over her reading glasses.

She touched him for the first time, just slipped her hand through his arm, allowed him to walk her to the lift. It was a long time coming. He looked up into her face. The light in the lobby was subdued, and her make-up was skilfully applied. She seemed to him to be flushed with youth, and sinewy. To the stranger in the city, far from home, she was beautiful.

More tourists spilled from the lift and were greeted by those in the lobby with cheers and laughter at their lateness. He liked the way the girl stood her ground and forced them to either side of her. It was only an hour since they had met. His second evening in the city and he had been sitting in the bar opposite the hotel, gazing into his glass, when she had come and taken the stool beside him. They had had three drinks; she had told him her charges for an hour or until midnight or until the morning; and he had learned and forgotten her name. Her name was unimportant to him, as unimportant as the false name that he

I

had given to her. In the lift, creaking towards the third floor, the girl slid her arms round his neck and eased her pelvis against his.

He would have run the length of the third-floor corridor from the lift to his room, if she had permitted him to, but she pouted a small smile to him and firmly held his arm, and made him walk at the pace dictated by her skirt. At the door of his room he fumbled the key from his pocket and twice failed to make it work before she took the key from him. There was no trembling in her hand. If he had looked then into her face, as the door swung wide, he would have seen the coldness of her blue-grey eyes, and he would have seen the tightness of her lips as if that were their natural repose, as if she were merely going to work.

The man's briefcase was on the hotel room dressing table against the wall opposite the turned-down double bed. A faint anxiety nagged at him. He had learned to be cautious because he had often been briefed in such matters. He was held in trust by his employers and those people demanded his caution in return for his freedom to travel on their business. He thought of it as a small betrayal of their trust to have allowed himself the temptation of a café whore. He laid his raincoat over the briefcase and had no reason to believe that the girl was even aware of it.

He paid her.

He shovelled the 100,000 lire notes into her hand. He gave her five notes, and she held the last one up to the ceiling light, then she grimaced, then she tucked the notes into her handbag. He watched as she placed the handbag on a chair beside the bed. He watched as she shrugged out of her hip-length coat. It was four years since the last time he had been with a European girl. The girls where he lived now were either Thai or Filipino, imported to lie on their backs.

The girl slowly and teasingly took the clothes from his body, and alternately from her own. When he stood in his underpants and vest, when she was naked other than her black-lace pants and brassiere, she broke away from him. She went to her handbag and took from under the banknotes a contraceptive sachet, and then she switched out the light.

2

He did not see her face again.

She took him by the hand to the bed.

There was a grey light in the room, filtered through the thin curtains from the street lights below, that played on the ceiling but her face was now close to his and in shadow. The quiet of the room was broken by the pursuit of the cars and buses in the street. For a short time he was aware of the raucous commentary on a televised soccer match from the room next door.

He emptied himself into her, into the contraceptive. He fell away from her. Before he slept he was aware of the caressing movements of her hands on his neck and shoulders. He slept easily, swiftly, because the girl had soothed away the exhaustion of his last journey. In four days he had flown to Paris and then travelled to the plants at Saclay and Fontenay-aux-Roses, and he had then flown to Genoa, where he had had crucial discussions with the director of a factory that specialized in the precision-worked equipment urgently required for his project, and he had flown to Rome. He slept now because his exhaustion was exacerbated by extremes of tension that always gnawed at him when he travelled on missions of secrecy.

He had no awareness of the girl slipping from the bed, dressing fast in the darkness of the bathroom. He slept on as she put the key to the hotel room into her coat pocket.

She closed the door with great gentleness behind her. For a moment she sagged against the wall in the corridor outside. Her own task was completed. The lift ahead of her opened. They were the same group of tourists who had seen her take the man through the lobby, and the same men gave her the glad eye, and the same woman stabbed at her with a glance of pure disgust.

The man dreamed.

Peshawar, under the forbidding weight of the climbing foothills of the Hindu Kush mountains, in the North West Frontier Province of Pakistan, where his father was a government administrator, had been his childhood home. He dreamed of cricket at a school presided over by an elderly white-bearded Englishman.

3

He dreamed of boundaries and rippling applause. He dreamed of the days before he went away to the college in Europe and university in Egypt.

The sun shone in the brilliant day of his dream.

He did not wake as the door of the hotel room opened, nor stir at the sudden flash of light from the corridor, broken by the rapid movement of two men, and then extinguished.

The girl had no place in his dreams. He was dreaming of his father standing by the pavilion steps . . .

He twisted on the hard mattress as the men crossed the room towards the bed, moving silently on the balls of their feet. The dreams of childhood were always abbreviated, cut away at moments of ecstasy. He had half woken.

A drab room in a small and drab hotel on a drab street behind the railway station. A pitiful place for a man to die. In the moments before he died, the man reached across the wide space of the bed as if he expected that his arm would come to rest against the bare white shoulder of the girl with the blonde hair.

They closed on him fast.

There was a hand across his mouth.

The scream stayed stifled in his throat.

There was a hand pulling the sheet over his body.

His legs thrashed and made a pyramid of the blanket above his knees.

There was a knife-blade on a short arc hard down into the sheet.

A pathetic place for a man to die.

There was the effort grunt from the man who used his strength to drive the knife down through the sheet, through the splintering ribcage. The narrow-bladed knife pierced the heart.

The man died with a choke in his throat. The sheet over his body soaked up the blood spurt of his last life-spasm as the knife was withdrawn. The man who had won distinction in his degree course at the University of Berne and fulsome praise for his doctorate at Imperial College in London and admiration for

4

his teaching at the University of Cairo's Department of Nuclear Engineering, lay dead.

A gloved hand lifted the man's briefcase from beneath his raincoat.

When they left, they hung on the outside door handle the notice requesting that the occupant not be disturbed.

By 9.30 in the morning when the director general of the specialized engineering firm of Ital/Int had waited in the hotel lobby for seventy-five minutes, when his patience was exhausted, he demanded of the hotel management that they should go themselves to find why his calls to the room went unanswered.

At 9.30 that morning, as the hotel room door was opened with a pass key, the briefcase was secreted in a diplomatic bag that rested on the knee of a courier. The courier sat in first class, the bag discreetly chained to his wrist, and the flight had been airborne for nineteen minutes.

Few in the city cared that Zulfiqar Khan, aged thirty-nine, resident of Baghdad, Republic of Iraq, last seen in the company of a woman presumed to be a prostitute, had been put to death. Fewer still would understand that a sovereign government had, at prime-ministerial level, sanctioned his killing in cold blood.

I

At the end of the road a boy was doing good business from the refrigerated box mounted over the front wheel of his bicycle. A crowd of forty, perhaps fifty, had gathered to watch the coming and going of the police and the counter-terrorism team. They stood quietly in the light rain, and more than half of them sucked at their ice creams.

The road that was blocked off was residential. There were good-sized villas hidden behind high whitewashed walls. There was the barking of guard dogs. It was the sort of road where the pick of the surgeons and lawyers and import-export dealers made their homes. Erlich paid off his taxi. He reckoned the boy had doubled the price for his ice cream because he was up at the smart end of town, not plying his usual pitch at the bottom of the Acropolis. Beside the boy an argument was developing between an overweight policeman and the auburn-haired girl who had parked her florist's truck across the end of the road. Erlich could see why she wanted to deliver her flowers. He reckoned the armful of red roses would have cost the policeman his week's wages. The girl held her head high. Her shoulders were back. Erlich didn't understand much Greek but he got her drift. Eventually the policeman was prepared to lose face. He stepped aside and the auburn-haired girl strode forward into the empty road carrying the roses loosely in her arm. Erlich shouldered his way through the crowd and went after her.

The policeman shuffled into his path.

Erlich said quietly, 'FBI, excuse me, please.'

He kept on walking. He doubted that the policeman had understood a word he had said. Perhaps the policeman had looked into Erlich's face and calculated that if he had not stood aside then he might just have ended up on his back. He stepped back and saluted. Erlich smiled and walked past the policeman, a dozen strides, into the centre of the road.

He had known Harry Lawrence since the fall of '88. There were not many in the Agency that he would call a true friend. He had thought of Harry all the way out of Rome to Leonardo da Vinci, all the time that he had stood in the check-in line, all the time he had sat on the Alitalia, all the time he had stood at Customs and Immigration at Athens International, all the time in the taxi out to the Kifisia suburb. If the policeman had stopped him getting close to where Harry had been shot to death then Erlich might just have punched him. He stood still, absorbing every detail of the street. Best done at the very start of an investigation.

'You poor old son of a bitch, Harry.'

A hundred yards down on the other side of the road a knot of men were gathered. The girl with the flowers stopped, looked across at the men, then turned into a front drive and was gone from sight.

It would have been a pretty road in spring, with the blossom on the trees that lined it. The leaves were down now. He knew very little of what had happened, had been out of touch since that first report had reached the Embassy in Rome and he had started running. They always sent a Fed when an American citizen was killed, and the Rome office covered Athens.

The men grouped together ahead of him were hunched against the drizzle. Erlich recognized from his balding head Harry's Station Chief. If that was where Harry had died, there should have been a big area quarantined off with tape. There shouldn't have been a cattle herd of feet trampling over the grass.

Erlich walked forward. He reached the group.

The killing had been early in the morning. The Station Chief would have come from home because he wore no tie and he was draped in an old windbreaker, probably the first coat to hand on the pegs by his front door. Killings never came convenient. The Station Chief detached himself from the group. He took Erlich's hand, as if he were a priest, offering his condolences. The Station Chief would have known that Harry Lawrence and Bill Erlich were close, that their friendship crossed the divide of Agency man and Fed.

The Station Chief pointed between the trousered legs and the shoes of the Greek police and security officials. There was blood on the grass, thin darkened streaks. The pointing finger moved on, away from the grass and over towards the pavement.

On the pavement were two patches of blood.

The Station Chief said, 'Harry had a contact with him – they were both taken out . . . Good to have you here, Bill.'

He didn't have small talk, not his way. Erlich said, 'This is unbelievable.'

'It's their backyard . . .'

'Has this place been cleaned up?'

'They got the cartridge case . . .'

'What else?'

'I don't know what else . . .'

'You happy with that?'

'Where was your Scene of Crime experience?'

'Atlanta, Georgia,' Erlich said.

'Listen here, Bill, this is sure as hell not Atlanta.'

'And you take that?'

The Station Chief's voice was low. 'We are foreigners, we are far from home. What I know from long and painful experience is this: we kick them, they go mightily obstinate. The harder we kick, the less we get.'

'I hear you.'

There was the rattle of iron gates behind him. Erlich turned. A woman came from the villa to which the girl had delivered the flowers. She wore a tailored two-piece grey suit and delicate shoes, and there was a scarf over her hair that came from Dior, minimum, and she carried the red roses. She walked in the rain across the road and round the group of policeman. Erlich

8

watched her. She went to the stained pavement, where the blood pools were washed by the rain spots. She knelt. Her eyes were closed, her lips moved. She crossed herself. The woman laid the roses on the pavement. She stood. For a moment she stared down at the stains and the roses, and then she walked away.

Erlich said softly, 'Thank you, ma'am.'

He didn't know whether she heard him, she gave no sign.

Erlich said to the Station Chief, 'I'd like to see Harry.'

Bill had been enough times to a morgue. He knew what they looked like, what the procedures were. A body didn't change if it had been blasted with an automatic weapon in a robbery on Lenox Square or gunned down on a sidewalk in Athens. Morgues were the same, bodies were the same. He fancied that the section of the morgue in Atlanta that dealt with violent death was cleaner, but it would be cleaner, had to be, because it was busier. The attendants stood back to allow Erlich and the Station Chief to go on their own to the centre of the room where the two stretchers were parked on their wheeled bases, draped with green sheeting. The harsh central neon light glared down onto the contours of the sheeting, and gouged back at Erlich's eyes from the white-tiled walls. He lifted the sheet nearer to him.

A pale, sallow face. A neat, dark moustache. A half-crescent of recently cut hair set round a receding scalp. A scraped discolouration on the left cheek.

'Where he fell – they were all body shots that took him.'

Erlich lifted the sheet further and studied the two gaping exit wounds.

'Who was he?'

The Station Chief said, 'Dissident, Iraqi. Price on his life, living in Damascus. Harry had met him before. The guy was back in town, rang Harry. Harry liked to pump him . . .'

He laid the sheet back over the face. He skirted the two stretchers, then raised the sheet of the second.

He swallowed back the bile in his throat.

9

It would have been a back-of-the-head shot. A low-velocity round tumbling against the toughness of the skull bone. The exit was a mess where the eyes and nose of his friend had been.

The mouth was what he would remember. Where the laughter was, where the good cracks were. Only the mouth told him that he looked on the face of his friend.

The Station Chief said, 'There are six wounds on the joker – Harry just took the one.'

'Which means?'

Erlich knew the answer.

The Station Chief said, 'Almost certainly it means, wrong place, wrong time.'

'Makes my day.'

'He wasn't the target, just in the way.'

'The Iraqis do their own people . . .'

'When they step out of line, sure, why not?'

Erlich drew the sheet back over his friend's wretched face. He would get autopsy details later. He didn't need more time in this chilled room. From what he had seen he estimated that the low-velocity rounds had been fired at a maximum of a dozen paces. It probably didn't matter whether his calculations were right or wild. A good man and his good friend was dead.

'As long as I am allowed to, I will follow this, Elsa. That is my most solemn guarantee, no backing off. If it takes a month, a year, ten years . . . Elsa, I promise.'

His friend's wife sat on the sofa. The two kids were against her, one on each side, and she had her small and narrow arms round her kids' shoulders and she pulled them to her.

It was five months since he had last seen her, since he had last been in Athens. Barbecue time late on a Sunday night on the balcony, and another Embassy staffer from the floor above leaning over his parapet and complaining about the smoke. She might have understood him, and she might not. She wasn't a pretty woman, but to Erlich's eye she was about the best there could be. OK, so he didn't have a wife of his own – but of the wives of the men he knew, Elsa Lawrence was the first in line. She had been weeping, he could see that, but there was no chance that she would cry now because the apartment was filled with Agency staff, four men moving through the small apartment, packing the family's belongings. In the fifteen minutes Erlich had been there, not one of the men had come to Elsa to ask her what case which clothes should go in. They were shadow walkers, emerging every few moments with a suitcase, bulging, from one of the bedrooms, stacking it in the cramped hallway.

'As long as it takes, Elsa.'

She took her arms away from round her kids' shoulders and held them out for him.

Erlich came close to her, kneeling on the rug he knew that Harry had brought back from a fast run to Beirut. Her arms were round his neck. He kissed her cheek. He could feel the wetness of his own tears.

He broke away. When he looked back he could see that once more she hugged her children to her. In the hall the Station Officer said, 'Good talk, fighting talk.'

'Not a lot else to say.'

'You're paid to do a job.'

'Yes.'

'Not to play Victim Counsellor.'

'Yes.'

'The same job whether you knew him or didn't.'

'Taken.'

'How many shots?'

'Twelve cartridge cases, seven hits.'

'How many weapons?'

'One weapon. Pistol, .22 calibre, with silencer. A professional's.'

'And are you sure that Harry Lawrence was not the target?'

'That's the way it looks.'

Erlich wrote it all down in a pocket notebook, longhand. The policeman sipped coffee. He was not welcome, Erlich knew that. He could hardly have been welcome, because when he had entered the senior police officer's room it had been with two aides trying to keep him out by every manoeuvre other than manhandling him. He'd got there, and he was staying . . . He hadn't been offered coffee.

'Do you have any evidence on which to base this supposition?'

'The aim of the shots.'

'Do you have an eyewitness?'

The grating of the cup on the saucer. A pause. The snapping of a cigarette lighter.

'That is a very straightforward question, sir.'

'Yes, Mr Erlich, I have an eyewitness.'

'Who saw it all?'

'So I understand, yes.'

'May I talk to the eyewitness?'

'Probably – at a suitable time.'

'Is tomorrow suitable?'

'I cannot say . . .'

Again, a pause. The smoke curled between them, eddied to Erlich's face. A telephone rang in an outer office. The policeman glanced upwards as if he hoped that the phone would give him an excuse to get rid of this intruder.

'Well, sir, what do you have?'

'What do I have? Put simply, Mr Erlich, I have an intelligence agent of a foreign country going about his activities without informing the local authorities of his work . . . Do you think, Mr Erlich, that if I went to your Embassy to request a detailed briefing concerning the work in my country of Mr Harry Lawrence, Central Intelligence Agency, that I would be shown anything, other than the door . . . ?'

'You have the hit car?'

'Burned out, no help.'

A welling frustration.

'We're on the same side.' The last time he had been in Athens, when the group that called themselves 'November 17th' had hit the Proctoer & Gamble offices with an anti-tank rocket, he had not been admitted to the presence of this big man. The warhead had not detonated, there had been no casualties. He hadn't been welcome then, wasn't welcome now, but he hadn't pushed his luck as hard when the target had been a corporation and no casualties, as when the target had been an American government servant, dead.

'Are we, Mr Erlich?'

'What do you have?'

'Lawrence and his contact walking in a quiet street. An Opel Rekord, stolen three days earlier in the Piraeus, pulls up twenty yards behind them. One man out, Caucasian, blond short hair. The contact shot. Lawrence blunders into the path of the bullets, is hit . . .'

'White?'

'Caucasian, Mr Erlich, white.'

'Is that it?'

'There was a shout from the car driver.'

'What was the shout?'

'The word "Colt".'

'What?'

'The shout was the one word. Please, Mr Erlich, be so kind as to excuse me. The one word shouted was "Colt". Only "Colt".'

He was Colin Olivier Louis Tuck.

Tomorrow would be his twenty-sixth birthday, but there would be no cards and no presents.

He sat and stared out over the skyline of the city in the chill of the evening. The first thing he had done when he had come into the apartment had been to turn off the heating system, and then he had opened the window in his bedroom and the window in the sparsely furnished living room. He hated to be boxed up. What had gone wrong he did not know. He had been met by the Defence Ministry people, who had taken him directly from the aircraft steps, but no one had said a word on the way into the city. There had been no pumped handshakes, no kissed cheeks, no backslapping, so something was wrong. And there was a man at the door, standing as if on guard. A man in a two-piece suit, and a thin cotton shirt and his tie knotted at the second button of the shirt. There was little light in the room but he wore wrap-around dark glasses. Colt had his back to his watcher, but could hear him shiver in the draught. They would say whatever it was they had to say in their own time. There was no hurrying them, that's what he had learned since he had been in Baghdad.

He ran his fingers hard through the cropped growth of his fair, light golden hair. He closed his eyes. He'd wake when they came. His day had started at 4.30 with the bleeping of his wrist-watch alarm. No breakfast, because he never took breakfast. No coffee. No food, nothing to drink. He had dressed. He had stripped the weapon, rebuilt it, satisfied himself, and then unloaded and reloaded the magazine. He always checked the mechanism before firing because the Ruger/MAC Mark 1 was now vintage and occasionally liable to jam. At 5.30 he had left his room in the west quarter of Athens, in the student sector. The car had been waiting for him.

As he lolled in his chair, not asleep but relaxed, he could remember that he had felt no tension, less excitement, as he had thrown his bag into the back seat of the car, climbed into the front carrying the Ruger with the integral silencer in a large plastic shopping bag. The driver was good, no sweat. The driver was from the Colonel's staff, and he had travelled ahead a full month before so that he knew the city, the back-doubles they might need and the side streets. Colt had known the driver for eleven months, and he knew he was good because the Colonel had told him how the driver had once handled an ambush.

Colt had been taken to the hotel where the target was staying . . . He had seen the target leave the hotel . . . It was his decision as to when he should take out the target. As the target had come out of the hotel, his hand had stiffened on the grip of the Ruger in the plastic bag and he had eased his weight towards the passenger door. But the taxi rank outside the hotel had been full and idle and the target had been straight into a vehicle. They had followed, and he had let his feelings rip when the driver had lost the taxi at a traffic light. The driver had stayed calm and quartered the streets until the taxi was picked up again two full minutes later. The driver would have known it was his first time, didn't take offence at the yelling. The taxi had stopped eventually at a crossroads in a suburb, and the target had paid it off and walked straight to a man who waited on the pavement. The target and the man had walked away up a tree-lined road. It was as good a place as any. No cars parked in the road, no pedestrians. The road was two hundred yards long and empty . . . It was as good a place as he could hope to find. He could remember the car pulling onto the verge twenty yards behind the target. He could remember calling out, because he wanted to separate the target from the man who masked him. He could remember the suppressed clattering noise of the firing on semi-automatic. The second man had lunged across the target, he could remember that, and he could remember that he had kept squeezing the trigger. He would have shot the second man anyway. It was too good a place to miss out on. But it would have been tidier if he could have separated them. It was just bad luck for the second man that it had been a good place. They had fallen, both of them, he could picture it exactly in his mind, and he could remember Kairallah, calling to him to get back to the car. There wasn't a great deal else to remember because it had all been pretty damn straightforward. Running for the car, the car going steadily, not too fast to the airport, and out onto the flight to Ankara. And even less to remember of the delay at Ankara before the connection to Baghdad. Actually, he had done well . . .

The thoughts, memories, lulled him. He had made his choice. For the time being it was a one-bedroomed apartment on the sixth floor of the Haifa Street Housing Project. It was an open window looking out onto the wind-rippled waters of the Tigris and across to the Al Jumhuriyah and Al Ahrar bridges and over to the tower blocks of the foreign-money hotels. It was his bed, and he would lie on it.

He heard the scrape of the guard's feet as the man scrabbled to get to the door.

He heard the rap at the apartment's outer door. He pushed himself to his feet. He stood with his back to the open window.

The Colonel was a thickset man. He smelled of lotion, from Paris. He was not tall, but there was nothing flabby about the weight of his body. He wore a plain olive-drab uniform, only the insignia of his rank on his shoulders, no medal ribbons. His calf-length paratrooper boots were not shined, they were streaked with the grey dust of the street.

He liked the Colonel. The Colonel, his patron, his friend, in his mind was without bullshit, but tonight there was no warmth, no smile even.

'Were you seen?'

'Seen? What do you mean, seen?'

'Were there any eyewitnesses to the shooting?'

'No.'

'Is there any possibility you could be identified?'

'Nobody saw me.'

'Think hard. Could anybody have seen you to associate you with the car even?'

'The road was empty.'

'You were seen by nobody?'

'Only by the target, and whoever was with him . . .'

'Whoever . . . ?'

'They're both dead.'

'Do you know who it was who was with the target?'

'I did not ask his name before I shot him, no.'

He stood very still. He knew that the target was a writer, an exile. He had been told what the writer wrote about the regime and the Chairman of the Revolutionary Command Council. He had been told also, in whispered confidence, that two attempts against the target had failed. He was the Colonel's card . . . Below him he could hear the passing wail of sirens, a familiar sound after dark had fallen over the city. The squads from the Department of Public Security always did their work at night, taking into custody those they claimed were a threat to the regime. And the sirens escorted their prisoners from the Department to the Abu Ghraib gaol, and those who had not survived interrogation from the Abu Ghraib gaol to the Medical City Mortuary on the other side of the Al Sarafiyah Bridge.

'You shot an American, Colt . . .'

'I killed the target.'

'A CIA American . . .'

The boy laughed out loud. He laughed in the face of the Colonel, and at the watcher standing against the door.

'So what . . . ?' he said.

'He was an intelligence officer.'

'It was a good street, got me? It was great. It was dead, there was no one. No nannies, maids, deliveries, really good. The target, he was already fidgety, I couldn't follow him all day, not a target who was that sharp. The street was right. If the American hadn't gone then he had my face, and he had the car. He had to go . . . and he should have chosen his friends more carefully.'

At last the Colonel smiled, and there was the gravel growl of his chuckle. 'And you did nothing stupid in Athens . . . ?'

'You taught me what to do.'

'. . . Nothing Colt-like, nothing wild? What did you do, Colt? No girls, no boasting?'

'You taught me. I'm clean. It was a good street, Colonel. There was an opportunity and I took it.'

'You could not be identified?'

'I'd go back, to Europe, because I know that I cannot be traced.'

The Colonel laid his broad hands on the young man's shoulders. He looked into the calm of the face, into the clear eyes.

'It was well done, Colt.'

Among those few who knew Zulfiqar Khan, and what work he did, news of his killing spread fast. And with the news, fear.

In Paris, an engineering specialist in deep tunnelling in heavy rock strata, home on leave, made up his mind there and then to turn his back on the remaining two and a half years of his contract.

The tunnelling that the Frenchman was paid – and handsomely – to supervise was off the road to Arbil, close to the village of Salahuddin, due north of Baghdad. The area so far excavated was the size of a football pitch, and deep enough for three levels of laboratories and workshops that would be concrete-lined. One more floor was required. The cavern was eminently suitable for the work intended for it. It was safe from air attack and shielded by the Karochooq mountain mass from satellite photography that would tell the story of the purpose for which this rock cave was fashioned. News of Dr Khan's murder had eddied amongst the foreign specialists on the project. By midday word had reached all the hard-hat staffers. By late that night, two of those staffers were at Baghdad International airport. They had driven the two hundred miles from their Portakabin compound in the village of Salahuddin at high speed. They waited for the first flight out of Iraq on which there were seats. It might be to Jeddah, or to Karachi, or to Budapest.

At the airport was an Italian who specialized in the fitting of the argon gas filters necessary for the hot cell boxes. The Italian sat close to his friend on the front row of the plastic-coated seats, and studied every two, three, minutes the TV monitor that would announce the next flight out. The friend had an office in the same block at Tuwaithah. The friend, who was an engineer involved in the precision shaping of chemical explosive, had that morning received a letter bomb which by chance had failed to detonate. They had been at the airport for six hours, waiting for a flight, any flight out of Iraq, going anywhere.

Erlich was breaking the rules. A Fed on assignment overseas with the ranking of Assistant Legal Attaché must always work through local law-enforcement agencies. Back at FBIHQ, where the book ran the show, they would have been climbing the walls in the Offices of Liaison and International Affairs if they had known that he was out on his own. At the very least, he should have had a local policeman with him. At best, he should have been waiting until the morning and then politely requesting a desk and a telephone and an interpreter somewhere in the back reaches of their Counter-Terrorism building. But Erlich was his own man. He had been his own man on the training run at Quantico and it had not been held against him there. And his own man in Atlanta, where his straight talking and his independence had won him his next posting. And his own man in the Washington Field Office, the CI-3 team, and putting in the longest hours and never a word of complaint, and that had won him the job in the Attaché's office in Rome. It was not his intention that he would spend the rest of his life as a Special Agent. Ten years, he had set himself, to running a Field Office. Twenty years, he reckoned, to an Assistant Director's desk in Headquarters. It was a break, coming down to Athens, and a good break should be grabbed with both fists.

The sadness was that it came from the killing of Harry. The excitement was that it was a really brilliant break. Sadness and excitement, both already seeking their own compartments.

At the edge of his flashlight beam he could see the dampened flowers, flattened now by the steady fall of rain. He wasn't interested in an examination by torchlight of the exact spot where Harry Lawrence and the contact had fallen. He paced out an arc of twelve paces, looked for the killer's place. He could be very thorough . . . A body on a garbage dump nine miles out west of Atlanta. Female, eighteen, black. Believed to be the victim of a serial killer, probably the fourth. She'd fought, her fists were bruised to show she'd fought, and there was nothing to work from. Over to the right of the dump was a high tree, holding the storks' nests. Erlich, rookie Fed, had demanded of the local police that they get a man up there, up to the nests, that they get each of the nests down, that they sift each of the nests on the very long chance that the storks had lifted a fibre of torn clothing to bind a nest wall. They'd done it, too, the police, and they'd found nothing . . .

After fifteen minutes he was crouched over tyre marks on the grass verge between the pavement and the road. Possibly the tyre threads of the Opel Rekord, that was burned through and useless for evidence prints.

After forty minutes, on his hands and knees, peering into the beam of the flashlight, he found the butt end of a small cigar. He had already found chewing-gum wrapping, sweet papers and cigarette filters faded by weather. The butt end of the cigar was fresh. Everything else he had collected he abandoned in the street drain. The butt end of the cigar was three paces from where the tyre treads were clearest, probably where the car had braked. He heard a shout.

He looked up. On the pavement opposite a small boy watched him. The shouting grew fiercer, and the gates opposite were thrown open. It was the woman who had put the flowers on the place where Harry Lawrence had died, and there was a small toy dog, a Pekinese, yapping by her ankles. The child went to her, reluctant to leave. The gates closed.

From his pocket, Erlich took a small plastic bag, and into it he dropped the cigar butt.

It was a beginning.

The wind came from the west. It blew hard on the beach and the militiamen who kept guard, protecting the Sheraton and the Ramada and the Tel Aviv Hilton against a landing by guerrillas, turned their faces from the stinging sand.

Two streets behind the seafront the cafés on Ben Yehuda were quiet. There were five of them at one table and they were the only ones still outside. The men drank beer from the bottles, and one of them passed round the cigarettes he had bought on the flight, and the blonde girl contributed a half-bottle of Stock brandy. They no longer talked about the substance of the mission. The debriefing had gone on through the afternoon and early evening in the soundproofed rooms of their headquarters. The mission was completed. They would probably not work as a team again, and certainly it would be many months before the girl, on any pretext, work or vacation, was permitted to leave the country. Drinking at a pavement café on Ben Yehuda was for each of them a way of signing off from the mission. There was the senior officer who had authorized the mission after assembling the detailed biography of Professor Zulfiqar Khan. There was his deputy who had collated the intelligence that gave the itinerary of the Pakistani. There was the girl who had played the whore and who would go home that night to her husband. There was the man who had killed Khan and who later would go barefoot into the children's room to kiss them and not wake them. There was the man who had been with him and taken the briefcase from the hotel room and who in the morning would go back to the Golani Brigade stationed on the Lebanese border and who would be chided by his fellow officers for having taken leave while the military workload was intense.

Only when the café owner remonstrated with them did they leave.

In the middle of Ben Yehuda they kissed each other. It was the only display, through the days and nights of tension, of their emotion. They kissed and they split.

The senior officer walked with the girl. When he waved down a taxi, he saw that her hand ferreted in her bag. As the taxi stopped, he saw that she pushed back onto her finger her narrow and plain gold ring. He opened the door for her.

'It was necessary,' he said. 'If we do nothing, if we sit back and watch . . . the State is finished. If that dwarf, Tariq, is permitted to build them a bomb . . .'

The senior officer of the Mossad drew his finger across his throat then quietly shut the taxi door, waved, walked away.

Colt went to the Khan Murjan in the old quarter only when someone else picked up the bill. This time he had the table to himself. The Colonel was paying.

Prawns and avocado, lamb, cheese, fruit, and French wine. It was his favourite eating place in Baghdad. There was a small band away from the tables, and the singer had started as he had begun his meat and called for a second bottle. He was not actually hungry, and it was rare for him to drink, but they were paying and he would make sure they noticed, and – apart from the singer – the Khan Murjan was a hell of a fabulous place. A great arched ceiling of close brickwork, carpets too beautiful to put a dirty shoe on. The singer was crap, but he could handle the singer, just switch that amplified voice off in his head, just as he could shake out of his head the recoil thud of the Ruger on semi-automatic . . .

He had walked through the old city with the guard a dozen paces behind. The city was his home, and the Ruger, and the Khan Murjan restaurant, they were as much of a home as he was now at liberty to make for himself. Light years ago, at his school, and Colt of course not a part of it but compelled to sit through it, *Murder in the Cathedral.* The troublesome priest. The Colonel had trusted him to rid the Chairman of the darts of the writer with the poisoned pen. Two had failed, he had succeeded. One had failed to penetrate airport security at Budapest, got himself arrested and deported. A second had failed on the streets of Zagreb, lifted by the Yugoslavs, locked up and the key thrown away. Colt had succeeded. He knew why he had been chosen. He was white, he was European, he had *access*. He had justified the Colonel's faith. He was the only European in the restaurant, because all the bastards who were in town to fight like cocks in a pit for the reconstruction contracts would be in the restaurants of the Babylon Oberoi and the Sadir Novotel and the Mansour Melia. He wore his better jeans and a laundered shirt, open at the neck.

He had shot an American. So what?

He drank deep.

When he had finished his meal, when he had collected his guard from the hard chair by the entrance, then he would stride back to the Haifa Street Housing Project, and he would chew on the pistachio nuts that were loose in his trouser pocket, and he would write to his mother.

2

The first of the November frosts had settled on the lawn in front of the house, and the Sierra was an age starting. There were some mornings, Monday mornings in particular, when it would have been as quick for him to walk to the main gates and then catch an internal minibus to his office block. On Monday mornings there was a solid traffic line at the junction where Mulfords Hill joined the main road from Kingsclere to Burghfield Common. But Frederick Bissett detested walking, and because his Sara's car was in the garage, and his own car sat outside overnight, he condemned himself to five minutes of scraping the ice from the windscreen and the back window and to revving the engine, blowing grey fumes away down Lilac Gardens. Sara seldom saw him off to work. She was generally too busy getting Frank and Adam ready for school.

His neighbour came through the front door of the house to the right. He was kissed. His wife always kissed him. His neighbour always wore grey overalls when he went to work. His neighbour was a plumber.

'Good morning, Fred.'

Frederick Bissett, Senior Scientific Officer, loathed being called Fred. He waved his de-icer without enthusiasm.

'Better mornin' for cuddling up – eh? What?'

His other neighbour was twelve years younger than Frederick Bissett, wore white socks inside his black shoes, and sold Heinz products into local supermarkets. His other neighbour's child-bride kissed her boy hero each morning, in her floating web dressing gown, as if he were going to the Falklands for three months. He drove an Escort XR3i complete with fluffy toys, and had moved to Lilac Gardens in the eye of the housing price slump, aided by the bequest of a dead aunt. Bissett had been told that often enough, about the dead aunt and her bequest.

He had very little to say to his other neighbours. He could live in a cocoon of his own making. That was the way of his work, and that was the way of his life in Lilac Gardens.

Bissett laid his old briefcase on the back seat of the car. The case contained only his sandwich box and his thermos flask of coffee. He drove out onto Mount Pleasant and was stopped at the temporary lights where the new sewer pipe was going in. He was held up again when he needed to turn into Mulfords Hill because no one would let him into the flow. The next hold-up was outside Boundary Hall where a stream of cars was emerging from his left and not acknowledging his right of way. He was stopped outside the Lloyds Bank by the entrance to Boundary Hall. It was far too early for the manager to be coming to work. An hour at least before the manager turned up to write his acid little letters.

There was a short gap between the cars sprinting out from Boundary Hall; he gunned his engine and surged forward. The Audi that thought it had a clear run had to brake hard . . . Excellent . . . He recognized the driver, one of the Principal Training Managers lodged at Boundary Hall, saw his annoyance and felt the better for it. Another hundred yards, and then held again at the Kingsclere–Burghfield Commons crossing. It was the same every morning, only worse on some mornings. Eyes into his mirror. He recognized the man with the white handlebar moustache sitting high in a ridiculous Japanese jeep, Health Physics branch, and he heard the sharp horn blast before he saw that the road ahead of him was clear. He took his chance and crossed the road. Another queue of cars at the Falcon Gate. They had the rods out with the mirrors. No end to it . . . State Amber Black at the Falcon Gate . . . He always left the newspaper at home in the mornings for Sara. He never listened to radio news in the mornings, and in the evenings he usually turned his chair away from the television set, so that he could read. He had an idea there had been a car bomb at another barracks. He did not know where, and did not particularly care, except that it meant that the Establishment was on Amber Black, and every car had to have the magic mirror wand shoved underneath the chassis. He was waved ahead.

He drove forward.

He was inside the perimeter fence of his workplace.

There are five such workplaces in the world. There is the Los Alamos National Laboratory in the desert uplands of New Mexico. There are the Institutes and Design Laboratories of the Ministry of Medium Machine-Building in the Chelyabinsk region of the Ural mountains. In France, there are the Centres d'Etudes of the Directions des Applications Militaires which is a subdivision of the Commission d'Energie Atomique at Ripault. There are the design facilities of the Ministry of Nuclear Energy at Lanzhou in Gansu province in the People's Republic of China. And in Great Britain there is the Atomic Weapons Establishment which has been built upon a World War Two airfield in the countryside of Berkshire, fifty miles from London and overlooking the Thames Valley.

When Bissett had left home the sky had been clear. No longer. The chill of the early morning was dispersing under the grey cloud base that spread in from the west.

He took the central avenue, along the old runway. Where he drove, surrounded by cars and bicycles and mopeds and minibuses, there had once been the strained drone of Dakotas pulling gliders into the air for the flights to the bridges and crossroads behind the D-Day beaches of Normandy, and for the flights to the Dutch town of Arnhem. He drove slowly down the wide Third Avenue. Grey concrete buildings that had been thrown up, always wherever they could be fitted in, on either side. The coiled wire above the fences that surrounded the A area where the plutonium was worked, and the B area where the chemical explosives were fashioned, and the contaminated areas, and the waste storage areas, all separated by their own grey wire barricades. The four great chimneys to his left spewing out their fumes into the grey cloud.

Bissett drove to the H area.

His workplace was H3.

The building was single-storey, red-brick walls, metal window frames, flat-roofed. The H3 building had been put up hastily in the early 1950s to get the scientists out of their first accommodation that had been little more than Nissen huts. There should have been a lifespan of twenty years for H3, but other priorities had been higher, and every four years since 1973 there had been a doctoring of the patient, a new lick of paint on the inside, an attempt to reinforce the roofing against damp, new wiring to carry the power of the computer that ran their lives. There was also a new fence around H area, all a part of the new security drive. Once more he showed his I/D card to the Ministry policeman.

Carol was at the coffee machine, stoking up for the day, the cover not yet off her typewriter.

'Morning, Dr Bissett.'

Wayne was lighting his first cigarette. He was the most recent recruit into H3, and only had a Lower Second from Aston. 'Morning.'

Reuben Boll was unwrapping the first of the boiled sweets he bought each morning in Tadley. The door to his office was always open. He was the Superintendent, Grade 6. He was the man in charge of H3, and he spoke with his émigré parents' guttural Central European accent although he had been born in Ipswich, and he had been in H area for twenty-six years.

'Morning, Frederick.'

Basil Curtis slammed the door behind him. He had been there since ever. Basil shrugged out of his duffel coat. The duffel coat would have been the one he had worn when he first came to work at the Establishment. There were no Civil Service retirement regulations applicable to Basil. The stitching of the rent in his corduroy trousers was his own work, the runs in his pullover were his cat's. Bissett thought him the most brilliant man he had ever met.

'Morning, Bissett.'

They were the first in. There would be others on the clerical staff who were always late, always pleading that the school bus hadn't turned up, or that their dog had to be walked. And others on the scientific level who would claim the excuse of a school run, or taking the wife to Surgery. Bissett was never late.

He went down the corridor that led off the central area. Third on the right. He unlocked the door with the key that was on his chain. His routine was invariable. Each morning he first switched on the power for his terminal. Then he took his sandwich box and his thermos of coffee from his briefcase. They went onto the shelf behind his chair, between the photographs of Sara and of the two boys. Then he went to his wall safe, opened it with the second key on the ring attached by a chain to his trouser belt, and took out his papers.

His Personal Air Sampler, the size of a small matchbox, hanging by a cord from his neck, banged on the desktop. It always banged on the desktop, each morning, before he remembered to tuck it below his tie.

Carol knocked, came in before he was able to tell her to. Her husband was a lathe operator in B area. She always said she could have done a better job running the place than the Director or his boss, Controller Establishment Research and Nuclear.

'This got delivered here, Dr Bissett.'

The envelope was marked Personal and Confidential.

As at Los Alamos and Chelyabinsk and Ripault and Lanzhou, the Atomic Weapons Establishment at Aldermaston is a workplace governed by secrecy.

Behind the grey wire, beyond the uniformed guards with their sub-machine guns and automatic pistols and attack dogs, 5000 people daily go about their work, to research, design, test and finally manufacture an independent source of nuclear weapons. Much of the work moving from the AWE consoles and design tables and laboratories and workshops is considered, by the few who so jealously guard their knowledge, as information too sensitive to be transmitted to any but those in the topmost reaches of government. Infinitely too sensitive to be shared, even in the most vague terms, with the general public, for whom the nuclear shield remains the ultimate defence.

Nine-tenths of the work done here would be known to the scientists and engineers at Los Alamos and Chelyabinsk and Ripault and Lanzhou. But Los Alamos and Chelyabinsk and Ripault and Lanzhou and Aldermaston form the club with the greatest exclusivity yet devised. No helping hand will be offered to newcomers. The door is closed to new members, and the membership protects itself against what it calls Proliferation with wire, guns, attack dogs, certainly, but above all with a suffocating cloak of secrecy.

It was noon.

He had arrived at the forward brigade post three hours earlier.

His car was mud-splattered, parked amongst the jeeps and armoured personnel carriers, a hundred yards from the helicopter pad. He was Dr Tariq. Dr Tariq had never liked the featureless flatland of the Fao peninsula before the war. After seven years as a battlefield it was now an unearthly, hellish landscape. Around the excavated brigade post were gun positions, and trench patterns, and mud. As a scientist, Dr Tariq despised the waste and confusion of the place. His back was to the waterway. He had no wish to look out over the Shatt al-Arab, the narrow glistening strip that divided his country from the Islamic Republic of Iran. He did not care to look beyond the semi-sunken hulks of the bombed merchantmen towards the clear flames rising from the refinery tower of Abadan. He waited. He paced close to his car. As far as he could see back up the Basra road were the headless date palms, lopped by the shrapnel.

As soon as he had received news of the death of Professor Khan he had requested a meeting with the Chairman of the

28

Revolutionary Command Council, at the Chairman's earliest convenience. As Director of the Atomic Energy Commission, Dr Tariq was familiar with the dark undercurrents of Iraq's body politic. He knew of the coup attempt of seven weeks earlier and he had heard the rumour that nine Air Force officers had been put to death. It did not surprise him at all that the Chairman's answer should come, hand-delivered, to his villa at four o'clock in the morning, and that the rendezvous would be away from Baghdad. He knew that the routine and itinerary of the Chairman were a closely guarded secret. Dr Tariq would not have said that he *liked* the Chairman of the Revolutionary Command Council, but he admired him. Nothing was possible, not any movement, without the clearance of the Chairman. He admired in particular the durability of the man, and his capacity to absorb succinctly presented detail, and his ability for work. So he awaited his summons without impatience.

Dr Tariq had rehearsed what he wished to say. When, eventually, he was admitted to the presence of the Chairman he would have perhaps fifteen minutes to explain himself. It was well known amongst that elite of which he was a part that the Chairman detested news of crisis. But the killing of Professor Khan, no doubt at the hands of Zionist agents, and a letter bomb to one of his scientists at Tuwaithah, that was crisis and had to be confronted. The defection of foreign personnel from his programme, that too was crisis. Like every man who had direct contact with the Chairman, Dr Tariq had a most sincere fear of his master. He knew of the disappearances, the torturings, the hangings. He had been told that the Chairman had with a handgun shot dead a general who had dared to argue with his strategy during the dark days of the war. So he had prepared his words with care.

The officer approached him.

Dr Tariq, five foot two inches in height, thin as a willow wand, stood erect. He raised his arms, to permit the officer to frisk him. Then, without fuss, Dr Tariq opened his briefcase for inspection.

He followed the officer, stepping through the churned mud, towards the concrete steps down into the brigade post, and the presence of the Chairman of the Revolutionary Command Council.

Not yet past the lunch hour, and Erlich had had his first argument of the day.

It could have been the second, but he had swallowed his pride when they had shown him the room that was allocated to him. It was scarcely a box. Just a table and a chair and a telephone that wouldn't be secure, and the room was two floors and the length of a ministry corridor away from the Operations Coordination Centre of the Counter-Terrorism section at police headquarters. He had accepted that. What he would not accept was the refusal to make available to him, face to face, the eyewitness. It was not suitable that he should meet the eyewitness, he had been told. He didn't know how much of his fury had been translated by the interpreter. The guys who had been up at Lockerbie, after Pan Am 103, working alongside the British police, they didn't know how lucky they'd been . . . Same language, same culture, same team . . .

But they had given him photographs.

He had on the desk the photographs that showed Harry and his contact on the grass and the pavement. Every goddamn way they had taken Harry's picture, so that he saw the part of Harry's head that was intact, and the part that was blasted.

They had given him one written statement. It was a photocopy and the name and address of the eyewitness had been omitted. He copied into his notebook all that his interpreter dictated. Harry and the contact walking and talking in 28th October Street. No traffic. Twenty-eight minutes to nine o'clock in the morning.

The silver-grey Opel Rekord pulling onto the grass verge, braking twenty yards away. No description of the driver. A fair-haired man getting out of the passenger seat, front. A shout from the fair-haired man. The targets turning. The fair-haired man opens fire. Pistol plus silencer. The contact hit. Harry blundering into the field of fire. The second shout, the driver's shout, 'Colt'. The car turning in the road, getting the hell out. Harry dead, and the contact dead when the first police and ambulance crew had arrived . . .

He left his desk as bare as he had found it.

He took a taxi to the Embassy.

He had to wait for fifteen minutes before he was admitted to the Agency's annexe.

Erlich told the Station Chief what he had. He was seeking to trade information, and he was going to be disappointed.

'I'm not opening up our file to you, Bill. It's nothing personal . . .'

'And it's not cooperation.'

'It's the facts of life. I give you a file, it goes into your system. You nail a guy, weeks ahead, months, and my file is evidence. My file gets to be prosecution material. Any asshole who wants it gets to read my file.'

'Is that final?'

'As I said, it's nothing personal.'

Erlich stood. He had the cigar butt in the plastic sachet in his pocket. He had not spoken of the cigar butt to the Station Chief . . .

'Bill, look at it our way, do me that favour. Harry Lawrence was your friend and I appreciate that, but Harry Lawrence was not the target. An Iraqi was the target, and it's your assessment and it's mine. We are in deep stuff, real deep. We have a big mission down in Iraq, during the war we did all we damn well could to make certain those boys didn't go under to the Ayatollah's shit-pushers. We gave them AWACS material, we put up satellites just for them. The enemy of Iran is our friend, got me? But we keep our hands dirty, we stay in touch with the regime's enemies. We don't make any noise about that . . .'

'Investigating a murder is making a noise?'

'You've got a job to do, OK, but don't make waves.'

31

'I want to know the identity of a man, I want to reach him, I want to put him in handcuffs and read him a charge of First Degree murder.'

'Beautiful.'

'With or without help.'

'Brilliant. You're a detective, you don't mix easily in diplomacy, neither does hustling for commendations . . . You go on like this and you'll find yourself short of help.'

'With respect, what I'm after is a result.'

Erlich walked out. Didn't even bother to close the door behind him. He walked straight through the outer office and out past the security gate and the Marine guard.

He headed for the main building, and the area of the basement where secure matter could be despatched back home.

As she filled in the forms for him, the girl in Despatch, big and black and at last a friendly face, told him she was from Mississippi, and sure as hell she hated Greeks, Athens, moussaka and retsina. In front of him, she sealed the cigar butt in the plastic sachet into a small tin box and then into the padded envelope. The package was addressed to the Laboratory Division of FBIHQ. Erlich, like every other Fed, had plenty to grumble about in the running of the Bureau, but the Laboratory was the best.

'You OK, Mr Erlich?'

He'd slept poorly. He hadn't eaten breakfast. The coffee at Counter-Terrorism was ditchwater, and he had been poleaxed twice. He should have been at the airport last evening to see Elsa Lawrence and her children off and the casket. For Erlich not much was allowed to get in the way of a job and he supposed that was why he had been sent.

She said she would get him some coffee, proper coffee, coffee from home.

While she was making the coffee, boiling her kettle, he glanced across at her *Herald Tribune*. He saw the Rome dateline. He read the name of the hotel, and the name of the street. He had been in that street two weeks earlier. He read of the death of the Pakistani nuclear scientist last seen in the company of . . . no leads . . . The coffee she brought him was great, kept him alive.

All through the morning there had been detonations and gunfire. Of course there had to be detonations, and of course there had to be shooting practice, but Monday morning was hardly the appropriate time. On any other morning, Bissett would have been able to live with the thudding blast of the explosives and with the crisp rattle of sub-machine gun and pistol fire. But not that morning, not on the morning that the envelope marked Personal and Confidential had lain unopened in his briefcase.

He had spent two hours in his room, at his console. By 10.30 he had gone down the full length of the corridor that ran past his office and he had then spent two and a half hours in H3's laboratory. He had achieved next to nothing in his own room, and in the laboratory he had been the victim of Reuben God Almighty Boll's sarcasm. So that every technician and every junior could hear him, Boll had enquired just how much longer before his present project would be completed, how much later than it was already.

Lunch hour, and quite suddenly, when it didn't matter, it was perfectly quiet. Boll would be in the Directors' dining room, Basil would have gone to see his cronies in A area, Wayne would have gone out with those as young and limited as himself to the Hind's Head in the village, Carol would be in the canteen wittering with the other Clerical Assistants and her husband.

He had drunk his coffee. He had brushed the crumbs from his desk top into his wastebasket. He screwed the top, that served as a mug, back onto his flask. He was determined not to rush himself. He had deliberately not used his home address.

He replaced the plastic sandwich box in his briefcase, and took out the envelope. He checked that his door was closed. He tore open the envelope. A fearful mess of it, he made, because his hands were trembling.

33

There was the letter heading. Imperial Chemical Industries.

'Dr Frederick Bissett, B.Sc. (Leeds), AWE, Aldermaston, Berkshire.'

He didn't look to the end of the letter first. He exercised his self-control. He began at the first line. He held the paper in both hands and he saw the paper waver in front of his spectacles.

Dear Doctor Bissett,

Thank you for sending your application for employment, dated October 19th. I do understand that because of the nature of your current employment your CV has remained narrower than would otherwise have been expected . . .

Idiot. Of course his CV was narrow. He had worked for twelve years on matters covered by the Official Secrets Act, of which, obviously, he was a signatory.

. . . However, I understand from your application that you have been concerned in your AWE work with the areas of Fluid Dynamics and Plasma Physics, but with the necessary somewhat restricted interpretation . . .

How in heaven's name could his interpretation be other than restricted? His work was concerned with the interplay reactions at the moment of implosion. The effect of micro-second synchronized detonation of chemical explosive onto beryllium, then onto uranium 238, then onto uranium 235, then onto weapons-grade plutonium 239, and then onto the innermost pit and the core of tritium/deuterium. In the innermost pit, if the work of the scientists in the H area had been successful, it would be assumed that a nuclear explosion would generate a heat in the core of tritium/deuterium of one hundred million degrees Centigrade. So, yes, it was somewhat restricted.

. . . Sadly, it has been our experience in the past that the most specialized work carried out at the Atomic Weapons

Establishment leads scientists into a cul-de-sac of research that has little, or no, relevance to science as practised in civilian life . . .

The science that was relevant to Frederick Bissett was the moment, too fast for any but the most powerful computer to register, when chemical explosive was driven by uniform spherical detonation against the fissionable material of highly enriched uranium and plutonium creating some millions of pounds overpressure per square inch . . . His head dropped. In front of him the page blurred.

. . . With regret, therefore, I have to inform you that we are not in a position to offer you employment in any research division of the company.

Yours sincerely

Arnold R. Dobson, Personnel Director.

(dictated, and signed in his absence)

He felt sick. He took the letter and the envelope out of his office and down to the abandoned area at the end of the corridor. He fed the sheet of paper and the envelope into the shredding machine beside Carol's desk.

He went back to his room.

Later he would hear Carol's laughter, and Wayne's giggle, and the clumping tread of Basil's iron-tipped shoes, and the coarse grate of Reuben Boll's voice. And later he would hear the dull punch of explosive detonations. He would work until it was time to go home, on the new warhead design that would replace the free-fall WE-177 bomb with an air-launched cruise system. He would work on the mathematics of implosion until, in the late afternoon, he cleared his desk, and took his briefcase, with empty sandwich box and empty coffee flask, to his car, and drove home.

In crisp early morning sunshine the Air Force plane touched down at Andrews Air Base.

Nothing hurried, none of the subterfuge of moving a body quietly and in the dead of night out of Athens. The networks were there, penned behind a steel barrier. The high-level officials from State Department stamped their feet on the tarmac and waited for the aircraft doors to open. There was a bearer party, old friends and colleagues of Harry's. The Director of the Agency and the Director of the Federal Bureau of Investigation were there.

The FBI Director said, 'My first man into Athens, a young man but a good friend of Lawrence's, has promised the widow that we'd go for the jugular on this one.'

The Agency Director mused, 'But, whose jugular?'

'Whichever.'

'Something tells me you may bump into a little politics on the way.'

The FBI Director said, 'Just this once, fuck the politics.'

The Agency Director said, 'I didn't hear that . . . but I wish you luck.'

They had brought Agency men back to Andrews, in caskets, from Europe, from Lockerbie, from Lebanon, from Central America. It was a regular run for the Agency Director, down the Capital Beltway from Langley to Andrews. He was used to shaking the hand, gravely, of a young widow. He was accustomed to dropping his arm round the shoulders of young and fatherless children.

The aircraft door was open, and the cargo hatch.

They saw, at the top of the steps, the small, intimidated figure of Elsa Lawrence, her children behind her. They saw the casket taken from the cargo hatch, and draped in their flag, and lifted onto the shoulders of Harry Lawrence's work friends.

The Agency Director said, 'You know what? Half the CBS story on Lawrence last night was time taken explaining where Athens is.'

When it came to their turn, both men shook Elsa Lawrence's hand, felt her limp grasp in theirs. And both men put their arms round the children, and felt them flinch from the touch of strangers.

*   *   *

Dr Tariq, frail and looking as though the gentle zephyr that came in off the Tigris might flatten him, could muster a savage temper when attacked.

He had been badly damaged when the Zionists had sent their commando squad with explosives to La Seine-sur-Mer, close to the French port of Toulon, to destroy the two reactors that were to have been shipped to Tuwaithah forty-eight hours later.

That had been twelve years ago, just one year after the Chairman of the Revolutionary Command Council had promoted him to Director at the Atomic Energy Commission.

They had hurt him again, killing el-Meshad in Paris in 1980, and frightening off the Italian companies who had been engaged to deliver hot cell boxes.

And ten years ago he had been hurt worst of all when the Zionist Air Force, the F-16s and the F-15s, had come to Tuwaithah out of the setting sun to put down 16 tons of explosive ordnance onto the Osirak reactor. He would never forget the great dust cloud that climbed over the reactor shell, broken like a duck's egg, after the jets had soared away into the June evening. Hundreds of millions of dollars blown away. Hundreds of thousands of working hours lost. And the ground defence system had not got one shot off in retaliation. He could remember lying on the floor of his office on a carpet bright with the shards of his shattered windows, and how he had howled in his frustration. Over long years, he had sought to rebuild the nuclear programme, as he had been charged to by the Chairman of the Revolutionary Command Council. In those long years when the war had taken priority, Dr Tariq had rethought the detail of the programme. On the day after the Cease Fire he had been granted an audience with the Chairman of the Revolutionary Council and he had argued his case for the revitalization of his dream.

And now the Zionists had attacked him again. Professor Khan had been a crucial cog in the great mesh of wheels that made up the whole for the creation of an Iraqi nuclear warhead. He was a foreigner, he had been bought, just as Frenchmen had been bought, and Italians.

In the brigade post at Fao, Dr Tariq had won his day. The Chairman gave orders for the military helicopter to fly the scientist back to Baghdad.

In spite of the headset that he wore for the flight, his ears were still ringing when he climbed down from the helicopter. Waiting for him was an army officer, squat and powerful, rocking on the soles of his paratroop boots.

The voice of the Colonel was faint, hard to understand, as they scurried bent low from the helicopter's hatch door to safety beyond the reach of the thrashing rotor blades.

'I am at your service, Dr Tariq. Whatever it is that you wish, I am instructed to provide.'

In the late afternoon, Erlich was back from the airport. Protocol and politeness had taken him out to the airport to meet the Temporary Duty men off the flight. It was what should have happened to him when he had come in from Athens, and hadn't. Nothing better than a smoothed way through Customs and Immigration, and ready transportation for the trip into a new city. They would be on the same corridor as him in the Embassy's accommodation annexe, and later they would talk through the case history together.

The three TDYs were all senior to him, all had done more than ten years in the Bureau. He hadn't met any of them before. That was the way of these things. Only a small chance that an overseas liaison Fed would know the guys coming in as firemen from Stateside. The one who was born Greek and fluent had lost his baggage, presumably in transit in London, and wanted action, and seemed to think that young Erlich would do the needful. Erlich smiled coldly at him and said nothing. All three were exhausted, and two, the older two, would crash out and try and sleep away the jet lag, and the Greek ethnic could shout all afternoon and all night into the telephone for his bags. What it came down to was that Erlich had one last evening as an independent, and that from first light, from waffles and coffee time, he'd be part of their team and doing their bidding. The senior man, who had come in from Los Angeles to FBIHQ after Erlich had left Washington, he'd be everybody's friend, he'd have them eating out of his hand down at Counter-Terrorism, he'd probably take out citizenship. The other older one had been in Chicago, moved to Washington less than a year back, and Erlich knew his name because he'd the distinction of having run the sting in the Board of Trade's soybean futures pit. He left them to get their heads down.

They were all top of the ladder. He didn't know their long-term histories, but each one of them would have had the break far back, hooked into it, started climbing. He didn't reckon to waste his last evening as an independent.

He had the Embassy driver take him out, again, to 28th October Street.

He told the driver that he would find his own way back.

He started on the left side of the road.

Some of the gates were electronically controlled. He had to identify himself from the pavement. 'I am Bill Erlich, of the Federal Bureau of Investigation in the United States of America. I would be most grateful if you could spare me a few moments of your time.' One gate that he could open himself let him into a front garden patrolled by two Dobermanns, but he was OK with dogs because there had always been dogs at his mother's home, and at his grandparents' home. He could talk his way past dogs. Some of the villa front doors were wide open to him. He talked to maids, struggling with his limited Greek, sometimes doing better in Italian, and to the camp boy servant of an old woman, he talked to wives and husbands and teenage children. Some gave him their answer at the door, others invited him inside and sat him down to ask his question. To a few he was a nuisance, to most he was merely a curiosity. As each door opened to him, he made the same statement. 'A colleague of mine, an American official of our Embassy, was killed here yesterday morning. Did you, or anyone in this household, see anything of the incident?' Some gave him their life history, then came round to saying that they were in bed, in the back of the villa, in the bath, already gone to work. Some were brusque. They had seen nothing, they knew nothing. It was dark by the time he had finished with the left side of the road. He thought that none of those he had spoken to could have told him anything of the killing. He believed their denials. But there was fear there, shrouded by some with belligerence, hidden by others with courtesy. It wasn't any different from what it would be back home. None of them wanted trouble. Erlich had been on his last months in Washington when he had read the lesson, digested it, that safe folks crossed the road from danger, and didn't mind who they turned their backs on. He was in Washington, and Mrs Sharon Rogers was living her life out in San Diego, California. Trouble was that Mrs Sharon Rogers' husband had been commander of the USS *Vincennes*. Down in the Gulf, the *Vincennes* had blown an Iran-Air jet liner out of the skies and killed more than 250 people. The hit squad blew her vehicle off the road, and she was lucky to have jumped clear before the main explosion. How did the good citizens of San Diego react? Erlich would not criticize a timid woman or a timid man in the Kifisia suburb of Athens . . . The parents of the kids at the school where Mrs Rogers taught had her barred from the school, in case the hit squad came back for a second try. If Americans didn't stand up for Americans, why should Greeks stand up for . . . ? He worked his way down the right side of the road.

Of course, he remembered the front gates. The front gates were across the road from where Harry had died.

The flowers were still there. The rain and the wind had done them damage.

He walked through the gates.

He felt a stabbing pain at the back of his ankle.

A Pekinese had hold of his ankle. He kicked hard with his free foot. He heard the dog whimper. His trouser was torn, and there was blood on his fingers when he rubbed the wound, and he wiped it away on his handkerchief. He rang the front door bell.

'Good evening, ma'am. Do you speak English?'

It was the woman who had brought the flowers to the pavement. He could sense her fear. She stood with her hands on the door latch, as if she were ready to throw the door back in his face.

'My name is Bill Erlich. I am an agent of the Federal Bureau of Investigation from the United States. Yesterday morning, an old friend, an Embassy officer, was shot dead in this road . . .'

'Yes.'

'It was very much appreciated, your flowers . . .'

'It was nothing.'

She wore good jewellery, and her hair was freshly made up. She was not attractive, her jaw was too prominent, and her eyes too close set . . . Steady, Bill . . . It was the twenty-eighth house he had called at. The pain had gone from his ankle, but a throbbing replaced the pain.

'I'm looking for an eyewitness, ma'am.'

'Somebody who saw . . . ?'

'Somebody who saw my friend killed.'

'Is that not the job of our local police?'

'Indeed it is, but it is also my job.'

He saw that she hesitated. She wavered. Perhaps she recognized him from yesterday. The dog was at his ankle, and wary of passing him. She must have looked down at the dog, and seen the bloodstain and the tear on his trouser. She must have understood why the dog hung back.

'Is it important to you, to find an eyewitness?'

'Yes.'

'Would you come in, please, Mr . . . ?'

'Erlich, ma'am. Bill Erlich.'

She opened the door fully. He walked into the hall, and brushed his feet hard on the mat. This was money, serious money. He could see the money in the paintings and he could see also the alarm wires leading to them. Money in the drapes, and in the pottery that had a shelf to itself by the wide, dark wood staircase. Money in the rugs over which her slippered feet moved. She didn't take him to one of the two formal reception

41

rooms opening off the hall. She went ahead of him into the living room. A television set was playing *Indiana Jones*. The dog slunk past him and settled in front of the electric fire and growled back at him. He saw a child's head peer round the wing of the comfortable chair, the child from last night. She switched off the film, she waved for him to sit down. She motioned for the child to sit on her lap. Erlich thought the boy was about eleven, could have been younger. She spoke quietly in Greek to the boy, soothing his annoyance at the turning off of the video.

'Mr Erlich, more than forty years ago my country was divided by civil war. My father took one side, perhaps it was the right side and perhaps it was the wrong side. He was killed by the Communists. Mr Erlich, no one came to ask in that village for eyewitnesses . . .'

She held her child against her.

'. . . He is a bright boy, Mr Erlich. We had an English girl as a nanny for three years. Andreas learned good English from her.'

Carefully, no sudden movements, Erlich took from his inside pocket his notebook, and removed the top from his ballpoint.

The boy talked.

It was before he had gone to school. He was in the front garden with the dog.

He had seen two men walking in the road. He had seen them through the gates.

A car had come fast behind them, a silver-grey car, and it had braked sharply.

A man had climbed out of the car. A white-faced man, with fair to golden hair. The man had in his hand a gun with a long and fat barrel.

The man had held the gun out in front of his chest with both hands, away from his body.

The man had shouted. In front of him the two men had separated, reacted to the shout, and then to the sight of the gun.

The firing of the gun, a soft thudding. The smaller man was hit first, and then the taller man had seemed to move across to him, and then he had been hit.

The man with the gun had stopped, stared. And the driver had shouted. The man with the gun had run back to the car.

The car had turned and driven away.

That was it. The death of his friend, told in the simplicity of a child's-eye view.

'What were the shouts, Andreas?'

'The driver of the car, he shouted "Colt".'

'You are certain?'

'Colt.'

'Couldn't have been anything else?'

'Colt.'

He believed the boy. The belief was instinctive. He wrote the word 'Colt' in his notebook, and each time the boy spoke the word Erlich underlined it again.

'What sort of age?'

'Old.'

'How old?'

The boy turned to his mother. 'As old as Nico.'

She said, smiling, 'Younger than you, Mr Erlich, perhaps twenty-five years.'

'How tall? Heavy or light built?'

The boy's response was immediate. 'Not fat, just ordinary height.'

'Hair?'

'Fair, like Redford, but shorter.'

Erlich paused. He let the words sink, and he wrote sharply, and his eyes never left the boy.

'The other shout, the shout of the man with the gun?'

'It was "Hey, there . . ."'

'How did he say it?'

The boy shouted, 'Hey, there.'

Erlich tried to smile. 'Did he say it like Harrison Ford would have said it?'

'English, not American.'

'You know that difference?'

'Like Nanny Parsons would have said it, English.'

'Andreas, this is really extremely important . . .'

'It was English, Mr Erlich.'

'I could waste an awful lot of my time . . .'

'English.'

The words 'Hey, there' were underlined and across the top of the page he had written in bold capitals ENGLISH.

He apologized for his intrusion. The boy had been good. He had no doubts about the boy. Because he had taught school before becoming a Fed he had some experience of kids. Erlich helped out with the Little League team in Rome that played and practised at the American School on the Via Cassia most Saturday mornings. When he was in Rome, when Jo was off somewhere, he enjoyed being one of the helpers. The coach liked having him there. The coach was an Embassy staffer in Rome and said that it was twice as good having helpers who weren't parents. The Little League baseball squad was fine relaxation for Erlich. It had given him the chance to go on talking to and getting to know children and he was sure he would know if a boy was telling him the truth. He said no to tea, thank you, or a scotch and soda. He walked down the driveway to the main gates of the villa. He crossed the road. He bent by the flowers, and tidied them. He went down the road to the junction to look for a taxi.

3

'That's all you've got, Bill, the testimony of an infant child.' Don was a Fed from his shined shoes to the loosened necktie at his throat. Old guard, old school. Don had led the 'rotten apple' investigation five or six years back. The arrest of that worm had been the greatest cross Don had ever had to carry, the most dangerous traitor ever in the history of the government's security service. Erlich remembered his face from the network news, bleak and uncompromising and shamed, when the announcement was made. Don pushed away the breakfast plate and lit his pipe.

'Ninety-nine times out of a hundred a kid will tell you what he thinks you want to hear,' Vito said.

Vito was too sharp a dresser to look like a Fed. Gold bracelet, sports shirt, and a small crucifix dangled from a 24-carat chain round his throat. The soybean sting in Chicago had been his. Fantastic to have run two agents inside the sealed world of the soybean futures pit. It was said in Washington, at the level that Erlich had worked, that Vito could tackle anything, other than Mafia. He'd have been good there, with his background, but his wishes were respected.

'You take the kid's word and you're going down a tunnel, might be a wrong-way tunnel,' Nick said.

Nick, the Greek, was first-generation American. His parents had left a village in the mountains near the Albanian border just after the Civil War. He had the language. More important, he worked on Counter-Terrorism programmes specializing in the Middle East. In '87, Nick had been in Athens as one of the team that lured Fawaz Younis to a boat out of territorial waters, and put the handcuffs on him, and read him the charges of Air Piracy and placing a destructive device aboard an aircraft and committing violence aboard an aircraft and aiding and abetting a hijacking.

Nick was wearing yesterday's shirt and the damp smell round the breakfast table told Erlich that Nick had washed his one pair of socks the night before. Nick wouldn't be contributing much that morning, he'd be out buying his changes. 'If it's a wrong-way tunnel,' he said, 'we start burning up man hours.'

'The boy is telling the truth,' Erlich said.

'You'd go to the wall for the boy's story?' Don said.

'Yes, sir, I would, and before you dismiss that story, I'd like to take you out there to hear it for yourself.'

Don's eyes seemed to devour Erlich's face. They would have been told, all of them, before they left Washington that he was a friend of Harry Lawrence. Vito was eating, he'd left the decision to Don. Nick had his back to them, was trying to attract the attention of the waitress for his third can of Coke.

'Suppose we go with what the kid says, what do you see as the next step?'

'We have a physical description, we have a name or a nick-name, and I believe he's English. We have to start asking questions in London.'

Don said, 'So go to London . . .'

Erlich took his hand, shook it. 'Thanks.'

'Nick, take him to the airport, give him what you can.'

And they were gone.

Vito had raised his dark brows in question.

Don said, 'If he's right then that's the best. If he's wrong, so what's an air ticket? Catch on . . . Lawrence was his friend. I don't want anyone with personal feelings stumbling across my path. Feelings is for Rita Hayworth, that's what I used to get told.'

They drove north out of the city, the guard, his sleepless ever-present shadow, at the wheel. The road took them between the old splendour of the Khulafa and the Gailani mosques, and

46

across the railway track that wound half the length of the country to Arbil, and out through Housing Project Number Ten, and through the concretescape of Saddam City, the Chairman's way of marking the end of the Iranian war.

Colt had heard it said that after the war the country's debt was eighty *billion* dollars. Now, that was a sum of money to be reckoned with. Eighty billion was a little more than the mind of Colt could cope with. Never mind the debt, the slogan seemed to be, get the show on the road. The show was all around, as far as the eye could see, any direction. New hotels, new flyovers, new housing, new monuments to the Fallen Martyrs.

Back home, in a small Wiltshire town, dear old Barclays was nursing an overdraft in the name of Colin O. L. Tuck, which was £248.14 at the last count. You'd have to add interest, of course, but even so he would take his hat off to a man eighty billion in the red who never stopped spending. On the other hand the great portraits of the Chairman of the Revolutionary Command Council were way over the top by Colt's reckoning. Usually he was in camouflage smock and holding an AK at the hip, and would probably have knocked half his pelvis off from the recoil if he had fired at that angle. Sometimes he was in the robes of a desert prince and the headdress of Joe Arafat, riding a white horse. Sometimes he was in a City of London pinstripe and showing off his new dentures. Colt didn't hold with the personality bit, but he knew enough to keep his opinion to himself. Not least because – although Colt didn't suppose that the Chairman had an inkling of his existence – Colt owed the Chairman his liberty certainly, possibly even his life.

When they were clear of the city's traffic, Colt eased himself back in the seat and lit a small cigar.

He wore erratically laced army boots, and olive-green fatigues, and a heavy-knit dun brown sweater.

His eyes were closed. It might get to be a bit of a bastard, the next few days, and then it might just get to be amusing. But then, Colt liked fun, fun on his terms, and he'd give the bastards a run. It would be the third time that he had taken part in the escape and evasion exercises of the Presidential Guard.

He was one day past his twenty-sixth birthday. In two weeks' time it would be one year since he had first come to Iraq.

Colt would have liked his father to know how he was spending the next few days. It would give the old man pleasure.

At the village of Al Mansuriyah, below the escarpment of the Jabal Hamrin, as the sun climbed, they were met by a jeep. Colt was given a rucksack filled with a sleeping bag, field rations, water, and a first-aid kit. He was given a map, compass, and binoculars. He was shown on the map the village of Qara Tappah. Two of the Presidential guardsmen were giggling as they pointed to the name of the village that was his target.

He told the guard, his minder, to get back to Baghdad. He told the troops to go and scratch themselves somewhere else. In the centre of the village was the square, dominated by a portrait of the Chairman. Colt sat at a table outside the café that saw everything that moved in the village. He asked for coffee and fresh cake. He put his feet on an empty chair. He closed his eyes.

He would move at the end of the day. He was that rare person. He was the person, taught by his father, who preferred darkness to light, night to day.

She was hurrying that morning. There was little enough in her life that she could honestly say was exciting, but that morning she was a little nervous, and, yes, a little excited. She wanted to get all of the washing out, then cross her fingers for a dry day with a bit of sunshine and a drying wind.

'Morning, Mrs Bissett.'

Little Vicky, and she'd be standing on tiptoe to see over the fence, and not even dressed yet. God alone knew what the girl did after the golden boy had gone off to sell his 57 varieties, heaven only knew why she couldn't get herself dressed before ten o'clock.

She had a mouth full of pegs. 'I've told you, Vicky, I don't answer to that.'

A hesitation, a smaller voice. 'Morning, Sara . . .'

'Good morning, Vicky.'

It was her own fault. If she hadn't been an awkward, obstinate bitch of a teenager, it would all have been very different. If she hadn't sulked with her father, fought like a cat with her mother, she wouldn't now be hanging up Frederick's threadbare underpants on the drying frame in a tiny back lawn in Lilac Gardens, Tadley. There should have been a nice young man on the Sunningdale marriage circuit, and then a nice house in Ascot, and probably a cottage in Devon, and two boys at a good preparatory school in Surrey. But it had been her choice. She had turned her back on her upbringing, but it didn't matter how many times she told Vicky. She was always going to be Mrs Bissett to Vicky, and Mrs Bissett to Dorothy on the other side.

'Got none of this 'flu, then?'

'Wouldn't have the time for it, Vicky.'

'You busy, then?'

She saw Vicky's face, over the fence, crestfallen. Poor little soul must be as lonely as sin. Come in, join the club . . .

She said cheerfully, 'Big day today, Vicky. I'm joining an art class.'

She didn't have to tell the girl. She didn't have to tell anyone. She hadn't told Frederick, there just hadn't seemed to be the right time.

'Oh, that's clever, Mrs . . . Sara.'

'Probably be a bloody mess.'

She should have stayed and talked with the girl, but this morning, unlike most mornings, she had a deadline to meet. Simply didn't have the time to make soap-opera conversation over the fence. It was their fence, and it was coming down, and she had pointed that out to Frederick, and she had known he wouldn't do anything about it, any more than he would buy himself new underpants. He said that he much preferred the money they could afford for clothing to go onto the boys' backs, and onto her. She thought that her father probably now earned more than £100,000 a year, but she did not know for sure

49

because it was nine years since she had last visited him, four years since she had last received a Christmas card from him. Her mother didn't even telephone. No reason for either of them to write or telephone, not after what had been said.

'It would be wonderful to be able to do pictures.'

The telephone was ringing inside the house.

She had the last of the shirts pegged to the frame.

She should have stayed to talk to the girl, but her telephone was ringing.

'Sorry, Vicky, another time . . .'

She ran inside. She went through her kitchen, past the pool of water. Dorothy's husband had plumbed in the second-hand washing machine for her, and refused to accept money, taken all Saturday morning doing it. Because he had refused to be paid she couldn't ask him to come back again to deal with the seepage. So it would stay leaking. She went through the hall. They needed a new carpet in the hall, and on the stairs. She picked up the telephone.

'Yes?'

It was the bank manager, Lloyds.

'Yes?'

He had written twice to Mr Bissett.

'*Doctor* Bissett, yes?'

He had written twice asking for a meeting, and he had received no reply. There were matters to be discussed that were really quite urgent. Would *Doctor* Bissett be so kind as to call back and arrange the appointment?

'I'll tell him you phoned.'

He would be very grateful if she would do just that

She rang off. She had seen the two letters. The first had arrived ten days before, and the second had been delivered four days before. She had seen him, ten days before and four days before, scoop up the letters from the kitchen table and put them in his briefcase. He hadn't remarked on them, and she had not asked. Each morning she had been too busy getting the boys ready to query the letters from the bank. It was years since she had last been to an art class. She didn't really know what she should be wearing, but that morning she put on an old pair of jeans. All of her jeans were old. She had dressed in a vivid red blouse and a loose woollen blue cardigan, and she had tied her long dark hair into a ponytail with an orange scarf. She hadn't been to an art class since she had been married.

She thought that she looked good, and she felt bloody good, and she wasn't going to let a telephone call from the bank manager interfere with her seldom-found excitement.

When it was dusk, Colt walked out of the village of Al Mansuriyah. The last light played on the cliff wall of the Jabal Hamrin, but by the time he reached the steep-sloping ground he would be covered by darkness. The sun's rays lingered on the one narrow minaret tower in the village behind him, and on the flat roofs where the corrugated iron was weighted down with heavy stones against the spring gales.

When he was clear of the goat herds and the sheep that grazed around the village, he moved down to the river that was a tributary of the distant Tigris. His boots were comfortable, had a deep tread. He scrambled down to the water's edge. With his fingers he broke away mud from the riverbank and wet it in the river. He smeared the mud across his face, and then across his scalp so that it matted in his close-cut hair. He layered more mud onto his throat and down to his chest and across his shoulders. Last, he rubbed it over his hands and wrists.

They had tested him in Athens, now they tested him again. He had no hesitation in telling himself that he would win.

Failure, he had often said to himself, was not a part of his life.

He had sat forward, in Club, because Tourist was full. The whole plane was full and Nick had done well to get him a seat at all. He had never before been through Customs and Immigration at Heathrow. Not a bad experience, because there was an Englishman with Erlich's name on a sheet of cardboard waiting at the entrance to Immigration. That was good. He wouldn't have his suitcase to show. The man had a card that did the work at the desk, saved them the queue, and it did the business at Customs too. They guy let him carry his own case and led him through into the concourse where the English driver from the Embassy pool was waiting.

That was OK. He hadn't reckoned on one of the Liaison team coming down from Central London just to shake his hand, talk baseball results, and drive him back. It was a good run into the city, against the outgoing commuter traffic.

They ended up close to the Embassy in a road called South Audley Street.

The driver gave Erlich an envelope with his name and the South Audley Street address on it. Inside a glass door he was met by a security man, plain clothes, not at all talkative, probably from Kansas. He was given a key and left to find his own way up two flights of stairs.

It was a room like any other room. It was what Bill Erlich, the bachelor, was used to, clean and soulless. Inside the envelope was a note from the London-based Legal Attaché. He was tied up that evening, apologies, and the rest of his team were out of town. Could Erlich be at the Attaché's office at eight in the morning at the Embassy?

Erlich was alone in a city that he didn't know. He dialled Jo's number in Rome, and grew lonelier and sadder as it rang on and on, unanswered.

Colt could easily have killed him. Colt thought that 'elite' was the most overworked word in the military dictionary. He reckoned that the word elite was usually applied to those who had the best publicity machine. In the *Baghdad Times*, the English-language newspaper, the Presidential Guard were always written up as an elite force. They had all the kit, down to the nightscope. They had bivouacs, sleeping bags and cold-weather anoraks.

He had found the observation post two miles beyond the outer rim of the Jabal Hamrin. He had skirted it and approached them from behind. Three troopers of the Presidential Guard.

They did two hours on, four hours off. It was the first obstacle in his route from Al Mansuriyah to Qara Tappah, and he could have ignored it, simply carried on, but that was not his way. He had waited, motionless, until the frost had settled on his body.

The gag was across the trooper's mouth, and the pressure of Colt's knee was into the small of his back, and the sheer strength of Colt's arm took the trooper's wrists up into the blades of his shoulders.

He trussed the trooper so that he could not move his feet or his hands. On top of the gag, he forced into the trooper's mouth the trooper's own filthy handkerchief.

Where he had been a child, when the fox came at night around the barricaded chicken houses then the old bugger always scented the chicken house sides, left his stink, boasted that he had been there.

And it would amuse the Colonel to hear what he had done to the President's elite guard.

He would have a ninety-minute start on them, maybe longer.

'I am afraid, Dr Bissett, that ignoring facts does not make those facts go away.'

It was a quarter past nine. It was a clear hour after Bissett would normally have been at his desk.

'Now, if we could, please, just go over the figures . . .'

He hated to be late. It was the way that he had been reared. 'Your salary as a Senior Scientific Officer currently runs at £17,500. I am correct?'

He had heard Carol, only the week before, say that the man who delivered coal to her house was paid £345 a week. For loading and unloading sacks of coal, and driving a lorry round the villages, that was £440 per annum more than a Senior Scientific Officer earned slaving for the defence of his country. That was the society they lived in. No account taken of intellect and value.

'Your wife does not work . . . Don't misunderstand me, I am not implying that she should be working . . . I sometimes feel that a great many of our social problems at the moment, young people rampaging, are brought about by mothers going out to work . . . So, there is no other source of income coming into the household? Correct again?'

She had worked in the supermarket off Mulfords Hill for five and a half months. It had been the first time that he had really seen Sara in tears. Adam had fallen over in the playground, hit his head on a bench, been taken to hospital. The school hadn't had his number at AWE. The teachers couldn't ask Frank where his mother might be because his class was out for the day on a Project Course. The first Sara had known of Adam's injury was when she had turned up to collect him at the school gate. She'd told him about the looks aimed at her by Adam's teachers. That was the end of her working, and anyway the money had been peanuts.

'Your mortgage is currently set at £62,500, Dr Bissett, which is slightly excessive for the salary you command, but I do quite understand that you bought at the top of the market and that interest rates were then not at their present level.'

They had made the move to Lilac Gardens in the summer of 1988. They had paid £98,000. They had known they were on the knife-edge, and interest rates had been at 8 per cent. Sara had said that she was just not prepared to live any longer in the jerry-built little terrace at the bottom of the village.

'Now, your salary works out at approximately £1460 per month, gross. Then, we've tax, insurance, local government rates, pension contributions, and the mortgage. I would estimate that, allowing for your outgoings, you have around £600 a month at your disposal. But that, of course, does not take into account the loan we made you at the start of the year. Six thousand five hundred, repayable over three years, plus of course interest. That's another £180 per month, without interest. You are behind on the interest, Dr Bissett, and you are two months behind on the repayment . . .'

The loan had been to buy the second-hand Sierra, and then had been topped up to cover repairs required by the

MOT; and then increased again when Sara's Mini had just died on her, expired in the middle of the village with 110,000 miles on the tombstone. Sara had to have a car. And topped up again to pay for the repair of the flat roof over the kitchen, and the man who had done the work should have been prosecuted for fraud.

'Dr Bissett, I hate to say this to a government employee, but . . . private enterprise round here is on its knees for skilled and qualified people . . .'

'What I'm interested in is no use to the private sector. And I'm a research scientist, damn it, not a yuppie.'

'So be it . . . Can you look for promotion, a better salary scale, a higher grade?'

'I've been *looking* for it for years, but I'm not in charge of promotion and the people senior to me in my department are some of the most brilliant minds in England, and elsewhere for that matter.'

The bank manager eased back in his chair. He was young and a butterfly, flitting from branch to branch and all the time climbing. His elbows rested on the leather padded arms of his chair, and his fingers were clasped comfortably in front of his chin.

'Something has to be done. We cannot go on like this, Dr Bissett.'

Sara said that the exterior woodwork of the house was a disgrace and needed painting, and that the kitchen floor needed new vinyl, and that the hall carpet was awful. Sara said that if they couldn't do better than last year's holiday, a caravan in the rain in West Wales, then it wasn't worth bothering . . .

Bissett stood.

When he was angry then the Yorkshire surfaced again in his voice, the grate of the harsh streets of Leeds. So bloody hard he had fought to get those streets behind him. All that struggle, just to have this jumped-up little man lecturing him.

'Try telling the government that "something has to be done". Try telling bloody Downing Street "we cannot go on like this".'

'Nobody forced you to buy that house.'

Bissett stared at him. 'Don't ever say anything as stupid as that to me again.'

In his adult life he had never struck any person, certainly not Sara, not even his children in anger. He stood, looming over the manager's desk. His forehead beneath his curled brown hair was reddening. His spectacles had shaken down the arch of his nose. His fists were clenched at the seams of his trousers. His breath came in short pants.

'Steady down, Dr Bissett.'

He could see that his bank manager was further back in his chair, almost cowering.

The bank manager waited until Bissett was at the door, until he was sure of his safety.

'I have to say it again, Dr Bissett, we cannot go on like this.'

The door slammed. The papers leaped on his desk. In fairness, the bank manager would concede, he could not see where the poor fellow could make another economy and continue to live a halfway acceptable life. But the man needn't have shouted . . . Anyway, the whole thing was ridiculous, maintaining that white elephant when every schoolchild knew that the Cold War was over and done with.

Erlich's morning was a write-off. He hadn't expected the red carpet to be unrolled for him, but he had thought that at last he would be at work, setting up his meetings, on the move. The Legal Attaché was once more apologetic, he had a late runner in his programme, a problem with a fraud extradition. There were problems with the warrant, and the Legal Attaché was going to be down at New Scotland Yard for the morning, and probably for the afternoon. Could Erlich manage eight o'clock the next morning?

He rang Rome, the Legal Attaché's office, and spoke to the girl who typed his letters and answered his telephone. He didn't know when he'd be back and she should cancel everything for the next several days. A lunch with the *Capo dello Squadro Anti-Terrorismo* that he had been waiting a year for, a session with a good guy in the *Guardia di Finanze*, and a squash game with Dieter who was number two to the Legal Attaché, and he just didn't know whether he'd be back before the Little League All Stars trip to Naples and the game against the Sixth Fleet which was the high point of the season which they played now courtesy of the Italian sunshine into late fall. Everything on his desk to go into Pending.

He had never been a happy sightseer and until his work was done, until Harry Lawrence's killer was identified and caught he couldn't see himself playing the tourist at the Changing of the Guard, or the Tower of London, even Poets' Corner which he had longed to see, as a passionate student of English poetry . . . that would have to wait. When this assignment was well and truly nailed he would ask Jo, long chance, if she could get over here. It would be a pleasure to share these glories with Jo. By mid-morning he had been through the day's edition of the *Herald Tribune*. Under the dateline of Rome, that caught his eye, he read that increasing mystery surrounded the murder of Professor Zulfiqar Khan. It was now known that the body of the Professor who specialized in nuclear physics had been claimed by the Iraqi Embassy in Rome. It was not yet known what had brought the Professor to the city . . .

By the time he had read the *Herald Tribune* from front page lead to back page comic strip, the maid had come to make up his room. There was a sniff of disapproval signifying that it was out of court for a grown man to be still in his bedroom in mid-morning, and not at a place of work.

Her vacuum cleaner drove him into the street, in search of a coffee shop.

Two espressos and a Danish pastry later, he was reduced to buying postcards. One for Jo. He had tried again in the early morning, and again the phone hadn't been picked up. He could have rung the CBS office in Rome, and asked where she was, where they'd shipped her. But Jo never rang him at work, and he never rang her office secretary to find what flight she'd taken. That was their way, their understanding. The *Herald Tribune* had told him that there was more confusion in Prague, more rioting in Zagreb, an OPEC meeting in Geneva, and a European summit starting that evening in Madrid. She could have been assigned to any one of them. He wouldn't have admitted it to Jo, but deep down he resented it when she was out of town and not picking up his calls. They met whenever she had a free evening and he had a free evening, and it wasn't often. It was even rarer that they could share a weekend in the villages round Orvieto. They spent their evenings together in a *trattoria* on the square beside the Ponte Milvio or down in Trastevere, before a couple of hours at his place, or half a night at her apartment. They each said that it suited them, that kind of relationship. He wrote, 'Jo, honey, will you pick up the goddam phone? It's me, your friend, and I need to hear your voice. Where are you? Maybe you're in London. Will look more closely at all the girls in future. Just in case.'

One for his mother. His mother had married Herbie Mason just three years after his father had been killed. They ran a hardware store and diner in the White Mountains of New Hampshire, serving the hikers and campers up on the Appalachian trail. He rarely heard from his mother, but he rang her each Christmas morning, wherever he was, and on her birthday, and he sent her maybe a dozen postcards a year.

One for his grandparents. They were his mother's people, they had an old weathered brick house close to the harbour moorings at Annapolis, Maryland. He was fond of them both. A bit correct for a small boy, a little formal, but they had been his proxy parents for school terms after his father's death, and after his mother had taken off with Herbie. Good people. They had never once criticized his mother's behaviour in their grandson's hearing. School terms in Annapolis, and holidays in the White Mountains, it could have been a lot worse. His grandfather was retired Navy, action in the Pacific and off Korea, where he had his own command.

If his father had lived he would now have been in his sixtieth year. Every time that he wrote postcards to his mother and to his grandparents memories of his father revived. Memories of a man going overseas in his best uniform. Memories of a man coming home for burial, with full military honours . . . Such a very long time ago.

He had once heard an Englishman say that what he knew of nuclear physics could be written on the back of a blackcurrant. It was an expression that still gave him pleasure and he would have used it to describe his own limited grasp of the subject, but it would have been wasted on the sparrow-sized man across the big desk from him. The Colonel had swiftly appreciated that if he needed to describe Dr Tariq's sense of humour the backside of a blackcurrant was all he needed, and to spare.

Soldiering was what the Colonel understood. As a young paratrooper he had fought in the north against the Kurdish rebels. It was where his reputation had been forged. It was his battalion's heroic defence of their positions on the Basra to Baghdad road, when the rats from Iran had swarmed in their thousands from the marshlands, that had given him his present renown. He had commanded a unit of the Presidential Guard which provided close escort to the Chairman of the Revolutionary Command Council. When the traitor scum, the creatures of the Al Daawa al Islamiya, last tried to assassinate the Chairman, six of the Guard had been killed, the Colonel had taken a bullet to the stomach, but the Chairman had survived untouched. Rewards followed. The rewards of the Chairman could be generous. But the Colonel had seen to it that his name did not go forward for promotion. He could learn from the fate of those who had climbed too high. He would never be a rival, he would remain the loyal servant of the Chairman. Now he directed a section of the Military Intelligence unit concerned with the security of the state from threats outside its boundaries.

Dr Tariq told him of the death of Professor Khan, of the defection of the two French engineers, and of the Italian laboratory engineers, of a letter bomb that had been received, correctly addressed, to the same complex, to the very building alongside the one in which he now sat. He was told of Dr Tariq's passage throughout the offices and laboratories, his attempt to steady the morale of the Germans, the Austrians and of two more Italians and of a Swede. He was told that the fear must be cauterized, that the defections *must* be stopped.

'I shall be frank, Colonel. I have no time to waste.'

'Of course.'

'We can delude ourselves, and we could delude others, as to the real situation here, and what do we achieve? Only a crucial loss of time.'

'I understand, Dr Tariq.'

'If this complex had not been bombed by the Zionists in 1981, then we would by now have the capability for the production of nuclear warheads. During the war with the Khomeini zealots, I could not command the necessary resources to reactivate the programme following the '81 setback. I now have the necessary resources. I have the commitment of the Chairman. But – and this is why I am obliged to require your cooperation – at a certain level there are gaps in my team. In specific areas of the programme I am short of men of the required experience. I had recruited abroad in those areas. Do you understand me?'

'I understand you.'

'I had recruited Professor Khan . . .'

'I understand you.'

The Colonel needed no instruction in the politics of fear. He had ordered firing squads into Kurdish villages. He had executed in public deserters from his battalion when it fought for its life on the Basra to Baghdad road. He had witnessed the death by hanging of two members of the Al Daawa al Islamiya who were believed connected with the attempt on the life of the Chairman. Much of his present work was aimed at silencing, by fear, the community of dissidents in exile. Silencing them or killing them.

'The Zionists murdered Professor Khan, they sent a letter bomb, simply to create an atmosphere of terror amongst the foreign nationals employed by me.'

'Professor Khan travelled . . .'

'Covertly, of course. Yet evidently they knew his itinerary. Just as they were able to single out an important member of my staff here, and address him by name.'

The Colonel lit his cigarette. He blew the smoke to the ceiling. 'Then you have more than one problem, Dr Tariq.'

Dr Tariq said, 'Quite so, Colonel. I have someone leaking information from inside Tuwaithah. And I have the problem of filling gaps from outside, from the top echelons of a scientific community that is growing more, not less, hostile. As I said, I will be frank. I recognize the extent of the problem.'

'Where can you fill such gaps?'

'No longer from France, I think. Not perhaps from Italy, though these have been our best recruiting grounds to date. The Soviet Union and China are not impossible, but we have not been successful there before. The United States is difficult. Their security services are watchful and their private sector pays inordinately high wages. In Great Britain, on the other hand, the position is very different. I should look to Britain, Colonel. I should look to the Atomic Weapons Establishment in the village of Aldermaston in the Thames Valley.'

The Colonel laughed out loud. 'I get a bus, do I? I drive a bus to the front door. I shout in a very loud voice that the Republic of Iraq will pay well for atomic scientists. I fill the bus and I drive it to the airport. Is that what you have in mind?'

He had been right the first time. There was not a jot of humour in the man. There was the thin voice beating at him across the desk.

'You are reminded that I have the backing of the Chairman and the Revolutionary Command Council. And the Chairman, who deigns to place a measure of trust in you, Colonel, anticipates that what I want you will make it your urgent priority to find. I want a scientist who specializes in the physics of implosion.'

The Colonel took out a notepad. He wrote 'physics of implosion.'

He arranged to return at the same time the next day to set about identifying the traitor in Tuwaithah.

He left behind him the scene, still shockingly evident, of the destruction by the Israelis of the Osirak reactor, the flattened mound of concrete. When his car was past the missile launchers, past the guards, he demanded speed. He wanted to be through Baghdad before the evening traffic. He was quiet in the car – none of his customary banter with his driver – as he digested the consequences of failing Dr Tariq. The spy in Tuwaithah would be an interesting challenge. For once the wielding of fear as a weapon would certainly be counterproductive. But the procurement of scientists from overseas as a novelty intrigued him. It was somewhat outside his province and yet, he thought, anyone who was willing to leave a Western nuclear establishment to help Dr Tariq build his atom bomb was either an idiot or a traitor, and traitors were after all his special subject. And to solve Dr Tariq's problems all he had to do was to find two traitors. One here and pray he wouldn't be yet another scientist who needed replacing, and one in the West. The Colonel had a momentary vision of himself being captured by the Special Forces of a Western army as he tried to recruit a physicist . . .

He wanted to be at the village of Qara Tappah before dusk became night.

The newest building in the centre of Qara Tappah had been built in 1934. It was the coffee house. There were oil lamps hanging over the verandah, and they threw black shadows towards the mosque entrance, and towards the shop where clothes were sold, long since shut. Across the square ran the open sewer of the village. The lamps from the coffee shop flickered on its silver, glistening surface. The coffee shop was abandoned, the square was empty. There was not one villager who had dared to emerge from behind his shuttered door, not since the foreigner had come to the village.

At the edge of the sewer, Colt lay. The pain racked his whole body.

The headlights of the Mercedes found him. He heard the slamming of the car door. He looked up into the face of the Colonel.

'Did you win?'

He had come to the village at last light bearing a balaclava helmet, a webbing belt and trousers, and a mess tin all belonging to the Presidential Guard. He had won because, over twenty miles of open country, he had eluded the patrols of the Presidential Guard. He had walked, dishevelled and mud-plastered, out into the square from the coffee shop and thrown at the feet of the Captain those trophies that he had lifted from three different observations posts along the way. He had come through the back of the coffee shop yard, through the kitchen, out on to the verandah. Colt had laughed at the Captain and the men around him, laughed until they took out their failure on him with the most savage beating he had ever received. He wondered how much the Colonel had wagered on his winning.

His voice was a croak. 'No problem.'

4

Erlich was content just to be on home territory. He couldn't imagine a government servant working abroad who did not feel that tug of pleasure when he walked up the steps of his embassy in a foreign capital. Past the locally employed security man, that didn't count, and up to the best-dress marine. The marine was where Erlich could believe he started to belong. Four minutes sitting in the big lobby and hearing the splatter of the ornamental pool and waterfall, and the lady coming to meet him. In each embassy he knew that had a Legal Attaché's office there was a lady who looked like everyone's mother, and who did the confidential typing and the greeting downstairs. Just about time to take in the portraits of the most recent Ambassadors before she was at his side, hair in a bun, flat shoes, blouse and cardigan, and shaking his hand and making him welcome. Up three floors in the elevator, and away down the long corridor that was chaos because the electricians were rewiring the floor, and on to the security gate into Bureau territory. There must have been a blueprint in FBIHQ for Legal Attaché's premises, because the set-up in London, the mechanism of the outer security door, was identical to the one in Rome.

Occasionally, behind his back, subordinates called him Desperado; to his face he was always Dan. Feds all used their given names, whatever their rank. The Director was the only one who was called by anything but his given name. That was part of the folklore.

Dan Ruane, the Legal Attaché, was at home in his office, as if it was an extension of his comfortable house in North London. The Indian wars prints on the walls were his; he had his own bookcases, his own imitation-Georgian partner's desk, and his own tilting leather-backed chair. He was politely apologetic at having had to cancel the day before.

'What have you got, then, Bill?'

'His accent is English. Either his real name, or the name he answers to, is "Colt". He works for the Iraqis. It's ninety-nine per cent sure he was the hitman for the dissident. It looks like Harry simply got in the way.'

'Harry?'

'Harry Lawrence, Agency, also a friend.'

'Friendships should be sidelined for an investigation. But you'd know that. What else have you got on the killer?'

'Nothing else, not yet.'

'What's the Agency say down there?'

'They say it's the Iraqis, but no one is going to lift a finger of complaint even, until the case is watertight.'

'What do you want here?'

Ruane's giant stockinged feet were on the desk. His chair was tilted back as far as it would go. From the cupboard beside the screwed-down floor safe, he had taken a mess tin in which he kept his shoe-shining kit. He rubbed polish in little circles onto the shoes that Erlich thought were impressively polished. A West Point cadet would have been proud of those shoes already. It usually took Erlich little more than thirty seconds to get his shoes presentable, but Ruane was burnishing now with a golden duster.

'I want the bastard named, then I want to be part of a team that goes hunting him.'

'Sounds about right.'

'And this should be the town where I get him named.'

'Did you get much help in Athens?'

'Excuse me, they pissed on me . . .'

The polish and the dusters were folded neatly back into the mess tin. The mess tin went back into the cupboard. He couldn't see Ruane's face because it was bent below the rim of the desk, as he put his shoes back on. The voice was a growl.

'You like that, Bill, being pissed on?'

'Didn't bother me.'

'Won't lose you sleep?'

'Not a lot does.'

Ruane took a key from his pocket that was fastened to his waist belt by a fine chain. He unlocked a drawer. He took out a small black leather address book.

'Do you know what the form is in this country, Bill?'

'Never worked here.'

'Right, OK, digest . . .'

The shoes were back on the desktop. Erlich could only see the soles. At least the soles weren't polished.

'. . . In London I work *through* three agencies – you note that I say that I work *through* – I don't know what you guys get in Rome, but here it is *through* . . . that's most of the time . . .' There was a dry smile. '. . . The three agencies are, first, Secret Intelligence Service who are involved solely in overseas intelligence gathering, same as the Agency. Second, the Security Service who are internal, have responsibility for counter-espionage and are deep into counter-terrorism. Third, Special Branch of the Metropolitan Police who have about the same job as Security but are more upfront, more visible. What sticks in their throats, any of those outfits, is if we start running around like it's our territory.'

'Meaning?'

'It means that I am in a liaison role here. It means that I have to work through these guys. It means that I don't play round here like a Wyoming steer in a glass shop . . . unless I have to . . . Enjoy your day yesterday?'

'No.'

'Pity, it may have been your last day off for I don't know how long.'

The feet swung clear of the desktop. As his weight came off it, the chair heaved upright. Ruane had his address book in his hand when he went to the office door. Erlich heard his instructions to the lady who had brought him up to the third floor.

66

Three names, three numbers, appointments required that day. No excuses, no nonsense about previous engagements, three appointments that day.

Ruane turned back from the door.

'I was your age once. I reckoned to get ahead. Back then, I'd have given my right arm to have had the opportunity you've collared. Do well and you'll be going places, cross me and you won't. You with me? Nothing personal, Bill, but just remember that I work in this town; and for me to work here then I need doors opening up for me. You foul my pitch and you'll be on the next plane back to Athens, whether Harry Lawrence was a friend of yours or not, whether that damns your record . . . Got me?'

'Got you, Dan.'

The whistle on the kettle and the front door bell went off together.

Major Roland Tuck swore peaceably under his breath. Nurse Jones was a busy woman and he valued the minutes he had with her over a cup of tea when she came down from the bedroom. He left her propped against the Aga. The kitchen was the warmest room in the house, apart from the sickroom. He went through the hall with the dog at his heels. The dog invariably followed him to the door, as if she expected, with each visitor, that her master would be back.

He opened the door.

There was a young man standing in the porch and looking around him. Not much to look at, because the front lawn and the drive to the Manor were a shambles. The leaves hadn't been swept up, and the gravel was alive with weeds. Behind the young fellow was a small van belonging to a household cleaning firm.

'Major Tuck?'

'Yes.'

'Could I come in, please?'

'What for?'

The man looked around him again, as if he expected that they were being watched. Tuck didn't think they were, not that day.

'I have a letter for you . . .'

'Good heavens, my dear fellow . . . come in.'

Each time it was a different courier, a different cover. The young man followed him into the hall, carefully wiping his feet on the mat. The dog had lost interest and was heading back towards the kitchen. There had been two letters that year. He wanted the letters, of course, yet each time they had the effect of shattering the quiet routine of the Manor. The boy was their son, God dammit, no escaping that. The courier took an envelope from his inside pocket and passed it to Tuck, and also offered him paper and a pen, so that the receipt could be acknowledged.

Tuck held the envelope in his hand, and his fist was tight, screwing at the paper.

'I've never asked this before.'

'Asked what, Major Tuck?'

'Could I send a reply back with you?'

'Don't see why not. I'll give it them, can't promise more than that.'

He told the young man to wait in the hall. He went to the kitchen and asked if the nurse would be so kind as to wait, just a few moments, and he was out of the room before she could tell him how tight her schedule was. He left the young man to admire the ibex head that was mounted above the hall clock. He went into his study and shut the door behind him. He opened the envelope. He gutted the four sheets of his son's writing. He sat at the desk, a French antique, and took a sheet of notepaper. He wrote a single sheet. The boy was a wicked little bastard, but he had a right to know about his mother's illness. He didn't know whether Louise would last until Christmas. He folded the paper and addressed the envelope with the one word COLT.

He went back to the hall. The young man seemed mesmerized by the gentle gaze of the beast on the wall.

'Please ask those who sent you to do their utmost to see that my son gets this letter as quickly as is humanly possible.'

He let the young man out through the front door. For a moment he stood with his hand on the courier's shoulder, as though that were a link, however tenuous, with his son. He closed the door. He heard the engine start up outside. He did not think that the house was watched that day. The dog usually knew if the house was watched. When she had the hackles high on her shoulders, when she whined and scratched at the back door, then the house was watched. He went back into the kitchen. Thank the good Lord for that Aga, for its comfort. Nurse Jones, bless her, had made the pot of tea. She poured her own mug, stirred in two sugars, and then she poured for him. He had known Nurse Jones for thirty years, she was an institution in the village.

'Just time for a quick one, Major.'

'How is she?'

'I've left a shopping list for you – just the chemist in Warminster, and the supermarket.'

'Mrs Jones, how is she?'

'Losing the will to go on fighting – but then you'd know that better than me.'

'Yes.'

He sat at the kitchen table. On the table was that day's newspaper, and the previous day's, neither unfolded. He cradled the mug in his hands. She told him when she would be back. She said that she would see herself out.

When he had finished his tea, he slowly climbed the staircase. She had just had the pains when Colt had last written, not been feeling herself.

Perhaps it had all been his fault. Country people who ran whippets and lurchers and labradors and terriers said that there was no such thing as a bad dog, only bad owners and bad breeders and bad trainers. As the recent months had passed, and as Louise had sickened, he felt the guilt more frequently. He knew many people in the village, almost everyone except the newly

69

arrived and the ones who used the village as a dormitory and who worked in Bath or Chippenham or Swindon, but he knew very few that he could classify as friends. The problem of living in the big stone-built Major House on the edge of the village, with the trees shielding it from the road, and the drive. He could think of no man, or woman, in the village that he could have gone to and talked with, and been reassured on the question of his guilt. As his wife, as his Louise, had slipped, there was no friend with whom he could share the sorrow he felt over his son. In his own time he had been a maverick, and for being a maverick his grateful sovereign had pinned on his chest the gallantry medal of the Military Cross. In the worst passages of his despair, Tuck could believe that the little bugger had learned to be a maverick from his father.

At the door of her bedroom, he paused. He loathed to be in the room now. It was the room they had shared for thirty years since they had moved in to claim his inheritance. He slept next door now, in his dressing room. He paused, so that he could shed the sorrow that had taken hold of him.

He was smiling when he went into the room.

'Good news, *ma petite fleur*, a letter from that young rascal of yours, a letter from Colt.'

The room was dim because the curtains were half drawn, but he saw the sparkle of her eyes. He walked to the bed, and he sat, and he took the gaunt hand in his own.

'I'll read you what the blighter has to say for himself . . .'

Erlich didn't know Englishmen. He had never had to work alongside them.

He thought this one must have escaped from the National Theatre down the road.

They were in a pub overlooking the Thames, a stone's throw from Century House, the Secret Intelligence Service offices. There was no way that SIS would allow Erlich into their tower block, Ruane had warned him in advance.

The stage Englishman wore a pink silk shirt and a lime polka-dot bow-tie. He was old and pompous. They were in the crowded saloon bar with the lunchtime white-shirt crowd, while the other bar was filled with the building trade. To Erlich, it was an idiotic place to meet. They were forced to sit so close that each wrinkle of the boredom on the man's face was apparent. The man seemed to think that everything said to him was excruciatingly tedious and barely worth his attention. Erlich drank Perrier, Ruane drank tomato juice. The Englishman drank two large gin and tonics, without ice, with lemon. Erlich gave him the name of Colt. He was told that it would be checked out.

Outside, watching the man stride away along the pavement, Ruane said, 'Just because they speak our language, don't imagine they do things the same way. Right, the Agency has an address, and a signpost at the right turning off the Beltway. These people don't exist, not here anyway. Very shy people . . .'

'Are all of them that exotic?'

'Colourful, I grant, but underneath that conspicuous plumage you will get to know, if you are as lucky as you are ambitious, a very down-to-earth bird. He organized, was control of, a mission into the Beqa'a Valley. He achieved with a marksman more than a Phantom wing of the Israeli Air Force could have, took out a real bad guy.'

Erlich said deliberately, 'Sorry I spoke.'

Major Tuck's letter to his son, by now encoded, was transmitted by teleprinter to the Defence Ministry in Baghdad. All matters concerning Colin Olivier Louis Tuck were dealt with in that small group of offices behind their own perimeter fence and guarded by their own troops. By the time that Colt's father had warmed a broth to take upstairs with the scrambled egg and toast that he would himself eat for his supper, the letter to his son would have been delivered to the Colonel's department.

Time, in Frederick Bissett's private world, the world of H3, was referred to as a 'shake'. Time was 'quicker than a shake of a lamb's tail'. A shake was measured at 1/100,000,000th of a second.

The nuclear explosive process that would obliterate a city involved a reaction taking place in a few hundred shakes. *Distance* was counted in new language, because it was necessary to be able to refer to the diameter of a unit as small as that of the electron that orbits the neutron in the core of the atom. The diameter of the electron is a 'fermi', named in recognition of the Italian scientist who achieved that mathematical calculation. There are 300,000,000,000,000 fermis in twelve inches. *Temperature* was talked of in the context of some hundreds of millions of degrees Centigrade, necessary for the stripping away of the electron from the hydrogen atom, vital for the removal of the hydrostatic repulsive forces of the nuclei, leaving them free to collide. The greater the temperature, the greater the force of the collision, the more complete the reaction. *Pressure* was worked on the scale of 'megabars'. The pressure in the pit of a nuclear explosion was one megabar times one million, equal to 8 billion tons per square inch. *Energy* was the release of such power that 2.2 pounds weight of the material, plutonium, could in the event of complete fission produce violent strength in the muscle of physics that was equivalent to the detonation of 20,000 tons of conventional explosive.

For his work among those Times, Distances, Temperatures, Pressures and Energies, Senior Scientific Officer Bissett, Grade 8, was paid less than his neighbour the plumber and his neighbour the tinned-food salesman.

Reuben Boll was at his door.

The man's voice boomed in the small room, would be heard down the corridor in the outer office where Carol lorded it over her clerical assistants.

'Tell me, kindly tell me, when is your material going to be ready?'

Bissett did not reply.

Each month the pressure of the work was greater. He should draw a graph of the increasing pressure upon his work.

The Trident programme had seen the start of the pressure, because the submarine-launched system was the priority programme at the Establishment. Everything was sacrificed to Trident. Bissett's own project had been shunted backwards, removing from him colleagues, laboratory time, engineering space, facilities. The staff shortages were the further factor. Fewer scientists, fewer technicians, fewer engineers. What sort of first-class science graduate would be recruited to AWE when he could earn half as much again or double in the private sector?

There might not be money for Frederick Bissett's salary or funds enough to supply him with badly needed backup, but by God, oh yes, there was money for the building programme. More than a billion for the A90 complex, and he had heard, and he believed it, that there was £35 million of money just for the new fencing and perimeter security equipment . . . money for that, money no object for the bloody contractors.

'Frederick, I asked when is the material going to be ready?'

He felt so hopeless. 'Soon, Reuben.'

'What is "soon", Frederick?'

'When it is ready . . .'

'I have a meeting in the morning, Frederick.'

'I am doing my best.'

The fact was that the facilities were not there. Computer time was not possible. Staff were not available. Every time he went across to A area, he was lucky to get half an hour of their time. He would be heard out, and he would see the shaking heads, and he would be told that facilities and staff were tied down, knotted down, on Trident.

'So, what do I tell them?'

'Tell them whatever the hell you like . . .'

He heard the door close.

Absurd of him, because at the end of the following week the annual staff assessments were due to be drawn up by the Superintendents. His own assessment was written up by Boll.

'Nice to see you, Dan.'

'And you too.'

'Wife enjoy herself?'

73

'Very much, apart from the prawns.'

'Ah, the prawns. Not universally successful, the prawns.'

Erlich sat back. The chair was not comfortable, but at least they were allowed inside the building. What a heap . . . They had come back across the river and they were in a street close to the Embassy. He had seen the building the day before when he lit upon a trattoria for his supper, without of course realizing what it was. He was learning. The lesson said that neither the Secret Intelligence Service nor the Security Service advertised themselves. There had been no sign on the doorway, just a number. Erlich wondered how men and women could work in such depressing surroundings. They had been allowed in, they had gone past the uniformed security, and then had had to sit and wait in a grey-painted lobby, watched by the plainclothes minders, before the man had come down for them. They were in the building, but only just. They were a dozen paces down a ground-floor corridor, and then ushered into an interview room.

'I'd like you to meet Bill Erlich, FBI.'

'I'm Bill, pleased to meet you.'

'James Rutherford. My pleasure.'

Erlich looked across the bare table at Rutherford. He saw a solid man, good shoulders on him and a squat neck and a good head of dark hair. He thought the guy would be about his own age, certainly not more than mid-thirties. His working clothes were bottle-green cords and a russet sweater worn over an open check shirt.

'What do I call you?'

'What you like, Bill.'

'Most people just call him "Prawns", "Prawns Rutherford",' Ruane said.

'James will do nicely.'

Ruane said, 'Christ, are we formal? OK, work time . . . Harry Lawrence, Agency, shot dead in Athens, am I going too fast for you?'

'I read the reports.'

'The bad news is that the trail leads right into your front garden. Tell him, Bill.'

Erlich told Rutherford what he knew of the assassin who spoke with an English accent, and to whom the word 'Colt' had been shouted.

'Is that *all*?'

'That's all I've got so far.'

Rutherford hadn't made a note. He had just nodded his head, and then returned to the talk about the social evening, and how difficult it was to be safe with prawns, and he had wanted to know if Dan and his lady would be coming to the Service's New Year's Eve party.

Out on the pavement, Erlich said, 'Thanks, Dan, but I wouldn't classify that guy as a picture of enthusiasm.'

There was a moment of sharp anger from Ruane. 'He's as good, for his age, as they've got, and his wife is one of the sweetest women I know in this town. If you just happen to stick around here you'll learn to sing his praises. He can be a friend, a really fine friend. Oh, and don't tell him your war stories because they might just seem trivial to him.'

Debbie said, 'But you've *got* to come . . .'

Sara shook her head. She pulled a face. 'Just no can do.'

'Sara, we are a group of middle-aged, well, nearly middle-aged, housewives, who amuse ourselves while the men are toiling, with a little bit of painting, sketching. There's no one in our cosy little set-up who has a quarter of the talent you have. I won't hear of it.'

'It's just not possible.'

Debbie persisted. 'We go after the kids are safely in school, we're back before they come out. Everyone's got kids. We'll be back in yonks of time . . .'

Sara looked away. She turned her back on Debbie. She looked out of the window. They were in the dining room of Debbie's house. She looked out through the big picture window and across the manicured lawn and down towards the ponds and away towards the line of birches at the bottom of the garden. It was a big house, at least four good bedrooms, and the garden must have been the best part of two acres.

'Is there a problem? I mean, tell me. Is it just because we're *amateurs*?'

The classes were at Debbie's house. When she had rung in response to the advertisement card on the board in the Tadley Post Office, she hadn't thought of where the classes might be. She had wanted to draw again, and to paint, and she had not wondered before the first class as to the group she would be joining. She was the outsider. She came from a housing estate in Tadley, and her husband worked at the Establishment behind the Falcon Gate. She had not stopped to think that she might be inserting herself into a social scene that she had walked away from when she had left home. Rich wives, with rich husbands, simply amusing themselves twice a week. She liked them, that was the trouble.

After the class they treated themselves to lunch, cold poached salmon the first day and the best cut of cold beef the next, and wine to go with it, and a raffle amongst the six of them for a bottle. Five pounds for each class . . . And there had been her materials. She could say, in all honesty, that she had looked out her college paints and brushes but they had been dried up and beyond recall. It must have been a dozen years since they were last used. For the first class she had just taken two soft pencils, and she had sketched while the others had mixed watercolours for the still life of a bowl of apples, oranges and pears. For that day's class she had taken her own watercolours, bought with the Visacard in Reading . . . They were going by minibus to London for the visit to the Tate Gallery, with a driver, and the transport alone was £15 a head.

Just a miserable mistake.

She had waited behind after lunch. She had helped Debbie clear away. She had wanted to speak to Debbie after the others had left, and all the talk over lunch had been of the trip to the Tate.

76

She could have bought each of the boys a pair of trainers for what she had spent on the watercolours.

'It's nothing to do with whether I'm good, whether I'm lucky enough to have been given more talent than you, the rest of you . . .' It was to do with money, bloody, bloody, money.

She turned back to Debbie. She felt dirtied in her old jeans, and her old student painting smock. The other women hadn't pulled something out of a bottom drawer to come to the classes. The other women, Debbie and her friends, would have been shopping in Newbury or Hungerford, run round the boutiques, for something careless and suitable. Debbie's husband owned a software business outside Newbury.

'Bloody hell, am I stupid.' Debbie's voice had softened.

Sara turned to her. There was a turquoise stone set in a pendant and hanging from a fine gold chain at Debbie's throat. The chain was long, too long, and Debbie had unbuttoned the two top buttons of her blouse so that the stone wouldn't be hidden. Sara thought the stone would have cost all of their own take-home money for a month after the mortgage was paid.

'It's boring old money, isn't it?'

Sara nodded. She should have been at home. She should have been thinking about the boys' tea, and about Frederick's dinner.

'Well, I have the solution,' Debbie said. 'You're going on the payroll, Sara. You're going on a freebie to the Tate because you're going to be our guide. And here, too, because when we need a model, you will be our model.'

She wanted so much to belong, could not help herself.

Debbie said, 'You're prettier than any of us, anyway. You'll be brilliant.'

Sara said, 'I really don't . . .'

'You're not *modest*, are you?'

The Chief Inspector was not a snappy dresser. If he had been working for three days and three nights then it was in the suit he was wearing now, and his shoes had mud on them, and Erlich didn't think Ruane would be impressed.

77

A yawn, then a big sigh. They were in a small office on the fourth floor, and one wall of the office was glass, and the heater was full on. Again the yawn.

'Now, what can I do for you, gentlemen?'

Erlich was getting sharp on the routine. He could get through it in a minimum of words. The voice was English, the face was Caucasian. Height, about five foot ten inches. Age, mid-twenties. Eyes, bluish. Complexion, tanned. Build, solid without spare weight. Hair, short and fair. The name he answered to, 'Colt'.

The Chief Inspector of Special Branch no longer yawned. 'An Englishman shoots a CIA staff man and an Iraqi journalist in Athens, that's a pretty bizarre setup, Mr Erlich. What's the motive?'

'Iraqi state-sponsored terrorism. Our opinion, they would have set it up, used your national as the contract man.'

'Can't be all that many Englishmen qualified for work of that sort, don't grow on trees. A single shot, you say, through the head at twelve paces. He ought to be quite an interesting young man.'

Erlich said, 'I want an identification.'

'I'm sure you would . . . Working for Iraqi intelligence? An Englishman? If we find him for you, I fancy we'd value a few minutes of his time ourselves, if we find him . . .'

And the yawn broke again on the Chief Inspector's face.

Erlich said, 'I'm asking for your best effort, sir.'

'Do what I can, can't promise more.'

Erlich thought that he wouldn't be doing anything before he'd put his head down. Trouble was, if he put his head down then he might not wake up again for twenty-four hours.

He went through the hallway of New Scotland Yard with Ruane, past the flame that burned alongside the Book of Remembrance. Outside, he braced himself as the wind lashed them.

'Will he do us the business, Dan?'

'Maybe. He'll do his best.'

78

Erlich said, 'I didn't get the message we were exactly priority.'

Ruane said, 'They may have a crowd in town from Abu Nidal. That's to say, they do have a very dangerous crowd, they just think they're Abu Nidal. They have no line on a target, but they have four addresses staked. He came off that to meet you.'

'Good to hear that somewhere at least the killing of an American matters.'

'No, it's not that . . . he owes me at poker.'

Colt was escorted into the Colonel's office.

He was invited to sit, he was offered a cigarette. He sat opposite the Colonel. He declined the cigarette, he lit for himself a small cigar. The Colonel beamed across at Colt.

Not for Colt to ask why he had been summoned to the Intelligence Section of the Ministry. He rarely asked questions of them. He had learned early on that they did not appreciate questions. They appreciated only answers to their own questions. He jolted. Away along the corridor from the Colonel's office, a man screamed. A rising wail of pure agony. And then a shorter second scream. And then silence.

Colt had already shut the sound from his head, and the Colonel showed no sign of having heard it. When a rabbit was in a snare, pinioned, and the fox closed in, then the rabbit screamed in fear and agony. Colt knew the sound, he knew the ways of the regime that was his host.

'Are you well, Colt?'

'Very well, sir.'

'Not damaged?'

'Girls I know, sir, could have hurt me worse.'

The Colonel smiled. 'I won a bet on you, Colt.'

'I hoped you would, sir.'

'I bet my friend, who commands the 4th Battalion of the Presidential Guard, that he could deploy fifty men and that none of them would lay hands on you. But you were impertinent to take their kit.'

'I hope it was a good bet to win, sir.'

'The favours of a Thai whore . . .'

Colt grinned, and the Colonel laughed. Colt sat upright in the chair, there was less ache in his spine that way, less of a throb in his kidneys. His body was still a rainbow of bruises.

'Colt, will you tell me about your father?'

He spoke in a flat monotone, suppressing all the emotion he might have felt. 'He comes from what in England is called a good family. His parents had status, what a good family means. He is seventy. Being of a so-called good family doesn't mean much these days, and the sort of money required to keep things ticking over a few years back doesn't get you anywhere now. After the war, when he was out of the army, he tried his hand at several things, and they were all pretty much a disaster. The money he had inherited with the house just wasn't enough. He tried business, just about anything. When I was a child he was selling insurance, then he was offloading imported sheepskin coats in the London street markets, then it was free-range eggs. None of them worked. I really don't know where the money comes from these days. They live, him and my mother, in one of those damn great draughty houses in the country. I suppose it's just about falling to pieces. It was after the war that he married. My mother is French, they met in the war. Truth is that everything that was best in my father's life happened during the war. He was a young regular officer, Brigade of Guards, at the start of the war, and he went to France with the Expeditionary Force. You'll have heard that they lifted the army off the beaches at Dunkirk. They took most of them off, but the rearguard and the wounded were left behind. My father was in that last line that protected the beachhead. When he knew they were going to surrender in the morning, he slipped away from his unit. I suppose you could say that he deserted. He moved out into the countryside, and eleven months later he was back in England. He had moved himself right across France and through Spain to get himself repatriated. Early in the war, in London, they set up something called Special Operations Executive, and my father was a natural for it. He was recruited. In the next three years he was twice parachuted into Occupied France. There are parts of France, used to be anyway, where he was almost a legend. Won't be too many places he'd be remembered these days, all those who could remember him are dead, or trying to die. He was an explosives man. Signal boxes on the railway, power lines, bridges. When they sent more men across, to liaise with him, it didn't work. He was his own man, never a team player . . . As long as the planes came to drop his explosives he didn't give a damn for the rest of the war effort. When it was over he was given a Military Cross by the British, and the Croix de Guerre by the French. It was the best time of his life, and everything since has been second best. He's older than his years and I don't know how much longer he can last.'

'You are proud of him?'

'We used to fight, morning, noon and night. Once with fists and boots and teeth.'

'Is your father proud of his son?'

He could remember clearly, when he had last been at the Manor House, the day he left. His mother had been crying as she had rifled the house for money for him, and as she had made sandwiches to put in greaseproof paper because it would be dangerous for him to stop at cafés on his way to the airport. His father had followed him from room to room, half a dozen strides behind him all through that late afternoon. When the telephone call had warned that Micky and Sissie had been arrested, there had been no option but to run. There was bound to be something in their squat that would lead the police to him. He had gone out through the kitchen door. He had left his dog tied to a drainpipe by the kitchen door, so that it could not follow him. At the end of the kitchen garden, by the stile to the open fields, he had looked back. They were framed by the kitchen doorway. His mother's head was bowed in her tears. His father had stood erect, his arm round his mother's shoulder. His father had not spoken a single word to him, just followed him around the house, not a solitary word. His mother had waved him on his way, not his father.

'I doubt he'd think there was much to be proud of.'

The Colonel bent to retrieve a sheet of paper from his brief-case, then pushed the decoded typescript across the desk towards Colt.

Colt read the letter that had been written that same morning, in haste, by his father.

'I need to go home, sir.'

James Rutherford, first thing after he had closed the door behind him, took a tumbler of malt whisky up the narrow staircase to his wife.

Penny said, 'If it doesn't kill the prawn bugs, it'll finish me.'

'Are we on the mend?'

'Reckon so.'

'Dan called by today. You're not alone, his missus has the same.'

Rutherford knew that his wife liked Dan Ruane, always had a good word for him. Service wives were not generally involved in the social scene, only when it was an American evening. Penny would have known more wives from the Agency and from the Bureau than she would have met wives from the Service. She was sitting up in bed, and she drank, spluttered, and grinned.

'Brilliant . . . what did Dan want? Sorry, sorry, wasn't thinking . . .'

She was the well-drilled Service wife. She had to be. Service wives did not grill their husbands about *bloody work*. She made it her rule that Belfast, the Provisional wing of the Irish Repub-lican Army, casual atrocities never crossed her lips, not after his last trip away, because the man who had come back to her from Northern Ireland had been frightened of his own shadow. She hoped to God that he would never have to go back there again. But James Rutherford didn't give two tosses for that particular tenet of Service discipline.

'The American killed last week in Athens, Agency man, looks like he was shot by a Brit.'

'You're joking?'

'No. Some sort of renegade, some dreadful little creature

looking for a cause to pin himself to, I expect. The Library's trawling for him.'

'And how was Dan?'

'Didn't really have a chance to talk to him. He'd a chap in tow who is doing the case. Civil enough young fellow, bit gauche, bit wet behind the ears.'

Penny giggled. The malt was working the colour back to her cheeks.

'Well, he's American, isn't he?'

Erlich sat in his quarters in South Audley Street. He had half an hour before Ruane took him to dinner. There was a card game next door whose progress he could hear through the partition wall.

When he had left the University of California, Santa Barbara, he had taught literature at a school in Battle Creek, Michigan. He taught the children of 'Cereal City'. Everyone worked for Kelloggs, and the plant turned out, each day, enough for ten million people's breakfasts. The kids didn't want to know about life outside Battle Creek. They wanted to get on the production line and turn out more breakfasts. They were enough to stretch a teacher who wanted them to learn the beauty of poetry. They'd stretched him, but they hadn't snapped him. While he had been kicking his heels yesterday he had spent an hour in a tiny book-shop in Curzon Street and had come away with a paperback edition of the Parsons *Rosenberg* and the Seamus Heaney and Ted Hughes's anthology. He had left home so hurriedly as to have packed not one of the poetry volumes that he was very seldom without.

While he waited for Ruane to be announced from the hall desk, he read.

> Red fangs have torn His face.
> God's blood is shed.
> He mourns from his lone place
> His children dead.

His father would never have heard of Isaac Rosenberg, an English poet, killed in the last weeks of the 'war to end all wars'. His father had died at somewhere called Duc Co that was somewhere in the Central Highlands in Vietnam. He thought of the cruel death of Isaac Rosenberg and the death of his father in the breaking of the siege of the Duc Co Special Forces camp.

> Move him into the sun—
> Gently its touch awoke him once,
> At home, whispering of fields unsown.
> Always it woke him, even in France,
> Until this morning and this snow.
> If anything might rouse him now
> The kind old sun will know.

This he could recite without the book, a poem of Wilfred Owen's which he had impressed into the minds of every one of his pupils in Battle Creek.

> Think how it wakes the seeds,—
> Woke, once, the clays of a cold star.
> Are limbs, so dear-achieved, are sides,
> Full-nerved – still warm – too hard to stir?
> Was it for this the clay grew tall?
> – O what made fatuous sunbeams toil
> To break earth's sleep at all?

He thought of his father, killed thousands of miles beyond reach, of Wilfred Owen, killed, of Harry Lawrence, his friend whose death he *could* avenge. And of Elsa and her children. He had made his promise. For Erlich there was no way that promise could be undone . . .

The telephone rang. Ruane was downstairs.

He went fast down the stairs.

'Have they got anything?'

Ruane said, 'One fence at a time, Bill.'

Carol had told him before he went home, so Bissett knew what to look for – Carol was the conduit of all the gossip for H3 – and it put him in his best humour of the day.

He made a detour to see it. Across Fourth Avenue, right up to the inner perimeter round B area. Through the close-mesh fence topped by razor wire he could see the wide double doors large enough to let a three-ton lorry into the huge earth mound. He saw the aerosoled message: 'WE WOZ 'ERE'.

As Carol had heard it, the Special Air Service had somehow broken through all the perimeter fences in the night, evaded the Ministry police and their bloody dogs, and reached the doors of the earth mound where the chemical explosives were stored. Carol had said that the SAS had also penetrated A area where the plutonium spheres were fashioned, walked right into the Citadel of the Establishment. Never mind about A area, in B area it was plain to any Tom, Dick or Harry. Bloody well done, the SAS. Bissett, along with almost everyone else at AWE, had a profound disrespect for the Ministry police. So many times held up at the Falcon Gate, so many times made to open his briefcase and his empty sandwich box and turn his empty coffee flask upside down when he was anxious to get home, so many times subjected to their questions when he was going about his business visiting other corners of the Establishment. He could see the savage glower on the face of the Ministry policeman some fifty yards ahead of him. So, the SAS had been in and demonstrated that the Ministry police security was a load of rubbish . . . Bloody well done, the Special Air Service. He imagined with pleasure the bollocking that would be administered to the men who had been on duty the previous night. Perhaps they would be a little less arrogant in future.

'In London, in 1934 when the knowledge of the power of the atom was a dream in very few minds,' Dr Tariq said, 'there was a Hungarian refugee. His name was Leo Szilard. It was he who first comprehended the potential of that atom. He foresaw a release of energy utterly beyond anything considered by scientists before him. He was standing on the pavement of a street called Southampton Row. The idea of this power, this energy, came to him as he waited for the traffic lights to change so that he could cross. If he had been able to cross immediately then perhaps the idea might never have formed in his mind. It was pure luck. But also his very great skill and his dedication – the fact that he was a Jew does not undo his skill and dedication – *earned* Leo Szilard his luck. If you work with great skill, Colonel, and with great dedication then you will earn your luck.'

The Colonel elaborated on the straightforward business of the reference section of the Ministry preparing for him a dossier on the British nuclear weapons programme. He also reported to Dr Tariq that he had put a London Embassy staffer, who worked directly to him, exclusively to following up one or two specific leads. He did not vouchsafe that this particular staffer was routinely tailed by the British secret services. They would all need luck, he reflected.

Dr Tariq did not vouchsafe to the Colonel the news that had reached him that morning, that a Frenchman, home on leave, had sent by letter his resignation. Nor did he tell that a German was now packing up his quarters, having refused to work another day. The Colonel, whose information on the morale inside Tuwaithah was by now almost as good as Dr Tariq's, was not surprised that this news was withheld. It would be one more damaging admission of cracks in his programme, and Dr Tariq was a vain man, his vanity complicated certainly by fear. Fear of failure. Fear, too, of the consequences of failure.

Dr Tariq saw the slackened jowl of the Colonel, he noted the way that the man dragged at the butt of his cigarette, his third, he watched the fidget of the man's fingers. It would be too soon, he thought, to remind the Colonel of the fate inescapably awaiting those who failed a mission which had the total support of the Chairman of the Revolutionary Command Council.

'You should seek, Colonel, to earn your luck.'

5

It was Justin Pink's lucky morning, that's what he would say afterwards.

What he called his workshop was a conversion of the roof space over the detached garage. He used it sometimes rather than go into the factory at Newbury. That morning there had been no reason to drive to Newbury. He prepared his papers, and the contracts, in his workshop.

Justin Pink was a winner. He was a winner, he realized, each time that he dressed in a Savile Row suit. His shirt was first time on, and his initials were monogrammed over his heart. His tie was silk, his hair was groomed. He felt vibrantly alive, he felt clean, scrubbed by Debbie in a long cold shower. He crossed from the garage loft to the great expanse of his brick-built house.

He passed the cars in the driveway. Bloody women, never could park . . . These women did themselves well, at least their husbands did them well. There was Bea's beautifully preserved E-type, not a scratch on it, Jill's Audi, Susie's BMW, Alice's Saab Turbo, Ronnie's Metro Vanden Plas, and one car that he did not recognize, a Fiat 127 with an A registration. There was rust on the bonnet and rust on the tail. He carried his briefcase into the house. They were out to dinner that night at Wally and Fiona Simpson's on the Kennet. That was a great house, four acres, nearly a hundred yards frontage onto the river, super fishing. Wally had rung to say that it was black tie, and he'd forgotten to tell Debbie. He went to the dining-room door. He had never actually seen what happened at Debbie's art class.

Bloody hell . . .

He stared over the shoulders of Alice and Susie and Jill. The table was folded away. The fire was lit, going well. They were in a half-moon, and all facing the fire. Alice and Susie and Jill had their backs to him. Bea on the left. Ronnie and Debbie on the right. They had all reacted to the door opening, as if he'd thrown a grenade into the room and they were frozen.

He stared at the woman. She sat on a hard chair. She was naked, not a stitch on her. She had long good legs, white. The legs weren't together. There was the black matt of the woman's hair. There was a little flabbiness in her lower belly, because she was a woman and not a girl, but she had a tight waist. Big breasts hanging, and the pink nipple buttons. His eyeline had not reached her face when Alice squealed and Bea had a giggling fit. The woman's hair was dark and loose over her shoulders. He looked into the woman's face. Her eyes didn't shift. Ronnie, who had carrot-red hair to go with it, had blushed pillarbox red. She was a great-looking woman, so damn relaxed. He had supposed Debbie and her cronies painted flowers, or bowls of fruit, or landscapes up on the Ridge. Damned quiet in the dining room, he'd thought, as he crossed the hall, and if Bea Smith was in a room and it was quiet then something pretty peculiar had to be happening. Her eyes never left his, the woman's, and she did not a damn thing to cross her legs or put her hands across her breasts.

He heard Debbie's voice, soft and amused, 'Get out, Justie, you dirty old thing.'

He muttered something in the direction of his wife, something about 'if she had a moment'. He stepped back outside. Inside, Bea led the choir of laughter and giggling.

Debbie was beside him. 'You are rotten, Justie.'

'Forgive me for breathing.'

She had hold of his hand, she marched him to the front door. 'Who the hell is *that*?'

There was the great breadth of Debbie's smile. 'Dump-head . . . You never listen to what I tell you. I told you about Sara . . .'

'Didn't tell me she was a stripper.'

'She's bloody clever, and poor as a church mouse. I told you, she's married to some pathetic scientist from Aldermaston. She's going to model for us so she gets grub on the house. You know what? You gave a very fair impression of a man who's never seen a woman undressed before . . .'

'Sorry . . .'

'So just piss off to your boring little job, and don't horn in on our fun.'

She kissed him. Her body was against his. Her tongue was in his mouth, until she broke away.

'Will you buy me a pencil set for Christmas?'

'Go away, you randy bugger.'

Justin Pink was at the M4 junction before he remembered that he had forgotten to tell Debbie that it was a black-tie job at the Simpsons'.

Colt hit the target with fifteen shots out of eighteen from a distance of twenty paces. The target was man-shaped, man-sized, and was moved electronically across the sandbagged wall at a brisk walking pace.

Only the instructor had done better and none of the officers who had come to amuse themselves on the range had more than a dozen hits out of eighteen rounds. Colt had not handled a weapon since Athens. He felt good. The act of firing was liberation to him. When he had inspected the target, when he had seen the envy of the officers who were gathered behind him, when he had received the instructor's grudging approval, then he walked to his guard's car. The suppressed sound of the gunfire was still in his ears, and the sweet cordite smell hung at his nostrils.

He was escorted by the Military Police into the Colonel's office. It was his luck that the Colonel had that morning been sent a report prepared by the Ministry of Transport and Aviation in conjunction with the Ministry of Finance.

Colt was told of a target and an address.

He was shown a blurred photograph, taken from a moving car, of a thief, an enemy of the state.

Colt had his ticket to London.

Erlich thought that the last week, waiting in the Legal Attaché's section, had been the slowest in his eight years with the Bureau.

Treasure that quiet first day, Ruane had told him, because it would be his last. There had been a whole quiet week. He had come to London to push an investigation, and the investigation was going nowhere. He had been twice into Ruane's office, and the first time the block had been polite, and the second time he had been told rather less politely to sit on his hands and wait, like everybody else had to. So for a full week he had sat in the outer office, and waited. There were four Special Agents in the London office, and they had plenty to do, so much so that the fidgeting intruder could just about be ignored. Erlich had offered to help them with anything they might shout for, and he had been turned down. That was fair enough. The extradition was still stalled; there was another fraud investigation involving a British defence equipment company that had been ripped off in an American takeover deal; there was a coke run in London that the Bureau in New York were interested in; there was a guy who was under surveillance and who was going to have a Grand Jury warrant out for him for chopping his girlfriend's mother into small pieces; there were investigations that were vaguer, and things that were closer. They didn't want his help, each one told him straight, because by the time he was briefed into what they were working on, then he would be away and they'd have wasted the classroom time. What he did learn was the coffee machine. Anything ever go wrong with a coffee machine, then send for Bill Erlich. Too much milk, too little sugar, too much chocolate . . . send for Bill. He had stripped the machine down. Not bad for a graduate in literature and one who normally took evasive action at the sight of a screwdriver. The lady who ran Ruane's office said the dispenser was giving them better coffee, better chocolate, than any time in the last nine years. If things didn't improve, then he would set about the central-heating system.

Jo was still not back. If he had been able to speak to Jo each morning before he left for the Embassy, he probably wouldn't have been such a pain in the outer office. His success with the coffee machine was acknowledged, grudged but acknowledged, but he had been made aware that there was an argument for calling in the professionals when it came to tampering with the thermostat on the air system. Trouble was that the professionals had had more than twenty attacks on the system. On the other hand, he had never touched a thermostat in his life.

He had the Intelligence and the Security and the Branch all burrowing in their computers for an Englishman called Colt who wiped people for the cause of the Republic of Iraq, and he had sweet nothing to do, unless he went eye to eye with the mysteries of the thermostat.

He read three newspapers a day.

He watched the network news on television in the evening.

He read poetry in bed at night, after he had rung and failed to connect with Jo.

He knew they were burying Harry that morning, and here he was, not an inch closer after a week in London, to solving his murder. Perhaps if he wrecked the thermostat, someone would think it worth putting a little pressure on their British friends.

'Bill, care to walk in?'

'Sure thing . . .'

Ruane always did his talking in his own office, like it was necessary to keep everything compartmentalized.

'Maybe it was time you got lucky, Bill . . . Branch has been on. You should get yourself down there.'

'Great, thanks . . .'

'Not much, it's a start, they'll tell you.'

Erlich turned to the door. He had shed ten years.

The voice growled from behind him. 'And let them know you're grateful.'

*   *   *

91

Bissett had been content, had worked intensely and well for the whole of the previous week. Reuben Boll had been taking the last part of his annual leave. He had even been able to purloin half an hour of Basil's time. That had been the highspot of the last week, sitting in his office, entertaining Basil, and showing him the problems that confronted him. Basil was magnificent. Every single scientist in the whole Establishment knew how exceptional he was. Bissett's difficulty lay in the time he had been allocated for his paper on the theoretical dimensions of the device. On any programme hitherto it had been accepted that the period between preliminary design and introduction to service could be as long as fifteen years. Fifteen years was quite adequate for the necessary stages of component research, reduction of options, testing of prototypes, laying down of a production line, through to full-scale manufacture. Nowadays everything was subject to time and motion study and fine scientists, original minds, were working to schedules created by smart alecks hired from private enterprise. And there was hassle over money, over facilities. It was a monstrous way to have to work in such a complex field. There had been two areas of particular difficulty. On the one hand the balance of tritium in the warhead pit, and on the other the weight of the carbon casing on the protective shield of the warhead. Half an hour of Basil's time had been a godsend. Of course, he hadn't come up with answers, but he had indicated where, in what directions, further work might pay the necessary dividend.

But that was last week and this morning his luck had run out.

The Sierra had not started. Not a cough, not one glimmer of a spark. Inevitably, he had flooded the engine, and then had to wait before he could try again, and still no sign of life. They had had a bitter, sniping quarrel in the hall, because Sara had said that she needed her car. He had even offered to run the boys to school, but, no, she had needed the car. She had been strange that morning, even before the row over the car, and dressed strangely. She didn't seem to be wearing a brassiere under her purple blouse. What the hell were they going to think of that at the school gates, any of the other parents or any of the teachers? He had to wait until nine o'clock to telephone the garage, and he had been told that they had no time that morning and would try to get down in the afternoon. He had had to walk to the Falcon Gate. The Ministry policeman who checked his I/D had been another one of those patronizing cretins who had obviously too soon forgotten the massive two fingers dealt them by the SAS. His raincoat was wringing wet, and he was drenched, when he stepped off the minibus outside H area. Now, Carol's noisy insistence that he take his coat into his own office and not leave it to drip on the communal coat-stand.

Bissett was two hours and twenty-five minutes late. On the balls of his sodden feet he advanced along the corridor to his room.

'Frederick?'

'Yes, Reuben.'

'I had hoped to find your paper on my desk.'

'Nearly there, Reuben,' Bissett said.

'I trust *some* progress has been made in my absence.'

Reuben Boll must have been down to the Canaries or Tenerife. He looked like a broiled frog, hunched over his desk, grinning and satisfied.

'Chemical Explosives were asking after you, B12 wanted you. I gather you have been chasing them for two weeks for their time. I said you would be over in thirty minutes, but that was an hour ago.'

Bissett went on down the corridor and unlocked the door to his room. He threw his briefcase onto the floor, into the corner, and with all his force he slammed his door behind him.

The contract was worth £1.31 million, and that was good money by the standards of the business owned and run by Justin Pink. It was his second gin, and they poured them so that they tasted like a horse's kick.

Justin stood with the Trade Attaché, and the Trade Attaché's assistant, and the Chargé had joined them. He knew perfectly well that the software was going into the Ministry of Defence, he had not asked to what use it would be put when it was installed, and he certainly hoped there would be more of the same. He knew that it would be going to the Ministry of Defence, but the paperwork submitted to the Department of Trade and Industry would state that the purchaser was the Ministry of Agriculture; Department of Trade and Industry rules said that manufactured goods could be exported to Iraq only if they had no military usage. Typical of the government's hypocrisy, in Pink's view, that it could bleat about the failure of exporters while at the same time putting every sort of obstacle in their path. He had been twice to Iraq. It was a good market, nothing more and nothing less. If the contract had been 'straightforward' then it would have been worth half the £1.31 million that he was to be paid. That it was not straightforward gave the deal an added excitement to Pink. He knew all about the Target Teams of Customs & Excise. He knew the wording by heart: *Attempt to export equipment with intent to evade prohibition then in force by the Provision of the Export Control and Goods Order and C & E Management Act (Section 68/2), 1979* . . . and he knew that the offence carried a maximum sentence of seven years imprisonment . . . Excitement was important to Justin Pink.

There were more junior officials around them, and Pink was the centre of attention. The Trade Attaché and the Chargé seemed to hang on his words, and he had the girl at his elbow with the Gordons in one hand and the Schweppes in the other. A great looker, and he may have shown his admiration because she had ducked her dark head in mock embarrassment and given him the slowest smile as she moved away.

'Beautiful,' the Chargé murmured.

'Charming,' the Trade Attaché sighed.

'The Ambassador's daughter . . .' the Chargé warned.

'To see her is to start the day well,' the Trade Attaché whispered.

'Actually, my own day started pretty well,' Pink said.

Their eyes were on him, enquiring. Yes, it was his day. His day to talk, their day to listen.

'You know what? I walk into my dining room at nine twenty-six this morning, just to say my goodbyes to the little lady. There's a woman sat there, in front of the fire, and she's stark naked. That started my day well, I can tell you.'

'Very privileged,' the Chargé said.

'May I visit you at home, Mr Pink?' smirked the Trade Attaché.

'Super-looking woman, didn't bat an eyelid. My wife has an art class for her friends twice a week, and this was their model . . .'

'Very smart.'

'Greatly fortunate.'

Pink thought that he felt the admiration of his audience, and they wanted more. 'She's the wife of a chap at AWE, sorry, I should explain, where I live we're right alongside the Atomic Weapons Establishment. This woman hasn't a bean, so she's going to pose for my wife and her girlfriends once a month or so, and she'll get the classes thrown in free. You won't have me up here again, not too early in the mornings, not on art class mornings . . .'

'Hasn't a bean?'

'Colloquial for penniless. It's extraordinary, really, but some of the best scientific brains in Britain are shut away there, at AWE, and they're paid peasant wages.'

'Extraordinary.'

'I tell you what,' Pink said, 'I'd prefer to be on a building site than be a government scientist in this day and age.'

'In our country a scientist is treated with the utmost respect.'

His glass was refilled, too much gin, not enough tonic. He grimaced at the Ambassador's daughter. He turned back to the Trade Attaché.

'He's probably a front-line scientist, and the family's on subsistence level. Still, if his wife is sitting in my dining room being a nude model it can't be all bad, can it?'

Pink was never aware of the man who hovered behind him. By the time Pink left the Embassy, worried now as to whether he was fit to drive, a Major who dealt only with Intelligence matters was preparing a report to send to Baghdad. The report would go directly to the desk of the Colonel.

'Please sit down.'

Erlich sat. 'What have you got for me?'

'Would you like coffee?'

Erlich said, 'I'd rather know what you've got for me.'

'Milk and sugar?'

Erlich said, 'No sugar.'

'Have to do it myself, my girl's off sick.'

Erlich had gone down to New Scotland Yard fast enough to be more than twenty-five minutes early for his appointment. They had made him wait. He had been taken to the fourth floor at exactly the time of his appointment. It was a bare working room. Erlich had seen nothing like it in CI-3, in Washington Field Office, where each room had photos of wives stuck onto cork boards, of kids, postcards from vacations all over the world, cartoons, clippings of headlines and a huge blow-up of a quote from an English thriller writer: 'The most suspicious, unbelieving, unreasonable, petty, inhuman, sadistic, double-crossing set of bastards in any language [are] the people who run counter-espionage departments.' Nothing like that here. Not even a picture in a frame.

The Chief Inspector came back in with two plastic containers of coffee. Erlich thought that the Chief Inspector looked, if it were possible, more tired. He thought that any Special Agent who dressed like this guy would be disciplined.

The Chief Inspector took his pipe from his pocket, filled it slowly, methodically, and lit it, and when the room seemed to Erlich dangerously full of smoke, he lit it again. 'For the last week I've had my head into Irish files, got me? In this country Irish files come first, and every time I'm into an Irish case I find myself cursing just about everything American, got me? American money keeps the Provos alive . . . And one more thing. We put a hell of a lot of time and effort into feeding your crowd detail on the Provos on your side of the water, and trying to get your judges to extradite the bastards back here is harder than getting water out of rock.'

'You'll have to forgive me, Chief Inspector, I've got a one-track mind and I'm here only to locate the man called Colt, the Englishman who murdered an Agency man in Athens.'

'Just so you know what kept us busy.' The Chief Inspector put flame to his pipe once more and under cover of the smoke-screen took a thin file out of the desk. 'We have a movement here called the Animal Liberation Front,' he said. 'It's made up of anarchists in part and in part middle-class softies. This is a free country and people are allowed to sound off about the fur trade, about vivisection, about experimenting with live animals. These people do all that, but they are also known to plant firebombs and rough people up who work in laboratories where animals are used for experiments. A couple of years ago, the ALF was getting out of hand. There were two department stores gutted by incendiaries; there was a laboratory where three dozen beagle dogs were "liberated"; a bomb was put under a car but failed to explode; a scientist who was trying to find an antidote for cystic fibrosis was beaten up. There was a special unit set up here, Animal Rights National Index, but these idiots had tight secur-ity, a good cut-off cell system, and it took us a hell of a long time to open the can. The breakthrough was a squat we turned over on the south coast, two years back. We found a set of initials there. We were able to put names to all the initials. Four males, two females. Three males and one female were arrested. The fourth male was identified as a boy named Tuck.'

'And that's Colt?'

The Chief Inspector ferreted again for matches.

'That's Colin Olivier Louis Tuck.'

Erlich said, and he meant it, 'Great thing, this special rela-tionship, and thank you very much.'

The Chief Inspector leaned over the desk; his voice hissed in anger. 'I'll tell you what I think of this so-called special relation-ship. It's whatever *you* want, and *when* you want it.'

Erlich did not understand the hostility of this man. He had been given a name. He had said what he thought was the decent thing to say, and had it chucked back at him.

'What's your problem, Chief Inspector?'

'My problem? By Christ, I'll tell you what my problem is. My son has been dead for three years. My problem, as you call it, is that he was nineteen and serving his first year in the Light Infantry, in the Bogside of Londonderry, and the weapon that shot him dead was an MI6 high-velocity rifle, product of America, put into the hands of those scum by scum in America protected by American judges.'

Erlich dropped his head. 'I'm sorry,' he said.

He was told that the liaison procedures were being sorted out. By tomorrow they would be in place.

Erlich let himself out of the room.

In the outer office a young detective intercepted Erlich.

'Mr Erlich?'

'That's me.'

'A Mr Rutherford has been trying to reach you. He said would you call by, Curzon Street, side door.'

The passport that the Colonel had given him was in the inside pocket of his anorak. The contact telephone number and the contact address he had memorized.

He was going home, and home meant to him no more and no less than the room where his mother was dying. The Colonel had no need to pressure him to return again to Baghdad after his mission was completed, and after he had visited his mother who was dying. They might as well have had a rope round his ankle. He was a fugitive from the justice of his own country. He knew the sentences that had been handed down to his associates. Twelve years the men, seven to the girl. Of course, he was a fugitive. His own country offered him only the deathbed of his mother, and twelve years' imprisonment. Of course, he would come back to Baghdad. It was rare for him to feel gratitude to any person, but the nearest was his feeling for the

Colonel. He had drifted into the Colonel's orbit. He had come from a bulk tanker that had tied up in the oil terminal in Kuwait harbour, thanked the Master who had allowed him to work his passage from the port of Perth, and gone ashore. He had gone because the great forward deck had in its turn become another confining space to him. Kuwait meant nothing to him, but the place was crawling with his countrymen, in the hotels and eating houses, on the streets and beaches. Brits were bad for Colt, so he had hitched a ride away from the city, to the frontier, and crossed over to Iraq. He had smiled at the frontier guards and kept walking with his rucksack slung over one shoulder . . . until the hand had clamped on his collar, and the boots had pitched him into a cell. Bruised and bloodied from days of interrogation on the floor of a cell that was an inch deep in his own shit and piss, the Colonel had found him and freed him. Of course, he would return to Baghdad. They had a need of him, he had a need of them.

At the gate of the security zone where there was access directly onto the apron, he formally shook the Colonel's hand. The Colonel kissed him on both cheeks.

'The Thai whore, sir, she was good?'

The Colonel hugged his shoulders, and he laughed.

'If you had lost the bet, sir, what would you have paid them?'

The hands moved to the back of Colt's neck and squeezed.

It would have been a long story, the warming of friendship and respect between the barrel-chested Iraqi Colonel and the young man from England who had proved he could stalk and kill. But a long story was an indulgence. Colt could only abide a short story. So it was a short story as he told it to himself, of an English runaway crossing the frontier from Kuwait, and failing in spite of many beatings to satisfy his interrogators until the arrival of the Colonel at the Public Security base at Basra. Colt seldom lied, not now, not then. He told the Colonel his life story between puffed lips, chipped teeth, and the Colonel was amused. He had been taken to the Colonel's bungalow. He had been told that he would teach two overweight, spoilt teenage boys the

English language. Colt, bottom of the class before he was expelled, now Colt the tutor. He had been lifted from a detention cell and given the job of English teacher because the Colonel liked a boy who could smile into the face of an interrogator who wielded a rubber truncheon. And Colt, after long days of torture, had recognized in the Colonel someone he could like, someone whose trust he would value.

'Until we meet, Colt.'

He was the last passenger onto the aircraft.

Rutherford sensed Erlich's impatience from across the room.

'Right, Mr Erlich . . .'

'Bill.'

'Right, Bill . . . concerning Colin Tuck, who we shall call Colt, I am your liaison while you are in Britain. Anything you want, you put in a request to me. Any actions you may think necessary will be vetted by me, any interviews you wish to carry out will be arranged through me.' Rutherford hoped that he spoke with sufficient polite force to nail the message home. 'Mr Ruane will have told you, no doubt, you adhere, most strictly, to the guidelines that we lay down. That way you get all the help and cooperation we can provide, any other way and you get shown the door. Are we quite clear?'

He saw the American rise. He was like the pellet-fed rainbows in the Fishery waters near Penny's parents. But the American rose and didn't take, had more sense than those daft trout.

'Thank you for hearing me out, Bill. Sorry for the claptrap, but the rules are important to all of us.'

'Quite understood. Tell me about Colt.'

There wasn't much to tell, and after Rutherford had finished he would leave the American in the room with the file and let him gut it for himself. He gave him the digest. He told the story of a loner, a drifter, a maverick boy who went from banner-waving at public meetings to protest at experiments on animals, all the way to incendiaries and assault and finally an attempted car bomb. And then the sudden flight and the disappearance of the boy from the face of the earth. He mentioned the request for information from the Criminal Investigation Division of the police in Western Australia, of a description received from Perth of a murder suspect, which might be relevant and might not, couldn't say.

'He went to the pub in the village where his parents live the night before he disappeared. He was in the pub, that we know. The next day his parents' home was searched, and the boy was gone. His parents have always refused to cooperate or even to discuss the boy.'

'Isn't that where we start?'

'The house is periodically watched, the mail is routinely opened, telephone calls are intercepted. We have no indication that his parents have had any contact with him since he disappeared two years ago.'

'It's still where we start, I'd reckon.'

Rutherford said, 'Would you not rather read the file first?'

Rutherford saw the determination, the jutted chin, of the American. If he had been working out of the Embassy in Washington, if he was being shunted round the FBI and the Central Intelligence Agency, if he had been twiddling his thumbs for a week, he might just have been a little determined himself. This was not a Lockerbie operator, that was clear. He had heard that the Feds at Lockerbie had been good as gold, working at the pace required, picking up on every small detail provided by the forensic team at Farnborough, where the 747 had been reconstructed. This young man was a bull looking for a china shop. He assumed Erlich to be ambitious, looking for results that would lift his career forward. He didn't care for ambition, perhaps he should have done. Rutherford found ambition a little vulgar.

He pushed the file across to him. He saw it snapped open. The photograph spilled out. Rutherford saw the way Erlich's eyes focused onto the photograph. It was a vendetta, any child would have seen that. This was Bill Erlich versus Colin Tuck, and anything that was personal in an investigation was going to be a bloody nuisance.

'I'll leave you to it. Be back shortly.' Not good form to leave Erlich alone in his office, but his safe was locked, and the drawers of his desk were locked, and he wanted to get to Accounts before they closed, to draw a float before setting off.

The Swede's office was on the second floor of the building. Outside his window there was a small garden, well watered on these warm evenings. The garden was often used by the target for a short relaxing walk. The distance between the Swede's second-floor office and Dr Tariq's ground-floor suite was sixty feet. The Swede had measured it.

He was at Tuwaithah because his much-loved sister had married an Israeli Air Force pilot. On his last visit home, to the university city of Uppsala, he had met with countrymen of his sister's husband. When he had returned to Baghdad, he had limped through Customs and Immigration to the car sent by the Atomic Energy Commission. He had leaned heavily on a stick. With his baggage had been a Sony music centre.

The stick, after the apparent improvement of his pulled tendons, remained in his office, always in the corner by the door where he hung his coat.

The stick concealed a rifle microphone, which, after much debate – over the alternative merits of contacts, spikes, tubes, any number of possible bugs – had been manufactured for him.

He could only use the microphone after his two Iraqi assistants had gone home. It was a huge risk, each time he unscrewed the base of the walking stick, took out the rifle microphone, plugged it to the small receiver that by day nestled in the back of his music centre, put on the headphones which on most days he used to listen to classical music. The fear, the terror of detection, each time, left him physically drained. But the job he had been given by the Mossad agents, who traded ruthlessly on his love of his sister, was a narcotic to him. He had become addicted to the terror.

He had twice before seen the Colonel walk through the

garden to Dr Tariq's office, but on each occasion his assistants had still been at work.

It was seventeen days since he had last locked the door of his office, turned down the lights, and unscrewed the cap of his walking stick, and heard Dr Tariq and Professor Khan discuss a series of meetings in Europe.

He crouched now beside the window. It had seemed so very straightforward at first, at the time of his recruitment. He was a techno-mercenary in the laboratory at Alto Gracia under the Sierra Chica mountains of North-West Argentina. Their first approach, late at night in his hotel room, came a week after he had received his sister's long and excited letter telling him of her marriage. Perhaps he had been bored, perhaps he simply hadn't believed in the danger. There were a number of Iraqis at Alto Gracia. They were the banker of the Condor missile development on which Argentina cooperated, with the further expertise of Egyptian engineers.

It had all been stage-managed by the Mossad. By a chance remark in passing in the Sierra hotel bar where the foreigners were billeted, a remark in the hearing of a senior Iraqi scientist, the Swede had let it be known that he found the missile pro-gramme tedious, that he really needed more challenging work. It had been true, and he often reflected, the work *was* challenging. For a bachelor, too, the working conditions and the pay were well above what he thought he could command elsewhere. Barely a week later an invitation had been made to him. He had thought, naïvely, of the excitement, and of his sister. But the conditions and the pay were long since beside the point. The point was the barbed hook of the Mossad in his nervous system.

The venetian blind was drawn down. The window was open. The microphone rested on the window ledge. Sharp and much too loud in his ears, the evening song of the birds and, between the calls of the birds, voices. It was hard for him, to catch the words, because the flowerbeds had just been hoed and the birds were raucous in their search for food in the fresh-turned soil.

'. . . Only H area, Colonel. Their A area, no, no, just engineers.

Their B area, that we do ourselves. He must come from H area, nowhere else . . . I don't want a chemist, I don't want an engineer . . . A scientist, Colonel, and he must come from H area . . .'

The Swede never attempted to assess what he eavesdropped. He passed it on verbatim.

Every shrill cadence of the birds' song, every soft utterance of Dr Tariq poured into him the high exhilaration of fear.

Colt flew into London on the last flight from Frankfurt. He had changed aircraft already at Prague. At Immigration he produced the Irish passport that the Colonel had given him.

He was nodded through.

No problem. And why should there have been a problem?

6

Saad Rashid was a shrewd man, good with figures, but it did not take his shrewdness to know that a sentence of death would have been passed upon him by those who had once been his colleagues in Baghdad.

It was a month since he had made the initial transfer. Twenty-nine days earlier he had personally visited the National Westminster Bank in Lower Regent Street, and in the office of the Deputy Manager he had ordered the movement of 500,000 American dollars from the account of Iraqi Airlines (London) to a numbered account in Dublin. Twenty-eight days earlier he had travelled to Dublin to transfer that sum to a second numbered account in Liechtenstein. Twenty-seven days earlier he had, by telephone, moved that same sum out of Liechtenstein and into the secrecy-shrouded computers of the Credit Bank of Zurich. On the day on which Saad Rashid had received the confirmation of the transaction from Switzerland, he had tidied his desk at the back of the Iraqi Airlines office, taken what few personal possessions he kept there and placed them in his briefcase, locked his door, pocketed his key, and told his assistant manager that he believed he was showing the first symptoms of the 'flu that was sweeping London. He had gone then to the Syrian Embassy and had applied for a visa for himself, for his English-born wife, for his two daughters. On that day, twenty-seven days earlier, he had travelled from the Syrian Embassy back to his rented home in Kingston-upon-Thames, and there he had, for the first time, informed his wife of their changed circumstances.

They had moved out that evening from the house in Kingston-upon-Thames. They had spent two nights in bed-and-breakfast accommodation before taking a month's let on a furnished flat close to Clapham Junction mainline railway station. Twenty-five days of suffocating in the one-bedroomed flat with his wife and the two children. He was a man used to taking his favoured clients to the Ritz or to Claridges. When he was on business away from home he stayed and entertained in the Hiltons and Sheratons and Inter-Continentals. The children wanted to go back to school. Zoë wanted to go shopping in Knightsbridge. He was suffocated. The third night, above the rattling progress of a late train, he had pummelled Zoë with his fists, and not heard the frightened crying of his children, when she had said that no fucking way was she going to be holed up for the rest of her days in bloody, bloody Damascus. It was the first time that she had forgotten the place of the Arab's wife. He had beaten her, cowed her, instilled in her once more the rule of obedience.

Zoë Rashid now accepted that she could not visit her mother before she flew out to Syria. She understood that she could only leave the flat to shop for food at the Indian-owned store at the end of the street. She accepted – rather, she understood – her position because she was never allowed from the flat with both daughters at the same time. Rashid had left the flat only once, to go by taxi to the Syrian Embassy to press further his application for asylum, and on that occasion, while he had talked and drunk coffee in an inner office his two daughters had sat outside with their colouring books and crayons.

It was prudent of Saad Rashid to hide himself and his family away. A Shia cleric, an enemy of the regime, had been shot dead in a hotel lobby in Khartoum. Qassem Emin, the political activist, who had made free with his denunciations of the Chairman of the Revolutionary Command Council, had been tortured and had his throat slit in Turkey. There was the wife of a Communist who had been stabbed to death in Oslo. There was Abdullah Ali, a businessman in exile, who was known to Rashid, and who had eaten in a restaurant in London with men he believed to be his friends, who had died in St Stephen's Hospital of a rat poison that had been sprinkled on his food during a moment of inattention.

What decided Saad Rashid to steal half a million dollars and seek a life of exile in a country reviled by his homeland was the telephone call from his cousin's wife. On a poor line from Baghdad he had been told, in a voice distraught with tears, that his cousin was under arrest, charged with treason, held in the Abu Ghraib gaol. It was their way, the men from the Department of Public Security, to take one man, and then trawl through his family for any small hint of the cancer of dissent.

It was twenty-seven days since Rashid had left his office at Iraqi Airlines for the last time.

With his two daughters, one holding each hand, he came down the long staircase from the top-floor flat. He had first checked from the window that the taxi he had telephoned was waiting. The passports, with the visa stamps, were waiting at the Embassy. He would fly that night to Damascus with his wife who had once been a dancer and with his children whom he loved. In his head was the account number at the Credit Bank of Zurich.

He closed the outer door behind him. He hurried with his daughters down the steps and towards the taxi.

He watched as the taxi pulled away.

It was twenty-eight hours since he had driven the clapped-out Ford Capri into the street, and counted himself lucky to find a space to park that was pretty near opposite the front door from which the man had emerged with his two small girls.

He would hand it to the Colonel: given the motivation they could, by God, do things right. Colt knew that the target was a thief, that he had been observed entering the Syrian Embassy when that Embassy was under regular Iraqi surveillance. Colt knew that the target had been followed to the house in Clapham. Colt knew his target at once from the photograph that he had been given. Colt thought it a serious mistake by his target to have gone in person to the Syrian Embassy.

He had found the Ruger under the mattress in his Bayswater hotel room, and with it the keys of the Capri, and the toolbox, and the overalls, plus the scrap of paper on which was the street and the number. The bill was prepaid, so that he was away from the hotel before the front desk was manned, and the car had started first turn.

For the whole day and all the previous evening, he had the hood up and tinkered with the engine. He worked his way through a bag of sandwiches and four cans of Pepsi. When night fell, he had slept in the back of the Capri, slept and dozed.

They wanted it over and he wanted it over. It was his deal with the Colonel, that once the business was finished then he was free to go west, head back to his roots.

He lay on his back. His head was under the outside front wheel housing. He could not avoid it, he took a lungful of the diesel fumes from the taxi as it pulled away. The pistol was under the main chassis, in a plastic bag, and the magazine was in place, and the safety was off. He had reached for the Ruger as soon as he had seen the taxi pull up, and he had had the Ruger in his grip when the front door opposite had opened, and he had loosened the grip when he had seen that the target carried no cases, only had his daughters' hands in his. He'd be coming back . . . The time would be when the target returned.

When the taxi had cleared the street, Colt pushed himself out from underneath the Capri. He pulled the woollen cap that had been in the pocket of his overalls further down over his close-cut hair. When he had lifted the hood of the Capri, and fastened the arm to hold it open, then he bent again and reached under the chassis to retrieve the plastic bag holding the Ruger. He put the plastic bag on top of the battery, always close to hand. The taxi, when it came back to the street, would be crawling because the driver would be looking for the number.

They were pretty children, Colt thought. Pretty clothes and their hair well brushed . . . Not easy if the target had hold of both the kids when he came out of the taxi.

* * *

It was as though he had come into work on a Sunday. Not that he had been to work on a Sunday for several years, but that was how he remembered it.

This one was a big strike. Different from the time the Radiological Protection Unit had been out, and different from the Boilermakers' stoppage. This was the real thing. This was clerical staff and Health Physics surveyors and instrument technicians, even the 'Ploot' grinders. They were all at the Falcon Gate, banners and placards, with the Transport and General Workers Union convenors haranguing them over loudspeakers.

It was hushed as a midweek chapel inside H3 because Carol and her typing tribe were all out in the rain with banners bearing crudely daubed exhortations to the government to raise their pay. Bissett had heard there was even talk of the fire cover being withdrawn.

Frederick Bissett was a member of the Institute of Professional Scientists, and a fat lot of good that did him. He had joined the Institute in his first year at the Establishment because at that time the organization seemed to have some sinew to it. He had been to the Top Rank entertainment centre in Reading when all the scientists had gathered one evening to formulate a demand for a 40 per cent pay rise. Whistling in the wind, that had been, because they had settled for half, and never recovered from the shame of behaving in the same way as the typists and fitters and laboratory assistants. Waste of his time, the Institute of Professional Scientists, which was why the annual assessments, prepared in his case by Reuben Boll, were so crucial. Be interesting, of course, if fire cover were withdrawn, because then they would have to rustle up the RAF crews from Brize Norton who wouldn't know their big toes from their elbows when it came to plutonium and highly enriched uranium and chemical explosive.

He had H3 almost to himself. Boll was over in F area because the Director had summoned all the Superintendents to a planning meeting. Wayne had rung in to say that he was sick, which meant that the little creep didn't want to drive past the picket line. Basil was in his office, probably hadn't registered that anything was different.

In the late morning he locked his safe, checked to see that all of his desk drawers were secured, and shut down his terminal. Because there was a strike, because their own laboratories were idle, the high and the mighty of A area were prepared to squeeze in a visit from lowly Frederick Bissett of H3.

He drove across Second Avenue, and past the new colossus that was the A90 building. The building was a great show box of concrete. He had never been inside the box, nor had he seen the Decontamination Centre that was alongside, nor the Liquid Waste plant. At least they were working on the complex that day, at least the civilian contractors had been able to bribe their private workforce to cross the picket lines. It was said that A90 and its ancillaries would end up costing the taxpayer £1.5 billion. He'd heard that stainless steel was going inside that box at such a rate as to absorb the country's entire annual output, and that the rip-offs were a scandal. It was being said that when A90 came on song there wouldn't be enough people to work it and there wouldn't be enough plutonium to make it work. Naturally, there was enough money for A90 . . . money, money, money . . . not a squeak out of the bank manager that week.

He cut across First Avenue. Ahead of him was what those who worked there called the Citadel.

The Citadel was the A area.

The Citadel was where nuclear warheads were made. Inside the Citadel, in Bissett's opinion, there was little that was innovative, much that was wasteful – but then what else could be expected of engineers? The Citadel was a sprawl of buildings, erected in various bursts of haste and always in secrecy since the early Fifties. Everyone who worked outside it said that the Citadel buildings creaked with age, improvization, and therefore danger. There was A1, in at the birth pangs of the British weapon, where the plutonium was heated in the furnaces so that it could be shaped into the melon-sized spheres for the inner workings of the warheads, and it was no secret amongst the

Establishment staff that a dozen years earlier cancers had been rampant amongst the technicians. There was A45, the Materials Assembly unit, where the plutonium sphere was wrapped in a second concentric sphere of highly enriched uranium before the sealing of the lethal elements in 22-carat gold foil. Bissett had once met the gaunt technician from A45 who had apparently received through a faulty glove a particle of plutonium the size of a pinhead and whose body had been cremated six months later before there could be an inquest. There was A12, Waste Management Group, where the plutonium and highly enriched uranium and beryllium and tritium were taken from weapons that had achieved their shelf life in the guts of submarines and the bunkers of Air Force camps, then reworked for newer and more potent devices. There were the open-air vats alongside A12 where acid burned out the plutonium before the sludge could be reprocessed.

Bissett had only to see the wire of the Citadel's perimeter, to see the smoke from the Citadel's chimneys, to feel a loathing for the place. He was required to leave his car outside the perimeter fence. In the walkway inside the high double fencing, an alsatian, an ugly and vicious-looking brute, dragged at its handler's leash. The dog, leaping at the wire, snarling its frustration, frightened him. The Ministry policeman, flak jacket unfastened over his chest, submachine gun hooked on a strap over his shoulder, checked his I/D card at the entrance to the razor-wire tunnel, consulted a list of the day's expected visitors, thumbed him through. The machine gun unnerved him, always had and always would.

At the second check, at the end of the wire tunnel, his name was searched for again, and he had to hand in his H area card in exchange for a temporary pass, and a phone call was made ahead. He was kept waiting. He could never have worked in A1 or A1/1 or A45 or A12. Every time that he had been inside the Citadel he went home as soon as his day's work was finished and scrubbed his body from toe to scalp. He could never have taken his urine and faeces samples once a week to Health Physics. He could not have endured the clamouring siren bells that marked an alarm and that caused A area to be sealed down, passage in and out of the Citadel suspended until the malfunction was located. He was ushered forward after cooling his heels for four minutes.

He met three men inside A45. For half an hour he took tea and biscuits with them, and discussed the problems of weight reduction through additional use of gallium worked into plutonium. Weight was the key to a warhead. He could have sat down with only one of them and achieved the same guidance on weight and machining capability, but three of them came to the meeting, which he thought typical of engineers. A sniff of tea, a whiff of biscuits, and there would soon be a crowd. Because of the shortage of plutonium, because of the call on plutonium by the Trident programme, he was required to reduce the warhead weight for the cruise system. As he left, the engineers were on their third cup and discussing last week's retirement party.

But he had had some valuable help.

He went out through the 'airlock' system of the wire tunnel. He was handed back his identity card. The dog was still there, still straining to break through at him.

It was always the same when he came out of there, he thought there was an itch at his back as if he had been *touched*. They actually wore, those engineers, four different samplers on their chests and pinned to their jackets or shirts.

He drove back to H area.

At least the post was not strike-bound. Carol, on her picket line, would be suffering in the knowledge that a whole delivery of post would escape her. A bundle of recycled internal envelopes for Boll, mostly journals and magazines for Basil, an OHMS for Wayne, a motley of envelopes for the technicians from H3's laboratory. He saw his own name on a plain white envelope.

Because Carol wasn't there, wasn't arching her head to see the contents of a letter, it was not necessary for him to take the envelope into his own office.

He read the neatly typed letter . . .

Dear Frederick,

Hoping this finds you well. As you will see, I am now the Professor of Physics here. In an effort to make life more interesting for our younger members of staff and our graduate element, I have been inviting past students back to lecture on *any* aspect of their current work.

Obviously much of what you do is restricted, but come and give us a talk on anything unrestricted that you think would be of interest.

You are something of a legend here still and would be assured of a fine welcome, a passably good dinner, and a bed at my humble abode – plus travel expenses.

Perhaps you could test the water at your end, and let me know when you could come. Thursday evenings are our best.

Yours,

Walter Smith

PS: What on earth do you do with yourself these days? Surely they must be about to close the bomb shop down.

Sara could see the raindrops falling from the bare branches of the apple tree in the garden, and she could feel the freshness of the wind on her arms.

She stood at the drying frame with her box of pegs and her tub of washing.

It was a strange thing, really strange to her, that she could feel her underclothes against her body. It was the third day after she had dressed, gone out, without wearing her underclothes, into her car, driving on the main road through Tadley, driving all the way to Kingsclere, knocking at the front door of the home of a woman who was almost a stranger, going into a house that she hardly knew.

Her underclothes had been neatly folded in the bottom of her handbag. No sketcher nor painter nor artist wanted to see the elastic weals on a model's shoulders and chest and hips and thighs, every model left her underwear off for as many hours as possible before posing.

The eyes of the man in the doorway had been a reawakening for Sara. It was more years than she cared to remember since she had last seen a man stare at her in frank admiration. When had she last seen Frederick stare at her, worship her? Back beyond memory. When she had been at art college, but that was just kids hunting for trophies, and they hadn't meant a toss to her. She had turned her back on the lot of them, and married Frederick Bissett, from a terraced house in Leeds, bright boy of the street. That was her statement to her parents, to her school, to her upbringing. She could not remember when poor old Frederick had last gazed in lust at her naked body, not like Debbie's husband had.

It had been better, a long time ago it had been better, when their loving had made Frank, and better up to the time of Adam's birth. Such excruciating pain and three weeks premature, and fast, but with the pain, and Frederick on his one and only trip to New Mexico.

Alone in her agony, she had vowed that the responsible bastard would go short . . . He'd gone short and the trouble was – she pegged his flannel pyjamas to the frame – that he didn't seem to care.

When she had finished hanging out the washing, before she went for the weekly shop at SavaCentre, Sara applied her lipstick, and around her throat she squirted the toilet water which she had had for three years and never before used.

Debbie's husband would have cared if he had gone short, oh yes.

Rutherford was in a poor humour, because the best that the pool could provide was a two-year-old Astra with 70,000 on the clock, and a ticket on the windscreen. He couldn't have been more than two, three minutes collecting Erlich in South Audley Street, but there it was. Accounts *would* be pleased.

He couldn't use his own car because they were going to be way out of radio range, and he needed the car telephone with the scrambler attachment. He had argued with the pool supervisor, but it was the Astra or nothing. He detested starting the day with an argument. At least he hadn't argued with Penny. She never fussed when he said that he was going down to the country and didn't know when he'd be back. Best thing that had ever happened to him, Penny.

Erlich had the passenger seat as far back as it would go and he still shifted his weight about as if he needed another six inches of legroom.

They had come off the M3 and were cruising on the dual carriageway A303. That was the Astra's optimum pace, a reasonably quiet 70 mph. It had no guts left in it. Pool cars were watchers' cars, and were hammered.

There was the fork ahead of him, and he slowed for a gap in the oncoming traffic.

The stones were wonderful. There was light shafting off the Plain ahead, cutting down behind the stones. He loved that place. He had loved the magic and mystery of Stonehenge since early childhood. On the way down to their holidays in Cornwall his parents had always stopped at Stonehenge for a slow coffee break while he had crossed the road to walk around the stones. Penny only wanted a West Country holiday, not the least ingratiating thing about her, and they took the same cottage that his mum had rented, and they stopped, he and Penny, for the same coffee and the same stroll round the monument. Well, nowadays you could get no closer than the wire cage around the perimeter, thanks to the hippies or the busloads of Americans or Druids maybe, who knew? He pulled into the car park.

'You want to stretch your legs?'

'Not particularly.'

'You want a coffee from the stall?' Rutherford gestured towards the open-sided van at the edge of the car park.

'No, thanks.'

'You want to see the stones?'

'I should?'

Rutherford said evenly, 'Those stones were cut and erected four thousand years ago. Each one weighs more than one hundred tons and was brought two hundred miles overland on rollers, by sea on rafts. We still don't understand how prehistoric man achieved that feat. Nobody in this much bullshitted century has achieved *anything* that can outlast what the men who laid out these stones did here. So, yes, you should, just for five minutes forget about being a policeman and be a human being. I do it regularly myself. It gives me a balanced perspective.'

The wind tore at their trouser legs as they circled the cage, and Erlich smiled his admiration of the great stone circle.

'Well, we mustn't lose time, must we?'

Rutherford said, 'Tell me, then, who in this age of miracles can be set against the master designer of Stonehenge?'

'I am afraid you will have to take account of the men of the Manhattan Project,' said Erlich through chattering teeth. 'They will be remembered as long as there is history. And now, mindboggling as this shrine of yours is, I think I need one of those coffees.'

Tork, Station Officer for Tel Aviv, always responded immediately to a summons from that office, cancelled whatever appointments he had. Tork's time there was never wasted. And after the affair in the Beqa'a Valley, he was trusted. A famous mission organized by Tork's London masters – an Israeli sniper with an English guide – had killed a PLO training-camp commander.

Tork was shown the transcript of a brief conversation. The text totally underlined in red ink, he was told, was that of the Director of Iraq's Atomic Energy Commission.

Tork had been Station Officer in Tel Aviv for eleven years. He had learned that there were no favours handed out. He had learned also that if there were a continuing nightmare in Israel then it was that an Arab enemy might one day possess the capability to strike out at the Jewish heartland with nuclear weapons.

'I'll get it off to Century at once.'

'But will they act on it?'

'It's not a lot to go on.'

'But you will give it a "most urgent" rating.'

'At my end, of course.'

She had lived all her life in the street running alongside the railway, and since she had retired from her late father's business, a haberdashery store in Wimbledon, since she had sold it to a family from Northampton for a good price, Hannah Worthington walked each day to the shop at the end of the street. She never bought more, nor less, than she would need for her housekeeping for the next twenty-four hours. It was one of the rituals of this lonely spinster's life that every day she would take her chihuahua to the shop on the corner and back again.

Miss Worthington was a small woman. In her winter coat she appeared to be little more than a central pole with a tent draped from her shoulders. She wore a dark grey hat taken from the store on her last day as owner, and that was seventeen years ago, and a plain grey scarf round her throat, and leather gloves that had stood a long test of time. In her flat and comfortable lace-up shoes, she made good progress on her daily outing.

She walked towards the shop.

In her wicker basket there was a shopping list for a packet of porridge, one pork chop, some oven-ready chips, a carton of frozen broccoli, one apple and one orange, a small loaf of wholemeal sliced bread, and an 8oz tin of Pedigree Chum. What she liked about the shop was that it was open for business on every day of the year. Even on Christmas Day, after church, she could walk to the shop and buy her necessaries.

Of course, the street had changed mightily in the years since her birth in 1909, the year King Emperor Edward the Seventh died. Before the Great War, and afterwards also, this had been a street where bank managers and principal shopkeepers lived. After the Second World War, the street had changed, and she knew that had brought sadness to her late father. He had talked about moving, but after his passing her late mother had simply refused to countenance what she had called 'evacuation'. Miss

Worthington often felt it would have been an unendurable sorrow to her parents if they had lived to witness the extent of the deterioration. To start with, every single front door in the street, excepting her own, was now festooned with illuminated bell buttons, marking the division of fine family homes into little warrens of flats. To go on with, in the former days, between the Great War and the Second World War, there would never have been men working on cars in the street, as if the place were a communal garage. She saw the taxi inching down the street. Between the Great War and the Second World War there were always taxis in the street, but not now. Taxi drivers came down her street in this day and age as if in fear of their lives.

Her dog sniffed for a moment at the ankle of the young man who worked at the engine of his car. She pulled the dog away.

The taxi passed her.

Her chihuahua was making its 'business' in the gutter, and that was a relief because it meant she wouldn't have to take him out again in the evening, and wait around for him. There was poor enough lighting in the street, and so many peculiar people . . .

'Good boy,' she murmured. 'Well done, little boy.'

She heard the taxi stop and the door open.

She heard the charge of feet behind her.

She heard the shout.

'Hey, there.'

There was a faint rattle, metal being drawn across metal. There was the slight sound, a light and muffled drumbeat.

Miss Worthington turned.

She thought the man was drunk.

It was the middle of the day, and the man reeled, staggered.

That's what had happened to her street, drunks in the middle of the day. She stepped out into the road. The man could barely stand. She would cross over.

The man fell.

She saw the man on the pavement, beside the driver's door of the taxi, and he was writhing, a thrashing fish. She saw the blood across the grey white of the man's shirt.

118

She saw two little girls, nicely dressed, running up the steps to the nearest house, starting to beat at the paint-scraped wooden door. She saw the man with the fat-barrelled gun held out from his shoulder. She saw the man with the gun shoot again at the man on the pavement. She was a dozen paces from the man with the gun, and she heard nothing. She saw his wrists jump from the recoil. She saw the man on the pavement shudder, and the thrashing cease.

She saw that the man with the gun had on his head a woollen cap. She saw that the cap was tilted. She saw the splash of short fair hair. The man with the gun turned. Eyes meeting. The eyes of a killer . . . and the eyes, masked by heavy Health Service spectacles, of a spinster in her eighty-first year. There was a moment, God's truth, she would not forget it, when the man with the gun seemed to smile at her, God's truth and she did not trifle with that.

She saw him run.

As he ran she saw the man working the gun into the front of his overalls, and she saw him also, with his free hand, drag the woollen cap back down across his forehead.

The chihuahua strained on its narrow leather lead to be clear of the shooting, and the shouting, and the crying of the little girls. The vet had said that the dog's heart was weak and that the dog should not be overexcited.

She picked up her dog, put it under her arm, and walked briskly to her home.

Safe in her own hallway, Miss Worthington bolted the front door, turned the master key. She could not bear the thought of returning to the street, going to the shop, to get the tin of dog food for her chihuahua's midday meal. She was in her first-floor sitting room, secure in her easy chair, when she heard the first sirens, saw the first police cars turn into her street.

It hadn't been real. It was like a disagreeable dream and she wasn't going to have anything more to do with it. She turned her armchair away from the window.

*   *   *

The body was gone. The blood was on the pavement. The children had been taken upstairs. The growing crowd was a hundred yards back, behind the white tape. The discharged cartridge cases were in the roadway and the gutter, close to the back wheel of the taxi.

The taxi driver said, 'You tell me he was shot, he looked like he'd been shot. I didn't hear no shooting. I heard a man running, but I ain't *seen* nothing.'

Of course, they started with a house-to-house, but it was the sort of street where most of the flats, bedsitters, were empty during the day. When a constable knocked on one door, at the extreme end of the street, he heard the distant yapping of a dog, but no one came to the door. He presumed the dog must have been left alone in the house. At the other extreme of the street, Mr Patel was able to confirm that a man had been working the previous day, and that morning, on the Ford Capri that was still there, still with the bonnet raised, still with a plastic bag on the battery. No, Mr Patel was very sorry, no, he had not seen the face of the man who worked on the car. When Mr Patel had passed, the previous evening and that morning, the man's head and shoulders had been underneath the car, and no, he had not come into the shop at all.

Later, an Anti-Terrorist Branch detective would tell his Inspector, 'Middle of the day, well-used street, and no bugger saw anything, not even the little kiddies, nothing that's half a description. It's hard to bloody credit . . .'

Just about the time they had seen the signpost, the rain had started in earnest.

Erlich's first impression was that this place was closed to outsiders. They drove the length of the village. Rutherford was muttering something about a bypass always changing a country community, as if he felt the need to apologize for the place. Erlich said that he wanted to walk.

Rutherford said that he would give him a twenty-minute start, then drive back through the village and collect him.

Erlich took his raincoat off the back seat, the heavy Burberry that he had paid a fortune for in Rome. He shrugged into the coat. He walked.

Small houses of grey and weathered stone on which the lichen had fastened; small windows to the small houses, some of them mullioned; gutters overflowing because they were clogged with leaves; tiny front gardens flattened by the ravages of the winter. He thought the houses, on the road, were low-set, as if for pygmies. A tractor powered past, pulling a trailer loaded with silage rings – shit – had splashed straight through the puddle round the silted-up culvert. Godammit! Mud on his Burberry, on his trousers, all over his shoes . . . Past a bigger garden piled high with abandoned cars. Past a small shop where there were farmers' boots and garden forks and rakes stacked outside despite the rain, and stickers in the window for frozen foods. Past a house that was larger, set back from the road, beyond a lawn on which the rain made ponds, and he saw the flash of an old woman's face at a window and then the falling of a lace curtain. Past the entrance to a farmyard rutted deep in soft mud, and he could see the slipped roofing of the barns where the fallen tiles had been replaced by corrugated iron. Past a gateway, and the wide gate had long ago subsided, and the driveway was leaf-scattered and weeded, and there was a house way back behind beech trees and the trunks of the trees were running green with water. There was the jabber of a car horn in his ear. He was looking up the driveway, trying to make out the shape of the house through the trees. It was the biggest house he had seen so far in the village. He damn well jumped. If he hadn't jumped then the car would have hit him. He jumped for the pavement and a small car swept past him. He saw a woman in the rich blue of a nursing uniform at the wheel. She didn't acknowledge him. She drove up the drive. Past more small, stone houses. A man came towards him. The man was elderly, bearded, bow-legged in his farm boots, and his old army great-coat was fastened at the waist with twine, and the man carried a broken shotgun across his forearm. The man didn't give way, and Erlich stepped into the road to let him pass. Past the pub, and the noise of laughter and the music of a jukebox and the bell chime of gaming machines. He was at the end of the village. He stood beside a muddy soccer pitch.

The rain dripped down his neck. His shoes and his feet were soaked. His raincoat was heavy with damp.

Colt's village.

He heard the car squelch to a stop behind him.

They drove back the way they had come. They stopped in the next village two miles away. They stopped at the modern bungalow that was the home and office of the local police constable. He was Desmond, he was young and bright and flattered that a man had come from the Security Service to see him, and agreeably surprised that a Field Agent of the Federal Bureau of Investigation had ended up in his stockinged feet in his front room. Desmond's wife brought them tea and a sponge cake that was still warm.

The rain drummed on the windows.

Erlich had out his ballpoint and his notebook.

Desmond said, 'I've never seen the lad. I was posted here barely a week after he went missing. But what you have to understand is that he's the biggest thing in these villages, so he has to be the biggest thing in my life. What I normally do is vandalism, poaching, driving without insurance, petty opportunist larceny. Master Tuck faces Attempted Murder, Arson . . . and if you're here then, I suppose, it has to be worse than that . . . Start with the name. Round here he's Colt. Not just because of his initials, but because of what he is, young, unbroken, wild. He represents something exciting to this community, two fingers to the authorities. OK, so he was involved with the Animal Liberation Front, serious crimes. What I hear, people talk to me, took a time but they do, is that the Front was just a vehicle for him, that there were no deeply held principles in it, more that he was in love with the danger, the risk of arrest. I'm not a psychologist, but I read, and I would say that attitude gives him a colossal arrogance.

'The Serious Crime Squad come down, and sometimes I'm

told when they're on my patch, most times I'm not, they keep the Manor House under observation, on and off, but they've not picked up any scent of him. Recently, they've been more often. His mother was big in his life and she's, well, she's not long to live, it seems. It's sad, actually, she's a very respected woman in the village. His father's respected, but in a different way. She's respected and she's loved. If Colt knew, then he'd be back, but it looks like he never made contact from the day he disappeared, so he won't know. He had a girl here too, but I doubt that meant too much, as wild as him.'

They had drained the teapot, finished the cake and Erlich offered his thanks. He understood more, much more, of the man who had looked into Harry Lawrence's face, and shot him dead.

They booked into a guesthouse on the far side of Warminster, and they had time to get into the High Street before the shops closed to buy Erlich a pair of wellington boots, and a rainproof coat that wasn't so City, and a hat.

'Absolutely out of the question.'

'It's not as if I'd ever touch on . . .'

'We do not go outside and give lectures.'

'Do I have to spell out to you how important this is to me?'

'Do you think you are the only one who is asked to give lectures? Myself, I get a dozen invitations a year . . . Basil, he must get fifty. But one doesn't give it a thought. One has no choice.'

'But this is absurd, it wouldn't be about my work . . .'

'Frederick, you are being truly stupid. Anything you talk about is of interest to outsiders, because of where you are employed. And how can you lecture about anything other than your work? What have you the chance to know about other than your work?'

'That's offensive, Reuben, and your attitude altogether . . .'

'Frederick, I am very busy, I have lost a day in meetings . . . I appreciate that your vanity was stirred by this invitation, and of course I understand your regret at having to decline it, but frankly I think your friend is a little jejune. He knows perfectly well what the rules here have to be.'

'Is that your last word?'

'My last word. Good night, Frederick.'

He had allowed himself to hope. He had looked forward to a day in the sun, the simple admiration of colleagues, young scientists. There were tears of frustration in his eyes when he was back in his office and scrawling his letter of regrets in longhand to his former tutor. He was a prisoner in the Atomic Weapons Establishment. The best years of his mind he'd sacrificed to this godforsaken place and precious little did he have to show for it.

7

He sat in the old chair beside the bed. It had not been re-covered since the black cat had massacred the upholstery, and the black cat had been buried under one of the beeches more than ten years. Colt's fingers played with the short lengths of frayed yarn.

His mother was still sleeping.

The sight of the lost flesh on her face had shocked him because he had not, quite, stopped to consider how she might look. Getting there, that had been his aim. Finding her alive, his only hope.

He was very still. His breathing was regular and matched the breathing of his mother.

They had done him well. The organization had been better this time than in Athens. An empty street, just the old woman. That wasn't organization, that was luck. The old woman had been looking not at him but at her dog. The taxi driver hadn't been looking at him either, head down in his change bag. A sprint to the end of the street, the cut through to the footpath. The lock-up garage. The small Bedford van, and the bag with the change of clothes. He had seen no one on the footpath, and no one saw him go into the lock-up garage, he would have sworn on that. Driving the Bedford van along the fringe of the capital, south to west, over Putney Bridge, hitting the small streets of Fulham, and all the instructions had been precise. A second lock-up garage behind an arcade of shops. The van into the second lock-up garage. The chance to squirm out of the over-alls, strip off the rubber gloves, discard the woollen cap, get into the new set of clothes, put the pistol in the pocket of the overalls in the bag. On the other side of the yard from the second lock-up garage had been the Escort. He had driven away. He had felt a new man. He reckoned that when they were sure he was clear they would send someone down to drive away the Bedford van, to retrieve the Ruger, and return it to the Embassy arsenal. He had driven out of London on the M4, past Heathrow, and then taken the Hungerford turning, and then turned again for Marl-borough. He had slept after he had killed the man on the road that led arrow-straight south of Perth. He had slept, back in the apartment on the Haifa Street Housing Project, after he had killed two men in Athens.

He had come off the Marlborough to Devizes road, bumped onto a mud track in a forestry plantation and slept so that he could be at his most alert when he approached home. He had slept while the evening had closed on the afternoon, until night had overtaken the evening.

There was a grey light seeping between the heavy drape curtains at the window. The room had been his childhood refuge. He had always come to this room when he was small and his father had made a play at disciplining him.

The light from between the curtains had settled on the mantelpiece above the fireplace. On the mantelpiece, in an old wooden frame, was the photograph of a bearded man wearing a battledress blouse and with a neckerchief knotted at his throat. His much younger father. It was the photograph that he saw every time he came back to the refuge and safety of this room. When he had been suspended from preparatory school, when he had been expelled from public school, when he had screwed up the Mendip Hunt and the Master of Fox Hounds had called to threaten his father with a civil court action, when he had taken the Stanley knife to the great ibex head trophy in the hall and they had wrestled and kicked and bitten on the hall floor, when he had had the call that warned him of the raid on the squat, he had come, each time, to sit in the old chair at his moth-er's side of the bed and he had seen the photograph of his father. His father had called him, successively, an idiot and a fool and a saboteur and a hooligan and a terrorist. What did his father expect? Colt was his father's son.

The dog stirred, sighed, stretched, lapsed again to sleep across Colt's feet.

The light was spreading in the room. He saw the marks on the carpet. It was the mud from the kitchen garden. It was the way he had always come back to the house when he came in secret. Through the hole in the kitchen-garden wall, where rain and frost had undone the mortar and the stonework, past the ancient privy now cascaded in ivy, to the back door where a spare key was always lodged above a beam and below the slates of the porch.

He heard a door open. He heard his father's first cough of the day. The dog heard his father's tread on the landing and settled closer to Colt's legs.

They were the first down to breakfast, and the first to check out from the guesthouse.

Erlich's Burberry was in the boot of the Astra with his shoes. He wore the new boots which he now realized were a size too large, and the waterproof coat. Rutherford wore a heavy sweater and ankle-length walking boots.

Once they were off the bypass, into the lanes, Rutherford drove fast. They surged out and past a lone milk cart. They squirted through the rain puddles in the road. Erlich saw the isolated cottages where the lights were only on upstairs, and he glanced down frequently at the map spread out across his knees.

It was a good time to be calling at Colt's place.

He had gone downstairs and had quietly called the dog and there had been no response. He had looked into the room off the kitchen where the washing machine and the freezer were, and he had seen the empty basket. It was after he had filled the iron kettle and set it on the Aga's hotplate that he saw the mud prints on the kitchen floor, and on the kitchen table, beside yesterday's newspaper, was a bowl with the dregs of cornflakes and milk in it, and in a saucer was the stub of a cheroot-sized cigar.

He boiled the kettle. He never hurried himself. It was forty-eight years since he had learned the lesson, the hard way, that hurrying was for fools. A bad night, a storm blowing hail onto frozen fingers, the railway viaduct north of Rouen, too much haste with chapped fingers, the jabbering French at his shoulders urging him to work faster, the connection between the command wire and the detonators not properly made. It had been a good night to get on the viaduct because the weather had driven the sentries to cover. The explosives had not fired. The weather had changed with the dawn. There had not been another opportunity to blow the viaduct while the sentries huddled away from the wind and the hail. Three weeks of reconnaissance and planning wasted.

He made the tea. He laid the tray and he put the bread in the toaster. He took an extra mug from the cupboard. While he waited for the toast, he wiped the floor clean with the mop. He carried the tray up the stairs, and twice he bent to retrieve lumps of drying mud. He went into the bedroom.

The boy was where he thought that he would be. He saw the boy's head tilt upwards . . . His son. His son beside his still sleeping wife.

He set down the tray on the dark space of the mahogany dressing table. He had not shaved, nor combed his hair. He was in his pyjamas and dressing gown and slippers. He cared not a damn. Never stood on ceremony, and not starting now.

He took his son in his arms.

He held Colt tight against him. God be thanked! No words aloud, nothing to say. He felt the broad sinew of the boy's back, and he felt the quiet breath of the boy against his cheek. This was his son, and he loved him. He looked from Colt's face, from the calm of the boy's face, down to the face of his wife. He wished that she would wake. He would not wake her. He would not interfere with the drugs that the nurse left, administered each evening, but he wished so fervently that she could wake naturally and see her son and her husband holding each other in love.

When he broke away, as the dog was belting his legs with its tail, it was to pour the tea.

He spilled the tea, made a hash of pouring it, because his eyes were never off his son's face.

He brought the mug of tea to his son. He thought that the boy looked well. He was tired, he could see that, hadn't slept properly for two, three nights, but still the boy looked well. And at that moment the smile froze from Colt's face and the hackles rose the length of the dog's spine, and he heard the grate of car wheels on the gravel under the window.

The door opened in front of Rutherford.

Erlich could see over Rutherford's shoulder, into the gloom of the hallway. The dog came first. Dogs didn't hassle Erlich. The drill with dogs was to stand ground, keep the hands still, avoid eye contact, act as if they didn't exist. Somebody must have told Rutherford, once, the same thing. Rutherford didn't acknowledge the dog. Whoever had opened the door was masked by Rutherford's head.

'Major Tuck?'

A deep voice in response. 'That's me.'

'My name's Rutherford, I'd be grateful if you would invite me inside with my colleague . . .'

He was a big man. Erlich saw him now. A big man in a big old dressing gown with his hair untidy and his stubble not shaved and his eyes sunken. The dog had retreated behind the man's legs, growling and blocking entry.

'. . . It's frightfully early, I do apologize.'

Erlich saw those deep eyes rove over the two of them. Their boots were in the car, and their waterproofs. From first light they had been on the high ground at the back of the house. They had been in the wood, under the dripping trees. They had scoured the windows of the house with binoculars. They had seen the lights come on, and damn-all else. Erlich smiled at the man, as if it was the most natural thing in the world to come calling at three minutes past eight o'clock in the morning.

'What do you want?'

'Just to come in, just to have a talk,' Rutherford said calmly.

'A talk, what about?'

Erlich looked into the eyes of the man, tried to read them, found nothing.

'Government business,' Rutherford said.

'What's government business to do with me?'

An edge in Rutherford's voice. 'I'm from the Security Service, Major Tuck. My colleague is from the Federal Bureau of Investigation. Government business is your son, Major Tuck. We'd like to come inside . . .'

'I don't entertain at this time of day.'

'I've already apologized, Major Tuck.'

'Don't go on apologizing. Just don't be any more of a nuisance.'

'You are the father of Colin Olivier Louis Tuck?'

'I am.'

Rutherford asked, 'Do you know where your son is, Major Tuck?'

The question hacked at the old man. 'No, no, I don't. I don't know where my son is, no.'

'Have you any idea where your son is?'

Composure regained. 'None.'

'No idea at all?'

'Absolutely no idea.'

'When did you last see your son, Major Tuck?'

'Two years ago.'

'No communication since?'

'No.'

'Aren't you curious, Major Tuck?'

'Curious of what?'

Rutherford said, 'Curious as to why a member of the Security Service and a representative of the Federal Bureau of Investigation . . .'

'I am not responsible for my son.'

Erlich said, 'Might I use the lavatory, Major Tuck?'

Rutherford said, 'We are investigating an incident of state-sponsored terrorism, murder.'

Erlich said, 'The lavatory, please, sir.'

'I won't have people storming into my house at all hours to use the lavatory, dammit. No, you can't come in. You'll find a public convenience, which I am sure Mr Rutherford will locate for you, behind the pub in the village. Good day to you both. I'll not be hounded because of my son . . .'

'Hounded, Major Tuck, surely not?'

'My house watched, my mail opened, my telephone . . . My son makes his own bed . . . Good day.'

When they were onto the bypass, when he could cruise without having to worry about shunting into a lorry round a blind corner, Rutherford said, 'I tell you what, I felt sorry for him.'

'You did.'

'Yes, I'm not ashamed to say it. I felt sorry for him.'

'Do you remember Walter de la Mare's "The Listeners"?'

'Hardly. Not since school . . .'

Erlich recited,

> 'But only a host of phantom listeners,
> That dwelt in the lone house then,
> Stood listening in the quiet of the moonlight
> To that voice from the world of men.

'I felt as if we were listened to, that's all.'

Dr Tariq had flown the night before with a Brigadier of the Air Force, a civilian attached to the personal staff of the Chairman of the Revolutionary Command Council, a laboratory technician, and four bodyguards from the Chairman's own squad.

The aircraft in which they had flown, an HS-125 executive jet, had had the insignia of the Iraqi Air Force removed from it. They had flown out over Saudi airspace, down the Red Sea coast, through Egyptian airspace, then south over the Sudanese frontier and into Khartoum.

They had slept on the third floor of the Hilton Hotel. There had been rooms assigned to Dr Tariq, the Brigadier, the civilian and the technician, and a fifth room for the bodyguards. At the other end of the corridor were the South Africans. On the floor above were the teams from Argentina and Pakistan. Two floors below, discreetly apart, were the Indians and the Iranians. Most professionally managed, as it should have been, because the Sudanese hosts had conducted such an auction before.

He had breakfasted in his room, relaxed in the knowledge that his laboratory technician would have been collected from the hotel along with the other teams' technicians before first light, and with his equipment taken to the apartment.

In mid-morning, Dr Tariq was driven to the international airport. The destination was an old aircraft hangar beyond the main runway. An oppressively hot morning, and inside the great tomb of a building the heat was worse. The technician reported that from the tests carried out with a remote-controlled drill, he could guarantee that the merchandise was indeed weapons-grade plutonium. He said, though Dr Tariq was more interested in the quality of the material than its origin, that the plutonium had come from a company in West Germany. The civilian in Dr Tariq's party was a senior member of the staff of the Chairman of the Revolutionary Command Council. His presence ensured that funds for the purchase of the 15 kilograms of plutonium would be available.

A grey-suited European, perspiring, masked by outsized polaroid dark glasses, moved amongst the groups who had taken their positions thirty paces apart on the circumference of a circle round the packing cases on the dust-drenched floor. The European moved from group to group, taking bids.

In less than ten minutes, Dr Tariq was the highest bidder.

He agreed the payment of $2,300,000 for each kilo.

And, within a further half an hour, five packing cases that held the containers, sealed with concrete and lead lining, were loaded onto his aircraft. Dr Tariq followed his delegation into the plane. He left the South Africans and the Pakistanis and the Argentinians and the Iranians and the Indians to haggle over what was left.

Nobody called him 'Sniper' to his face, only behind his back – the older ones with a taint of envy, the younger ones with a slight sneer. But they all acknowledged that Percy Martins carried weight.

Martins said, 'Tork's trouble is that he's been there too long.'

The Deputy Director gazed at the slow movement of the barges and the dredgers and the pleasure craft on the river. The Desk Head (Israel) drummed the blunt end of his pencil on the highly polished table.

Martins said, 'He's gone native, become a bum boy for the Israelis.'

Percy Martins could say what he liked these days, and he did. But everything about the Service, everything about Century House, had changed since he had run a mission into the Beqa'a Valley of eastern Lebanon in which a marksman had taken the life of the murderer of a British diplomat. He was a hero of the good old former times. The fiasco of the capture by Iranian Revolutionary Guards of the Desk Head (Iran) while pottering about after archaeological remains in Turkey, the disastrous consequences of his interrogation in an Iranian gaol in Tabriz, the loss of an entire network of Field Agents, ensured that all was now different. Martins, OBE, hero of the Beqa'a, had established his reputation before Whitehall had put a stop to any mission that smacked of derring-do or risk.

Martins now headed the Desk that watched over Jordan and Syria and Iraq, and he was safe until he cared to retire.

'That's not entirely fair,' Desk Head (Israel) said.

The Deputy Director said gently, 'I tend to agree, Percy, not entirely fair.'

Martins said, 'What have we got? We have H area, A area, and B area. Tork is pushing the Israeli belief that this means

Aldermaston. Maybe they are right, don't get me wrong, but where else are there H and A and B areas? Shouldn't we be checking at Sellafield or Harwell? And at the French nuclear centre, and in America, and in South Africa, and in Pakistan for that matter?'

The Deputy Director inclined his head. He was already fifteen minutes late for his weekly session with Personnel. 'I believe Percy has a point.'

Martins powered on. 'A typical Israeli tactic, involve everybody else with their difficulties. They love it, having everyone rush around doing their work for them.'

The Desk Head (Israel) snapped, 'A serious warning, strongly suggestive of an attempt on the part of Iraq to steal nuclear secrets or possibly to entrap or seduce one of our own nuclear scientists, is not to be taken lightly.'

'You call this a serious warning? It's altogether too airy-fairy in my view.'

The Deputy Director took his cue. 'I think we may justifiably request, via Tork, more detailed information from our friends in Tel Aviv, yes?'

'So, you'll do nothing?' The Desk Head (Israel) began to riffle his papers together.

'Speak a few words in a few ears, not make a panic.' The Deputy Director smiled. 'Good enough, Percy?'

Martins tugged at his small moustache. 'If the Israelis want us to spring about in every direction they will have to share with us something rather more concrete.'

Carol, of course, was back, holding court in the outer office, back from her day at the Falcon Gate replenished with gossip. On the picket line she had gathered more weapons-grade scandal in a day than she would normally have accumulated in a month.

Bissett's open door was well within range.

Carol said . . .

The A90 building was awash with Department of the Environment fraud investigators.

Carol said . . .

The best bit was that – you're not going to believe this – a bulldozer had been ordered on the Establishment account, but delivered to A90 when it should have gone to the man's home where he ran a landscaping business. Wasn't that *awful*?

Carol said . . .

On the A90 site, it had been decided that 3500 metres of ductwork to carry nitrogen into the glove boxes where the plutonium would be worked, *if* the place ever worked, was going to have to be ripped out and replaced because the 2000 welds connecting the ductwork weren't up to scratch, couldn't be repaired. Five million taxpayers' pounds down the plug. Wasn't that dreadful?

Carol said . . .

He heard the rise and fall of Carol's voice as she distributed her precious discoveries from the picket line. The door opened across the corridor. Boll going for a late lunch in the Directors' dining room, taking a short break from the annual assessments. Bissett hunched himself over his desk as Boll went by. Thanks to Carol's shattering revelations, thanks to the bank manager's renewed assault, thanks to his humiliation at Boll's hands over the lecture invitation, it had not been a productive morning. How would he, indeed, assess himself? 'The work of this gifted, original physicist is undervalued in the Establishment.' Was it? He was no longer confident of that.

'I won't jump, not for those patronizing bastards.'

'It's a simple warning, and one to be acted upon.'

'I wouldn't cross the road for them, not if one of them was being mugged for his last pound coin.'

Barker was head of D Branch. D Branch included the Military Security section. The Military Security section was Hobbes.

Barker said, 'Come off your cloud, young man.'

Hobbes said, 'They snap their bloody fingers, those bastards, and they expect us to come running.'

Barker said, and it was not like him to be cruel, 'No doubt if they had accepted you then your attitude would have undergone the old sea change.'

Hobbes said, 'Very catty. Anyway, I haven't the manpower left.'

Barker said, 'I don't need a bulletin on the 'flu casualties. Do me a favour, stop fucking about, just nominate somebody.' He understood young Hobbes's dislike of the Century House crowd, and in truth shared it to a degree. One day, someone would take the lad aside and tell him just how lucky he had been to be rejected by the Secret Intelligence Service and to have squeezed into Curzon Street instead.

'I suppose Rutherford could do it.'

'What's he up to now?'

'Nannying an FBI fledgling.'

'That American thing . . . ?'

Dickie Barker was 64 years old, one year off retirement. He would have served, to the day, forty years in the Security Service. He had worked in the Watcher Service of A Branch, the Personnel Vetting section in B Branch, the Soviet Satellites section of C Branch, the Political Parties (Left) section of F Branch. In his run-up to retirement he headed D Branch with sections working to him that dealt with the Civil Service, Government Contractors, Military Security and Sabotage Prevention. Many newer men, Hobbes among them, had not been too proud to seek him out for advice on this and that. He had a deep well of experience and, when his PA wasn't off sick, a constantly patient and amiable manner.

He had helped Jim Skardon interrogate Fuchs. He had been among the watchers who had tailed Alan Nunn May. He had been in the team that kept the bungalow home of Peter Kröger under surveillance. He had observed Bossard, he had prepared the case against Bettany who had worked only two floors below him in the old Leconfield House building. If he had had a very good evening, he would talk of the days when the FBI heavyweights were over in Leconfield House, running riot through Registry, shitting on the Service and playing the game that every Briton was subversive. It was said of Dickie Barker that second only to his contempt for the Secret Intelligence Service was his dislike of the American agencies.

'I could tell Rutherford to put the American on hold.'

'Yes, Rutherford would do. Tell him to park his pram, preferably in the middle of Oxford Circus. Have him in here before the end of the day.'

Erlich spoke fast, didn't hide his excitement, said what he wanted . . . He listened. He replaced the receiver.

Ruane was across the room, getting off his coat, back from lunch.

'You all right, Bill?'

Erlich looked up. He looked into Ruane's face. There was a quiver in his voice.

'I'm being pissed on, Dan.'

Ruane gestured him to follow, walked smartly into his office. He held the door open, closed it behind Erlich. A growl in his voice. 'What sort of shit talk is that?'

Erlich said, 'They gave me a liaison. There is a shooting in London, an Iraqi, former government employee, is killed. I'm not informed, I am left to read it in the newspaper. I react. I ring my liaison and I tell him what I want . . .'

'*Want?*'

'Want, Dan, because I am here to investigate a murder. Yes, I tell him what I want. I tell him I want every detail on the investigation into this local killing. Anything they've got on identification, etc. etc. My liaison said he was *unavailable*. He said he had *other work*, and would be back to me when it was finished. What do I do, Dan?'

Ruane had ducked out of sight. When he reappeared it was with the box of brushes and polish, and his stockinged feet swung to the desktop.

'When I know what I want and no one will give me what I want, then I go and take it.'

'Thanks . . .'

'You screw up, and I never heard of you. You hear me?'

*   *   *

Colt was still sitting beside his mother when his father returned to the bedroom in the early afternoon.

When his mother had woken he had leaned forward to kiss her cheek, and she had smiled. Her eyes had closed again, but then, at least, her breathing had been steady, and from the time that she had woken he had loosely held her hand. Her peace brought a calm to Colt. His thoughts were of memories long buried, of the family holidays, and laughter and merrymaking at Christmas in the Manor House. Only the good memories concerned him.

It was good she was asleep. If she had been awake then she would have wanted him to talk. He would not have wanted to tell her of the two boys to whom he had taught English, and who had learned nothing, but who had shed their puppy fat and their conceit and learned to pitch tents and make campfires and shoot a rabbit at a hundred paces with the Colonel's Kalashnikov rifle, and skin the animal and cook it and eat it. Through teaching those boys his own freedom he had further taken the eye of the Colonel and dictated his own transfer from the uplands of rock and desert around the army compound and the Colonel's bungalow to the prison cell that was the apartment on the Haifa Street Housing Project. She would not have wanted to hear that he had been taken from the wild happiness to the capital city to be trained as a killer of targets. Best that she was asleep.

His father carried a tray into the bedroom. Three soup bowls, some buttered toast cut into fingers, a jug of orange juice and three glasses.

His father said that he had been into Warminster to the bank, and that he had needed to do the shopping. Colt thought that his father had found an excuse to leave son and mother together.

His father lifted his mother, propped her high against the pillows, fed her soup with a spoon, and he talked as if she could not hear him.

'They were Security Service and the FBI . . .'

'I heard the voices.'

'I sent them packing.'

'You don't want those bastards in your house.'

'. . . I told the American to go down to the pub because I couldn't let him inside, because the lavatory door is beside the kitchen door and because this is obviously a non-smoking house, and because on the kitchen table you had left a saucer with a revolting little cigar end in it.'

Soft, murmured words, as he fed the soup into his wife's mouth, and after he had given her each spoonful he wiped carefully at her chin to remove what the shake in his hand had spilled.

'Thanks.'

'You always were a careless little sod.'

'What did they want?'

'When I'd seen you, where you were.'

'What did you tell them?'

His father looked into Colt's face. 'That I wasn't responsible for your actions. They said it was about state-sponsored terrorism, I said that you had made your own bed . . .'

'Did they believe you?'

'I didn't ask them . . .' A coldness in the whispered voice. 'Isn't political murder a cut above your league?'

'If you say so.'

'I mean, that's not running around with those animal loonies . . .'

Colt said, like it was an explanation, 'He got in the way. He wasn't the target. He was CIA.'

'They won't ever let up after a trick like that.'

Colt said, 'I'll never be taken.'

'The idiots all say that.'

'You could have turned me in, when you were in Warminster this morning.'

'Could have done . . . should have done. Could have let the American in before breakfast, for that matter.'

'But you didn't.'

'During the war there were men who died under torture, rather than give my name – your soup will be cold – I would never inform, even on a stranger.'

Colt's glance caught the wartime photograph. There were the clear features of his father and behind were the fading faces of his colleagues in arms. One of them, on the extreme right, had been his mother's uncle. He wondered which of those blurred figures had been taken and tortured, and had held his silence that his father might live.

'Thank you for sending for me.'

Erlich said, ever so gently, 'That's just terrific, Miss Worthington.'

'It's only what I saw. You see it or you don't see it.'

'And again . . .'

'So that you can write it down, Mr Erlich. He had fair hair, cut close, not shaven like those skinhead types, I don't suppose you have them in America, cut very tidily. He was wearing this woollen cap. If it hadn't slipped, just for that moment before he straightened it, then I would not have seen his hair. Rather golden fair hair.'

'And you'd know the face again?'

'Oh, yes, Mr Erlich.'

'Positive?'

'He looked at me, he smiled at me. When you've seen a man kill another man, then that man smiles at you, well, you are going to remember that face.'

'And he said . . .'

'He said "Hey, there". That's when I looked up. The man, the foreigner, you see I thought that he was the worse for drink, and I started to cross the road. I had heard nothing. As long as I live it will be with shame, because I thought he was drunk and I started to cross over so that he wouldn't involve me. Then he fell and I saw the blood. Up to that time the man in the boiler suit had stood away from him, but then he went closer. I don't hear very well these days, I heard nothing. The man lying on the pavement, he just stopped moving, and I shall never know if I could have done something for him or not, but I was just going to get out of the way because I thought he was a drunk.'

It was the old training from Quantico that an interrogator

never showed excitement. Didn't matter if he was getting the laundering system of a crack baron, or a confession to serial murder, the Fed was taught at the Academy not to show excitement. To show excitement was to lead. Never lead. He shouldn't have told Miss Worthington that she was terrific. That was a slip. It was the fifth house that he had called at in the street. He had knocked on the door. She was just inside the door and he could see her shape through the glazed glass. He had knocked and rung the bell, but she had been a long time answering. He had sensed she was faint, that the small dog was frantic. His intuition, that she was a prisoner in her own home. The shopping basket with the list in it had been on the carpet by the front door. It had been his intuition and his understanding. Nothing said. He had taken the basket, gone to the corner shop at the far end of the street. He had bought a packet of porridge, one pork chop, oven-ready chips, a carton of frozen broccoli, one apple, one orange, a small loaf of wholemeal sliced, and an 8oz tin of Pedigree Chum. And after he had ticked off each item on the list he had asked for two ½lb bars of milk chocolate and a small bunch of chrysan-themums. He had come back to the house. He had allowed her to peck in her purse for the coins to reimburse him, but not for the chocolate and the flowers. He had cooked her meal, fed her dog. He thought that if she had not been standing near the door at the moment he had knocked, if she had been in the recesses of the house, then he would never have been admit-ted. She was 24-carat gold dust.

'Miss Worthington, my paper says that the police do not have a description of the assassin.'

'I really couldn't say.'

'Haven't they been to speak to you, Miss Worthington?'

'I wouldn't talk to them.'

'Why not, if that's not impolite?'

'I wouldn't open the door to them . . . You're different, Mr Erlich, and you're American.'

'Do you have American friends?'

'Two of my best friends are Mr Silvers and Miss Ball.'

Well done, Phil Silvers, well done, Lucille Ball, he thought, and he took the photograph from his inside pocket.

'Miss Worthington, I am going to show you a photograph of a man. You really have to be very honest with me. If you don't recognize him, you must say so. If you do recognize him . . .'

He laid the photograph on the table beside her, where there was a book and her reading light and her close-work spectacles.

She changed her glasses, took off her heavier pair, replaced them delicately from the table. He didn't prompt. If she said what she thought he might wish to hear, then he could face weeks of wasted effort. She glanced at the photograph. She didn't bother to hold it and peer at it.

'You're very clever, Mr Erlich.'

'Clever, ma'am?'

'Of course that's him.'

He was up from his chair. He kissed her on both cheeks. When he stepped back he saw the flush of colour in her pale face.

She said gravely, 'It was a terrible thing he did in our street, and he could have hurt those dear little girls.'

'And before that he killed a man who was my friend.'

'You'll go after him?'

'That was the promise I made to the widow of my friend.'

'Do you go to chapel, Mr Erlich? No, I don't expect you have time. I will pray for your safety, young man. Any person who can take the life of any of God's children, then smile at an old lady, he would have to be very dangerous. What is his name?'

'His name is Colt.'

'The best of luck to you, Mr Erlich. I have so enjoyed your visit. And, I will be praying for your safety.'

'What are we going to do?'

'I don't know.'

'Well, think, Frederick.'

'I don't know.'

142

'That is just a pretty stupid answer.'

'If you shout, Sara, you will wake the children.'

'Just how bad is it?'

'How bad . . . ?' He laughed out loud. His voice was shrill, matching hers. 'How bad do you want it? ICI have turned me down. That bloody man at the bank is turning the screws. Boll is doing annual assessments now and I'm behind on my work project, and getting nagged.'

'They wouldn't put a bailiff in . . . ?'

'For what?' he scoffed.

'Frederick, you have to tell me what we are going to do . . .'

They could take the cars, his and hers. They could take furniture. They could take their clothes off their backs. Christ, it was obscene . . . All the lights were off in the house except for the bedside lights in the children's room, and the strip light in the kitchen. The heating was off, because the boiler was shut down. They couldn't take the television set, because it was rented.

'I'm going to say good night to the boys.'

'Frederick, we have to talk about it.'

'Something'll turn up.'

He stood at the bottom of the stairs. He thought that she was beautiful with the tired frightened anger in her eyes. He did not know how to talk to her. A dozen years of marriage and he knew nothing that mattered about her. If she ever went away from him, abandoned him, he could not have survived. Yet he did not know how to talk to her, and he loved her. Yes, something would have to turn up.

'Is that the best you can offer?'

'That something'll turn up, yes.'

Bissett groped his way upstairs towards the bar of light under the boys' door. He had always provided for his family. He had not expected that his wife should go out to work. That was his upbringing. Old-fashioned, yes. Working-class, yes. He had been the bright star of his college, he had a first-class degree in Nuclear Physics, he was a Senior Scientific Officer, he lived in the house that he and the building society had paid £98,000 to buy, yet he would never escape from his upbringing. It was his responsibility alone to provide for his family.

Something would turn up, yes. He paused outside the boys' door. He could hear them larking about and giggling.

Away up the road, up Mount Pleasant, up Mulfords Hill, across the Kingsclere to Burghfield Common Road, were the arc lights and the fences of the AWE. It was Boll country, Basil country, Carol country, a world of fraud and waste and burnt-out hopes, of excruciating effort, constant danger, trivial rewards, Ministry police with machine pistols country. Less and less did it feel like Frederick Bissett country.

'Now then, you naughty little blighters, time for sleep.'

8

He drove out of London, with a road map across his knees. He might just get the New York posting if he fouled up. Some of the instructors at Quantico said that hunches were good, and some – more – said they were crap. Ruane had been out when Bill had got back to the Embassy and his hunch told him to get down into the country again. New York-based Agents earned less than the city's garbage collectors, and the only worse posting than New York HQ on Foley Square was the regional office at Brooklyn-Queens. If he really fouled up it would be the fast heave out of Rome, and if he fouled up really bad then it could be Brooklyn-Queens, New York City.

He edged his way along amid the commuter traffic flow.

The Quantico bible, verse one, chapter one, said that Proper Prior Planning Prevents Piss Poor Performance. The seven big Ps. He had two P's worth on the back seat of his Ford along with his waterproof coat and the wellington boots. He had bought himself some thermals and a sleeping bag and a camouflaged bivouac cover.

The motor was fine, cramped but he could cope with that and where he was going was just right for a dismal-looking little motor. Once he was past Reading the traffic had thinned. He drove carefully, and the light had gone by the time he could take the turn off the motorway for the cross-country route to Warminster.

Erlich was a town boy. He had lived in Annapolis, Maryland, with his grandparents, then he had gone to Santa Barbara, University of California, then to Battle Creek and the town school, then to Quantico and on to Atlanta and Washington. Country was not his place. There was big, raw, country where his mother now lived, out on the White Mountains and on the long trail, but he had never felt at home in country. He did not know the way of the country, nor the pace of the country. Or the *suspicion* of the country.

Two miles short of the village, his headlights picked out the gate. The entrance into the field had been solidified with stone chips. He reckoned it was a good place for him.

He parked the Ford in the field, hard against the hedge. The hedge was thick holly and would screen his car from the road.

In the darkness he put on his boots and slipped on his waterproof coat. He rolled his sleeping bag tight inside the camouflage bivouac screen. He felt in his pocket, checked that he had his monocular glass.

Between the trees ahead he could see the dull gold glow of the village lights.

When the Serious Crime Squad boys came down to the village and bothered to announce themselves then, they always asked to see Desmond's log. His wife was in the kitchen and his supper would be up in a quarter of an hour, and the small ones were in bed. It was a useful time for Desmond to get his log up to date.

The log listed as many of the visitors to the Manor House as he knew of. Pretty dull reading it made, but it was what Serious Crime wanted.

He knew about the flowers being delivered because the van driver had called in at the shop to ask directions. Desmond knew just about everything involving the shop because he had won Mrs Williams' gratitude when he had put two kids in court for breaking her plate-glass window the last New Year's Eve. Nothing surprising about the flowers because obviously Mrs Tuck was very ill. The young constable felt he was a coming man. How many policemen in the Wiltshire force could boast a visit from an FBI Special Agent plus an offer from the Security

Service? He wondered what poor Mrs Tuck's son had done to warrant the attention of the Security Service and the FBI. Properly speaking, that visit would have to go into the log too, and Serious Crime could make what they would of it.

He wondered, too, whether that pig of a son would come back to see his mother before she died.

The flowers were on the compost heap and the voluminous cellophane wrapping and the ribbons were in the rubbish bin beside the back door. He wouldn't have the bloody flowers in a vase and on display. She was upstairs and dying, his wife, and he was damned if he would allow their bloody intrusion into his life and into her death.

'You owe them nothing . . . They make a joke of your mother's illness. Flowers, damn them, just to get a message to you. How can you owe them more than you owe your mother and me? How could you involve us in the infernally dangerous mess you are in?'

'I'll be gone by the morning,' Colt said.

He *was* involved, Major Tuck was most emphatically involved. He was involved because before he switched on the light in any room he first went to the window and drew the curtains closed. He was involved because he cared for his son's freedom. He was involved because in the late afternoon dusk he had walked the dog around the garden and known that the dog would show him if the house was watched from the kitchen garden wall and the paddock hedgerow or the front garden wall on either side of the front gates.

'Will I see you again?'

'Will I involve you again?' Colt asked, and there was the careless smile at the boy's mouth.

God's truth, he'd miss the little bugger. God's truth, he wanted him gone because when he was gone then at least he knew the boy was safe and at liberty. God's truth, the smile on his wife's face, as the boy had sat with her and held her hand, had been the best thing in his life for months. God's truth, he could no longer remember how he had been at that age, in France, alone, a satchel of gelignite for company.

'If you can come again . . .'

'I will.'

She took the pheasant from the snare. She loosened the wire from its throat. In three of her snares there were strangled pheasants, two cock birds and a hen. She could move in the fields without light, her father had taught her well – it was six years since the keepers had last caught him, since he had last been before the magistrates in Warminster. Her footfall was without sound, her breathing was silent. She was a wraith moving in the care of the darkness, back towards the village.

He came past the empty keg barrels that were piled as haphazardly to await collection by the brewery as they had always been. He came past the oil tank and the rusted plough that had been at the back since he could first remember. He went through the outside back door and through the gents toilet.

Colt came into the back bar.

The beer smell was in his nostrils. The cigarette smoke was in his eyes. The jukebox music was in his ears. He paused in the doorway.

He saw the faces and he saw the astonishment. He might not have been away. Two years back, and they had all been in the bar. Billy and Zap, the brothers who worked in the bike garage in Frome . . . Charlie on the dole and proud of it . . . Kev from the farm on the Shepton Road . . . Dazzer who had tried to be a postman but who wouldn't pack in the evening drinking and couldn't get up in the morning . . . Zack, who had done time for sheep-stealing from Home Farm, three months in Horfield . . . Johnny, whose grandfather had left the plough at the back to wipe off his slate twenty years before, at least . . . and old Brennie. He was back two years. Old Brennie by the guttering fire, where he had been two years back, where he had been with the German Shepherd sleeping on its side at his feet when Colt had last come to the pub. The village boys were around him. Billy and Zap, Charlie, Kev, Dazzer, Zack, Johnny, all around Brennie. Christ, and old Brennie had on the same brown Windsor soup jacket that he had worn that night two years back. Fran was the only one who hadn't seen him. She was beside her father, with her back to the door.

They were all staring at him. As if he was a ghost. Not a word spoken.

Fran turned. She swung her shoulders to see what had killed the talk around the fire. Her face lit up, then she frowned and her eyes blinked, like they weren't sure.

As she stood, her heavy coat was caught for a moment against her father's leg, and the lining showed and the deep pocket and a cock pheasant's head jutting from the pocket. For a moment, Fran's fingers clung to old Brennie's shoulder, because it could not be real.

He stood his ground in the doorway.

Then the explosion of her movement. She ran across the room. Four feet from him, she jumped. Her thighs were on his hips, her arms were round his neck.

Not a word said. Not a word from any of them.

Colt kissed Fran. Fran kissed Colt.

Old Brennie grunted something, and none of the kids knew what he said. But Old Brennie went to the bar and he slapped down his pound coin, and told old Vic to get up a bitter dash.

Colt felt the pulsing energy of his Fran and her warmth. And when he had let her down, then he held her face in his hands, let his fingers rest on her cheeks, and he kissed her lips and her chin and cheeks and her nose and her eyebrows and her ears. He kissed her until old Brennie shook his arm and handed him the pint. He held her against his chest, and he drank the pint straight down, and tossed the glass at the group of them, and Zack caught it, and old Vic was already pulling his pump.

They were all on their feet and round him.

Zack said, 'Shit, boyo, you shouldn't be here . . .'

Kev said, 'Colt, the filth watch for you, they're here regular . . .'

Dazzer said, 'There was a Yank in the village . . .'

Charlie said, 'You show yourself here, Colt, you're for the fucking jump . . .'

Billy said, 'The pretty boy, the copper, he's always sniffing round your house . . .'

Johnny said, 'What we heard, they've guns when they come looking for you . . .'

'Have you come back for your ma, young 'un?'

'Yes, Brennie, I came back to see her . . .'

'I was sorry to hear about your ma.'

'Thank you, Brennie.'

Old Vic had come into the bar from behind the counter. He carried the filled pint sleeve glass to Colt. Old Vic went to the main bar door and he pushed it shut and he set the bolt across. Colt saw it in old Vic's face. He was expected to drink up, and he was expected to get his arse out. Old Vic wouldn't want trouble. Old Vic had taken his position by the counter, his arms folded across his chest. He was waiting for Colt to be gone.

'Where have you been, Colt?' Kev asked.

Colt drank.

Where he had been, what he had done, that would mean nothing to any of them. Old Brennie used to claim that he had never in his life travelled further than Warminster and the Magistrate's Court. Billy and Zap had been as far as Southampton, to watch football, and given that up as a waste of weekend drinking time. Zack had been to Bristol for Crown Court and prison. Australia was the moon, Iraq was the stars. Kev had been to the special school in Warminster that handled pupils too disruptive for the comprehensive.

'I've been around,' Colt said. 'Here and there . . .'

His father would not have known the names of any of them. His mother would have known their mothers through the Institute. They were the dregs of the village, Colt's father would have said.

Fran said, 'Are you going to drink, or are you going to come walking?'

She took off her heavy coat and slung it to her father, and the pheasant spilled on the flagstones.

Nothing changed, not in two years. The poacher's daughter was tall, big-boned, big-hipped. She had red flame hair that would have been on her shoulders if it had not been caught in a ponytail with an elastic band. Strong as a bullock, old Brennie had said. She took Colt's hand and walked him to the door. None of them would tell on him. Most likely, they'd have one of old Brennie's snare wires round their neck if they did.

They went out through the yard at the back of the pub. They crossed two fields, bent and close to the hedgerows.

There was a pillbox on the high ground above the village, to the west. There were brambles across the entrance, and under one of the gun-slits there were the diggings of a badger sett. It was where they had always come, it was where they had been two years back.

'Is the American for you?'

'Yes.'

'What does he want with you?'

'First choice would be to kill me, second choice would be to take me.'

'We'll give him a run,' she said.

It wasn't raining now and Erlich used the bivouac cover as a groundsheet. He was a few yards back into the trees, but he had a clear view down the slope of the fields to the house. He reckoned that he was six hundred yards from the house. An image intensifier would have been a help, but he would have to make do with the monocular glass. From his vantage point he could see the high narrow window on the stairs and he could see the kitchen window, both lit. The rest of the house was dark. The bedrooms were on the front of the house.

The isolation oppressed him. He must have been mad to have taken himself off to a God-awful lonely wood where the birch saplings were dripping and the cold rainwater splattered from the big oak branches. He thought of Don and Nick and

151

Vito and their so far empty bulletins, and imagined their warm, convivial evening in an Athens taverna. He saw Colt's father, clear, come down the stairs. He saw him framed in the back door at the kitchen, and he thought he saw the dog come past the man's legs, and a few minutes later the door was opened again, then closed. The kitchen light went out. And then the stair light. After those lights had gone Erlich's spirits sank. He felt dismally alone. The shouting from the car park at the pub carried to him, and the revving of car engines, and after that only deeper silence beyond the sighing of the wind in the trees above him. He was scared. He nearly jumped out of his sleeping bag when a young roe buck passed ten feet from him, hugging the edge of the field. And he muttered an expletive in fear when a pigeon, alarmed by the slight shift of his body, exploded out of the trellis of branches above his head. He heard a fox vixen call, and once he heard the death screams of a rabbit and didn't know what predator was at its throat. There had been a moon to start with, occasional and in between the fast-moving cloud formations, but that moon was lost in thick cloud. When it started to rain, he wrapped himself tight in the bivouac cover. He lay still. It was the first time since he had left Washington that he had missed the comfort of the sharp shape against his chest of a standard issue, .38 calibre, Smith and Wesson revolver.

Good loving, just as it had been two years back.

She said that she had known he was back when she found the car hidden away in the old barn at the edge of the twelve acre. She had known he was back and had carried three bales of straw to the pillbox.

She had stripped him off, she had stripped herself off.

They were on the rough straw in the pillbox.

She was great and she cared about nothing, other than getting the condoms on him.

The third time, she tickled him to life, so he could be useful to her again, with a stalk of straw.

Her on Colt, Colt on her, her back on Colt.

Soft and gentle loving, and fun.

And the talk was soft and gentle. Not heavy and not serious, because that wasn't their way, but fun . . .

'Do you remember . . . ?'

When they had gone to the pheasant pens on the estate, let the lot out, screwed up the whole season's shooting for the posh crowd.

When they had been out at night, the night before the hunt had been due on the estate and the Home Farm land, and they had laid the trails with the aniseed in the sacking bag, and they had sat the next morning on the high ground and watched and laughed till it hurt at the chaos, and the Master looking as though he'd do his heart.

Fran hadn't joined the Front. Fran had said, after Colt had taken her to one meeting, that the ALF were a load of ponces and poseurs. What she had meant was that the activists were too serious. She couldn't be doing with serious.

When Colt was flat on his back with the goose-pimples working up the bareness of his thighs, and when there was the big warmth of her breasts on his chest, then Colt told his Fran where he had been and what he had done. It was natural for him to tell her. He told her about the rush out of the Manor House, and the flight out of Heathrow before the law was organized. He told her about Australia, and about the man who had tried to roll him when he was sleeping rough off the highway down to Fremantle. He told her about his escape from Australia on the tanker where they used bicycles to get from bow to stern. He told her about Kuwait and making his way into Iraq. He told her about a job teaching English to the children of an Iraqi Colonel, about his friendship with the Colonel's family, about his recruitment and about the shooting of two men in Athens, and the shooting of a man in south London. He told her about his life since they had last been, naked and cuddling, in the pillbox overlooking the village that was their home.

Fran told him what she knew, that there was a car parked behind the holly hedge of a field on the Frome road.

*   *   *

153

Desmond was shaving and his wife was still in bed and the little ones were still asleep when he heard the rapping at the front door. If he hadn't already wiped his face then Desmond wouldn't have recognized him. Mud from head to toe, like he had been crawling in a gateway where the cattle had churned the ground. A line of rips in his coat, like he had been caught in wire and hadn't the calm to unpick the barbs. The American's chest was heaving. He was at the end of his tether. Obviously not a time for talking, because the American was already walking towards the panda car in the carport. Desmond grabbed his coat and his keys.

The place was halfway between the police house and the village. The hatchback of the Ford had been forced. The jack from the Ford was abandoned in the mud beside the car. Close to the car, on the field side of the holly hedge, were the four wheels. The Ford was beached, stranded. He could have laughed, but he hadn't the nerve.

Rutherford thought it was the sort of job that he would be looking for when he was that age, a cosy little number.

He sat in the Security Officer's room on the top floor of the main block of F area. 'I tell you, Mr Rutherford, we have a happy community here. I'm not talking about the general workforce, I am referring to the senior scientific and engineering staff.'

'Quite.'

'And you would do well to consider that while Defence has had traitors, so has your Service, so has Intelligence, so has GCHQ ... Atomic Weapons Establishment has had no blots on its escutcheon at all.'

'Of course not.'

'The loyalty of our scientists and engineers is the last thing I shall be losing sleep over. They are first-class people. They know what their job is and they get on with it.'

'It's just a general warning ...'

To Rutherford, the place reeked of complacency, but it wasn't his concern. He was just the messenger, packed off on the errand of communicating a 'general warning'.

'The Iraqi Atomic Energy Commission, you say.'

'That's where we believe a threat to security *might* come from.'

'. . . They would need very specialized knowledge. They'd have to know who they were looking for, where that individual worked, and then they'd have to compromise him. Not the least of their problems, you see, Mr Rutherford, would be in identifying one of our scientists. Practically impossible. The Establishment prides itself on its discretion.'

'That's very gratifying.'

'They couldn't even trawl around and fail. The slightest approach made and that scientist, that engineer, would be straight in here, my door is always open. Government has done very well by this place. Conventional forces may be feeling the draught what with the changes in Eastern Europe, but we've been left untouched. Everybody here has job security.'

'It was a general warning and I've passed it on.'

'And I've noted it . . . Don't get me wrong, Mr Rutherford. Anyone, *everyone*, here would be appalled at the suggestion that a regime as bestial and madcap as that of Iraq could get its hands on nuclear weapons. They will not get any sort of help from anyone at AWE. Now the French, that's another matter. The Italians, I am afraid, quite a different kettle of fish. On the other hand, Mr Rutherford, if your people come up with something a little more specific, by all means be in touch again.'

'I'm sure you'll do what's necessary.'

'Well, we won't be scaremongering.'

Rutherford said quietly, 'The sort of people who could help the Iraqi programme, how many are we talking about?'

'Twenty, not more.'

'It would be good if you keep a weather-eye on them, those twenty.'

'Mr Rutherford, take a message back to London . . . Those twenty men and women are some of the finest brains employed in government science. They are all, each last one of them, people who deserve society's respect. If you think that, on the basis of some intelligence tittle-tattle, I am going to order phone intercepts, mail opening, bank statement access, against our foremost individuals, then . . .'

Rutherford stood up. 'I'll tell them in London that the Iraqis will have to look elsewhere.'

Again, he could not fault them. He presumed they had learned from the Soviets, but then they might just as well have learned it off the British. They told him enough for him to know that it was foolproof whether it had come from the Soviets or from the British.

They told Colt, the two men that he met in mid-morning in the puddled car parking area on Wimbledon Common, that they had used the scatter and disperse procedure. They told him that there would always be at least one car from the Security Service or from Special Branch watching the front of the Iraqi delegation's building. They told him that their tactic was to overwhelm the watchers. The Military Attaché and two Second Secretaries, who were sensitive and known to the Service and the Branch, had left the building one after the other. One had turned right down the street, two had gone left. Three trails to follow, two cars at most for the job . . . Two minutes later, the two men had left the building. They had come via taxi, underground train, mainline train, and taxi again.

He called the taller of the two Faud, and the shorter Namir. Faud had joked that he was listed as being on the staff of the Cultural Centre in Tottenham Court Road, and Namir had said that he was listed as a chauffeur to the Commercial Attaché. Faud had pointed out the rubbish bin in the car park that was emptied on Mondays and Fridays. Namir had said that a message could be left there on any Sunday or Thursday, and that the bin would be checked by himself on those evenings. Faud had shown Colt the decoded telex from Baghdad, Namir had burned it with his cigarette lighter when Colt had read it.

Colt had the address. He had his start point.

And he was told that he had done well, that he was a favoured son, that there was great pleasure at the sending to Hell of Saad Rashid, the thief.

The Metro Vanden Plas went first.

He was down the road, on the verge. Straight after the Vanden Plas came the Saab Turbo. He saw the BMW come out and cross the traffic and it was nothing short of miraculous that it missed the gravel lorry and when the lorry driver hammered his horn she gave him two fingers. There was the E-type and the Audi. He had time to smoke a small cigar before the Fiat crept out of the gates. The Fiat with the A registration, that would be the car. His engine had been idling. He allowed a van and an estate to get in front of him before he came off the verge. Colt did not know the name of the woman, only that he was to follow her because her husband worked as a scientist at the Atomic Weapons Establishment. He followed her off the main roads, and through a housing estate. When he saw her at her front door, her sketch pad under one arm and rummaging in her bag for her key, Colt thought her a good-looking woman.

On every house there was a Neighbourhood Watch sticker. Colt had driven to Newbury and had bought a calculator and an accounts ledger and a book of receipt dockets. He sat, now, in the car in Lilac Gardens. He had positioned himself directly under a street light. He invented receipts, and he entered those receipts in the accounts ledger. He wore a clean shirt and a tie. He was the sales representative clearing his day's paperwork. He was the rep who had found a quiet place to get his paperwork tidied up before his last appointment of the day.

He was seventy-five yards from the front of the house, under the light, positioned so that he faced the junction of Lilac Gardens with Mount Pleasant. He had seen the wife again. He had seen her go out in her car, and he had watched her come back with her two small boys. It was important for him to know the numbers of the household, and later he would watch for the bedroom lights so that he would know where the family slept, but that would be later. He watched the men of Lilac Gardens coming home from their day's work. He saw a Cavalier pull into the forecourt of the house to the right. He saw a flash Ford, a newer model than he recognized, accelerate up the cul-de-sac, brake, and turn squealing into the opened garage of the house to the left. Colt thought that he had never before watched the herd of workers actually come home. He saw the lights of the Sierra. He had never, himself, worked in his life, he didn't count the part time that he had thrown in with the farmers around the village, harvest-time tractor driving. The Sierra was slowing. There had always been money from his mother for what he needed, beer money, cigarette money, petrol money. He had never gone short, even in Australia, always picked up a bit here and there. Now of course he had in his hip pocket the fat brown envelope that had been handed to him in the car park on Wimbledon Common. The headlights of the Sierra caught his face then swung away, turned onto the concrete and stopped behind the Fiat. He saw the man who came out of the car.

There was a light rain. He flicked the windscreen wipers across once, killed them.

He saw the sports jacket. He saw the dark hair. He saw the man run with his briefcase to the front door. Colt saw the face of his target.

An electric fan purred in the corner, its face traversing a narrow arc, and every few seconds the papers on the desktop gently lifted, then fell back.

There were filing cabinets, each drawer with a solid padlock fastening it. There was a floor safe, old enough to have carried the papers of the founding fathers. There was a desk, and hard chairs against the walls. No decorations of any kind. Typical of them, Tork thought. That room symbolized everything that he admired about the men of the Mossad. No frills, no bullshit.

'What you are suggesting is blatantly ridiculous.'

'I'm not their apologist,' Tork said.

'Are they too stupid to interpret the threat?'

'I simply cannot say what they have or have not read into it.'

'If the Iraqis were prepared to use chemical agents against their own people, their Kurds, would they hesitate to use a nuclear device against us? They have the Condor missile, capable of reaching any of our cities. A missile with Condor's range is not designed to carry a sackful of conventional explosive.'

'We must assume that Century is au fait on Condor and its current state of development.' With his hand Tork flapped away the smoke from the Israeli's cigarette. If he ever developed cancer of the lungs it would be from passive smoking in the offices of the Mossad.

'And do they also know that Dr Tariq has recently purchased fifteen kilos of weapons-grade plutonium?'

'Has he now?' Tork wrote a sharp note in his pocket pad.

'And they want an even bigger picture drawn for them?'

'I think what it is, is that Century, in consultation no doubt with the boffins, regards it as inherently improbable that the programme directors at Tuwaithah would dream of targeting a *British* scientist. So much so that they – well, obviously there are more plausible targets – want something pretty specific before they are willing to turn Sellafield or Aldermaston upside down looking for Iraqis under the bed. At least, that's the gist of it.'

'So, they will do nothing until there is a warhead on the Condor, the Middle East at Baghdad's mercy? Most politic.'

'In a separate communication,' Tork said, 'my own Desk Head asked particularly that I should say that he hoped very much that you would be in a position to give them something more. Then he'll go straight in to bat. That's to say . . .'

'Yes, yes, we know all about batting, Tork. This is not cricket. This is survival.'

There was a cursory handshake. He was escorted from the building.

He liked to walk. He felt that when he walked on Ben Yehuda, and on the other arteries of Tel Aviv, then he could soak up something of the atmosphere of the society on which he had reported to London for the last eleven years. There was much in that society which he disliked. His private opinion, never expressed, was that the Israeli military had demeaned its reputation in its handling of the *intifada* war against the Palestinian teenagers. And there was much in that society which he admired. His private opinion was that the men and women of the Mossad left his own Service for dead. But they were ruthless, the case officers of the Mossad, and he wondered what poor devil, living a buried life of danger, would be ordered to produce 'more' that the hesitations of Century might be quelled.

'I'll take them,' Frederick said.

'Are you sure?'

'I'd like to.'

'I've got a splitting headache.'

'I'll take them.'

'It would be marvellous . . .'

'I'll do it.'

She couldn't quite believe it, that Frederick would take the boys swimming. He never took them. Not to Cubs, nor to the Saturday morning soccer.

'Has something happened?'

'Should it have done?'

'At work?' Hope in her voice.

'Just another bloody day in another bloody factory.'

She turned away. She didn't want him to see her disappointment. She went to get the boys' costumes and their towels. When she came downstairs again the boys were at the front door, and she could see the way they looked at their father, hesitant because of the change in a precious routine. They were super swimmers, that's what she'd been told last month at the pool, and they should be encouraged. Well, that was encouragement, their father taking them.

'Watch Frank's freestyle, won't you? Adam, you'll show Daddy how you can do backstroke now?'

Sara kissed Frederick's cheek.

She saw them through the door.

She waved them off. It was three years since she had last packed her bag and started to fill suitcases with the boys' clothes. It was before they had put the small house on the market and moved to Lilac Gardens. It hadn't been a particular row, just an accumulation of tension and frustration and the slow building of the ice wall that blocked communication with each other. As she had packed and filled the suitcases and bags she had not thought through where she would have headed for. Not her mother's home, where she would have been crippled by the recrimination of what had taken her into this ill-fitted marriage, God, no. Not any friend's home, because she had no friends with whom she was close enough to share the agony of a failed relationship. It would have been a bed and breakfast place somewhere. And that afternoon he had come home early because he was sickening with the 'flu that was going round, and she had kicked the bags under the bed. She had decided that she would stay, that they would exist together. There was still the sensation of Frederick's cheek on her lips. So stiff, so taut, as if the muscles of his face were in spasm. God, the poor man. Poor old Frederick . . .

He sat in the gallery above the pool, watched the man who walked alongside the pool calling encouragement to a small boy struggling with a backstroke. The man walked barefoot, carrying his shoes with his socks hanging from them.

He could have done with something to eat. He hadn't eaten that morning, nor that afternoon, nor that evening. He'd have to find time to eat, because if he didn't eat then the motion of his stomach would wake the dead. What he would really have liked to have eaten was a bowl of pistachio nuts and a plate of lamb grilled with rosemary and spiced rice at the Khan Murjan.

His eyes were never off the man, not for the seventy-five minutes that the man was at the pool with two boys.

*   *   *

161

'So, it's Indian country.'

'Down there, Custer would be messing his pants.'

'Hostile natives . . . ?'

'If you'd jumped out of a hit Phantom over North Vietnam then you'd get a better welcome than down there.'

Ruane had his shoes on the desk, spotless and polished. 'Did he do it?'

Erlich said, 'Not necessarily, according to the local lawman. He says that it might have been thought a police car, or they might have thought it was Customs and Excise snooping to check whether the farmers are using their tractor diesel in their cars . . . They're just not very friendly people down there.'

'Do you think he's there?'

'I don't know . . . but I know he's close. He shot that Iraqi in Clapham Junction, that's for sure, Dan.'

Ruane pushed back across his desk the five-page report that Erlich had hammered out once he had returned from the country. Each page was now initialled by the Legal Attaché for transmission to Washington and Athens. Erlich was calm now. His anger had been steadily dissipated in the bath at the policeman's house, and on the platform of the railway station, and on the train back to London, and in the accommodation on South Audley Street where he had hung out his wet clothes and changed into clean, and when he had sat at his desk and punched out the report on the hard scene of Colt in London and the killing. He thought Ruane was great, no post-mortem about the car, not a word about going off alone without consultation. He only said, 'Where do you go next?'

'Back to Rutherford, in case he's forgotten me. I'll put some hassle under him.'

Ruane said, 'They like to piss on us, Bill. If they do then you catch it in a bucket and chuck it back at them.'

9

The cat eyed Colt.

It was marmalade and huge, with a fluffy tail. He had seen it put out of the house with the Cavalier.

As he came up off the roadway, flitted towards the garage door, the tomcat was watching him. Its back arched briefly and there was a fast spit from its mouth, just to warn him. He was the interloper on the tomcat's territory. The tomcat scented, tail lifted, against a rear wheel of the Sierra, then relaxed, came and rubbed its head against Colt's shin. The brute had a purr like a lion cub's growl. It was a hell of a cat . . . He didn't need his torch, not until he was inside.

The whole of the cul-de-sac was quiet. It was past two o'clock and three hours since the cat had been put out. There were no lights on in the houses on either side of the target's house. There was a light on the landing of the target's house, no bedroom lights that he could see from the front, no downstairs lights. He stood in shadow at the side of the house. He took his time, looked steadily and carefully around him. Neighbourhood Watch country. He peered across the cul-de-sac at the houses opposite, those from which he was visible. All the curtains were motionless, drawn tight.

He reckoned the time was as good as any time would be. There was no door through the wickerwork to the back of the house, so he went past the Cavalier, to the garden door of that house. Not locked. He was in deep shadow once he had pulled the garden door to behind him. His torch battery was old, little more than a glow thrown, and that was good enough to show him the watering can and the wheelbarrow and the dustbin. He avoided them all. He came down the passageway between the house and the garage wall. At the end of the passageway, he came to the fence that divided the gardens of the two properties. It too was wickerwork, and in a terrible state, five foot high and all over the place. Big breath. Colt held two panels gently then firmly apart and stepped through.

There had been no alarm box on the front, and there was no box high on the back wall.

He could see into the kitchen. There was light coming from the upper landing into the hall and through the kitchen door. He crouched down on the patio by the kitchen door and listened. There was occasional distant traffic on the main road that was beyond the bottom of the garden and the line of houses beyond. He couldn't see those houses because conifers had been planted when Lilac Gardens was built. He could see the washing-up left in the sink for the morning, and he could see the frame over which were draped the towels and the swimming trunks. He had learned what to do from Sissie. Sissie was better at it than Micky. Sissie had the small neat fingers, and the patience. Before they had gone to the home of the bastard who made his living from experiments on animals, before they had beaten the shit out of him, Sissie had shown Colt how to pick a mortice lock. Sissie had told him that people put a Chubb and a Yale on their front door, and economized on the back with a simple mortice, and she had been right about that bastard's house, and she would have been right about this one. Poor little Sissie, doing seven bloody years . . . Straight, simple, opening the mortice with three inches of wire.

The door opened.

Don't hurry, that's what Sissie and Micky had said. He sat on the doorstep and took the thick pair of wool socks from his anorak pocket, drew them on over his trainers. Colt eased the door far enough open for his body to pass inside, then pushed it to. He went through the kitchen. What he wanted would not be in the kitchen. He went through to the hall and the bottom of the stairs. Again, he listened.

He heard a boy's cough, and the creak of movement in a bed. He thought the boy coughed in his sleep. The sitting room and the eating area ran the length of the house. The curtains were drawn at each end of the long room. Torch on. Papers on the table, letters and blank sheets that had been covered with pencilled columns of figures and an account balance sheet. Thin rubber gloves on his hands, bought from the all-night chemist in Reading before he had gone for the burger to stop the howl in his stomach. Sissie would have thrown up in her cell, would have cried her heart out, if she had known that he had actually sunk so low as to go for a fast-food burger. Poor little Sissie . . . Don't ever hurry. She'd been the one who always took most care over her personal security. He'd never known how they screwed up, what took the filth to the squat. Sissie would have been taking her time, would never have rushed as she moved around a target's house, and she had taught him well.

Under the calculations, under the account statement, was a bank letter. The bank letter was addressed to Dr F. and Mrs S. Bissett. He had a name for them: F. and S. Bissett. He read the letter. He took a notepad and a pencil from his pocket. He copied the dozen lines. His father used to have letters like that. His father didn't sit up in the evening, goaded by such a letter, and try and sort out his balance. His father used to chuck that sort of letter into the fire. Colt copied the letter in full, and he wrote down the balance sheet's final debit figure. A bonus, but not what he had come for.

He searched the downstairs area of the house. He found a briefcase, initials F.B., in the kitchen. But it was empty.

Onto the stairs. The landing light was on.

He had to go up the stairs, he had to go towards the light. His footfall was on the side of the stairs, on the painted woodwork. The child coughed again. The cough was from the second front bedroom over the hall. It would be a pig if the boy came out of his room to go to his mother, or to go to the bathroom for a glass of water. He came up the stairs. He could feel the sweat of his face under the wool of the balaclava. A right pig, if the boy came out of his room . . .

At the top of the stairs were four doors. Three bedrooms and a bathroom. The bathroom door was wide open, and he could hear the drip of a tap. Two bedroom doors ajar, the small bedroom onto the front of the house, and the third bedroom onto the back. The door of the main bedroom was shut. He was at the top of the stairs. Bad moment . . . Switch off the landing light and the sudden sensation of darkness might disturb the kids, wake them. Leave the light on, and when he went into the main bedroom, where he had to go, then the light would follow in with him when he opened the door. Could have done with Sissie. Sissie would have known. He turned off the landing light. He eased open the door. God, the room was dark.

When he had come into the bedroom of the bastard who lived off experimentation with animals, Colt had carried a pick-axe handle. He had the torch in his hand. He had to use the torch. Her breathing was light, regular, his breathing was harsh as if his sleep were as thin as frost ice. He stood at the end of their bed and he turned his back to them so that his body would shield some of the torchlight. The torchlight moved across the room. Across a dressing table that was covered by jars and bottles and hairbrushes. Across a chair that was draped with her trousers and her blouse and her bra and her pants and her tights. Across a wardrobe with twin doors. Across a chest on which were photographs of two small boys and a handkerchief and loose change. There was a second chair beside the bed, his side. For a moment the torch beam showed, in dulled light, the man's face. It would have taken an earthquake . . .

She moved. He froze, pushing the torch beam into his chest. She was on the further side of the bed. She shifted again and there was a soft cry from her. He was rock still. She subsided. She might have been dreaming. He waited.

Colt was statue-still for a full minute.

The torch beam found the chair beside the bed, his side. His trousers were folded over the seat of the chair. His sports jacket was hung over the back of the chair. Each footstep considered, tested, before the weight was committed. There was a wallet in the inside pocket of the sports coat. Colt drew the wallet from the pocket. He opened the wallet. He found the bank card . . . What he looked for was not in the wallet.

The boy hacked his cough again. She moved again. Again he froze. No cause to hurry.

The first side pocket, not there, just car keys there and a spectacle case.

The second pocket. He felt the length of cord. He felt the smooth laminated skin. He eased from the pocket an identity card, issued by the Security Office of the Atomic Weapons Establishment. In his notebook he wrote down the name on the card, Frederick Bissett, the serial number of the card, the authority given by the card for access to H area, the date of expiry of the card.

He returned the card to its pocket.

It was what he had come to find.

He closed the door behind him. He switched back on the landing light. He went down the stairs. He crossed the hall, and the kitchen.

The kitchen door was open, wider than he had left it.

He closed it after him.

He used his wire to turn the mortice lock.

Colt stood on the patio, let his breath come in great gasping surges, and the sweat under his balaclava ran to his chest and the valley of his back.

Sara shovelled herself out of bed. Frederick had his eyes open, lay on his back.

'A good night?'

'Great, good sleep.'

'Didn't sound like it . . .' Sara was at the door, dragging on her dressing gown.

'What do you mean?'

'Weren't you up?'

'No.'

'I heard you.'

Frederick pushed himself forward on his elbows. 'I was never up.'

She didn't want a fight, not at three minutes to seven o'clock, not when she had the boys to get up, and his sandwiches to do, and the washing basket to clear, and last night's supper to clear away.

'Sorry, must have been dreaming, forget it . . .'

He heard her going heavily down the stairs. He heard her running the tap in the kitchen to fill the kettle. He heard her shout of pure anger. He heard the opening and the slamming of the back door.

Sara came back up the stairs. 'For God's sake, Frederick, can't you be more careful when you lock up? You shut their bloody cat in.'

He was only half awake. 'I did?' Yes, he had worked late . . . No, he could not remember opening the back kitchen door . . . She didn't stay to argue. No time in the morning of a weekday to stand around their bedroom and argue.

Half an hour later, two pieces of toast wolfed down, Bissett presented himself at the Falcon Gate, watched as the Ministry policeman peered down through the opened window of the Sierra to check the I/D hanging from its cord round his neck.

The first joggers were out on the Common, and the first riders urging their ponies into a canter, when Colt left his message underneath the rubbish barrel.

He had copied for the text of his message all that was on his notepad.

He was just another motorist who paused on the Common for a breather, just another motorist who had a plastic bag full of litter in his car, who tucked it into the rubbish bin on his way to work.

He was quite unremarkable, quite unnoticed.

*　　*　　*

Rutherford was usually early at his desk, but the Clerical Assistant to the section always beat him in. She handed him two message dockets. Erlich, twice. He found Hobbes, arguing with the sandwich machine.

'How did you do?'

'I delivered your warning and was lectured on the exceptional quality of the Establishment's security.'

'Wonderful.' Hobbes had extracted a sandwich, salami and Stilton. 'Now *that* is a triumph of intellect over incalculable odds . . .'

'The American's jumping up and down, two calls this morning already.'

'Yes.' A long pause, in which the sandwich machine gave a little heave and a tinkling avalanche of coins, like a fruit machine, seemed about to issue an improbable windfall, but it proved a merely internal matter. 'Keep him happy, and try to keep him out of trouble.'

Rutherford hadn't made himself comfortable in his chair before his telephone rang.

'Hello, Bill, I was just about to call you . . .'

Bissett heard the exchange from his office. His door was open because he had just come back from the laboratory at the end of the corridor to collect the first sheets of his paper for checking against the latest results produced by the technicians.

'But it isn't convenient,' Boll protested.

'Don't tell me, tell him.' Carol, enjoying herself.

'Only me and Basil?'

'That's what he said, the two of you from H3, ten o'clock sharp.'

'Why not Bissett, can't Bissett go in my place?'

Carol said firmly, 'He wasn't asked, only you and Basil.'

At ten minutes to ten o'clock precisely, on Bissett's watch as he stood near the window of the laboratory, Boll and Basil were to be seen hurrying across to Boll's car, bent against the wind. Bissett had no idea where they were going, what was the summons that was of such importance.

*　　*　　*

Erlich said, 'What I want is a hostile interview facility. I want to turn him over, jazz him so he doesn't know what day it is, shake him.'

'That's not easy, Bill . . .'

'It's not supposed to be easy, for fuck's sake. Nothing is easy when an American government servant has been murdered.'

Rutherford swivelled in his chair. Rutherford's body was positioned between Erlich and the floor safe . . . Good form, so that he couldn't see the combination that Rutherford used on the dials, typical . . . Rutherford turned back. He opened the file that he had taken from the safe. Rutherford was turning pages, not offering them for Bill to read.

'He has a Military Cross.'

'So?'

'He has the Croix de Guerre.'

'So?'

'They are gallantry medals. They aren't the sort of decorations picked up in little adventures down in Panama or Grenada, or for cocking up in Beirut. Here, he's a war hero, that would be how we would regard Major Tuck.'

'His son's a killer.'

'We don't know that for certain.'

'Well, I know it. I can't prove it of the Athens killing, though I am sure of it, but I am one hundred per cent sure of it for the Clapham killing.'

'Bill, I'm sorry, it's not by any means certain that Colt shot Saad Rashid.'

'I have an eyewitness, dammit.'

'Who is not saying to the Anti-Terrorist Branch what you say she said to you. Nevertheless . . .'

'They don't know their business.'

'Nevertheless . . . , I will request on your behalf a "hostile interrogation facility" with Major Tuck. I will also, and you're pretty damn lucky for that, accompany you down to that nasty little village so that we can conduct surveillance without you falling on your face in the mud, so that the Embassy of the United States doesn't run too short on transport.'

There were times, yes, in the small brick bungalow in the foreigners' compound that he dreamed of walking away from the danger and the fear. Occasions, now, when he took his twice-yearly leave to Europe and met with the Mossad men and did not have the courage to tell them, face to face and one to one, that his nerve was exhausted. He thought it would require more courage to quit than to go on.

He had guessed that from the first day of his arrival at Tuwaithah, and from the first day that he had used the courier.

He was cut out from the courier. The cut-out was a post-restante box at the new Post Office on Al Kadhim Street in the old Juafir district of the city. He had a key to the post-restante box, and the courier had a matching key. They would never meet.

He read the message. He came over once a week to Baghdad and shopped and took lunch at the Ishtar Sheraton, and walked across the Jumhuriyah Bridge and towards the old circled city and into the new Post Office on Al Kadhim Street.

He drove back towards Tuwaithah.

They had never before asked the chemical engineer from Sweden for more complete information.

They were all Grade 5 and Grade 6. All divisional heads and their Superintendents.

They were from Mechanical Engineering and Weapons Electronics and Assembly and Special Projects, from Applied Physics and Materials, from Chemical Technology and Explosives and Metallurgy. Reuben Boll and Basil had come over to F area from Mathematical Physics in H3. Twenty men and women had gathered at the Security Officer's summons, and there was coffee and biscuits.

Not one among them, none of these senior engineers and chemists and scientists, would have claimed that he was glad of a summons to the Security Officer's conference room. They all worked in areas of great secrecy. Their papers were marked with the highest classification used at the Ministry of Defence, Top Secret (Atomic). They were subject to positive vetting. They were encouraged not to discuss their work either with wives or with colleagues. They were all signatories to the Official Secrets Act. Their knowledge was hardly shared, and only a handful of civil servants in Whitehall had anything that approached a full picture of their work, while the number of elected members of government who were trusted to be taken into their confidence was tiny, a small Cabinet subcommittee.

The Security Officer had been the rounds in the Intelligence Corps before being invited to quit two years before his army retirement date. He had held the rank of brigadier, with an OBE as reward for thirty years of service. He had served in Aden, in Whitehall; he had been deputy to the senior intelligence officer at the Land Forces HQ at Lisburn, outside Belfast; Germany for two tours; the Ministry of Defence again. He had been offered the position of Security Officer at Atomic Weapons Establishment. He was answerable to the Ministry of Defence and the Controller Establishments Research and Nuclear, but a call from Curzon Street was adequate cause for him to jump.

'Good morning, gentlemen, I very much appreciate your finding the time to attend, and at such short notice . . .'

In the Directors' dining room he most often ate alone because he came early to the table. He was joined only when there were no other chairs available. He had long ago realized that his office would leave him friendless and an object of suspicion. There was nothing formidable in his appearance, a bright bald scalp, small and close-set eyes.

'. . . Just a warning, nothing more serious. It has been brought to my attention, and I am duty-bound to pass it on, that there is a remote possibility that the Atomic Energy Commission of Iraq may attempt to recruit personnel from the Atomic Weapons Establishment. I expect that sounds quite ridiculous . . .'

A chemist giggled. There was a general release of tension.

'. . . In my own view, not so much ridiculous as preposterous. Some of you may remember talk a few years ago about the Iraqis putting together a nuclear device, and that led to the bombing of their reactor by the Israeli Air Force. Last year, of course, there were further rumours that the programme had been reactivated; unsubstantiated rumours. What has now crossed my desk is a somewhat unspecific warning that the Iraqis may be attempting to recruit top-grade scientists from abroad, and I would be failing in my job if I did not, without overemphasis, pass on that warning. Obviously, I am not for one moment imagining that any single one of you would entertain such an approach should it be made . . .'

There was a ripple of muttered conversation.

'. . . but I do ask that you come straight to me if any attempt is made to approach you. From what we read of recent happenings in Iraq, an individual would have to be clean off his or her whistle, certifiable, to entertain an offer, however lavish, from that quarter, but, as I say, we are warned. That's all, and thank you again for your time.'

There was laughter. The Security Office smiled warmly. He had done his bit, and now he could return to the very much more pressing anxiety of vetting the construction workers from the Republic of Ireland currently employed on the fitting out of the A90 complex.

'That was balls,' Basil said. Boll was at his car door. He'd brought his keys out of his trouser pocket along with a fistful of change that was spinning in all directions on the tarmac.

'I beg your pardon.' On his knees now, reaching under the chassis.

Basil said, 'The man's an idiot, couldn't catch his own tail.'

'Who's an idiot?' Boll brushing himself down, finally unlocking the doors.

'Security officer. He implied that the Iraqis hadn't the technology, the quality of workforce, the capability, that's just balls. If he thinks we are the sort of people they'd be after, that's balls too. We're yesterday's men, Reuben, the administrators and the paper pushers. If they are serious, the Iraqis won't be looking for geriatrics like you and me, they'll be after the youngsters . . .'

Boll drove back to H area. He didn't speak. He was rather offended that Basil, the acknowledged brain of the Establishment, should regard him as geriatric. But he never quarrelled with Basil Curtis, because he, Reuben Boll, was one of the few who were privy to the tragedy of the man's life, who had known Basil's wife, who had comforted him after she had died at the wheel of her car. What love Basil Curtis still possessed was now vested in the atrociously smelly cat in his quarters at the Boundary Hall accommodation complex. He made every allowance possible for Curtis's behaviour, which wavered between the eccentric and the spiteful. Somewhere, there was a son, who would be middle-aged now, and Boll had heard that all contact with him had been cut.

Anyway, Grade 6 and Senior Principal Scientific Officer Boll, with the title of Superintendent, certainly did not regard himself as a 'yesterday's man'.

Erlich stood. He had the telephone at maximum stretch. He shouted, 'It's just great, great to hear you, Jo.'

'And you, Bill. How are you?'

'Surviving, you could say that.'

'In London, and that's all you're doing. What's it about?'

'It's an open line, Jo . . . Shit . . . It's about Harry.'

'It's what you've been waiting for.'

'Yes.'

'When you'll get noticed.'

'Yes.'

'That's what you want, important.'

'But it's about Harry.'

'That was bad . . . Why are you only surviving in London?'

'They don't love me here.'

'You giving them too much Pepsi culture?'

'Prickly crowd.'

'Let them know who's boss, Bill, like you always do. Let them know they're just the hired help, eh . . .'

'Too right . . . Jo, I been calling you each day, twice a day.'

'Got in this morning.'

'Where from?'

'You could have called the office, they wouldn't eat you . . . Bucharest.'

'Christ, where?'

'Bucharest, airhead. They ran a facility down there to show us a new housing project. It's a real fun place, you'd love it. We got one slot on the Breakfast, two others are holding pending the trash can, and I'm scratching all over.'

'What's Bucharest like?'

'Creepy, horrible . . . When are you coming home?'

'I don't know.'

'I'm lonely already . . .'

'Get yourself a stud off the beach.'

'The stud I've got, he's pulling my panties off now . . . Love you, Bill, that sort of crap.'

'Take care, Jo.'

'Come home.'

'*Ciao*, Jo.'

Perhaps he should have told her that he loved her. He sure as hell *missed* her, but they weren't supposed to love each other. When they were together, great. When they were apart, too bad. Jo wasn't going to throw up a Field Producer's job with a network to shuffle round after a Fed. They were just career people, and busy. And he had forgotten to ask her what was the result of the game in Naples. She was on the edge of that scene with him, bringing in a picnic in the summer and a thermos of soup when the Saturday mornings came colder. He thought that theirs was what was called an 'adult relationship', and the best they could manage. Rutherford had a wife at home, lucky old Rutherford. Rutherford had his shirts washed and his trousers pressed and his meals served up on demand. Erlich put together his boots and his waterproofs and his bivouac. Rutherford would be waiting for him, down on the street in the car.

Colt found himself a room on the south side of Newbury.

He paid £80 to the man, and because he hadn't jibbed at the £40 a week, two weeks in advance, he thought the man regretted not asking for more. The house was virtually new and the builders were only a hundred yards away putting roof beams on for the next phase of the development. There were worry lines on the man's face, and he had passed the notes straight to his wife who was behind him, holding a baby.

He stood in the room. The man was by the door. A bed, a table, a chair, and a wardrobe which didn't close properly.

Colt said, 'I've moved up from the West, looking for work. I may be on days or nights. I just don't know at the moment what my hours will be. I hope you don't mind that, me coming in and out at all hours. But I'll be quiet. Is that all right?'

'No problem, mate.'

The door closed on them. He had found a room in a quiet street. He could come and go at will. He was only eight and a half miles from Tadley. He kicked off his shoes. He lay on the bed. He would rest until it was dark.

Sara had seen them through the sitting room window, working the far side of Lilac Gardens.

'Yes?'

She had her coat on and she was in time, if she left quickly, to get to the MiniMarket before turning up at the school gate.

'Good afternoon . . .'

'Can I help you?'

The older woman had a pale face, shoulder-length auburn hair tied in two plaits and she wore a long overcoat tightly buttoned. The younger woman had short-cut fair hair with a parting and was bright in her yellow raintop and mauve shirt. Not Salvationists, not Jehovahs. The younger woman carried a clipboard and she stood behind her companion with a pencil poised. Sara really, actually, did not have time to be polled on detergents or politics or . . .

The older woman smiled. It was the sort of smile that was taught in charm classes, wide, brilliant and signifying nothing.

'We're from PARE.'

'Do you want money?' Of course, they wanted money. Why else would anyone tramp round tedious Lilac Gardens if not for money. How much would it take to get rid of them? She had three £10 notes in her purse, and damn near nothing in small change. Could she give them a tenner, and ask for nine in change?

'We just want to tell you about PARE.'

'Oh, I am in rather a hurry.'

'We think it pretty important. Cancer in general, leukaemia in particular. We think it's worth a few moments of your time. May I ask what your name is?'

'Bissett, Sara Bissett. I am in rather . . .'

'Mrs Bissett, do you have children?'

'I've two small boys.'

'Then of course you'll be interested in PARE.' The younger woman smiled, the same smile.

The older woman said, 'We are from the Tadley action group, People Against Radiation Exposure, I expect you've read about us.'

The younger woman said, 'The cancers round the Aldermaston base and the Burghfield Common factory . . .'

The older woman took her cue. They were well rehearsed. 'The cancers are way above average in this area.'

'That's child cancers, which is mostly leukaemia, and testicular cancer for male adults.'

'I don't know whether you are aware, Mrs Bissett, that you are living very close to such danger.'

'Both Aldermaston and Burghfield Common have quite appalling safety records.'

'Into the water, into the air, they're just spurting out poison. Nobody knows the long-term effects.'

'When the new building at Aldermaston is working we esti-mate that it will produce two thousand drums of solid waste a year.'

'And it will produce a million gallons a year of liquid waste, and where does that go after it's been *treated*? It goes, Mrs Bis-sett, into the Thames.'

'Already the leukaemia rate in this area is six times the national average, and it's going to get worse.'

Sara was calm. She rather surprised herself. She just wanted to be rid of them. She wanted to do her shopping, and she wanted to be at the school gate to collect her children. She had no sense of loyalty to Frederick, not at that moment.

'That's a pack of lies.'

The older woman's mouth tightened. 'Statistical evidence shows . . .'

'Lies.'

The younger woman's voice keened, 'You know what we've got here, Deirdre, one of the "little women" whose husband works there.'

Sara said, 'That's right, so just piss off.'

'If you think that learning about the risk of leukaemia in children is wasted time . . . ?'

'She'll just parrot her husband's distortions, Deirdre.'

'God, why can't women think for themselves . . .'

They turned away. The younger woman minced to her com-panion, 'If I were married to a man working at that place, spreading leukaemia around, I'd have left him.'

For what? Bed and breakfast with the kids on Social Security, new schools, no roof? She would never leave, not now . . . She was late. 'I don't have time to hang about listening to your lies and distortions,' Sara snapped.

They had their shoulders back, as if to make their point that they could take abuse and survive. In a few moments they would be at little Vicky's door, and half frightening her to death. Sara locked her door behind her. No, it hadn't been out of loyalty to Frederick. It should have been out of loyalty to him. She should not have sent them packing because she wanted to get supper from the MiniMarket and still be on time at the school. She should have kicked their behinds off her front step for slagging off her husband, and her husband's work. She sat in her car.

Sara knew what she should have done, and she had not done it. And she should not have sat in her car before switching the ignition, and rejoiced that it was her art group again in two days and wondered if Debbie's husband . . . she should straightaway have made up the lost time.

It had taken them time, but they were getting there.

They were a good team and there was nothing that an investigation could throw up that, between the three of them, they had not confronted before. No rush, but the hours had been worked, and the picture had emerged.

The pieces had started to slot together when Don had received from Ruane, down the wire from London, the photograph of Colin Tuck. Don thought that young Erlich had done well to have gotten the name of Colt, and the photo. He had made an asshole of himself at Athens Counter-Terrorism, nothing but criticism for closing down that source, but this was good work. Don had sent Vito and Nick out with the photograph, and he had booked the best table at the best restaurant in the Piraeus, and he had treated the head of Counter-Terrorism to the sort of meal that was going to lift an eyebrow or two when the docket reached Administrative Services Division. Smoothly he had opened the doors that had been slammed in young Erlich's face. Opening the doors had given the team a good young liaison who would go anywhere with them, get past any block, and was at their disposal from the time they woke to the time they hit the sack. The Agency's Station Officer, across on the other wing of the Embassy, said that no one had ever oiled such cooperation out of those Greek mothers as Don had. With the doors open and the liaison in place, Don could sit back in the office and collate what came in. They had the place, the rented room, where Colt had spent the night before the killing, and they had a kind of identification from a Yugoslav who still stayed there, but the room had been cleaned and there were no prints that helped. Vito and the liaison had done the airport. Every check-in desk for every flight that had gone out from Athens that morning and that afternoon, and when that showed nothing, then he and Nick had worked the lists of the cabin crews of all the Olympic flights. A stewardess, a week later, back from the mid-morning flight to Ankara had been shown the photograph. She had remembered the man in the photograph as a passenger. He had refused coffee and refused food. She had given Vito and Nick a seat number, and the airline computer had given them a name, and the name and the Irish passport had been checked with the Emigration officers on duty that morning. They had had a flight to Ankara. Of course, the passport was rubbish, not important . . . Pleasantly calm for Don, Athens, once Vito and Nick had flown to Ankara. A round of golf in the Ambassador's four-ball, a cocktail party at the Station Officer's home. Vito, through on secure communications from the Embassy in Ankara, had reported that he had found the check-in girl who had done the duty that late afternoon. The check-in girl had nodded when shown the photograph. The Iraqi flight had been delayed. There would have been a passport switch in transit at Ankara, a British passport used. She remembered the British passport, and she remembered that she had been shown the Iraqi visa. Ankara airport didn't carry a passenger list for the flight, and they weren't inclined to go asking the Iraqi officials if they had a flight list. Didn't matter . . . They had him, the little bastard, out of Athens and into Ankara transit, and they had a passport switch, and they had him on a delayed flight to Baghdad.

It had taken them time, but they had gotten there.

They sat in the room they had been allocated at the Embassy, and they had a portable radio playing in the room and they talked under the sound of the radio. Old professionals, doing it the way it should be done.

When he had finished the longhand draft of their report, Don read it back.

Nick said, 'That's shit in the fan, guys.'

Vito said, 'Respectfully, Don, that's for the Director's desk.'

Don said, 'I'm not arguing.'

Nick said, 'It's just too clean, too well-organized, for Colt to be hitting for an asshole group.'

Vito said, 'It's state-sponsored, and what Big Wimp will want to do about that, I just don't know.'

Don shuffled the sheets of paper together. The Athens end was over.

Don said, 'We shouldn't take that kind of crap, least of all from a government.'

He reached for the telephone. He rang the restaurant down in the Piraeus to book the table by the plate-glass window with a view over the yacht harbour. Next, he rang the Station Officer to say they'd be gone in the morning.

After dark, Colt left the house and walked three streets to where he had parked the car.

Colt was the moth, his mother was the flame. He headed for his home and for her bedside.

10

'Of course, I wanted her to see you but, God help me, I don't want you taken . . .'

'If you shout, you'll wake her, and she needs all the sleep she can get.'

Damn you . . .'

The boy was his agony. Still so clear in his mind, the dawn raid of the police. He and Louise in their dressing gowns in the hall while uniformed men and detectives swarmed over the house. The detectives had carried handguns when they had run through the hall in the moment after he had opened the front door. The armed detectives and uniformed men, who carried pickaxe handles and sledgehammers that would have taken down the door if he had not immediately opened it, had ransacked their home in frustration. The whole village had known. The road outside the main gate to the drive had been blocked for an hour, and there had been more guns outside, guns carried in the garden and in the fields beyond the paddock at the back. That was what the boy had done for them, sentenced them to the dropped lace curtains when they walked the village street and to dropped voices when they used the shop that was also the Post Office. After the raid there had been the surveillance and the clicking interruptions on their telephone line and the delay on their letters that most often took four days from postage to delivery.

'You're just a bloody fool to go to the pub.'

'Nobody'll tell on me.'

'You're so bloody arrogant, and so bloody naïve.'

'They're my friends.'

'Friends? . . . You don't have any *friends*. They're junk, trash. You have your mother, and you have me . . . You have no one else, Colt.'

His mother's hair had still been fair, soft sunlight gold, when the police had come that early morning. Now it was grey-white. The medical people that they had traipsed to see, from one specialist to another, searching for better news, said that extreme stress hastened the spread of the cancer. The raid had only been the worst. There had been the time when Colt had stayed away a week, and the papers and the radio had carried the story of the bludgeoning of an animal scientist in his own home. Nothing had been said, but they had known.

After the raid, the two of them, together, had tidied the house. Neither of them had mentioned the boy's name, not for hours, not until the work was finished. If he had mentioned the boy's name she would have broken. But he wasn't a rogue dog that he could have had put down if it bit the postman, he was their son. There was no escape from the love, whatever the agony, whatever the confusion.

'Is there anything you want?'

'I didn't come here to take anything. I came only to see my mother.'

'Do you want money? I could go to the bank . . .'

'I need nothing. I have more money than I can spend.'

'You're a whore . . .' And he bit on the word. He stepped back because for the briefest of moments he wondered if his son would strike him. Facing him was only the total calmness of the boy. It was, he thought, as if Colt had been through hell and fire and tempest and to be called an abusive name was merely trivial. God, and he loved the boy. Colt's voice was gentle. 'Were you happy in France?'

'I had a cause, I had something to fight for.'

'You didn't think that then.'

'It was right what I did, I knew it was right.'

'You never thought about that.'

'What do you think I did it for?'

'Because it was freedom.'

His freedom had been being hunted, and never believing that he would be caught, tortured, shot, never believing that. Freedom had been making up his own rules, far from the armchair warriors at SOE, from the buggers who had never slept in a cave and never stripped a belt-fed machine gun and never run like the wind from a wired shunting yard.

'We're the same, Dad. You have to see that . . .'

He looked down into his son's face. God, and how he loved the boy.

He said, 'Before you go, if you can come again, please . . .'

The boy kissed his cheek. He hugged the boy.

He stood on the landing and watched his son lope away lightly down the staircase.

The shadows had gathered around him, and his age and his loneliness. As he went back into the bedroom to prepare the night medicines he heard the kitchen door close on his son's back.

A wild and awful night, a night when the badgers moved without threat of disturbance, when the rabbits crushed their bellies against the ground and fed fast, when the fox coughed a hoarse bark to bring a screamed answer from a vixen, when a tawny owl clung with talons extended to the ivy skein of an old oak.

A night on which an Astra car was parked for safety in the driveway of the local police constable in the adjacent village, across the parish border.

The night for a man who gloried in the wild and who would never be trapped. Colt was at home. He was at one with the darkness and the elements. He was as free as the badger and the fox and the owl in the oak above him.

Standing in the black doorway of the pillbox, he did not consider what error of his had brought men from the Security Service and the FBI to the village. In his mind were images of animals transported to the slaughterhouse; of beagles with masks on their heads so that they breathed only nicotine smoke all the way to the first shadows of lung cancer; of a polar bear, its brain damaged by captivity stress, in the zoo at Bristol; of chickens reared in confinement so close that they could not walk nor beat their wings; of a gin trap tight on a bear's leg, and the animal in its pain gnawing at the limb that it might find crippled freedom. Fran was close to him. With a slow and deliberate movement she pointed away to his right, to the fringe of the wood, to where the wood was directly behind the Manor House. He saw the movements.

> 'Tis a dull sight
> To see the year dying
> When winter winds
> Set the yellow wood sighing:
> Sighing, O sighing!'

'For Christ's sake, Bill, shut up.'

'Edward Fitzgerald, perfectly good poet, didn't hit the big time like Tennyson, but . . .'

'You'll wake the whole village. Is that what you want?'

'Just didn't want you to be bored.'

They had been in the wood for two hours.

'I'm going to shift a few hundred yards along to get a clear view of the side of the house. Do you see the corner of the wood? I'll be there. Sing out if you get lonely. Otherwise I'll be back before daybreak.'

'Yeah, OK . . .' Erlich hoped his regret wasn't plain to hear.

He felt the shake of the bivouac as Rutherford crawled away, and heard the sounds of his body scraping away through the leaves. He heard the wind sigh and whistle after the sound of Rutherford's movement was gone. He heard the rain splatter onto the bivouac. At the house, through his monoglass, he saw nothing.

Rutherford took pleasure in his slow progress along the wood's edge. Knees. Elbows. Knees. Elbows. And all the while sweeping the twigs from his path, stopping every two or three minutes to study the house and sweep his binoculars over the gardens. He found a patch of leaves, almost dry, under a beech close to the furthest edge of the tree line and shrugged his way down into their cover. He settled into a nightmarish reverie of long nights of surveillance in Armagh. He wondered what absurd notion had possessed him to leave his flask behind. A gift from Penny's father. This was the last time he'd go on night exercises with windy Americans without his flask. Anyone who talked that much had to be scared. Probably allergic to rabbits.

The scream . . .

Shit . . .

The scream was desperation.

He was on his feet. The scream was in the air and in the trees. Where, where was the scream?

The cry. Had to be Erlich.

The cry was pain and terror.

He charged, blundering through the trees, through the low branches and the brambles. He couldn't see a blind thing, and he ran with his arms outstretched in front of him, barging off trees and fighting and kicking his way through the undergrowth. Gasping and running, knowing that he had heard Erlich's screams.

A lifetime to where he had left Erlich, through the lashing branches and the catching, tearing bramble undergrowth. And he hadn't a weapon. He had nothing more lethal than a pencil torch in an inner pocket.

He saw them, silhouetted against the fainter light of the night sky, two of them.

He saw the punching and the kicking, the frenzy.

He closed on them. No way that they could not have heard his approach, the bloody elephant's arrival. They must have heard him, and yet had not faltered from the blows and the kicks into the heaving and writhing shape of the bivouac. He had no gun and he had no weapon, and he didn't think about it. He hurled himself forward to get them away from the

American, he threw himself at them. His hand flew at an arm, caught a sleeve, rough cloth. The two figures separating. He staggered from a kick to his shin bone. His hand scrabbled to stop himself from toppling, found material, clung to it, and a fist, gloved, smashed at his face. He was falling, tumbling, out of their reach.

He yelled, 'Stand or I shoot . . .'

And they were gone. Good fucking bluff. He didn't see them go. He was on his back, no shadows above him, no silhouette bodies. They were gone without a sound. He listened for them. He heard the silence, and the wind gale in the trees and the rain driven around him, the moan of the American's pain.

He found the pencil torch in his inner pocket. He wriggled forward. He pulled back the bivouac cover. He shone the torch on his own face, so that Erlich would see it, know who was with him, then he swung the torch down. It was a long time since he had seen the face of a man who had been systematically beaten and kicked.

That was Ireland. Not in Ireland now. In the English country-side, for God's sake. Blood all over the face, and an eye closing faster than paint dried. Rain falling on the face. Erlich was doubled up, knees against his chest, and his breath came in sharp hissed sobs.

'It's OK, Bill, they've gone.'

'Thank Christ for the cavalry.'

'Anything bust?'

'God knows.'

Gently, he pulled Erlich upright. The blood ran from the cut over the American's right eye and from his nose.

The covert stuff, that didn't matter any more. There seemed to be a dog barking in the Manor House as they made their way across the field. Too late to worry about being spotted from the village. He limped from the blow on his shin bone, and because he had the full weight of Erlich on his shoulder. He had Erlich's arm wrapped round his neck and his throat, and the man was solid. They sloshed across the middle of the field and the wind and the rain lashed their faces. They ploughed through a gateway and into another field, and the lights of the pub car park came slowly to meet them. Rutherford's fear and shock gave way to anger that Erlich had let himself be jumped. He had probably been reciting Wordsworth. But greater than anger was his amazement. The man was a wreck, done over fit to break. Why? What in God's name *for*?

And he hadn't the heart to tell Erlich that at least one of them had been a woman. When he had gripped at a sweater his fingers had caught a bra strap. Might just ruin Erlich's night altogether.

A car came past them fast, sprayed them with road water, heading away from the village. It was a long two miles to the next village, to the policeman's house.

Dr Tariq sipped at his fresh pressed juice, as he waited for the Colonel to be admitted. Dr Tariq had little respect for the military men of his country, but his contempt was kept concealed. They were the power of the regime, they were the provider of resources. He had no interest in the executioners and the torturers and the interrogators of the regime. He was a scientist, he was responsible only to his work. A laboratory technician had come to him the previous month, spoken of a cousin taken into custody and no word of him had been heard by the family. Could the Director, please, please, use his highly esteemed influence? He had not picked up the telephone. It was not his business. Only his work was his business.

The Colonel, too, was all business. No niceties with the Colonel of Intelligence, Dr Tariq thought. The Colonel said the name. The name was that of Frederick Bissett.

He repeated the name. 'Frederick Bissett of the Atomic Weapons Establishment at Aldermaston.'

'And his rank?'

'Senior Scientific Officer.'

'His department?'

'His identification card gives him access to the H3 building.'

He stared out of the window of his office at the broken upper structure that had housed the Osirak reactor. The jagged, wrecked shapes of the crippled reactor were never far from his thoughts, as present as a most recent bereavement.

'H3 is where a most acclaimed team of scientists work on the study of implosion, Colonel . . . Bissett, how could he be attracted?'

'Money, no doubt.'

'You know that?'

The Colonel opened his briefcase. He passed to Dr Tariq a transcript of the message from London.

Dr Tariq read it and smiled faintly. 'A Senior Scientific Officer, in that department, I would want him, Colonel, subject to your being absolutely satisfied that you are not importing a foreign spy into my team. To have any scientist from Britain's best team would be so exceptionally unusual as to create suspicion on this score, but I will grant that the circumstance of your discovering his possible willingness to join us are themselves so, well, so exceptionally unusual that I believe luck will be on your side.'

Dr Tariq outlined the terms that could be offered to Frederick Bissett, and stated that he would have prepared, by that evening, a list of questions to be put to Frederick Bissett, before a deal would be struck.

The Swede was crossing the garden, when he saw the Director ushering out the Colonel. He recognized the Colonel. He saw that the Director wore no necktie. He saw the insignia on the Colonel's shoulders and the medal bars pinned on his chest, and he saw the holstered pistol at his hip.

'Good morning, Director,' the Swede called out.

He was ignored. He hurried on his way. It had been demanded of him that he should seek more complete information. The Colonel had returned to Tuwaithah. The Colonel had come on business so pressing that he had made his appointment before the Director had shaved and before he was fully dressed. Under

189

his breath, as he greeted the members of his laboratory workforce already at work, he cursed. An opportunity had been
missed.

Reuben Boll said from the doorway of Bissett's office, 'I really
must have something on my desk tomorrow morning.'

'Well, I honestly don't know if . . .'

'My desk, tomorrow morning, latest.'

'I'll do what I can.'

'Work through the night if you have to. You know what, Frederick? In the old days here, when a man had work on his desk,
then he did not go home until it was finished. Before your time,
of course, but that was the old attitude.'

Quite simply, he had not the courage to tell Boll. Sara was
out that evening, at the parent-teacher meeting at school. She
had cleared it with him, that morning, that he would most
certainly be home in good time to look after the boys. So he
could not work in his office until midnight. He had promised
Sara.

'No sweat, Reuben, by hook or by crook it'll be on your desk
in the morning.'

Penny was still in her dressing gown, and she was half falling out
of that, and there was the warm and sleep-battered look on her
face that he loved, before she anointed herself with all the garbage.

'Good grief, what's the cat brought in *this* morning?'

'Darling, this is Bill Erlich. Bill, this is my wife Penny . . .'

'What in God's name have you two been at?'

'Just be a love, and clean him up.'

And don't ask any silly questions. Don't even consider enquiring whether the guest has gone three rounds with a pissed-off
buffalo.

She was a State Registered Nurse. She'd have seen worse.

'If she hurts you, Bill, just scream, and I'll come and thump
her.'

Penny directed Erlich up the stairs, and Rutherford made for the sitting room. He pulled the curtains back, tidied the newspaper from the floor. He preferred to drink in the pub in Shepherd Market, but this morning he poured himself a good measure of whisky. He drank. He had two hands tight on the tumbler. He heard the cascade of the bathwater upstairs. He drank again. They had reached the policeman's house as the first cut of light was coming under the rain clouds. They had powered away in the Astra after five brisk minutes of the policeman's time. Did Desmond, the village constable, know of two young people, one male and one female, capable of administering a cold-blooded beating and kicking? Not much change from the local policeman. It was a rough and tough community. Could have been any one of a dozen males and any one of half a dozen females. Not much sympathy from the policeman, disturbed from his sleep and his wife also woken, and his children crying. A blunt suggestion that Mr Rutherford might care to spend a Saturday night with the police in Warminster when the pubs turned out if he thought a beating and a kicking were exceptional.

It was the least he could have done, to have brought Erlich home. No way he was going to take an FBI man into the Casualty Out-Patients of a National Health Service hospital, no way. All the way home he'd talked and the American had mouthed through his swelling lips. They couldn't be *certain* it was Colt.

Between them they should have nailed at least one of them and then they would have been certain.

Penny came down the stairs.

She was carrying Erlich's clothes.

'He's nice . . .'

Rutherford said, 'He behaved like an idiot, lucky not to have got himself killed.'

'He was hit hard, down under.'

'Did you get in the bath with him to see?'

He could see her looking at him, questioning. He had the glass in his mouth, held in two hands.

'I examined his penis and his testicles for injury,' Penny said. 'They're quite nastily bruised.'

'Was it Colt or was it not?'

The man had said his name was Hobbes.

Rutherford was behind him, subdued, chewing on a peppermint.

Erlich was wearing one of Rutherford's shirts, too small at the collar and with the tie trying to cover the gap, and a pair of Rutherford's socks, and Rutherford's wife had tried to clean his trousers and his jacket. And she had washed the cut on his face and even if he looked like a bum his spirits were a good deal restored. Not every day of the week you get a bath *and* a hot breakfast from an English nurse.

'I don't *know*, but nothing else that I can think of makes sense.'

'You don't know, but yet you request an interview to be arranged with Major Tuck?'

'I want to turn him over.'

'You will have a meeting, you will most certainly not have "a hostile interrogation facility".'

'Just a *meeting*?'

'Only that, and I would suggest a change of clothes first.'

Colt slept. Deep and undreaming sleep. He slept in the small room in the small house in the quiet road on the outskirts of Newbury. The man he had beaten had been staking out the back end of his home, and the man was American, an agent of the Federal Bureau of Investigation, and that was not sufficient to disturb his pitch-black sleep. Because of the man, because of the implication of his being in the wood at the back of his father's house, he would not go back. And the farewells and the partings in the dank small hours of the morning, neither were they able now to disturb that depth of sleep. He had held his mother's hand, he had shaken his father's hand, he had ruffled the loose fur at the collar of his dog, and he had gone. He was his own man, waking or resting, and many years since it had been different.

His own father and mother had never gone to the evenings at his school when the teachers sat at their desks and discussed the performance of the pupils. His own father had once said that he was buggered if he was going to change from his work clothes into his funeral and wedding suit, and put on a clean shirt, to spend an hour listening to the patronizing chat of schoolmasters, and his mother for once had not contradicted him.

Her mother and father had been to every open day at her school, come down in the Bentley, picnic hamper in the boot, that's what Sara had told him.

As he drove the length of Third Avenue, he thought it was just the difference in their backgrounds. He had not telephoned her to say that he must work late. He had not asked her to miss her evening at the school, but he had left his desk only when he had known that Sara would be waiting for his return.

The floodlights and the gates were ahead of him. He was held in a column of traffic. He edged forward.

He was already rather tired, he would be in good shape, if he didn't fall asleep, and he had warned Carol that he would need someone in early to type up his paper. He slipped forward, low gear.

'Identification, please.'

The Ministry policeman was bent towards the car's side window.

He produced his card. He held it up. He saw the rain-spattered face against the glass, and the grey toothbrush of the moustache.

'This is a security check, Dr Bissett.'

'Jolly good, and we had the same yesterday, all our yesterdays.'

'Were you checked going out of H area, Dr Bissett?'

'I was not.'

193

'Do you have a briefcase, Dr Bissett, an attaché case?'

Shit, derision, fuck . . .

'Yes, yes, I do . . .'

'Could I see inside your briefcase, Dr Bissett?'

'My wife is waiting, if you don't mind . . .'

'Just see inside, thank you very much, Dr Bissett.'

'I really am in a very great . . .'

'Then the sooner I've seen inside your briefcase, Dr Bissett, the sooner you'll be on your way.'

'Don't you people have anything better to do?'

'Very droll, Dr Bissett. Now, could I please see inside your briefcase?'

His car was flooded with light from the cars behind. He turned and he looked through the rear window. He thought there might be twenty cars waiting their turn to come through the check. It was almost a year since he had last been stopped, last asked to open his briefcase for inspection.

There was the great sinking weight in his stomach.

'I've a great deal of work to get done by the morning.'

The Ministry policeman said briskly, 'Please, Dr Bissett . . .'

He was down in the low seat of the Sierra. The Ministry policeman was above him. He could see the face, and the veins in the cheeks and the hair in the nostrils, and the rain falling from the rim of the helmet. His briefcase was beside him. His briefcase was stamped by the lock in faded gold with his initials. He reached for the briefcase.

He undid the catch fastener.

He had the briefcase on his lap, and he opened it. There was his empty sandwich box, and there was his empty thermos flask, and there were the two files of papers. There was the sticker, red letters on white background, on each of the files. The letters made the word that was SECRET. Oh, shit and derision . . .

The barrier was down in front of him. For a moment the Ministry policeman straightened, and Bissett could hear him talking into his personal radio. He felt sick. He felt the sweat damp on his back. He felt faint . . .

The politeness was gone from the Ministry policeman's voice, a sharp bark.

'Get that car over to the side, and hurry it.'

The Security Officer was on the point of leaving his office, locking it, going to his weekly meeting with the Director. He rather enjoyed these sessions. A glass of sherry, a general chat, a chance to sit with the one man in the whole place who did not seem nervous in his company.

His principal telephone rang.

He picked it up, he listened. He did not interrupt.

'Thank you, Inspector, thank you. I'm not able to get down for a bit, might be an hour. Just put him on ice. No access, no telephone, don't attempt to question him. Just let him sit and reflect for a while, until I can get down. Yes, it will be as soon as possible. Thank you, Inspector.'

The Security Officer put down the telephone. He gathered up his coat from the chair by the door. His face showed neither excitement nor sadness nor anger. It was this mask-like quality in his face which chiefly made his colleagues uneasy. He walked the corridors and up the stairs to the Director's office. For the life of him, he had not an inkling who Frederick Bissett was.

An hour after he should have been home, half an hour after she should have left for school, at the time that she should have been sitting in the classroom with Frank's and Adam's teachers, Sara went upstairs to change out of her suit.

'Aren't you going, Mummy?' A small voice from the bottom of the stairs.

'No.'

'Why aren't you going, Mummy?'

'Because your father is not home.'

'Don't you want to hear about us?'

'It's just not possible.'

'Where is Daddy?'

'I don't know, and I don't bloody care . . .'

II

It was a room bare of decoration except for the requisite Annigoni Queen and the tyre company calendar, the one with rural views of his country. At least it was not a cell.

Bissett sat on a straight-backed chair at a small table, his head in his hands. He didn't care, any longer, to look up at the Ministry policeman standing, arms folded, impassively, in front of the door.

It was the most shameful hour of his life. He had been directed out of the line of cars to the side of the road by the Falcon Gate, up against the high wire fence. There had been two of them at the car door when he had opened it, and one had put a hand on his sleeve to ease him out of the car, and one had reached inside for the briefcase. Another Ministry policeman had been waving through the cars behind him. He had seen all their white staring faces, through their rain-dribbled windows, as he had stood in the wet. People who recognized him, and people who did not, staring at him, wondering why he had been hauled from his car.

He had started, of course, to try to explain when they had shovelled him into the back of the police van. He had been ignored. Two blank, uninterested faces in the back with him. He had tried anger, and he had tried being reasonable, no response. He had been taken into the police building. More faces turned to him. The faces of Ministry policemen on the front desk, and on the staircase and in the corridor. Faces that looked him over, stripped him to the quick.

They had sat him in the room. An Inspector had been brought in to see him. Bissett had recognized rank and status. Right, fine, at last time to talk to someone with an ounce of common sense, someone in charge of these cretins on the gate. Again, he had explained. Perfectly straightforward, pressure of work, need to complete a paper, wife going to a parent-teacher evening, him minding the children. Couldn't have been more reasonable, should have been the end of it . . . hadn't been the end of it. The Inspector hadn't argued, hadn't said anything at all, the Inspector had just walked out. He was left with the Ministry policeman for company.

He had asked if he could telephone his wife, because she was expecting him, and the Ministry policeman had shaken his head. He *needed* to telephone his wife, he'd said, because she was going out that evening, and again the shake of the head. God, she'd be furious, and for once that was going to be the least of his troubles. He sat with his misery and his shame.

It would be half round the Establishment by the middle of the next morning . . . Frederick Bissett caught at the Falcon Gate, taken out of his car, marched to a police van, taken off for questioning.

He heard the footsteps approaching in the corridor.

The Security Officer came in with the Inspector behind him. The Ministry policeman was dismissed and the Inspector stood in his place. The Security Officer came forward and took the chair at the table. Bissett could smell the sherry on his breath. The small eyes pierced him. He doubted there were more than a dozen out of the 5000 who worked at the Establishment who would not have recognized the Security Officer. The eyes were bright, sparkled at him.

'Dr Bissett, Dr Frederick Bissett?'

He had to strain forward to hear the softness in the voice. 'Yes, that's me.'

'Senior Scientific Officer?'

'In H3, yes.'

'And how many years have you been with us, Dr Bissett?'

'Since 1979, that's when I joined . . .'

'So you're not a new boy?'

'No.'

'You know the procedures?'

'Yes.'

There was a slow, dead silence in the interview room. The Security Officer's eyes never left his. When he moved his head right, left, dropped it, those eyes followed his. It was what they said a stoat did with a rabbit, first capture its eyes, then create terror, then kill.

'You are a signatory to the Official Secrets Act, Dr Bissett?'

He stammered, 'Yes, yes I am . . .'

'And you are cognizant of the security measures applied at this Establishment?'

'Of course, I am, yes.'

A quiet whiplash in the voice. 'What were you doing taking classified papers, that should under no circumstances leave the Establishment, off the premises?'

He felt so utterly feeble. He explained. The pressure of work as dictated by his Senior Principal Scientific Officer, Reuben Boll. The pressing need for this paper to be completed by morning. The parent-teacher evening at school. His wife having agreed to attend, his having to be home to be with his young boys, his intention to work at home, through the night if necessary, on this badly needed paper.

'Has this happened before?'

'What? Being stopped and searched, do you mean?'

'No, Dr Bissett. I mean, is this the first time you've tried to smuggle classified material out of the Establishment?'

'I can't have that. I'm sorry. I won't have "smuggled" . . .'

'You are asking me to believe that your behaviour was not criminal, merely crassly stupid?'

His head was in his hands again. Unless he laid the weight of his head on his hands he thought his body might keel over from the chair and down to the linoleum-covered floor.

'I have been very stupid . . .'

'Just stupid?'

He raised his head. He looked into the eyes of the Security Officer. What the hell was the bloody man talking about? What in God's name was the bloody man at?

'What else?'

'To work at home with those papers would be stupid, to have any other purpose for those papers could be criminal.'

He pushed himself up from the table. He felt his voice surge. 'That's idiotic, and I'm not having it.'

'What's idiotic, Dr Bissett?'

'The suggestion that I'm a criminal ...'

'I don't think you heard me say that, Dr Bissett. I don't think you heard me accuse you of any such thing. I expect you'd like to go home now, Dr Bissett.'

From the upper window of the interview room, through the marginally raised venetian blind, the Security Officer watched Bissett, a pathetic creature, led from the doorway of the police building to a car.

Before he left the police building, he congratulated the Inspector on the vigilance of his men, and he took away with him the files marked SECRET.

Before he left for home, he put through a call to the Night Duty officer of the D Branch of the Security Service to request that a telephone intercept procedure should, immediately, be commenced on the home receiver of Frederick Bissett, 4 Lilac Gardens, Tadley, Berks. Merely precautionary, he explained, probably this Bissett was overstressed, no more. He would review the request in a week.

The Inspector's men, some of the younger and brighter members of his force, God willing, would be sufficient to keep a covert watch in Lilac Gardens overnight. And the rest could wait until the morning.

The boys were in the living room, watching *Dynasty*. It was past their bedtime, and they were still dressed. Neither of them had looked at him. They were both bright, they both did well at school. They would both have been given high marks by their teachers if their mother or father had been at the meeting tonight. Neither looked at him. He loved those boys, and there were too many times when he did not know how to show them his love.

Sara was not in the dining room, and she was not in the kitchen. His supper was on top of the oven. A plate covered by an upturned plate. The sausages had died, the beans congealed, the mashed potato was the colour of lead. The plates were stone cold.

He climbed the stairs, and went into their bedroom. She was in bed, and she had her shoulder turned away from the door. There was the prettiness of her hair upon the pillow, and the clear white of her shoulder against the hair. Her light was off.

He sat on the bed beside her. He tried to take her hand, but she wouldn't give it him.

He told her what had happened. He told her of the paper that had to be finished by the morning; of his intention to work at home while she was at the school; of his arrest; of the long wait in the police building; of being interviewed by the top Security Officer. He told her what the Security Officer had said to him.

She turned to face him at last.

'He was quite right. "Crassly stupid", on the nail.'

'He said I was stupid, not a criminal.'

'You wouldn't have the balls to be a criminal, but I don't suppose *criminal* is what he had in mind. If they sent for the top man I expect they were more fussed about you being a spy or a traitor. Well, I could have reassured them on that front as well.'

He left her in the darkened room, and went down to the kitchen to see if any alternative could be found to the supper on offer.

The courier was brought from Heathrow to the Embassy by a car carrying CD plates. In the Embassy basement, next to the coding and enciphering room, was the secure Communications Area. The Communications Area was no more than a metal box that measured twelve feet by twelve feet by seven feet high. It was the one area of the Embassy where the Military Attaché felt able to discuss the confidential aspects of their work with Faud of the Cultural Centre and Namir who was the chauffeur to the Commercial Attaché. The box was regularly scanned with a voltmeter and a spectrum analyser. The briefing from the Colonel was read by each of them in turn. From the briefing's requirements, a list of priorities was drawn up. A message was prepared, to be taken that night to the drop on Wimbledon Common.

When they were out of the suffocating atmosphere of the box, Faud took a taxi to Sussex Gardens and the home of the Trade Attaché. Once there, he requested in a whisper that the Trade Attaché immediately, despite the late hour of the evening, telephone Mr Justin Pink and arrange a meeting in the morning, on a serious matter involving a contract.

He had wondered whether they would come again in an early-morning call with their handguns and sledgehammers. Instead there came, by messenger, a handwritten letter from the Home Office addressed to Major R. Tuck, MC, C de G, inviting him, civilly enough it had to be said, to lunch at the Reform Club. The signature, spelled out in capitals underneath the scrawl, was of a name that he did not know.

After he had seen that Louise was sleeping as well as possible, he had laid out a clean shirt and he had brushed the dust from his best double-breasted pinstripe and he had sponged his Brigade of Guards tie. And while the dog was out for the last time he had bossed his black shoes to a gleaming shine. Years since he had last dressed up, probably not since Louise and he had gone to the school, seen the headmaster, pleaded awkwardly for the boy's expulsion to be cancelled, and been turned down flat.

He doubted if he could have found an excuse that would have satisfied them. The letter had made it clear that an arrangement had been made for the District Nurse to be at the Manor House for all of the hours he would be gone. They obviously knew his circumstances backwards.

That night, before he climbed into his cold bed, he drank two and a half fingers of whisky. He wanted to sleep decently, for once, so that he would be alert, when he was at the Reform, when the agenda was his son.

'If I ask too much of you, Frederick, then you must say so.'

Bissett stood in front of Boll's desk. He had the two files in his hands. He had been to the Security Officer's room, first thing, and they had been handed back to him without comment.

'We are a team here, Frederick, and a team is only as good as the weakest link.'

He had scarcely slept. Sara had not spoken to him as she had prepared the children for school. He had made his own breakfast.

'While we want for nothing here, every other civil service department complains of cutbacks. Only through being an outstanding team can we justify our privileged position. You understand that, Frederick?'

There was something nauseating about the reasonableness that Boll play-acted. Obviously the Security Officer had been in contact with Boll. They all knew, he was sure they all knew, because Carol had not told him that he was late for the typist that he had booked. Carol had merely told him that Boll was asking for him.

'. . . Do you hear me, Frederick?' Bissett had lost the thread altogether, but he mumbled his assent. 'There are too many now who are prepared to deride our work here as mediocre. There are too many who say that original thinking in this Establishment gave out ten years ago. There are too many who say that we only survive off the backs of the Americans. But we are not a backwater and I want the best from the people who work for me, only the best.'

'I hope to have my paper completed by lunchtime, Reuben.'

'The silly episode of last night is now forgotten, Frederick.'

'Thank you, Reuben.'

*　　*　　*

Forgotten? Not quite forgotten.

The Security Officer might well have been inclined, on reflection, and on Reuben Boll's say-so, to forget the matter of Dr Bissett's taking classified documents off Establishment premises. He would have entered a short note in his file and that would have been that. But it would not now be left solely to the Security Officer's discretion. He had made a request for a telephone intercept to be put on all calls from Bissett's house, and he had asked for covert surveillance from the Ministry police. By 9.15 the Security Officer knew that Bissett had driven straight home, had not used his own telephone, nor gone out to use a public call box, nor made any stop on his way in to the Falcon Gate. If there had been anything sinister in the affair, in the Security Officer's belief, he would at some stage last evening have warned a contact of his temporary arrest. The Security Officer had gone through the Personnel file.

Bissett was a junior scientist in the mould of most of his contemporaries. Pretty bright, judging by his assessments. Absolutely no sign of erratic, even eccentric, behaviour. Everything about the record of Dr Bissett was reassuring.

But the matter was not going to be forgotten because Curzon Street had rung and left a message to inform him that that prig Rutherford would be back, later in the day. Just a precaution, of course.

'You'll come?'
     'I don't know, it's not . . .'
     'Got to come.'
     'It's not easy getting someone to babysit.'
     'Find someone, go on, make the effort.'
     'Well . . .'
     'Just a few friends, let our hair down a bit, nice people.'
     'I'm not sure that Frederick . . .'
     'Drag him along, don't take any excuses.'
     'He's not very . . .'

'He'll be all right. We have great parties, Sara. May not be able to do much else, but we do throw a great party.'

Sara smiled. 'OK. We'll be there.'

'That's the girl.'

For a very brief moment, Pink's hand brushed against Sara's hip. Debbie was in the kitchen, heating the coffee. The girls were in the dining room, setting up their equipment.

'Got to earn the old crust.'

'I'll see you this evening, then, and thank you . . .'

Erlich toyed with *The Times* and stared around him. The great expanse of the hall and the gallery and the gathering of clubland for its lunch. It looked to Erlich like a cross between a Hollywood set, with any number of David Niven look-alikes, young and old, mostly old, and the Rome Stock Exchange. He was surprised by the noise. He thought London clubs were for sleeping, even dying, in.

Major Tuck cut a good figure. He wasn't the shambling old man who had refused them entry at his front door. He looked good, well turned out too, and he sat straight in a high-backed leather chair, ignoring the throng round about him. He had a handful of what looked to Erlich like military journals on a table beside him and he devoured them one by one. He had never once looked up. He was letting them come to him. And, by God, Rutherford was taking his time, but if they were keeping him waiting then Colt's father didn't seem to give a damn.

> Had he and I but met
> By some old ancient inn
> We should have sat us down to wet
> Right many a nipperkin!
>
> But ranged as infantry,
> And staring face to face,
> I shot at him as he at me,
> And killed him in his place.

I shot him dead because
Because he was my foe,
Just so: my foe of course he was:
That's clear enough; although . . .

Erlich shifted in his chair, to settle the dull pain in his crotch. Contemplation of the melancholy figure opposite, who in a different world, thought Erlich, would have been a man he would have liked to know, wet a nipperkin with, whatever that was, gave way to thoughts of Penny Rutherford looking him over in the bath.

'Are you Erlich?'

Erlich looked up. A small man, thinning with age, a stoop in his shoulders. His suit seemed a size too big. He had a grey, gaunt face and his sparse hair was brushed down in tracks over his scalp.

'I'm Bill Erlich, yes.'

'That's rather a nasty bang you've had. Rutherford said I'd recognize you.'

He said his name was Barker, Dickie Barker, actually. Only when he could see into Barker's eyes did Erlich find any strength in the man. The eyes were good, the rest of him looked worn out.

Erlich was up from his chair. 'Are you with Rutherford?'

'Rutherford is sometimes with me . . .' A glacial smile. 'Out of town today, his section head tells me. It's his section head that answers to me . . . Come on then, Mr Erlich.'

'Aren't we going to talk it through first?'

'Just ask, young man, whatever questions you have to ask.'

'Did you speak to Mr Ruane?'

Barker didn't wait. He strode across the hall. Erlich hurried to catch him. He was at Barker's shoulder, a pace behind him, when they reached Colt's father.

Barker spoke.

'Major Tuck, good day to you, I hope we haven't kept you. I am most grateful to you for coming up today. I heard about your wife's not being well, and I am very sorry for that . . .'

Erlich watched as Colt's father laid his magazine aside, took his time, and stood up. No handshake.

'I'm Barker, I run D Branch, Major. We've met before, but you won't remember the occasion. Nearly forty years ago, a course on survival in hostile territory. You gave us the benefit of your very considerable experience obtained in wartime France. This is Mr Erlich, Federal Bureau of Investigation. I believe you've met.'

Erlich saw that Colt's father looked straight through him.

'We offer what help we can to our friends across the water, whenever we are in a position to be of assistance. What would you like, Major, a little gin, a vermouth and something, whatever suits you?'

Barker ordered a gin and Italian, Colt's father said he'd have Campari and soda, Erlich asked for a Perrier. Before they went through to the dining room, Barker led the conversation. He talked about the train service from the west of England, and about the frightful business of maintaining old and valuable houses without local authority grants. Erlich said nothing. It was one hell of a place, Erlich thought, to be entertaining the father of Harry Lawrence's murderer. Barker discussed the menu with Colt's father, and he advised Erlich that the fish was his best bet. Barker and Colt's father assessed the political front, the economy, the prospects of the winter touring party, and never addressed a word to Erlich.

After the meal was finished, Barker led them up the staircase into the gallery, and with a show of courtesy he pointed out the libraries to Erlich. They helped themselves to coffee from urns and found an empty corner.

Barker said, 'Right, Erlich, get to work, earn your lunch.'

'I work for the FBI out of Rome, Major Tuck. I was sent to Athens two weeks ago because an American government servant had been shot dead there, in the street, murdered in cold blood. Your son took that man's life, Major.'

No reaction. No flicker of the eyelids, no looking away, no twist of the tongue across the lips.

'Last week he came to London and killed again. He shot an Iraqi in London. Those are facts, Major, and the evidence that supports those facts is now at the FBI's headquarters in Washington. I should add that in Athens he also killed an Iraqi dissident, a brave writer, an outspoken opponent of a brutal regime. Your son, it seems probable, is a hired gun for the government of Iraq . . .'

He sensed Barker's awkward glance about him to see that they were not overheard. Tuck looked back at him, mildly interested, no more, as if it didn't involve him.

'It's the FBI's job, Major, to track down this killer, bring him to justice for the murder of an American official. I'll put it to you very simply: are you sheltering your son?'

'You've tried barging into my house already, Mr Erlich.'

'Shall we stop fucking about, Major? Just give it to me straight, yes or no, are you harbouring this psychopath you are proud to claim as your son?'

Barker said abruptly, 'I won't have that kind of talk in this club, Erlich.'

'Not cricket, eh, Mr Barker? Well, I've had all the cricket I've got the stomach for for one lunchtime. And I will, by Christ, have an answer to my questions, and you, sir, will sit quiet until I have them.' Erlich turned his back on Barker and said to Tuck, 'Has he been in your house?'

'When?'

'Last week, last seven days, has he been in your house? Has he been home to see his dying mother?'

He saw the choke rise in the throat. He saw him swallow fast.

'I want a fucking answer, Major. Has the little shit been home or not?'

The eyes were no longer on his. The old head, and the well-swept grey hair, had ducked.

His voice lifted. 'An answer, home or not?'

'He's gone.'

'He's been and he's gone?'

The tears were in the eyes. There was a handkerchief at the eyes.

'That's enough,' Barker said.

'Is he coming back? Will he come back again to see his mother?'

Colt's father stood. The tears were bright ribbons on his cheeks. 'You're too late, Mr Erlich. My son has been at home. He has seen his mother. He has made his goodbye to his mother and to me. I do not expect to see my son again. Now, you will excuse me. No. Don't get up. I'll see myself out. Good day to you.' He nodded curtly to Barker, and dealt Erlich a long stare, full of pride, full of loathing. He was very erect as he walked away.

Barker said, 'Erlich, you are a complete and utter shit.'

'If you people had done your job properly that wouldn't have been necessary.'

'Oh, don't take offence, young man. You did well. You got what you came for, I suppose. Ruane will be proud of you. Myself, I find unmannered and pushy young men nauseating company. Tell me, you won't mind my asking, who gave you those fearful bruises? The waitress couldn't take her eyes off you, I expect you noticed. Any young man I would consider knowing, if he had taken such a thrashing, would have learned to curb his conceit.'

She was very firm, she brooked no argument. Bissett had not been back in the house ten minutes before she told him what she had arranged. 'I want to go, and we're going.'

It was the middle of the week, they never went out in the middle of the week.

'We never go out anyway, whether it's the middle of the week or the end of the week.'

What about the boys? The boys just couldn't be left.

'All fixed, Vicky said it would be a pleasure, and she doesn't care what time we are back.'

He didn't know them. She knew, didn't she, that he loathed going to parties where he didn't know anyone.

'They're nice people, really nice, and it'll do you good to get out. You won't get any hassle, they're all solid Tory. They won't be like those bitches I had to field on the doorstep.'

She'd told him about the women from PARE. Little made him overtly angry. That sort of woman did, but it was one of the reasons why he avoided casual contacts outside the Establishment, that he hated being backed into corners and hectored by the nuclear danger lobby.

'I want to go, Frederick, and you are coming with me.'

He could think of no further excuse. His paper was in, typed up, and would now be in Boll's safe. Would probably be there for months before it was read.

'What would I have to wear?' he said.

'God, I don't know. Is everyone in that bloody place like you, can anyone make a decision? How do you get anything done?'

'Well, as long as we're not back too late.'

They were already there when Colt drove into the car park on Wimbledon Common.

He sat in their car. Faud talked, Namir was silent in the back. They explained what was required of him. Bloody hell . . .

Surprise spilling on his face in the darkened car.

'You want me to do that . . . ?'

Those were the instructions. He was not given the opportunity to argue, or to back off. He assumed that either Faud or Namir would have a handgun. If he had refused, then he wouldn't have made more than a dozen paces from the car. The car park was empty. And where was there for him to run to? His only refuge was Baghdad, when they were good and ready to give him the means to get home to the apartment on the sixth floor of the Haifa Street Housing Project. Home, was that, after all, home?

And if he failed, sure as fate, they would disown him. He had recognized that he was already distanced from his immediate past in Iraq. When the Colonel had identified Colt's potential usefulness he had, at the same time, removed Colt from contact with his family, with his sons. He missed the boys, who had been arrogant, aimless brats when they had first come under Colt's care, who were now toughened from hard hiking into the desert and foothill wilderness around the military compound. He thought they would run to fat again in no time . . .

The instructions were repeated again. A new contact procedure was arranged.

'I want a gun. I shall have to have my Ruger again,' he told them.

From the window Rutherford could see the stream of cars and buses edging out through the Falcon Gate. He had been in the office alongside the Security Officer's room since early afternoon. He had been given the Personnel file on Bissett to read, which was as thin as a wafer, and speaking of wafers, he'd been given nothing else at all, not even a cup of tea. The Security Officer was pleading pressure of work. Well, obviously, panic stations the previous evening, a wild splatter of backside-protecting telephone calls, and nothing but an embarrassing calm the morning after. He wasn't welcome. Simple as that. His rank did not flatter the Security Officer.

He could understand, too, why he had been called into Hobbes's office and told that he was not required at lunch at the Reform Club, and that he should get himself down to Aldermaston. Dickie Barker was taking over. Barker wanting to be in the dogfight as referee, to see that no harm came to the famous old war hero from Buffalo Bill Erlich.

He heard the rolling stamped footsteps.

'All right, Rutherford?'

God, the man had an unpleasant voice.

'All right, as far as it goes.'

'I think it's gone far enough.'

If he had been offered one solitary cup of tea, leave aside a biscuit, a sandwich, or two fingers of Famous Grouse, then he might not have been so bloody-minded. Or been allowed to be at the lunch at the Reform where he *should* have been . . . He swivelled in his chair. 'We'll just have to poke about a bit and see, won't we?' he said.

'I am satisfied that Bissett was just an ass.'

'When I've talked to him, I dare say I will share your satisfaction.'

'I don't think that will be necessary.'

'You called us in, sir, so we're here. When we start, then we finish.'

'I don't need you to run my department, Rutherford.'

'You know better than me, sir, with your long experience, that Curzon Street has a sticky touch . . . I'm not paid to be easy to get rid of, and this,' he picked up and dropped Bissett's file, 'which it took all of four minutes out of the four hours I have been here to read, would *satisfy* no one in Curzon Street of *anything*.'

'It was a one-off. I've discussed it with his department head. The man's behind with his work, he was just extremely stupid . . .'

'And when I've talked to him, then I'm sure I will be able to endorse that.'

'It'll have to wait until the morning.'

Rutherford smiled, sweetly. 'No problem, sir, I've all the time in the world, all the time it takes.'

And he kept smiling. The Security Officer outranked him, of course. Equally, he understood that the Counter-Intelligence division of Curzon Street had access wherever it wanted to go, whenever. So here he was, his feet were under the table, and here he would be staying until he was damn well finished . . . and if the Security Officer didn't like it, he could go suck peppermints.

'And I'll want to see his Superintendent, and perhaps some of his colleagues.'

'I'll not have a hand grenade thrown in here. You don't have my authority to disturb the work of very able and very dedicated men.'

'No, indeed, sir, and nor would I need it.'

'You got my phone burning,' Ruane said.

'The British, Dan, they're a race apart. What did that asshole Barker say?'

'He said he could use a tough operator like you in his department – mind you, he didn't say what for – and he said to watch my ass, you'd be after my job first chance I gave you.'

'I got him to admit it, Colt *was* there.'

'You got more than that, Bill . . .'

Ruane slid a fax across his desk. Erlich read. The smile was spreading on his face. The report of the laboratory in Washington. The analysis of saliva on a cigarello tip. The DNA print. Great stuff. Getting better. Analysis of a tobacco leaf. Produce of Iraq. Grown in Iraq. Manufactured in Iraq. Linkage. That was very good indeed.

'You find your Colt, you match that saliva, and you got yourself a case. Meanwhile, and it may be the last thing we wanted, we've a case against those sweet-talkers in Baghdad.'

He should never have come. He should have let Sara go on her own. He was out of the range of his pocket, here, out of his *class*. The women talked about school fees and holidays and 'little places' in the West Country. The men talked about the Market and tax schemes and the hideous price of commercial property. That was before the champagne got them going. He was welcome, of course, because he was Sara's husband. Poor Sara, married to that nobody. He was asked where his boys went to school, failure. He was asked where he had been on holiday, failure. He was asked where he lived, failure. After that they made no effort in his direction, that first group. He could see Sara. He'd seen her glass filled twice. He watched her laughing. The man she was laughing with was the man who had answered their ring at the front door. The man wore midnight-blue corduroy trousers, and a green silk shirt. The man had his hand on Sara's arm, and he made his Sara peal in laughter.

He drifted from the group. They didn't seem to notice his going. He forced himself. He penetrated a second group. Across the room he saw that Sara blushed, and that she giggled, and he saw the man's head close to her face, saw that he whispered to her.

He stood his ground in the second conversation. Noise

growing all around him. The babble of the voices, and the heavy beat of the music from hidden speakers. The hostess, the one called Debbie, was at his elbow, more champagne. These were the chosen people around him. The ones who were never breathalysed. The ones who knew the back doubles in life. These weren't the people who would have themselves stopped, where everyone could see, at the Falcon Gate. These were the Thames Valley Triangle people. There was the sweep of lights through the window, thrown from another car in the drive. These were the new rich, and he couldn't think for the life of him what he was doing here . . . There was a ring at the front door. He saw the back of them. Sara's back and the man's back, going out into the hall. A man asked him if he knew that club in Barcelona where the girls stripped in feathers, feathers would you believe it? Bissett said, to general merriment, that he was willing to believe anything he was told of Spanish strippers. Could no longer see Sara, or the man.

He thought it must be the guest that Debbie Pink had been waiting for. A tall, younger man, in jeans and a faded denim shirt. He managed a surreptitious look at his watch, not even ten, Christ . . . 'Oh, Freddie, someone for you to meet . . .'

'Hello, I'm Frederick Bissett.'

'This is Colin Tuck.'

The young man smiled. 'I'm usually called Colt,' he said.

Bissett tried to grin, 'You want to be called Colt, you can be called Colt.'

The introduction had eased him out of the conversation group, and Debbie had moved away, more glasses to find and fill.

Colt said quietly, 'This sort of crowd makes me want to throw up.'

About the best thing he could have said to inch his way to Frederick Bissett's affection.

It was Debbie's bedroom. He held the picture in front of her. The picture was of herself, sitting in front of the fire, in the dining room downstairs. The drawing had been framed in a simple black border. He held it for her to see herself. He put the picture down on the arms of a chair, where it faced the bed. She could have walked away. She could have pushed him away. Slowly, he began to unbutton the front of her blouse. He slipped the blouse from her shoulders and reached behind her to unfasten the brassiere. She could have walked out through the door, slammed it on him. He pulled the zip on her skirt, and the skirt fell. She kissed him. His hands on her hips, and pushing down on her pants, and her stepping out of them. Her tongue in his mouth. Sara pulled the shirt off him, she had his belt open, she drove down at the waist of his trousers. She crouched. She pulled off his trousers and threw his shoes aside and peeled at his socks and underpants. She stripped him. Still not a word was said.

He led her to the bed, Debbie's bed. There was the photograph of Debbie beside the bed on the small table. Beside her own bed, Sara's bed, was the photograph of Frederick with Adam and Frank. She looked away from the photograph of Debbie. She lay on the bed and she threw out her thighs and she lifted her knees.

'Oh, you're there, are you? Must be fascinating work.'

'It has its moments.'

'Well, that's the best brains in the country.'

'Some of them.'

'Well, my privilege . . .'

'Thank you.'

The food was in the dining room, and there was a slow movement towards it. Colt had manoeuvred Bissett towards the corner of the room away from the dining-room door.

'What I heard, people work in that place for peanuts, lifetime of sacrifice on the altar of science.'

'Well . . .'

'If true, it's scandalous.'

'I wouldn't say that we're . . .'

'Look at this crowd . . . Does any of them do anything that is remotely valuable? Yet the drive outside looks like this year's Motor Show. This country's got its values upside down.'

'I wouldn't disagree.'

Colt reached for the bottle. A splash for himself, a fill for Bissett. The man didn't look like a successful drinker.

'All the rewards go to the tax dodgers, the system buckers, the free enterprise merchants. And the best brains in the country? Ground into dust.'

'We're not paid well, it's true.'

'Understatement of the year, Frederick. You're very loyal, but you're paid awful money. One wonders if it will ever get any better.'

'I'm afraid we've missed out. World's upside down and Frederick Bissett's on the bottom.'

'It's like a trap, really, isn't it? And it's difficult to know how to break free.'

Her back arched, her thigh muscles taut. Reaching for him, rising to him. Him deep in her.

Oh, the fucking goodness of it, of him. When was it last as fucking good? Was it ever as fucking good with Frederick fucking Bissett?

Grinding her slowly away, breaking her will to compete with him. He was marvellous. Taking her with him. Best ever . . . better than the Ceramics tutor, and that was forever ago. Don't match him. Let him do it all, because that's what he was telling her. Kissing him, holding him, running her fingers on his back. She was falling, she was letting her legs slide from against his hips. She was his. Slow, so slow . . . Taking her as she had not been taken. Slow, slow, till she'd scream. Oh, oh, fucking good . . . Her head thrashing on the pillow, Debbie's pillow. Hearing her own voice. Recognizing Sara Bissett's voice. Little shouts, slight calls. She moaned. He came inside her, deep inside her. She cried out.

He rolled away. Bloody hell, and the light was still on, the door was still open, and she could hear the shouting and the laughter shimmer up the stairs, and the rattle of plates, and the thump of the music. Didn't care, didn't give a damn. She played patterns with her fingernail in the hair on his chest.

Her husband was downstairs with the voices and the food and the music, and she didn't give a damn.

They were still in the corner, left to themselves. To Colt, he was just a target. He felt no emotion towards the man, no pity and no contempt. The time was right. The timing was the gamble. It was his alone to choose.

He said, 'There is another way.'

'I don't know it. God knows, I've looked elsewhere. Too high-powered, too specialized, that's the trap.'

'Go abroad.'

Bissett said, 'It's against the rules.'

'You go abroad and you don't tell them where you're going.'

'That's . . .'

'That's looking after yourself, Frederick. You go abroad where your work is accorded the respect it deserves, and where it is *paid* what it deserves.'

'What you mean . . .'

'I mean, where you are a top man, head of a department. I mean where you are paid a hundred grand a year, no tax.'

'I beg your pardon . . .'

'A team working for you, superb working and living conditions.'

'I really don't know . . .'

Colt said, 'Dr Bissett, you can leave here tonight, you can go to your security people, you can report this conversation. I'll be in shit, and you'll be a hero and poor. On the other hand, you can agree to meet some people, you can discuss a work offer, a meeting without strings. Which, Dr Bissett?'

He recognized the wife. She came across to them. She said nothing. A beautiful woman. She looked as though she had had one too many.

Colt wrote down a telephone number on a sheet of a

216

notepad from his shirt pocket. He looked into Bissett's face, he saw the trust brimming in his eyes. He handed the paper to Bissett.

Bissett said, 'I think it's time we went home, Sara, don't you?'

12

He had had the same fierce throbbing ache – and the same sense of shame – the morning after his 'stag night', just him and the junior physics lecturer who had agreed, after having his arm twisted, to be his Best Man. And, once before, when he graduated. Breakfast this morning was absolutely out of the question. Sara had followed him round the house when they were back inside. Had he enjoyed himself? Just a little? It hadn't been too frightful, had it? He wasn't sure it hadn't. And she hadn't worn her nightdress when they went to bed and she had clung to his back, and all he had wanted was to keep the room from rocking.

He could hear the clatter of plates and mugs, and he could hear her shouting up the stairs for the boys to hurry themselves.

As he shaved, and then as he dressed, there were the moments of truth remembered from last night. He asked himself what had got into him that he had accepted the telephone number of the young man who called himself Colt. What in Christ's name had he done that for? Why? Well, obviously he'd drunk too much. No . . . not just because he had drunk too much, and he was committed to nothing, absolutely nothing. Of course he wasn't committed to anything, it was a conversation at a party . . . That was utter rubbish, and a Senior Scientific Officer at AWE didn't have to have it spelled out to him.

He went downstairs. The boys were down already and in their school pullovers, and bubbling to their mother because Vicky had let them sit up and watch television till late. He loved those boys. Sara protested he must eat his toast, the boys hooted

218

with laughter, and the pain of the noise drove him, almost at a run, out of the house.

The young man had been a very pleasant young man, and he'd talked good sense. No strings, no commitment, just a conversation.

The Ministry policeman on the gate, he'd know that bastard. Same bastard. He produced his I/D card. The man said, 'Once more into the breach, Dr Bissett?' and all the way to his office Bissett hunted in his aching head for a stinging, annihilating riposte, but all the best lines seemed inadequate for use on the policeman.

Carol was handing the day's internal post to Basil. Basil had his bulging briefcase on the floor beside his feet as he flicked through the brown reusable envelopes. Basil wouldn't be stopped by any bastard of a Ministry policeman when he cycled to H area from Boundary Hall. The Clerical Assistants were shrugging out of their coats, squeezing lipstick onto their faces, filling the coffee machine . . . and there was the young man. The young man sat close to Carol's desk and he had a raincoat over his knees, and an attaché case that he held close against his chest. The young man seemed to be mesmerized by Basil.

'Morning, Dr Bissett.' Carol's singing greeting.

'Morning, Carol.'

The young man's head didn't jerk. There was nothing obvious in his reaction. The young man's head tilted upwards. A good-looking young man, Bissett thought, didn't look as though he was from the Establishment, might be down from London, the tie was London. Carol was handing him his own mail. He sensed that the young man watched him. He dropped three of his four envelopes into Carol's bin. He headed down the corridor, for his office.

He heard Carol say, 'The problem is, Mr Rutherford, that Mr Boll may not be coming straight in. His diary's locked in his room. If he's a meeting first thing then I don't know when he'll be here.'

He was at the door of his office, reaching for his keys.

A quiet, pleasant voice, 'I'm not in a hurry. On the other hand, if that's coffee that I see being brewed . . .'

He could listen. If he listened and did not like what he heard then he could walk away. Frederick Bissett was his own master. He could control what he had begun. Why should he not be able to control his destiny?

A little past eleven o'clock, he left his office. He felt quite calm. He locked the door behind him and he walked down the corridor. He paused by Carol's desk. He didn't have to speak to her. The young man was still sitting in the easy chair near to Carol's desk. The young man was watching him. He didn't have to offer an explanation to Carol as to why he was leaving H3 in the middle of the morning.

'I'll be gone for a few minutes, Carol.'

The young man looked to Bissett like a civil servant, perhaps from the Property Services Agency, perhaps from the Director-ate of Defence Services, another of the creatures who came down from London, knowing nothing, to pry into the efficiency of the Establishment. The young man was watching him.

He would only be a few minutes because that was all that it would take for him to drive across to the main canteen area where the public telephones were.

The telephone shrilled below him. The woman shouted at her baby to be quiet, and he heard her answer the telephone.

She came up the stairs to him. She knocked and opened the door. She seemed to him broken by the poverty, anxiety, of her life. She looked at him with a sort of longing. Not how Fran looked at him. It was as if she knew that he was free, and she was not free. She told him that there was a man on the phone for him. He went down the stairs fast.

Bissett, poor bloody Bissett.

'Hello, Dr Bissett, very good of you to call me. Inconvenient, not a bit . . . You would? That's excellent. Of course not, no, just a talk . . . That's grand.'

Colt said where they should meet, when they should meet. He put the phone down. She might have thought that he was free, but what did she know? Free to go back to Baghdad, to the Haifa Street Housing Project, when he had *finished* and there he would die a little until the next time he was called to the Colonel's office. And his future? That was a big word, too big for Colt. Too far away, anyway, to think about.

The woman was still trying to calm the baby's crying.

It was Frederick on the telephone. It was so rare for him to use an Establishment telephone that her first reaction was that it must be catastrophe . . . He told her that he would not be home until late, that he had a meeting, that they were working through the evening. He was always curt on the telephone. She didn't quiz him, and she wasn't sorry that she would be spared the effort of making conversation with her husband that evening.

And she hadn't called Debbie. She would have to be braver before she could speak to Debbie, thank her for the party, tell her that Frederick had enjoyed himself.

The party was still just a bad dream, and in the nightmare was the beauty of Justin's loving. She went back to the kitchen, back to turning the collars on the boys' second school shirts. Odd, really, that Frederick had actually seemed to enjoy himself, hadn't bitched all the way home.

Oh, but he'd been good, better than anything ever before, Justin Pink and his loving.

Colt spilled his information. They heard him out. They talked between themselves. When they switched back to him they explained what they wished of him. Faud shook his hand. Namir kissed his cheek.

Faud's question. 'But why, Colt?'

'Why what?'

'Why does he come to us?'

'Money.'

'Just for that?'

'Well, he's flattered, too, but most of all he wants the money. You saw the state of his accounts.'

'You're of his country, don't you mind?'

An absurd question. Colt didn't care. 'All that nationalist crap is for the birds.'

They did not understand the world of the mercenary, they did not understand how a Senior Scientific Officer would agree to meet with agents of a foreign power. They couldn't understand it because in their own country the traitor was going to fetch up in the cells of the Department of Public Security and from there straight on to the Abu Ghraib gaol, and from there, no change, the Medical City Mortuary. Either that or they were shot in Athens, or in London. That's what they did to their own.

They said it would all be in place. They went over again what Colt had to do. They said the arrangements were in hand to provide him once more with a pistol.

Rutherford asked Boll to tell Carol that no calls should be put through. He reached for the radio on the window ledge, tuned it to classical, turned the volume halfway up. The Senior Principal Scientific Officer hadn't apologized for keeping him waiting the whole of the morning, so he didn't ask his permission to switch on the radio.

He hadn't messed with any Home Office nonsense. He had told Boll that he was from the Security Service, he had invited Boll to check his credentials with the Security Officer, which of course, he had.

'Frederick Bissett . . .'

The antagonism cut across the room. Nothing new and he could cope with it. Nobody loved the man from the Security Service.

'What about Bissett?'

'Just running a routine check.'

'As I understand it, the matter at the Gate was cleared up to the complete satisfaction of the Security Officer.'

'Well, you know the form, you working for government just the same as me, these things sort of have a way of developing their own momentum . . .'

'Come to the point . . . What do you want to know?'

'I just want to talk about Dr Bissett.'

Rutherford didn't have a notebook out, and he hadn't wired himself with the pocket cassette recorder that he carried in his attaché case.

'What about Bissett?'

'His work.'

'You're not cleared to hear about his work.'

'Let's say, the quality of his work . . .'

'It is quite satisfactory.'

'But he needed to take work home.'

'We are not all time servers, Mr Rutherford. When we have a job to do, then we get it done.'

'Would it not have been more natural for Bissett to have requested permission to take those two files off the Establishment?'

'I can't recall exactly the circumstances that day, perhaps I wasn't here.'

Rutherford noted it, the hesitation. He would remember that. It was safe to assume that the Security Officer had spoken to Boll already. The man gave away that he had been warned.

'Is he a good worker?'

'I've no reason to think otherwise.'

'A good member of the team in this building?'

'Quite . . . satisfactory.'

'A man who makes friends?'

'It's difficult, Mr Rutherford, to be well liked here. We're not a soccer squad. We are a group of expert nuclear scientists. We have our own work to get on with, that's how we live. Is this a social club? No, it is not. Do we prop up a bar all night? No, we don't. Most of us, from the style and nature of our work, are private people. I doubt, Mr Rutherford, that where you live you are the life and soul of your neighbourhood.'

Point scored. Rutherford took it. Penny always said that he was so private that the rest of the street wouldn't know he was alive.

'I am merely trying to establish the motives of Dr Bissett, in taking classified files out of his office, in direct contradiction of standing instructions.'

'Then you'd better ask him.'

'I will. Is Bissett in line for promotion?'

'I don't know, not my decision.'

'Would you recommend him for promotion?'

'I haven't made up my mind.'

'Would this business affect his chance of promotion?'

'I would have thought the quality of his work would determine that, not a moment of silliness.'

'To your knowledge, are his financial affairs in order?'

'I haven't the faintest idea.'

'There are usually signs . . .'

'That's something else you'll have to ask him.'

He was at the door. He could be ingratiating when it suited him. He thanked Boll for his help.

'I will be seeing Dr Bissett, but I will be seeing other people first. I don't want the nature of this enquiry discussed at all. I can count on your cooperation, I know.'

He had been with Boll for thirty-five minutes, and in that time he had heard not a kind word about Bissett. No praise, no affection, no support.

James thought that to be interesting.

Colt had parked on Praed Street, in Paddington, close to the hotel. He had booked and paid for the room. He had arranged for the canapés from the kitchen, for the whisky and the gin and the splits.

He wondered if Bissett would show.

Much of the work was routine, and it was just routine that it should be recorded that the radio signals that afternoon from the Defence Ministry in Baghdad to the Embassy in London had increased above their usual volume. It was also noted that the code used was of a different pattern to that usually employed. The signals were recorded at the Government Communications Headquarters at Cheltenham in the west of England. In the Middle East Department priority was at that time given to transmissions from Iran and the guerrilla groups in the Lebanon, but notification of the traffic surge was filed.

Likewise, it was basic routine that a tape would be sent each evening from the Telecom exchange in Newbury to Curzon Street. With the many intercepts ordered by Curzon Street, it was impossible to detach someone from the Service to monitor each interception. For those intercepts that did not have the highest priority a tape recorder, installed only by senior management, could be hooked to a number and activated by incoming and outgoing calls. The tape would be messengered to London each evening. Just routine.

'It's good of you to see me, sir.'

'We'll get this straight from the start, Mr Rutherford. If 5000 people here think it good enough to call me Basil, then Basil it will have to be for you as well.'

Rutherford couldn't help but like him. The Security Officer had told him that Basil Curtis was the principal innovator on the Establishment. He knew that he lived in Boundary Hall, permanently cramped into a single room, that his only company was the one cat allowed in the accommodation block, that he rode a bicycle, that when he went to Los Alamos he was considered too valuable to be sent on a commercial flight and had to put up with an RAF transporter. And the Security Officer had said, first time the creature had smiled, that Curtis was paid more than the Director because some joker in charge of Special Pay Additions at the Ministry had evaluated his work, compared his salary with American salaries, and put in the extra so that he wouldn't defect to Los Alamos or Sandia or Livermore. The Security Officer had added that Curtis would have worked at the Establishment, just as happily, just as successfully, for a machine fitter's weekly money.

'Well, Basil, thank you anyway.'

They walked on a sanded path that ran through copses of birch alongside the edge of C area, towards the Establishment's power station. It had stopped raining, and the late afternoon skies had cleared. There was a sharp wind. Rutherford was shivering in his raincoat, whipped cold. Curtis wore thin slacks and old leather sandals and an open sports shirt under his pullover. There was an air sampler barging against his barrel chest. There was a pipe clamped in his mouth. His heavy chestnut hair flew in the wind. Curtis wasn't tall, wouldn't have made it into the old Metropolitan Police, but he exuded strength and presence. Rutherford wasn't paid to like people, he rarely did at first sight, but he instinctively warmed towards this man.

'So, you're a spycatcher . . .'

'On the bottom rung.'

'A hunter of traitors . . .'

'A washer of bottles, really.'

'And you're investigating the unhappy Dr Bissett . . . ?'

'That's about it.'

'We've never had a spy here, nor a traitor.' A throaty chuckle. 'Well, if we have, we haven't known about it.'

'Did you ever meet Fuchs?'

'Cocky little Klaus Fuchs, no, before my time. He was never here, of course. He was before this place was set up. "I *am* Harwell", that was his boast. Dead now, poor old thing, plonked away in East Germany somewhere. He would have hated to see Honecker and his gang given the bird. And it's just as well he's dead, because it's come out since that most of the stuff he bunged at the Soviets was false. Turns out they learned more from sampling air particles from the atmosphere after the American tests than ever they learned from Fuchs' material. That's enough to make a man frightfully depressed, when he's spent nine years in gaol and thirty years in East Germany for his efforts . . . They're not relevant now, Fuchs and Nunn May and Pontecorvo, they were committed to a political ideology that's gone up the chimney . . .'

'So, what's today's spy?'

Curtis stuffed the bowl of his pipe. Rutherford's help was enlisted. They huddled together to shield the flame from the wind.

'He's a greedy little beggar.'

'Just that?'

'Greedy, and resentful . . . We were lectured, you know, by our resident Gauleiter to be on our guard against seduction by the Iraqis. He had it all wrong, he said that we – the senior buffers – were the ones at risk . . . quite untrue.'

'Who is at risk?'

'If it was the Iraqis who were headhunting then you'd have to know their personnel structure. You'd have to know what knowledge they were short of. Could be a scientist, could be a chemist, could be an engineer . . . you'd have to know what hole they were trying to plug. But it would be a youngish man, on the way up.'

Rutherford stopped. 'Greedy, resentful, a youngish man on the way up, is that Bissett?'

Curtis smiled quietly. 'Isn't that for you to decide, Mr Rutherford?'

'Would it surprise you?'

'I'd prefer to answer a question that you haven't asked, if you'll bear with me. To some, the Establishment is a beach of shipwrecked dreams. Hear me out . . . Many young scientists arrive here believing that we have not changed from those rather exciting days of twenty years ago and more. At that time, this place harboured the cream of our scientific community. We were the innovators, belting at the horizons of knowledge. A young man comes here, and can be sadly disillusioned. We're a factory, Mr Rutherford. We are making do on the minimum of innovation. We're not at the top of the tree any more. We are a frightened gang of time servers, hoping to get our pensions before what's left of this lifestyle is taken from us . . . When young Bissett came, with his very pleasant wife, he believed he had *arrived*, his enthusiasm was almost embarrassing. Have you met Boll? Of course you have. Boll could stifle the enthusiasm of a puppy. Bissett's dreams were beached. There was no wonderful and vigorous community of science, only a gossipy inbred society. He gave a fork supper once. He sent out at least two dozen invitations, and I was the only one who turned up. They learned. Am I helping you at all, Mr Rutherford?'

'Friendless, lonely Bissett, is that relevant?'

'Fuchs was actually much loved, there were enough people surprised by him, and by Alan Nunn May and by Pontecorvo. Don't these flotsam always surprise those who are closest to them . . . ? But you've asked for my opinion . . . Not to be held against me?'

'Of course not.'

Curtis said, 'I'm rather ashamed of myself. I see him every day, sometimes several times a day. I'd like to be more support-ive of a colleague, but I am afraid my answer is rather negative. You see, I just don't know.'

They turned. A second conversation, and the second absence of a single word of praise, affection, support, for Frederick Bissett. They walked in silence, with the wind pecking at their legs, back towards H area.

There were three platforms at which Bissett could arrive from Reading. Colt stood at the end of the middle one of the three.

Three trains had come in from Reading, all within the time window that Bissett had given him. He had watched 500 faces pass him, perhaps 1000 faces, and he had not found Bissett's face. As his impatience rose, Colt was cursed with the thought of his mother. She had been asleep when he had gone. He had told his father that he would not return. She had been asleep and he had gently loosened his hand from her fingers. She was the only person that he cared for in all the world.

He saw Bissett.

He saw the dark curled hair on the high forehead. He saw the broad tortoiseshell-rimmed spectacles. He saw the heavy check shirt and the tweed tie. He saw the sports jacket. He saw the raincoat carried over his arm. He snatched his mother from his mind.

Bissett had to walk the length of the platform. Colt saw his eyes roving, saw the tension in his eyes. Just a little man looking for a big break, and scared shitless. He stood his ground. He let Bissett come close to him. The eyes were going right, left, behind, ahead, as if everyone in front of him and everyone tracking him was police or security. Frightened out of his mind.

But he had shown . . .

Bissett walked right past him.

Colt turned.

'Hello, Frederick . . .' He thought the man nearly died, frozen shock, eyes half out of his head. 'Come, I'll take you to our friends . . .'

The Colonel had come to see the Director twice that day, and on both occasions the Swede's staff had been in his office.

At the end of the working day, the lights burned on in the Director's suite. Most evenings at this time, with the dusk sliding fast over the Tuwaithah complex, the chauffeur would be idling in the garden, waiting to take the Director to his living quarters, tossing small stones for the cats to chase. Tonight the chauffeur had not come. The Swede told his assistants that he would be working late. Obvious enough something was coming to a head, but it was impossible for him to know if the Colonel would return. The Swede prepared the rifle microphone, wired it to the receiver, draped his jacket over it and sat at his desk in the gathering darkness. He heard every footfall in the corridor, every closing and opening door in the block. He heard every voice in the garden outside. He listened to every vehicle pull up or draw away. And in his gut, as he waited to see if the Colonel would return, was the grinding, piercing fear of discovery.

The technicians at a monitoring station outside Tel Aviv roved over the wavelengths that linked them to the transmitter in Baghdad. They were listening for the fast jumble of sibilant notes that would bring them the call sign from one particular radio operator. They were all young, these technicians, they were all children of the state of Israel. Of course, they could not know the detail of any message recorded in code from Baghdad, but each of them appreciated that such a transmission might be critical to the survival of their country. A desperate and rising tension climbing amongst the young technicians. They sat in the subdued wash of light in the monitoring station with the headsets tight on their ears, waiting and watching. They willed on the unknown agent . . .

They were on their feet as one when he came into the room, all three coming forward to greet him, hands outstretched in welcome. Three of them advancing on him. He saw their confidence. It was the moment when he might have turned and run.

The door closed behind him. Colt walked past him to the television set. He heard the tinsel applause of a game show.

They introduced themselves. He heard the names and he lost them. He felt the flush on his face and the sweat on his back and the nervousness that locked his legs. He was asked if he wanted a drink. Couldn't speak, shook his head. He saw the exaggerated disappointment. Surely, a small drink, just a very small one. Colt poured. Heavens, it would have felled a bullock. All of them with drinks, except Colt, who had gone behind him to stay beside the door, and their glasses raised to him.

'It is very kind of you to come to see us, Dr Bissett . . .'

'It is a great honour, Dr Bissett, to meet you . . .'

'We much appreciate you giving up your valuable time to us, Dr Bissett . . .'

They raised their glasses to him. He sipped at the whisky and the trembling of his hand swilled the drink down. He coughed and spluttered. There was one amongst them who took the lead. He remembered that this one, dapper and scented, had prefaced his name with the title of Major.

'Dr Bissett, we represent the government of Iraq. We meet you here today at the direct instruction of our Head of State, the

Chairman of the Revolutionary Command Council of Iraq.' He thought of the manager of the Lloyds Bank on Mulfords Hill in Tadley. 'Your time is valuable, and I would not wish to waste it. If certain matters are satisfactory, I have the authorization to offer you employment by my government.' He thought of the Personnel Officer of Imperial Chemical Industries and his stinging letter of rejection. 'That is to say, the opportunity to head a far-reaching and generously funded research division at our Atomic Energy Commission. Your talents would be given full rein.'

He thought of the close-set pig eyes of the Security Officer. He thought of the bland, cool faces of the Assessment Board that would consider him for promotion, that would have in front of them Boll's annual report on his performance.

'Should you consent to join us, we are able to offer you the salary of $175,000, paid in American currency to any bank of your choice.'

It was a fantasy, a dream . . . more money than he understood . . . His voice was hoarse, his throat was scraped dry by the whisky. 'What would you want of me?'

'That you should join a magnificent team of scientists, Dr Bissett, that you should develop your own considerable gifts as a part of this team. The Atomic Energy Commission of my country means to be in the forefront of world science. We are working, you understand, not for military goals alone, but to throw back the frontiers of knowledge. We are reaching for excellence, Dr Bissett. To achieve excellence, we request that you join us.'

He heard the quaver in his own words. 'I'd, I'd have to, well, consider it, think on it.'

There was the satin smile of the Major. He glanced down at the sheets of paper he held. 'Your discipline, Dr Bissett, is implosion physics.'

'It is.'

It was the first step over the chasm.

'You are the man we need, Dr Bissett. With us, you will be a man of importance and you will be a man of wealth.'

He could go back on the train to Reading. He could go directly to F area, and he could speak to the Night Duty Officer in the Security wing. He could report the proposition that had been made to him. He could turn his back on them ... or he could hold out his hand to them.

'I'll come back to you.'

The second step into the void.

There were smiles as smooth as silk. There was a murmured explanation. 'Expenses, Dr Bissett,' and an envelope was passed to him. He felt the sinewy bulk of the envelope.

'All I've said is that I'll come back to you.'

'Come back to Colt. We are grateful to you, Dr Bissett, just for the opportunity to meet you, to have the honour of inviting you to join us.'

'I'll think on it.' He slipped the envelope into his inside pocket. Colt held the door open for him.

13

R uane said that what Erlich needed was a bit of home comfort. A couple of minutes past seven a.m. and the phone
had gone. Breakfast was across in Grosvenor Square, sharing a
table with two marines coming off night duty, surrounded by
the clerical staff and the juniors who used the place. Waffles and
syrup and a Mexican omelette and as much juice as he could
drink and good coffee.

Straight from breakfast into the Embassy car park round the
back. Over on the far side of the car park, on a recovery trailer,
was the Ford that had been sabotaged outside the village. If
Ruane saw it, he didn't care to mention it. He sat Erlich in the
passenger seat of his Volvo estate, and pushed into his hand a
two-day-old copy of the *Los Angeles Times*, and he didn't say
where they were going.

They were against the traffic. They made good time. When
they were out of the city it was a fast road.

Erlich kept his head in the paper. He read about the scandal
of the slow movement on the post-earthquake reconstruction in
San Francisco, the new programme of the DEA to block the
importation of Mexican brown across the border into San
Diego, the real estate slump throughout California, a preview of
the weekend's football, a profile of Tom Cruise . . . No mention
of London. Nothing on the Middle East. Nothing from Athens,
nothing from Rome.

The town they had reached was called Colchester. He laid
the folded paper down on the heap of coats on the back seat,
and saw the rifle pouch that was partly concealed under the
coats. They passed a garrison entrance, and there was a proud

233

flag flying, and he saw the armed sentries in their camouflage smocks. They turned into the entrance to the range.

Ruane said, 'Time for some fun, Bill, to take that grim expression off your young face. Get some fresh air into those bruises, too.'

It was a bright morning, hellish cold, and a sharp wind took the big red warning flags. They were Ruane's friends who were waiting for them. Erlich was introduced . . . There was a USAF major from the Mildenhall base. There was an American who had been twelve years in England, who worked in corporate security for Exxon and who had done time in the New York Police Department. There was the range marshal. They were friends and they made Erlich welcome and no one said anything about his face. They loaded the Volvo and bounced out across the rutted track to the faraway butts.

The targets were the old ones, what he knew from the range at Quantico, the outline of a charging infantry man with a Wehrmacht helmet. Erlich hadn't been on a range in the two years since he had left Washington. He thought he might make a real fool of himself.

There was an Ingram sub-machine gun, the close-quarters blaster with the 50-round magazine, he could have taken it. He was given first choice. There was the Armalite carbine that Ruane had brought down in the carrying pouch, and which he had fired twice, an age ago, at Quantico. There was a G-3 German infantry rifle, standard infantry issue for their army, which he declined. There was a Smith and Wesson revolver, .38, four-inch barrel. It was the Smith and Wesson that he knew. It was the Smith and Wesson that he should have had in the tree line overlooking the Manor House, then there wouldn't, by Christ, have been the beating and the kicking. The Smith and Wesson came with the USAF guy, and there was a cardboard box of slugs and there was a neat small holster to thread through his trouser belt. He understood what Ruane was at. The Smith and Wesson felt good in his hand.

The range marshal read the riot act, just as the instructors at Quantico would have done. Erlich was listening with half an ear, he was sliding bullets into the chamber of the Smith and Wesson, he was checking his own 'Safety'.

Away from him, behind the tail of the Volvo, there were the first cracks of the G-3, and the first blast roar of the Ingram, and the snap of the Armalite. He could hear the whoops of the guy who was in corporate security. He went through his drills.

He unzipped the heavy weatherproof coat Ruane had allocated him and walked to a butt that was fifty paces off. He took up his position. What they said, the instructors, was that each practice must be made to count. Deep, hard breathing, punching the oxygen into his lungs. Not on a range outside a country town in the east of England . . . going down an alleyway, threading past shop doorways, moving into a house. Into Condition Yellow, unspecified alert. Getting the adrenaline to pump. Into Condition Red, armed encounter. The trembling in the hands and the lead stiffness in the knees. Into Condition Black, lethal assault in progress. The takeover of the 'flight or fight reflex'. Tunnel vision on the target. The sense of hearing gone, no longer aware of the beat of the Ingram and the sharp shooting of the G-3 and the Armalite carbine. The target was not a paper cut-out. The target was Colt. Colt in front of him. Adrenaline, epinephrine, bursting into his muscles. The swing of the hip, the open jacket thrown clear of the holster. Right hand on the Smith and Wesson's stock. The revolver coming up. Left hand over the right hand. Isosceles stance. The triangle of two arms extended and meeting on the Smith and Wesson. 'Safety' off. Arms rigid. Knees bent. Eyes over rear sight and front sight. Index finger squeezing . . . the belt of the firing in his ears. Three shots fired, rapid. 'Safety' on . . . Colt was still charging him, Colt with the rifle and the heavy helmet down over his forehead. He was seven paces from Colt, and the bastard was still coming at him. He had hit a man-sized target at seven yards with one shot out of three. There had once been a jerk in Chicago, the instructors had said, and he'd needed thirty-three hits to finish him, and another jerk that they talked of who had taken thirteen hollow-point slugs before he dropped. He had hit Colt once, and the target was still coming at him . . . The swivel again, the coat flying clear of the holster. The Smith and Wesson in his hands. 'Safety' off. Condition Black, lethal assault in progress. Three shots fired, three hits, three .38 slugs gouging into the paper and the hardboard that was Colt.

He loaded eight more times. He loaded at speed. He always fired in the Isosceles stance, not the FBI crouch, not the Weaver position. He ripped the shit out of Colt. Every time three out of three.

He walked back to the Volvo. They were waiting for him.

Ruane had a small smile playing at the side of his mouth. It was all right for Ruane, because he had been there, he had fired and he had killed. Ruane was getting a picnic box out of the tail of the Volvo, and cans of Budweiser.

'Don't go losing that . . .' Ruane said.

'. . . Or I'm for a Court Martial,' the USAF officer said.

Rutherford was in the canteen of Boundary Hall, listening to the conversation around him.

Penny wouldn't have allowed him a breakfast like that, not even on his birthday . . .

'. . . There's no problem with the Christian ethic, none at all. It is perfectly proper for the Christian to arm himself with a nuclear deterrent. We've had peace for forty-five years in Europe because we've had the bomb. We love our neighbours, that doesn't mean we have to lie down in front of them. Sinners grow bold if they don't think there's punishment round the corner. I've a quite clear conscience with my Maker . . .'

He had a photocopy of the Personnel report, and he had a digest from the surveillance and from the telephone intercept.

'. . . I cannot for the life of me see why more people don't join. There's just about everything to be caught in the Decoy pond. It's a unique opportunity, all those police to keep the poachers at bay, no families with squealing brats at your shoulder, no dogs running round fouling the banks. You've got carp, roach, tench, bream, pike, all queuing up to be hooked. What more do people want? Quite frankly, if it wasn't for the fishing I'd die of boredom in this place . . .'

He went through each question that he would put to the little cretin that nobody liked, and who hadn't the bottle to tell his Superintendent that he could get stuffed, that he'd get his paper when it was good and finished, not before. But he wasn't bitching, because the alternative to being given the run-around in Aldermaston was chasing round the countryside with Erlich.

There might be some who rejoiced in the prospect of the collapse of the intelligence-gathering agencies of the Russians and the Czechs and the Poles and the East Germans and the Bulgarians, but not everyone was cheering in Curzon Street. It was going to be damn dull without the old friends. Boundary Hall breakfast went on around him. He was ignored. Wouldn't have been ignoring him if they had known he was Curzon Street, but they didn't know and they chattered on.

'. . . Spain, Portugal, Tenerife, you can keep them. My sister and I, it'll be the thirty-fourth year, consecutive, that we've been to Looe. I've done all the travelling I ever want to. When we came back it was Christmas Island to Honolulu. Honolulu to Vancouver. Vancouver to Greenland to Brussels. Brussels to London. London to back here. Christmas Island was a real pig of a place. We were in tents for four weeks before the Test. That's no joke, not enough fresh water to keep clean in. Couldn't swim, currents were treacherous, sharks and all out there. Mind you, we had a shark in Cornwall once . . .'

He wondered how often the others had heard it all. If he'd had to share their table morning after morning, he would have hidden himself behind a newspaper or given up breakfast.

Time to go and ring Penny, and then time to go and find out whether Frederick Bissett was a fool or a traitor.

He felt the cold of the barrel against the nape of his neck.

He slipped his hand behind his head, and took the pistol that had been under his pillow while he had slept.

His fingers nestled loosely round the grip. He held the Ruger .22, and his eyes wavered over the sights towards the bulb in the ceiling. He couldn't be sure that it was the same weapon that had been given him for the hit in London, because all their weapons had the serial smoothed off, but it was a Ruger/MAC Mark 1, .22 calibre, and wavering towards the light bulb was the snake body shape of the integrally silenced barrel.

It was as if it was his reward. Been good, hadn't he? Delivered little Bissett right into their laps so they could fill him with whisky and bullshit, and drop a thousand in notes into his inside pocket. If it had been the one that he had used in London then they had cleaned it since he had abandoned it in the lock-up garage, and their work was there for him to see, oil on his hands, and oil on the sheet under the pillow.

He put the Ruger into an unmarked plastic bag. He took out two magazines, unloaded them and slowly loaded them again and then wiped the twenty or so Long Rifle hollow-point bullets that were spare, folded them back into the dishtowel and put them into the plastic bag. It would go everywhere with him. Meanwhile he would wait for the call. The call might come that day, might not. Might come the next day, might not.

Nothing more to it, than to wait for Frederick Bissett to make contact again.

Rutherford knocked. He stood in the corridor outside H3/2, holding his sheaf of papers behind his back. The door opened. Bissett was a mess. He had cut the edge of his nostril shaving and there was still a staunching peck of cotton wool on the wound. His hair wasn't combed. His shirt was unironed.

'Good morning, Dr Bissett. Could I come in, please?'

'Who are you? I'm sorry, I don't know . . .'

'My name's Rutherford, James Rutherford.'

He could see into the office. More confusion. Paper on the floor and over the desk, and around the console, and covering two of the chairs.

'I don't know who you are.'

'Mr Boll said you would be willing to spare me a few minutes.'

Rutherford walked in. The door was closed behind him. He looked around him. He had been careful not to step on any of the printout sheets.

'What can I do for you?'

Rutherford smiled his ingratiating smile. 'You could find me somewhere to sit, Dr Bissett . . .'

He thought the man had scarcely slept the night before. He had dark grey shadows under his eyes, and his cheeks were pale as death.

Bissett cleared the papers off one of the chairs.

'A few minutes, what for? I've got rather a lot on, well, as you can see.'

It would be a brisk interview, that was how Rutherford had planned it over breakfast. Businesslike, straight to the point, no introductory chat.

Bissett had his back to him, was picking his way through the paper minefield, towards the chair behind his desk.

'Dr Bissett, I'm from the Security Service . . .'

The man froze for several seconds and when he reached his desk and turned, the man looked poleaxed.

'. . . I'm here to deal with your attempt to take classified documents off Establishment premises . . .'

Bissett put his hand on his desk, as if to steady himself. He seemed to topple into his chair.

'I've . . . surely, that's . . . already . . .'

'Your Security Officer called us in.'

'I was told, my department head, Boll, that is, told me it was all finished, cleared up.' A wind-blown reed of a voice.

'How would you rate the material in the files you were attempting to take out?'

'We've been through all this, for heaven's sake. It's low-grade, my own work.'

'Dealing with what exactly?'

It was as if, all of a sudden, some confidence returned to the man. 'Do you understand nuclear physics?'

'I don't.'

'Then you won't understand the interaction of a fission explosion.'

'I don't, no.'

'Then there is not a great deal of point in my explaining the material contained in those papers. Anyone here will tell you it was low-grade.'

'Have you ever been approached, Dr Bissett?'

'*Approached?* I beg your pardon. I don't know . . .'

'You don't need to be a nuclear physicist to know what that means. Have you ever been approached by an outsider, anyone outside the Establishment, for information concerning your work?'

'That's ridiculous.'

'Just answer the question. Yes or no?'

Rutherford thought the man was hyperventilating. Straight question. Should be a straight answer . . .

'No.'

'If you were to be approached, Dr Bissett, what would be your reaction?'

'That's hypothetical.'

'Then hypothesize . . .'

'I suppose, well, I'd go, you know, I'd go to the Security Officer.'

'But you haven't been approached?'

'I have not.'

Rutherford watched Bissett's hands. Bissett's hands were moist. He watched Bissett's lips. The tongue was flicking. If he hadn't been from Curzon Street he might have thought there was something to be made of damp hands and dry lips. But he had learned that the very mention of the Security Service frightened perfectly innocent people into irrational anxiety, even outright fear.

'How are your personal finances, Dr Bissett?'

'My what?'

'Your personal finances.' Good grief, the man was an imbecile.

'I work here . . .'

'I know that. Just answer the question.'

'If you worked here, then you'd understand. We happen to live in the most affluent part of the country . . . Don't you work for the government, Mr . . . I didn't catch your name?'

'Do you have an overdraft, Dr Bissett?'

'Do I have an overdraft?'

'Yes or no . . . ?'

'Yes, I have an overdraft. Is this the sort of question you . . .'

There was a pattern emerging. It didn't matter one way or the other to Rutherford whether Bissett said he had an overdraft or whether he did not. The pattern was more interesting. Every question bred a return question. Not too much to read into it, that the man threw questions back at him, buying him space to think. Interesting . . . He glanced down at his notes. He had the transcript of a telephone call in front of him.

'Were you at home last night, Dr Bissett?'

'Where was I?'

'Were you at home, Dr Bissett?'

'When . . . ?'

'Last night.'

'No.'

'Where were you?'

'I worked late.'

'The Security at the gate will tell me what time you left.'

'Then I went out, I wanted a drink.'

'What pub did you go to, Dr Bissett?'

'Well, I didn't actually. I thought of going for a drink, but I didn't . . .'

'What did you do, Dr Bissett?'

'I just drove around for a bit. I stayed in my car.'

'Why was that, Dr Bissett?'

He saw the anger. He had the transcript of Bissett's call to his wife, the claim that he was working late, that he would be home late. He already had the log from the Falcon Gate that told him that it was early evening when Bissett had driven through the checkpoint. He saw a lonely and frightened man in front of him, a man who could not count as a friend any one of his colleagues.

'I just wanted to be on my own.'

'Wife trouble, Dr Bissett?'

His fists were clenched. For a moment Rutherford thought he might just come over the top of his desk, launch himself. Bissett exploded.

'It's not your bloody business, is it? Get your bloody nose out of my life . . . Get out at once. Get out of my bloody office.'

'Thank you, Dr Bissett, I think that will do for the time being.'

He sat at his desk, his head buried in his hands. He squeezed at his temples and he could not rid himself of the pulsing pain. Desperately and cruelly frightened. The fear was a barb inside him. His door was closed, and it offered no protection from he fear. The sweat ran on his spine, was clammy in his vest. The sickness was in his throat, he could not shed it. When he moved from his desk, he went to the radiator by the window, and he carried the envelope that he had been given in the Great Western Hotel at Paddington station. It was as though the envelope was the sure sign of his guilt. He had not opened the envelope, not in the train, nor when he had reached home and climbed the stairs to bed and found Sara already asleep, nor in the morning. The envelope was his guilt, to open the envelope was to secure that guilt. He could not judge what the man from the Security Service knew. His world, Frederick Bissett's world, was crumbling. No strings, no commitment . . . tell that to the bloody Security Service. Easy enough to say it, whisky in his hand, flattery in his ears . . . no strings, no commitment. All around him was the calm, slow, complacent life beat of the Atomic Weapons Establishment, around him and beyond his reach. All he knew was fear and pain and sickness. As far as he could push it, he stuffed the envelope down behind the radiator under the window.

* * *

242

It was the sort of meeting that Barker detested. It was the White-hall machine at its wretched best. The Deputy Chairman of the Joint Intelligence Committee was referee. Barker knew him as the former commander of an armoured division in Germany, brought home with the cutbacks, tidied into an area that he knew nothing of to work through to his pension.

He had Hobbes with him, to make up the numbers.

Martins he had met on a handful of occasions. He knew of the reputation of so-called 'Sniper' Martins, that the man was a celebrity at Downing Street. He thought him second-rate. And the meeting shouldn't have been held at Century, it should have been at JIC's quarters, the annexe to the Cabinet Office. But Barker quickly understood why the meeting was held at Century. The Deputy Chairman was lunching with the Deputy Director General in the executive suite on Century's nineteenth floor. The Deputy Chairman and the Deputy Director General were distant cousins, had been at school together, and then at Mons Officer Cadet College together. Barker didn't have any cousins who were worth knowing, had been to grammar school, had been rejected for military service because of a right leg shortened in childhood by a polio virus.

The stenographer cleared away the coffee cups. The Deputy Chairman took his place at the head of the long table. Martins eased himself down opposite Barker.

For Barker to start . . . marvellous. He would start, Martins would follow. They would kick it around. He would do his summary, and then Martins would have the last word.

Hobbes had written the paper that Barker paraphrased. There had been a shooting in Athens, an Iraqi dissident killed, and an Agency man, who was with him, killed too. The killer's driver had shouted the name of 'Colt'. The shooting in Clapham of an Iraqi whose hand had been in the state airline till. The face of the same killer *might* have been identified. In both killings the weapon had been a silenced .22 calibre pistol. This Colt was British, a fugitive from justice, already wanted on a charge of attempted murder. Colt had recently been in Britain, might still be within the jurisdiction. Iraqi involvement clear-cut. Another matter – not connected – but the warning of a prospective Iraqi fishing expedition amongst the staff of the Atomic Weapons Establishment . . . What to do? When and where to stamp on the Iraqis? '. . . And the Americans, of course, wish for a result.'

A dry smile from 'Sniper'. Wouldn't have been even the ghost of a smile when Barker had first met the man, before that lunatic escapade in the Beqa'a, no more than a cringing little arse-licker he'd been then.

'And that has very little to do with us.'

'I merely state the position.'

'You don't have enough to go to court.'

'That's for the Director of Public Prosecutions.'

'I'm simply observing, Deputy Chairman, that he'd be laughed out of the Central Criminal Court.'

'I wasn't aware, Deputy Chairman, that Mr Martins had any experience of British criminal law.' The Deputy Chairman flapped a hand down the table, as if to wave the combatants apart. 'We have, in my view, enough to justify the expulsion of at least five or six members of their embassy staff,' Barker snapped.

'I would most strongly oppose that course of action, Deputy Chairman.' Martins cracked his palm down onto the sheened table surface. Another new gesture, acquired since the man had dined with the Prime Minister, Barker supposed.

'With or without evidence to satisfy a jury, we cannot tolerate Iraqi terrorism, state-sponsored terrorism, on the streets of London.'

'Talk is cheap . . .'

'That is insulting and unwarranted.'

'Have you the faintest inkling of the consequences of the action you propose?'

'I am interested solely in the security of this country.'

Martins turned so that he faced the Deputy Chairman. He ignored his adversary.

'We are, damn near, near as makes no difference, in a state of war with Iran. We have, because of quite colossal bungling, no network inside Iran. We are blind in that country, and deaf. What little we know of the political goings-on inside Iran comes courtesy of the intelligence agencies of Iraq . . . is that point taken? I make another point . . . Iraq is currently rebuilding her entire infrastructure. They have billions of oil dollars to spend, they are hunting high and low for contractors with the expertise they require and, God willing, contracts will come our way . . . And yet here we are being asked, on the flimsiest of evidence, to march up to their front door and toss half a dozen accredited diplomats out of the country. I lose my major intelligence-gathering source in Iran, my country loses – and the French and the Germans will pick them all up – billions of dollars' worth of trade, all because the Americans want a result.'

'Your attitude is craven.'

'Your way, I'll tell you what will be achieved, sweet nothing . . . except that we lose contracts, lose goodwill, lose good information. I won't sit back while a painstaking process is sacrificed for a wasteful gesture. Century is the real world, apparently Curzon Street is not.'

Barker looked to Hobbes for support. Hobbes looked away.

'Gentlemen, gentlemen . . .' said the Deputy Chairman. 'And you have not, Mr Martins, addressed the issue of the Atomic Weapons Establishment . . .'

'If indeed, sir, it is an issue. The Israelis have been asked for more detail. They have been unable so far to provide it. It's in their court.'

The Deputy Chairman smiled again. Barker thought that if such a man had ever commanded an armoured division then the army needed winding down.

'So what is your suggestion, Mr Martins?'

'Pretty simple, isn't it?'

'Do please enlighten us,' Barker snarled.

Martins beamed. 'Find this Colt and shoot him . . .'

'You're not serious?'

'Find him, shoot him . . . and bury him deep.'

245

He carried the day. Barker had seen the eye of the Deputy Chairman brighten. He had seen the bully confidence of 'Sniper' Martins win the hour. It did not go into the stenographer's notebook, of course, but that was the decision of the meeting, two votes to one, and Hobbes was not asked his opinion.

Colt was to be found, shot, and forgotten.

Would Barker resign? Would he hell! He was a man who took an order.

The technicians had put on their heavy coats and taken their bread and goat's cheese and their sweet tea out onto the verandah below. The Swede was often alone in his office for that hour of the day. Today there was the music of Beethoven in his ears, the Seventh, and even that beloved symphony was not enough to calm him. He could set his watch from the time they left to the time they would return, his two assistants. He would be alone for an hour. The Colonel had not, so far as he knew, come back. He could hope for a telephone call, and hope that the rifle microphone could pick up whatever was said by the Director if he were to be telephoned by the Colonel.

For every second that the microphone lay, assembled, against the window side of his desk, he experienced an agony of fear.

The Swede knew the fate of spies working against the regime. A German chemist had told him, and sniggered as he said it, that spies did not even suffer a *clean* death by hanging. Spies were stood under the open-air gallows in the execution yard at the Abu Ghraib gaol on a shallow stool. When the stool was kicked away then the spies would kick and strangle to their deaths.

It was because he detested the despot regime of cult and fear that he could justify what he did. He had taught the Pakistani how to play golf. Khan had thought him his friend and Khan was dead. The Swede had felt no regret when Khan did not come back from his European journey. He had not expected that he would.

He knew that security men had been seen, had been

interviewing the Iraq-born scientists and engineers and administrators in the office complex in Tuwaithah. They were searching for the source of the leakage of information. If he went now, and failed to return from leave, the finger would be pointed at him. Where would he run to, that was beyond the reach of the thugs of the regime? Not to a desk in the Chemistry Faculty of the University of Uppsala, not to a hi-tech factory in California. Would they want him in Israel? Would they want his expertise in the Negev desert factory of Dimona? Very probably not. It was enough to make him laugh out loud in his office, his bungalow, the thought that he was safest at Tuwaithah from assassination.

Tonight was Bridge night in the compound, at the bungalow of the physicist from Salzburg. He knew the dates of the Austrian's next leave, his skiing holiday, and he wondered who would take over the little brick bungalow two down from his own if, as he expected, the Austrian did not return from his leave.

There were no calls received by the Director during his technicians' lunch hour. The agony was wasted.

The Swede had gone to the limit of the hour. He was barely back at his desk, the rifle microphone returned to its hiding place, when the technicians came back into the office.

He had come downstairs in his stockinged feet in answer to the woman's shout. They must have been getting used to him in the house because the woman didn't bother to come up and knock at his door, just yelled from the hallway.

There was the breathy voice. He wanted a meeting. No, he did not want to go back to London. No, he wanted only Colt. He sounded to Colt like he was going through hell.

Bissett gave him a rendezvous. A pub at Stratfield Mortimer, beside the Foundry Brook, just across the stream from the railway station. And a time. Colt said he'd be there. The telephone purred in his ear.

* * *

247

Barker had not been back in Curzon Street five minutes before the summons came for him to take a sandwich and a bottle of Malvern in his Director General's top-floor office.

A fierce and rare sunshine splayed through the arms of the blind. The Director General was tiger-striped.

'. . . You'll do what you're bloody well told, Dickie, and if I don't have, right here and now, your total commitment and support then you have exactly thirty minutes to clear your desk. But before you do anything rash, let me put you in the picture. In the time it has taken you to get back from your meeting Century House has been alerted by their man. He has talked to the Chairman of the JIC and he has called me. Everyone is giving the decision arrived at at your meeting the go-ahead. You won't have a friend in the whole wide world. Is that understood?'

'However you dress it up, whatever illusion of national security you invoke, it is still *murder*.'

'Thank you, Dickie. Your point is made. Now get me Rutherford in here. Get Rutherford back . . .'

'I'll not have my name on any bloody piece of paper.'

'Pipe down, Dickie, and get me Rutherford.'

Rutherford was in the small room next to the Security Officer. He was deliberating whether to call Hobbes and recommend that one more day was needed at Aldermaston. He didn't know, that was the problem. He wanted someone to talk through with him what he had assembled. He simply didn't have the experience in this sort of investigation. He hadn't known Bettany, hadn't been involved in the case at all. He didn't know what had made Bettany *different* to any of the rest of them. He hadn't worked on Prime, because he had still been sharpening pencils when the team had gone down to GCHQ to root through the Soviet agent's past history. He had only the book to fall back on. The book said that the danger was MICE. MICE was Money, Ideology, Compromise, Ego.

Money was an overdraft. Under this government everybody had an overdraft, but Money was worth looking at further. *Ideology*, post-Cold War, was pretty ludicrous. He couldn't see the International Brigade and the Fight against Fascism, or the Fight against Communism, for that matter, making any sense *à propos* Iraq. Ideology was probably better off in the British Museum, and he'd have to have a word with the instructors and have them dig up a new acronym. *Compromise* was cash or sex. What they said on the course was that anyone could be reached by cash or by a woman's thighs. Anyone, all the way to an ambassador. He didn't know, not yet, just how critical was Bissett's financial crisis. Sara Bissett he'd seen, the night before when she had come home from the school. Good-looking woman, very pretty if she hadn't been creased with worry lines. He'd have been willing to bet that Bissett was going short, and he'd have bet more that Bissett wasn't complaining . . . *Ego* was the key. Ego, in his case, was carrying around the damn great chip on his shoulder, believing that the world was selling the big talent short. Maybe he had seen disappointment, but he hadn't seen arrogance and he hadn't seen vanity. Bissett was alone, maybe not of his own choice . . .

He was called to the secure line in the Security Officer's room. There must have been a meeting in progress, because there were half a dozen men and women filing out of the office, including the Security Officer. This was one way to make himself popular. Probably half the Establishment would have defected, anywhere, before old Pig Eyes called for help again from Curzon Street.

'That you, Rutherford?'

Yes, it was James Rutherford.

'Get yourself back here.'

He hadn't finished. There were a few loose ends.

'You got a goodie?'

No, he didn't *think* so. No, there was nothing *positive*. But if he were to be thorough . . .

'Don't ask me why, starshine, but the Director General wants to take tea with you, and I don't think he means tomorrow.'

There were no regrets expressed when he informed the Security Officer that he was called back to Curzon Street. 'Basically, Mr Rutherford, the lesson you should carry away with you is that we know how to run our affairs at Atomic Weapons,' the Security Officer told him.

As he accelerated away down the Burghfield Common Road, Rutherford thought he'd have to find some polish for his shoes, after tramping round in the rain-splashed compounds of Aldermaston, before he presented himself in the Director General's office. And that the pubs weren't closed, and he'd get a drink before he reached the motorway. And Bissett – was he a traitor? Well, that could wait, that was apparently on the back-burner. Erlich would probably recite, 'Theirs not to reason why', some crap like that.

'It's your decision, Dr Bissett.'

'I used to love it, the work there.'

'Used to?'

'I'm treated like dirt now.'

'Then that's your decision made.'

'I'm certain of it, I'm passed over for promotion this year.'

'That's unthinkable, a man of your potential . . .'

'You probably cannot understand, it's hideous to work when you are accorded no respect.'

It was dark in the car park of the pub at Stratfield Mortimer. Their faces were briefly lit by the headlights of the cars of the first customers. Each time they were caught in the lights, Colt ducked his head away, and Bissett was like a rabbit held in a flash lamp's beam.

'Then you walk away.'

'That business last year, I read something, that report from the Human Rights crowd.'

'The Israelis interfering again, just their propaganda. Me, I'm not aware of torture, that sort of thing. I wouldn't be there if I didn't like the place. Heh, Dr Bissett, you don't believe what you read in the gutter press . . . ?'

'What sort of life would I have?'

'What they told you, Dr Bissett. You'd be head of a whole department. It would be a good life, good accommodation and good facilities.'

'And Sara, my wife, and the boys?'

Colt gagged . . . Corrected himself. 'You'd take them?'

'Of course.'

'They'd have a great life. They will be happy. It's a very modern country. Good British community, international school, everything . . .'

Colt didn't know what the living conditions were like at Tuwaithah, he didn't even know where Tuwaithah was. He knew there was a small British community, but he had never moved in it, and he had never been within a mile of the British Club. He didn't know, but he thought that the International School might be the pits.

'I don't know what to do.'

Colt said quietly, 'It's your life.'

'It's so difficult . . .'

'You take your chance, or you turn your back on it.'

'You know, Colt, when I came here they all said that I was brilliant, that I had an original mind. I was coming to the place where there was the best original thinking in the country. That's the way it used to be. It used to be a real community of endeavour, but that community's dead now. It's not a place for scientists any more, it's for accountants, penny-pinchers. You want to get on, you have to be a politician and a safe bureaucrat. It's twenty years since anything outstanding came out of here. They suffocate brilliance and they've strangled me. Brilliance would threaten the little pedestals of the empire builders. They dragged me down, Colt, they squashed out my brilliance . . . What would I be, there?'

'Your own master, if you go.'

'Would I be a traitor?'

Colt's head sagged back against the seat. So what the fuck would the frightened little bastard be?

'Just a word, Dr Bissett. Words don't mean much. If you go, then you are in charge of your own life. If you stay then you are their slave, till you drop, till they give you a gold watch.'

'There's something I should tell you.'

'What's that?'

'I've had a little . . . difficulty.'

'What sort of difficulty?'

'I was interviewed this morning by a man from the Security Service.'

Colt was straight up in the seat. His eyes roved across each of the cars parked close to the Sierra. Mind going flywheel speed. Looking for a Watcher, looking in the darkness to see if he could isolate the shadow shape of a Watcher . . . fucking hell . . . As cool as he could make it. 'Why was that, Dr Bissett?'

The blurted answer. 'I had to work late, but I couldn't be in my office because I'd said to Sara I'd look after the boys. I was taking papers home. I was stopped at the gate check. I was interviewed by the Security Officer, but there's been another man down, from London, from the Security Service. He was awful, terribly aggressive . . .'

The hard cut in Colt's voice. 'Did you satisfy him?'

'How would I know?'

Colt said, 'If you're to go, you'd better be going fast.'

'I don't know, so difficult to know what's best.'

'I have to know your answer.'

'I tell you, I wouldn't tell another living soul, I'm just so desperately frightened.'

Colt's hand rested on Bissett's arm. It was a gesture of friendship, a touch of solidarity. 'I go out with you. I am with you each step of the way when you go out.'

'I'll ring you.'

'Tomorrow.'

'I'll ring you tomorrow.'

Colt slipped out of the car. He moved back in the car park so that he would not be caught in the headlights as Bissett drove away. And he was sick, sick as a dog, onto the loose chip stone of the car park. He thought he was the small bird over which the fine close-mesh net was thrown. If he flew now, he could escape. If he stayed, he would be trapped. There was quiet around him, there was the fading of Bissett's car in the lanes. Bissett had attracted the attention of the Security Service . . . He retched onto the gravel behind his car and before he collected his pistol and searched all the cars in the car park he retched again until there was nothing more for him to bring up.

She heard the Sierra's engine and she broke off the conversation. Sara put the telephone down.

Beside the telephone, on the little table in the hall, was the post that had come after he had gone to work. She had learned to recognize the type used by the bank.

She heard the car door slam shut.

She was quivering. Through all her body there was a tightness. Debbie's voice was still in her ears, all of Debbie's regret and Debbie's pleading with her. She opened the front door. He was bent into the back of the car and he was lifting out his briefcase and his raincoat. It was the saddest thing she could remember, telling Debbie that she would not again be coming to the classes . . . She saw the way that he looked around him after he had locked the car. He looked to the right up Lilac Gardens, and he looked left. She thought he looked like a fugitive. He came fast over the few paces from the car to the front door, and he almost punched her out of his way as he came through the front door and into the hallway. He kicked the door shut behind him, used his heel, and the hall echoed with the rap of the front door closing and latching. She had told Debbie, no explanation, no justification, that she would not again be coming to the classes . . . The television was on in the sitting room, it was where the boys were. Any other day and he would have nodded to her, forced a smile, hurried past her. Any other day he would have gone up the stairs to change out of his jacket into the cardigan that he wore on cold evenings. Any other day, not that day. He clung to her. The angle between the arm and the lens frame of his spectacles gouged at her cheek. So long since he had held her in that way, so fiercely. As though he was struggling to reach her. She felt the trembling in his body. She couldn't see his eyes, she didn't know whether or not he wept. When she broke away it was with the muttered excuse that the supper would be boiling over on the cooker's rings, and that he should greet his boys. She went back into the kitchen. She left them, her husband and her sons who had come to him in the hallway that needed new carpeting . . . Thank God she had rung Debbie. Thank God it was over . . . When she came back into the hall, Sara could see Frederick's face. Like he'd aged ten years since he had gone to work that morning.

Sara said that supper would be a few minutes.

He said that after supper they would all play Scrabble, then he saw the letter from the bank. She watched as he tore the envelope, unopened, into small pieces.

The Kurd from the city of Kirkuk had been under surveillance for a week, and it had been observed that he had come to the new Post Office and been seen at the post-restante boxes on three days of the last seven. The man was arrested as he came away from the new Post Office on Al Kadhim Street in the old Juafir district.

He was one amongst the four million Kurds struggling for a life-hold inside Iraq. He was of the people that had been shelled and bombed and attacked with the odourless gas canisters. The man was a member of the 'Peshmerga', the guerrilla army that fought, poorly armed, to hold back the regime of the Chairman of the Revolutionary Command Council. The man was also a field agent of the Mossad. Because he was a Kurd, he had always run the risk, in Baghdad, that he would come under observation.

There were three of them. They carried their Makharov pistols under their coats. They had closed on him. He saw them. He might have stood his ground. He might have stated, baldly, that he awaited a letter from a cousin living in Turkey, he might have spun any tissue of lies . . . He had run.

He had burst past them. He had turned once to see how far behind him they were. He had turned as he ran and he had seen them reaching for their handguns from their shoulder holsters. He had collided into the woodframe stall, pushed on old pram wheels by the seller of pistachio nuts. He had fallen.

The sirens howled across the city, and the Kurd was held in the basement cells of the Department of Public Security.

It was the best day Erlich had known since he had come to London. A good breakfast, good company, a good picnic, good shooting. After the picnic he had let go a magazine of the Ingram, and he had fired the G-3 through a telescopic sight and he'd had a better group than Joe from corporate security and he had a $20 bill, proper old greenback, to prove it. He had told Ruane, until the big man looked tired of hearing it, that he was grateful for his day.

He stood on the corner of South Audley Street and Grosvenor Square, searching for a free taxi. He held the paper bundle against his chest. The bundle was a shirt that he had been lent, and a singlet and a pair of underpants and grey socks, laundered and ironed. A taxi veered across to the kerb in front of him.

He had the weight of the Smith and Wesson, in its holster, pulling at his belt, and he felt good.

'You're Rutherford?'

'Yes, sir.'

'You did well in Northern Ireland.'

'Thank you, sir.'

'Tell me, Rutherford, why did you join the Service?'

'I thought I would be doing something worthwhile.'

'Do you still believe that?'

'If I didn't, sir, I'd leave.'

'Committed to the Service, Rutherford?'

'Yes, sir.'

'What's the hardest thing about maintaining that commitment?'

'The enforced privacy, sir.'

'It's true. We're a lonely breed. Can you cope with that, being outside the pale?'

'I hope so, sir.'

'The Service has to be first, always first.'

The Director General walked to his cabinet. He knew that young Rutherford had been drinking already, could smell it. No concern of his. If he had run an abstainers' show then Curzon Street would have been as empty as a cemetery at night. He poured two whiskies. He added a splash of water.

It was his pleasure, from time to time, to chat with his junior Executive Officers. Something to do with growing old, he supposed. He liked their company, he enjoyed their certainty.

'The American, Erlich, what do you make of him?'

'He's an ex-teacher, not the usual FBI material, and not terribly skilled – you couldn't imagine him surviving a day in Belfast, for example. I have no doubt this is his first major assignment and he wants to make double certain it works for him. Career-wise, he doesn't intend the grass to grow under his shoes. He's a curious mixture. He'll go through a brick wall and back, he's belligerent and impatient, and he knows more Victorian poetry than I can bear to listen to.'

'Not your run-of-the-mill gunslinger, then?'

'Oh, he'd shoot, sir, shoot first, ask questions afterwards . . . that's metaphorical, of course.'

'And the feelings of Erlich for the Tuck boy?'

'It's become a very personal thing, sir. The Agency man who was killed in Athens was Erlich's friend. And some days ago Bill Erlich was jumped – we were watching the Tuck place at night – and got himself pretty badly beaten. That looked like Colt's work, too.'

'He'd want him dead?'

'If he had the chance, sir, no question.'

The Director General had started to pace. They were good strides, they would have graced a fairway. There was a swell in the filled tumbler and then a trail behind him of whisky splashed on the carpet. He couldn't call in a committee to evaluate the competence of young Rutherford. Young Rutherford didn't fidget, and he liked that. Young Rutherford stood his ground. It was his decision. If he was right, well, then, he would receive no praise because his decision would never be known of. If he was wrong, well, then, disgrace . . .

'Major Tuck told Mr Barker and Erlich that his son had been at home. He said that his son was now gone.'

'Did he, sir?'

'If this boy, this Colt, were still in Britain, where would you look for him?'

'His mother's dying, sir. That's where I'd look for him.'

'Find him, please, Rutherford, and take Erlich with you.'

'Yes, sir.'

'What will you do when you find him?'

'The local PC is a very good man, sir . . .'

'No, no, no. I wouldn't do that, Rutherford.' The Director General gazed into Rutherford's face. He thought this could have been a pleasant young man if he had had a proper job, if he hadn't chosen to work in Curzon Street. 'The political implications here are as long as your arm. The Iraqi connection, etc. etc. No, the best way out of this hornet's nest would be to get Erlich to kill him. No publicity, please, just dead.'

14

The fire was heaped with coal, burning well. He sat in the easy chair and the cat was on his lap. It was a woman's room, he could see that. There was a neatness about the small pieces of furniture and the light-coloured curtains and the delicate china ornaments and the arrangement of the print pictures on the walls. It was a room to be at home in, and there was the smell of the witch hazel.

Bill had not known such a room since he had left his grandparents' home, down by the yacht harbour at Annapolis, since he had gone west to college at Santa Barbara. The room was where to end a great day.

She had poured him good wine. She had cooked him tortellini, good sauce. She was just a hell of a fine girl, she had welcomed him into her home and sat him by the fire, and she had rubbed the witch hazel into the yellow dark bruising of his face and his crotch.

She heard the taxi before him. She cut herself short in her description of how it was to be married into the Service. She had been sitting on the sofa, her ankles tucked up beside her, her skirt tight above her knees.

The taxi drove away. She had stopped talking and her head was raised, listening. The cat hadn't moved. The cat didn't care who came, who went, as long as the lap was warm. Erlich heard the scraping of a key at the front door. He had to grin . . . James Rutherford coming home, and not able to get his key in the hole. Hell of a start to your evening home. The third failure with the key, and she swung her legs off the sofa and stamped out into the hall in her stockinged feet.

Erlich heard the front door opened.

He listened.

'Hello, darling.'

'You're pissed.'

'Good cause, darling.'

'Always a good cause.'

'Blame the D-G.'

'Come the other one.'

'Honest, darling, he had me in, really. He had me in, he poured me a killer.'

The softening in Penny Rutherford's voice, anxiety. 'Are you in trouble?'

'You don't get half pints of Scotch if you're in trouble.'

'What did he want?'

'You won't believe it . . .'

'Try me.'

'He wanted to talk about Buffalo Bill . . .'

Erlich heard the relief of her laughter.

'*Who?*'

'You know, chap in your bath, Erlich.'

'What did you tell him?'

Erlich heard the bright chime of Penny Rutherford's giggle.

'I said that he was impetuous, more. I said he was too scholarly for the Service, too poetical, really, and anyway, I said, you turn your back on him for the length of a cornflake and he's in the bath with your wife. No, I blackballed him, ha! ha! ha!'

'Come on in, before you fall down.'

Penny led. She had the mischief in her eyes. Erlich thought that Rutherford would be struggling out of his coat, and there was the thudding of his overnight bag onto the polished floorboards in the hall. She was beautiful, and the mischief in her was explosive. Rutherford came in.

Rutherford stopped.

'Oh, Christ . . .'

'Evening, James,' Erlich said.

'What the hell are you doing here?'

Erlich said, quiet and easy with a bit of a drawl like he came from cattle country, 'I came to take a bath.'

'Come on, you two. We'll watch James have his supper. I think you've had enough to drink, darling. Go and sit down and I'll heat it. Bill, catch him if he looks like falling.'

Rutherford stood straight. He stood like he was on parade. He even straightened his tie.

'Apart from the bath . . . .?'

'I was bringing back your laundry, for which, again, thanks.'

'Ah, yes, the laundry . . . I hope they haven't used starch on my shirt,' Rutherford said. 'The rest of it is fixed, by the by. We're given carte blanche to track down Colt. This is my full-time priority. No more sideshows, you'll work alongside me because that's the way you'll get to Colt . . .'

Somewhat later, they both kissed Penny Rutherford good night, and slipped out through the front door into the street.

Rutherford let him drive. When he wasn't dozing, when he wasn't giving the directions for the turn off the M3 onto the A303 and the right-hand fork at Stonehenge, he thought of Penny. That was the trouble, too much thinking about Penny, not enough time to do anything about Penny. Pretty Penny, the wife left at home . . . Bedrock of Curzon Street, the wives that were left at home. On his floor, in the D Branch, he knew of four men who had moved out of their suburban houses that year, and exchanged their own homes for an inner London bedsit, bachelor apartment, studio, or whatever . . . She could have warned him, she could have whispered and pointed to the sitting-room door. Perhaps it was her bit of fun, pretty Penny's little laugh, to let him lead with his big foot. Actually, all jokes aside, they were washed up. All the excuses could be tripped off. But, no, she hadn't warned him because she hadn't given a toss that he had made a rude bore of himself. He just thanked his stars he hadn't given away the true gist of it. The hair rose on his neck at the thought of it. Still, some comfort there. Tight as an owl and still a good Service man. A good Service man and a piss-awful husband. Go on the way they were heading and he'd be for the bachelor flat in no time, sure.

They both pretended to be asleep, and they were both awake. Midnight chimed on the clock downstairs in the living room. Sara knew the problem was new. He had slept after the last session with the bank manager, and he had slept after he had come back from being held by the Establishment police. He had played Scrabble with them, and he had made sure that it was always either Frank or Adam who won. He had been like any other parent. He had been like the fathers she saw at the school gate meeting their kids. Beside her, he twisted and turned.

She reached to touch his shoulder, felt him start away from her.

'What is it, Frederick? What's happened?'

It flew from him in a torrent.

'Whatever I've done is for you and the boys. Whatever I am going to do, is only for you and for Adam and Frank. Only for you, only for them. Whatever I've done, whatever I'm going to do, don't listen to anyone. It's only for you . . .' And then nothing more.

Her questions rebounded from his angular shoulder.

The car was where it had been the last time, in the driveway of the policeman's house, left in front of his darkened windows. This night there was more light, half a moon and broken quick-moving cloud, and they had skirted the village and come to the wood from the east side.

He heard the crushing of the dead leaves.

He lay in the wood loam. He was using his bivouac as his groundsheet. There was a big wind up high, but where he was the trees shielded him from the cold. There weren't trees heaving, not this night. He hadn't heard the collapse of a falling branch. It wasn't a branch, broken off, that had crushed the leaves. Rutherford was off to his left, beyond reach. From where he was, Rutherford could see the front gate of the Manor House, and could look over the outbuildings of the place, what had once been the pony and trap sheds, right to the front gate. Erlich watched the light on the stair window and he could see the kitchen door. There was a light on in the empty kitchen.

He heard the cracking of a twig.

He heard a soft, dried-breath throat growl.

Fast, sudden movement. The weight buckled down onto Erlich. The blow of the weight onto his shoulders and his back. The stab of pain at his neck. Groping for the holster. The weight was on his back and heaving down onto the fist that scrabbled for the handle of the Smith and Wesson. The throbbing roar in his ears, and the torn hurt in his skin. Hand on the gun, the gun clear, twisting and rolling. The weight and the pain following him as he twisted, rolled. The gun out. The gun pressed against his chest. Foul breath spilling at his face. The growl roar, and the weight, and the pain.

He fired . . .

Kept firing . . .

Erlich kept firing until there was no more noise, until the weight was gone, through the six slugs in the Smith and Wesson chamber, and on round, until there was just the sound of the hammer hitting dead cartridge heads.

Rutherford was above him, and Rutherford's torch played over the tree branches and roots around him, and over the bramble undergrowth. Rutherford asked if he were all right. He heard the concern in Rutherford's voice. Yes, he was OK. There was pain in the back of his neck, and the breath had been sucked clean out of his lungs by the weight, and his ears were blasted from the deep-throat growl and the hammered gunfire. But he was OK. The torch wavered, came close to him. The torch found it. God, the bastard was huge. Laid out, its full length stretched, and there was blood at its mouth, blood on its teeth. He'd only once seen a bigger German Shepherd, half pulling a warden over, at the Federal gaol at Marion, Illinois. There was a head shot and there was a chest shot, and there was a shot that looked to have broken the dog's right rear leg.

They heard the advancing footfall. There was no attempt at concealment. The footfall drove without hesitation through the undergrowth, from the depth of the wood. Goddam fingers shaking. Revolver up, cylinder out, palm of the hand belting the barrel to shake the spent cases clear. The footfall closing on them. Prising the new cartridges into the chamber.

The torch picked her out. There was her dirt-smeared oil jacket, the jeans and the big boots. There was the rich red flame of her hair. Erlich went to the crouch and to the aim. He could see that she carried no weapon, but he went to the crouch and the aim and his right index finger was crooked level with the trigger. Rutherford held her in the beam of his torch. She never slowed. She seemed to see through the power of the beam that dazzled her. Erlich remembered, too damn well, the beating and the kicking. He remembered his own screams. He remembered the smell of her, when she was a foot from him as he crouched and aimed. She never looked at him.

She picked up the dog. She picked it up like it was a sheep, or a dead deer. It must have weighed forty kilos. She slung it across her shoulders, and the blood from the dog's mouth dribbled down her jacket.

She looked at him then, and he felt the hate in her.

She walked away, back into the depth of the wood.

He was crouched, he aimed at her all the time that the torch beam held her.

The sounds carried over the fields where the light frost was gathering. He heard all of the shots fired.

He had only slept fitfully since his son had last sat with his wife, held her hand. Not a poacher's shotgun, not a hunting rifle. He had recognized the full chamber of a revolver discharged. There were no revolvers in the village, none that he had ever heard of. Revolvers were for soldiers, and for armed policemen.

He lay on his back in the cold and companionless bed.

A man had told him once, a friend of his father, a man who had shot game in Tanganyika between the wars, that the most dangerous animal in the bush was the leopard. The man had said that a leopard was only safe when its head had been sliced off. He thought that the American at the Reform Club would have thought of his boy as a leopard. And if the bruises on the man's face were anything to go by and the screams in the wood in the night a week ago, then the American was right about the leopard. And six shots were for killing. Six shots were what he would have fired, nearly fifty years before in France, for killing.

He lay on his back, he stared up at the darkness of the ceiling. He would be told, they would come to tell him. He listened for the scratch of car wheels on the gravel of the drive.

The shots were heard all around the village.

Every living soul fed from the gossip that Colt had been home, that a car had been stripped of its tyres, that an American had been savaged until he screamed for his life in the high copse behind the Manor House, that Colt was watched for.

Billy and Zap and Charlie and Kev and Dazzer and Zack and Johnny, and the bank manager from Warminster, and the solicitor from Shepton, and the District Nurse, and old Vic in the pub, and the woman above the Post Office, and the tenant of Home Farm, they all heard the shots, and they all thought of Colt.

When Fran reached her home, the cottage on the dirt track past where the church had once been, old Brennie was in his chair beside the stove. Fran stood in the doorway with the dog, her Rocco, on her shoulders and she saw the anger that he shared with her. They took a spade, and the flash that he used for pinioning rabbits in their fear, and they went to the old tumbled stone wall that marked the edge of the disused cemetery of the church. There had been enough rain to make it easy for deep digging. They took their turns, they dug in silence.

*   *   *

To Erlich it was pointless that they should stay, but he wasn't going to be the first to call a halt. He had picked up the cartridge cases, they had scraped leaves over the dog's blood, they had moved a hundred yards east. It was still just possible to see the kitchen door of the Manor House, and most of the driveway.

At the first grey dawn smear Rutherford broke the long silence between them.

'Where did you get that thing?'

'I got it, and I'm keeping it.'

'It's a miracle half the county's police aren't scouring the woods for you. Perhaps they are. They won't make a hundredth of the noise you made.'

'What would you have had me do?'

'Bloody good covert surveillance, a real A-team.'

'Don't piss on me. I'm not some Rambo kid out of the mountains . . .'

'No, indeed.'

'You'd have had me use a kitchen knife? That monster would have had my throat.'

'I was merely observing that we have gone rather public.'

Erlich said, 'But there's nowhere else.'

Rutherford said, 'That's the pity of it. It's where we have to stay.'

'Every goddam night till he comes . . .'

She didn't have to look so damned surprised. He had only said that he would take the boys to the school gate, drop them, and then drive to the Establishment. She didn't have to look as though he had suggested running naked round Buckingham Palace.

It was Frederick Bissett's decision to take the boys to school and to arrive fifteen minutes later than usual at the Establishment. He would decide when he should telephone Colt. He would decide whether or not he would accept their offer of employment.

For once she didn't argue with him. Just that once she didn't dispute her husband's authority. She wasn't going to dispute *anything* when he was head of a department, when he was running a research unit, when he was rich and respected.

He drove the boys to the school gate. He did his best. He talked about the Liverpool team, and their new striker. He talked about the cricket side for Australia. He stopped at the newsagent on Mulfords Hill and he bought them each two comics . . . They'd settle, they'd work it out. Plenty of families went abroad to work and took their children with them. It was their future that he was concerned about, their future and Sara's.

He dropped the boys. They didn't kiss him. He would have liked them to show him affection. They ran from the car and into the school playground . . . There was one thing he'd miss, by God, he'd miss it: the chance to see the faces of Reuben Boll and Carol and sickly little Wayne and the Security Officer when they discovered where he had gone.

On the first floor of a decaying building in the ancient Old City, the part of Baghdad settled twelve centuries before by Abu Jafar al-Mansur, the radio transmitter was found. It was the discovery of the transmitter in the room where he lived, alone, that redoubled the torture inflicted on the Kurd, and doubled, too, the number of officers who now involved themselves in the investigation.

With the arrival of each new officer at the Department of Public Security's interrogation cells, so the demand for confession grew, so the screw was turned.

By the time that the Colonel reached the basement cells, the Kurd, and it was all he prayed to his God for, was close to death. The Colonel had seen the carnage inflicted by the traversing machine guns on the human waves of the enemy outside Basra. He had seen the heads of men blown apart by revolver fire; he had seen the kicking death throes of those hanged from makeshift gallows. But even the Colonel was nauseated, felt the bile rise in his throat, when he saw what had been done to the Kurd.

266

They had taken the fingernails from his hands, the toenails from his feet. They had beaten the soles of his feet with rubber truncheons. They had used the *al-mangana*, the clamp on his toes that was tightened. They had torn off one of his ears. They had pounded his penis to a bloodied prune. The cell echoed with the Colonel's fury. He had the Kurd taken down from the manacles that suspended him from the ceiling. He demanded that the doctor be brought immediately. He had no feeling for the Kurd, but he had uncontrolled anger for those who had supervised an interrogation that had lost them their suspect.

The Kurd had not talked. And even as he was lowered from the ceiling, his prayer was answered and, sinking deeper into wave after wave of pain, he died. It was twenty-one hours since his arrest.

The Colonel demanded continued discreet surveillance of the post-restante box. It was all they had. He promised a charge of treason for any man who failed in his duty.

There was a knock. His door opened. It was Boll in the doorway.

'Ah, Frederick, you have a moment?'

Funny, but actually he wasn't frightened of the man any more. They would make him suffer when it was discovered that he had lost a Senior Scientific Officer.

'What can I do for you, Reuben?' He heard the coolness in his own voice. There had been times when he had stood up when Boll came into his room.

'That man who came . . .'

'What about him?'

'I wanted you to know that I thought his investigation here disgraceful.'

'I expect that he would have said that he was only doing his job . . .'

'That is extraordinarily reasonable.'

'. . . Nevertheless, I told him to get the hell out.'

'You told him to get out?'

267

'Oh, yes. That's what I told him. He went too far, frankly. I'm not sure I didn't offer him some violence. Anyway, he went, as instructed.'

He saw the surprise on Boll's face. 'I just wanted you to know that you had my sympathy.'

'Thank you, Reuben.'

'Oh, and you should know that I rated your paper very highly. Good work . . .'

'Thank you again, Reuben. I hope you have a pleasant trip to the United States.'

He stared at the closing door.

If he went fast, if he went when Colt wanted him to, then Boll would just have arrived at Livermore or Los Alamos, or wherever the bastard was feting himself. Just have got his feet under the table when the alarm button would go. A Senior Scientific Officer from H area disappeared, that would get Boll's fat little feet under his fat little arse scurrying back onto the plane home.

It was time to make his call.

From her desk by the window Carol saw everything that moved at the front of the H3 building. She saw Frederick Bissett go and she realized that he must have left the building through the emergency fire door beside the entrance to the laboratory section. She saw that he was hunched, as if he were frozen cold, as if he had compressed his neck into the collar of his raincoat, almost as if he tried to hide his face. Boll was on the telephone, staring out of his window. Boll saw him get into his car, and thought, with fresh amazement, of Bissett's throwing the man Rutherford out of his office.

Basil was performing the painful weekly duty that distressed him, still, after so many years at the Establishment. Basil was sealing the plastic bags that held his faeces and his urine. Basil detested going to the lavatories of Health Physics to perform, and he had the dispensation to provide his weekly samples wherever he chose. Basil rapped at the window. The tyre of his bicycle was punctured. He banged on the window and shouted.

He wanted Bissett to take his samples over to Health Physics, not too much to ask. But Bissett had his raincoat collar turned up past his ears and he hadn't heard. Basil watched in irritation as the Sierra pulled out of the parking area.

Colt wrote down what time Bissett hoped to reach Paddington station, told him at all costs to avoid being followed to the station.

There was the faint threshing of fear at his gut. He hated the fear. Colt wanted to be out, gone, beyond the reach of fear.

If she had not seen the E II R insignia on the Englishman's briefcase, the landlady might well have called the police. They were two filthy creatures. They tramped their mud across her hallway, across her breakfast room, up her stair carpet, and all over two of her bedrooms. The Englishman had given as his address, in her Registration Book, 'c/o Home Office, Queen Anne's Gate, London', and the American had written, 'c/o Embassy of the United States of America, Grosvenor Square, London'. Well, anyone can invent an address and there was mud all over their faces, on their hands and their clothes. *And* she hadn't lived in Warminster all her life that she couldn't recognize the smell on the waterproof jacket of the American. Mr Erlich *stank* of cordite. Well, obviously, they had been playing army games at the School of Infantry and Mr Erlich might have been the dirtiest American she'd ever seen, but his manners were lovely. And Mr Rutherford had paid a week's booking fee in advance, in cash.

Through the morning and the afternoon the landlady was alone in the guesthouse with the two sleeping men. Her usual guests, commercial representatives for the most part, would not be back until the time she served her early supper. The Englishman and the American had said they would not be eating in.

In the late afternoon, after she had taken her retriever for a walk, she went up the stairs with her plastic watering can to annoint her geraniums. She had seen the American, wearing only his boxer shorts, come out of the Englishman's room and carry a portable telephone through his own door.

It was her joy, her pleasure – her late husband used to call it her vice – to overhear the conversations of her guests.

'Jo, I can't. I just can't . . .'

The American's voice was surprisingly soft and wheedling for such a big man, she thought.

'. . . Jo, that is not reasonable. You want to go to Mombasa, great. I would like to go to Mombasa. You can, I can't. End of story . . .'

He was getting rather cross, and she didn't think she liked this Jo. Here was poor Mr Erlich up to his ears in mud and guns . . .

'Jo, don't go on, don't get goddam scratchy. The beginning and the end of it is that I cannot break away. No, no chance. Heh, Jo, did you hear what happened to the All Stars in Naples? . . . That's too bad, that's dreadful . . . Listen, it is not my choice. Get that into your head . . . You want to go to Mombasa, you go to Mombasa. That is not fair, Jo . . . Yes, you send me a postcard, you do just that . . .'

She glided to the far end of the landing. She heard the American come out of his room, walk to the Englishman's door.

They were gone at dusk, as the first of her evening guests checked in. The Englishman was brusque, as he had been that morning. The American was subdued, poor thing, and seemed to jump about two feet when the dog came out of her sitting room and sniffed his trousers. She had never been outside the United Kingdom for a holiday, but she thought it must be disappointing for the American not to be able to take time off from his work to accompany his Jo to Mombasa. On the other hand, she always said, life was not complete without disappointment, and she had learned in long widowhood that this was true.

The Chairman of the Joint Intelligence Committee was not liked by the Director General. He had taken early retirement from the bench of the Court of Appeal. He was typically aloof, the

Director General thought, an arrogant, high-climbing judge, and utterly out of place in the corridors of Curzon Street.

'I will brief the Prime Minister. You may rely on me.'

'It is my department that is affected.'

'Not exclusively true. Century have a position too, as you have yours. Better that a third party should speak for both of you.'

'This could get very *messy*, and frankly, we're not happy.'

'It will just be the Prime Minister's ear, no others. I assure you that there will not be fallout, provided that your people perform satisfactorily.'

'You're taking a huge risk . . .'

The former judge, a man accustomed to the craven subservience of his court, bridled. 'I don't think the Prime Minister will see it that way. I don't. We want this creature dead. Unhappily, we want our relations with that country intact. And we want the Americans off our backs. This course satisfies all three requirements. Where is the difficulty?'

'Shooting people, even Englishmen who inconveniently kill Americans, is the difficulty.'

'Quite honestly you astonish me. I had not expected to find anyone in your position squeamish.'

The Director General said flatly, 'It's in motion, if he's still in the country and if he can be reached then it will happen.'

'First class . . . You have my support, and you will have the Prime Minister's, provided your people do the job properly.'

'You ask a lot of my people . . .'

'Quite right, too. And you won't be able to convince me that you have never carried out an execution. I imagine your department is full of experienced people. I certainly hope so.'

When the Director General left, it was as much as he could do to stop himself slamming the Chairman's door. He walked out into Whitehall from the Cabinet Office. He dismissed the car. He walked back to Curzon Street tailed by his bodyguard. He wanted to be alone, he wanted to think. He wanted to consider James Rutherford, junior in D Branch, on whose inexperienced shoulders so much had been laid. So much was asked of his people, of young Rutherford, and of the American whom he had not met and didn't want to know.

Colt stood beside the hotel room door because he knew where the camera was secreted inside the wardrobe, behind the fractionally opened door. He knew that the door of the wardrobe cut out all vision of him from the video camera.

Bissett had nearly kissed him when they had met at the end of the platform at Paddington station. He had pumped his hand, he had clung to his arm all the way across the concourse of the station and into the Great Western and across the hotel's lobby to the lift and the ride up to the room.

Colt listened.

He was behind Bissett.

There was the Military Attaché and the Assistant Military Attaché and Faud and Namir. It was their job to do the talking. Colt's job was to have brought Bissett, and to escort him away. That was the extent of his job. They'd put a drink down Bissett, and Colt had seen the nervousness of the man as he had held the glass in his two hands and still slurped it from the side of his mouth and down his shirt front. They had filled his glass again, and they had sat Bissett down and they had gone through the questionnaire. Like a job application ... not that Colt knew anything that mattered about job applications. They were pushing to be certain that they had the real thing. The questions and the answers roved over Colt's head. Place of work: H3 building ... Work to: Reuben Boll and Basil Curtis ... Current work: Implosion physics ... Specific current work: Development of cruise warhead as replacement for WE-177 bomb drop warhead. ... Detail of current work: Physical interaction of material elements at detonation macro-second ... Colt didn't know what was tritium, and he didn't know about beryllium. He had not heard of gallium. He had no concept of a fashioned plutonium sphere. He saw that confidence was restored in Bissett. Bissett had the message. These chaps hadn't a clue about tritium, either, or beryllium or deuteride-oxide or gallium or plutonium, they were just working to a brief that had come in code off the teleprinters. Bissett's confidence was growing because even he could fathom that the questions had been supplied to them. Bissett was the swot at school with all the answers. Bissett blossomed.

The Military Attaché left the room. He carried away with him the question papers and the answers that Bissett had supplied. Bissett was asked by the Assistant Military Attaché if he would please to be patient. Namir fed him another drink. There were no canapés this time.

Bissett was talking too much, like the drink had got to him and like his self-importance had overcome the fear. He was asking all the questions. Where would he live? What would be the work area? Who would his working colleagues be?

They seemed to take it in turns to give him the bullshit. He would live in the finest accommodation, fitted with the best European appliances. His work area would be the most modern and sophisticated that money could build. His colleagues would be the finest scientists who had come from all over the world to join the team that had very many distinguished achievements to its credit already and would welcome the arrival of Dr Bissett. The Assistant Military Attaché, Faud and Namir, soaped the bastard, and all the time they flattered him. They had Frederick Bissett eating out of their hands, and the drink flowed. After an hour the Military Attaché returned.

He stood stiffly in front of Bissett, and he shook the pathetic bastard's hand.

'We are sincerely honoured.'

The glasses were raised. Colt could see the flush of pleasure spewing on Bissett's face. Not Colt's problem, not if Bissett wanted to go and bury himself in Iraq when he didn't have to.

'You will be a most valued member of our scientific community . . .'

Colt said, 'Sooner rather than later. We have not offered Dr Bissett any opportunity to tell you that he has been under the scrutiny of the Security Service, and that he was interrogated yesterday morning. It would be advisable to move him fast.'

Bissett gabbled his explanation. There was the anxiety on their faces.

Colt said, 'We just lift him out, before the net closes.'

Bissett was just the package. He was left to his drink, and his embarrassment. Around him they talked flight times, schedules. He had been propositioned, he had accepted, he was no longer the centre of attention.

The Military Attaché said, 'Tomorrow night, we can hold the aircraft.'

Colt said, 'He works tomorrow, perfectly normally. He leaves work. I'll pick him up, get him to Heathrow.'

The Military Attaché nodded. 'Tomorrow night.'

Bissett cut through both of them, his head was shaking, his finger jabbing. 'Hold on a minute. You're forgetting . . . I mean, well, my family . . . arrangements have to be . . .'

The Military Attaché said, 'You tell no one, Dr Bissett. You make no arrangements. You have the normal day.'

'But I can't just . . . My wife, she has to . . .'

He supposed that it was where all such things ended up. A grubby little man with too much drink and not enough food in his stomach standing and whingeing his confusion in a hotel bedroom. No time now for flattery, no time to make arrangements, to talk the wife round. And way too far down the road to back off.

Colt said, 'If you don't do as you're *asked*, Dr Bissett, you'll go down for twenty years.'

In his unlit office, the cold bristling through the opened window, the Swede heard snatches of the conversation.

'. . . He could be better, he could be worse.'

'He wants to come, Dr Tariq . . . Wants to, surely that is important?'

'He is not a senior man, but then senior men are buried with administration . . . You have done me well, Colonel.'

'It is the privilege of all of us to serve the Revolutionary Command Council.'

'The putting together of a team is a delicate affair. This man is not, in himself, important. But to the overall performance of the team he is quite vital.'

His fingers, in the darkness, were clumsy on the dials of the receiver. He could almost hear the slow turning of the spools.

'My people say he is very impressive, a good man . . .'

He had the left side of the headset clamped on the ear, he had the right side behind the ear. With his left ear he heard the talk, as best he could. With his right ear he listened for any footstep in the corridor. Each slow minute was the worst, each last minute was torture. With his handkerchief he mopped at the sweat gathering on his forehead. They wanted more, and he had as yet so little. He heard the jangle of a telephone in his left ear. Then only the drone of an air conditioner. Then in his left ear the Colonel's report. 'He's coming. It is confirmed. Dr Bissett is coming tomorrow night. We will hold a plane, if necessary; he will be on the flight from London tomorrow night.'

'You are to be congratulated, Colonel.'

'There has been an unexpected difficulty with Bissett's security, Dr Tariq. That is why he must leave at once.'

'You would not lose him, Colonel?'

'The hands on him, Dr Tariq, they are excellent hands . . .'

The Swede gulped at the air. So worn down by the late evening vigil. He gulped at the air, and his sigh sang his relief. He had what they wanted of him. Feverishly he dismantled the rifle microphone, and the receiver, and the aerial. He reached between the slats of the blind and drew his window slowly shut.

Fifteen minutes after the Colonel had reported to the Director of the Atomic Energy Commission that Frederick Bissett would travel from London to Baghdad the following evening, the Swede walked from his workplace to his small bungalow. The tall, shambling, blond-haired figure was familiar to all the

275

guards who patrolled the area between the offices and laboratories and the accommodation area. He was not challenged and
he was not searched.

'This is just dumb, James.'

'Wouldn't have thought a hero from the Bureau would have
noticed a drop of rain, a little breeze . . .'

'Notice? I can't even notice the face of my wristwatch.'

'It's eight minutes to two o'clock.'

'That's all you know. I reckon your watch got drowned an
hour ago. It feels more like time to go back to bed to me.'

The wind crowed in the treetops and the rain fell steadily. For
a long time neither spoke, nor moved. Only watched. Once,
twice, the bedroom lights came on. And the second time Rutherford watched the old man go down the staircase and the kitchen
light went on and when he went back upstairs the kitchen light
stayed on.

Erlich suddenly said, 'I rang my girl this afternoon. She's with
CBS in Rome. Sorry, but you're paying for the call . . .'

'If we do all that's expected of us, young Buffalo, I don't
suppose they'll kick up much of a fuss.'

'She wanted me to go to Ruane, tell him that I needed a vacation, get myself down to Mombasa. I mean, that is just idiotic.
Wasn't even friendly when I said I was tied up here. Do you
know what I'll do when this business is over? I'll go into the
mountains. My mom is up in the mountains. Got a hardware
store and a diner with my stepfather. Do a bit of walking, bit of
shooting, never read a paper, put the television in the garbage.'

'They all say that. It's impossible . . . Heh.'

'We haven't gone on vacation together in months . . .'

'Heh, Bill.'

'Never her fault when she can't synchronize with me, always
my fault when I'm working and she's free. That's women . . .'

'Bill, *shut up* . . .'

Erlich stared out into the night. The rain was on his nose and
in his eyes. And the kids going all the way down to Naples and

having the game scratched because it rained. Can't have been rain like this. He saw the car headlights coming slowly, then almost to a stop. He saw the lights swing and they caught at the big trees. Erlich rose to the crouch on his knees.

'Got me, Bill?'

'Got you.'

'We struck lucky, Bill?'

'Right.'

Erlich drew the Smith and Wesson, .38 calibre, from his waist holster. He checked it, he could do that by feel in the darkness. A clean bill for the Smith and Wesson.

'You OK, Bill?'

'Never been better.'

They left the tree line. They came out into the force of the wind and the teeth of the rain. They started walking. Down the long field sloping to the Manor House. Lights coming on downstairs in the big building. They walked to the first hedgerow. They trotted to the second briar and thorn line.

'You got him, Bill.'

'Damn right.'

Both of them running, both sprinting through the mud to the Manor House ahead, to the target man.

15

'You'll deal with the dog?'
'I'll do the dog,' Rutherford said.

They were at the wall of the vegetable garden. Rutherford showed his watch; on the luminous dials it was twenty-five past two. He didn't know why Rutherford had to show him the time of night. He clipped the revolver back into its holster. Rutherford made a stirrup with his hands and Erlich slid a boot into them. Rutherford heaved, levered Erlich up. It was an old wall, and the mortar came away as Erlich steadied himself on the top. He reached down, took Rutherford's hand and dragged him up. They were both on top of the wall and bent low.

'You ready, Bill?'
'As I'll ever be.'

He turned and took Rutherford's outstretched hand and lowered himself down a carpet of ivy to the ground. Rutherford was beside him, crouching, in a second. He unholstered his revolver and Rutherford motioned him to follow. Rutherford was a pace ahead of him when they reached the kitchen door. He was flattened against the wall beside the door with his Smith and Wesson up close to his ear. His hand was tight on the revolver handle. His breath came in great controlled surges. His heart was going like a hammer and he thought that if the wind hadn't roared through the trees around the house the dog would surely have been alerted by now. Rutherford's hand was on the door handle.

'Locked?'
'We'll try the front . . .'
'Where he came in.'

Again Rutherford was in front. First they withdrew twenty yards into the kitchen garden and then looped along the back of the house, past old flowerpots, past an overturned wheelbarrow. They stepped through the loose coil of a watering hose. They came up the side of the house, along a narrow path. He was at Rutherford's shoulder, as if it were important to him to be close to the Englishman. They were at the corner of the house. He thought that the front light's bulb, the light above the front door, must have blown, because the front door was in darkness. There was a small car parked near to the door, but it was outside the crescent beam thrown by the skylight above the door. And across the lawn beyond the gravel there was a narrow shaft of light where it pierced poorly drawn curtains upstairs.

'Upstairs . . . ?'

'Where his mother is.'

Rutherford turned the doorknob. The door eased a fraction of an inch. Rutherford was looking at him. It was his choice. There was the dead weight of the Smith and Wesson in his hand. He could go inside fast, he could leave Rutherford to handle the dog, he could finish it. Rutherford was waiting on him. His choice, because he had the weapon. He could feel the shake in his hands and the hard panted breathing in his lungs. He knew his breathing was too hard, too fast. He held his breath, on his terms and in his time he let the breath hiss from his lips. That was what they taught on the StressFire course. That was what they taught when the student was going into Condition Black. One more time. Hard in . . . and wait . . . slowly out. Then he drove his shoulder into Rutherford. He push-punched the front door open.

He was on his way.

He was going.

He was committed to shooting Colt, to killing Colt.

Across the hallway, the bloody great animal seemed to fly at him off the wall. Erlich ducked, the loose carpet scudded from under his feet. There was the moment he stumbled. He caught at the end of the bannister rail for his balance. He was at the bottom step of the staircase. Behind him he heard the first barked shout of the dog, from the kitchen. He went fast up the stairs, stamping his feet for speed. He could see the blood pool in the rain where Harry Lawrence had fallen. He pulled himself with his free hand on the bannister round the corner halfway up the stairs. He could see the pale and hollow cheeks of Harry Lawrence on the stretcher in the Athens mortuary. He hit the top of the staircase. There was the door ajar, with the light behind it, ahead of him. The dog was making pandemonium, blocked at the bottom of the stairs by Rutherford.

He went in fast and crouched and turning.

'Safety' off. Isosceles stances. Finger hooked beside the trigger guard. His arms were out to their limit, his body was bent forward, slight angle. His legs were loose, not locked, so he could turn right, turn left. His eyeline was over the sights.

He saw the man beside the window. He saw the woman sitting in the chair beside the bed. He saw the woman, frail shape, eyes shut, lying propped by pillows on the bed.

Holy God . . .

Christ, no . . .

He saw the man, Major Tuck, guest at the Reform Club, father of Colt, stare at him, unable in shock to speak.

He saw the woman, dressed like a nurse, rising from her chair, and her fury had bitten at the plumpness of her face.

'Who are you?' The snarl of the woman's voice.

'Where's Colt?'

'I'll have you know there's a patient in this house.'

'Colt came, his car.'

'Nonsense . . . Put that ridiculous thing down. It's my car, and I came alone.'

Holy God, Christ, no . . . He saw that the woman in the bed was conscious, gazing at him in horror, perhaps in disappointment, her mouth fallen open, her eyes searching past him. He eased the hammer of the Smith and Wesson down. His thumb flicked the Safety upwards.

'Where you come from, don't you have any respect for the sick? Go at once, and go quietly.'

He didn't apologize. He had nothing to say. He turned and he went out through the door. He closed the door behind him. He came back down the stairs, stepping carefully in the wet mud footprints of his ascent. He thought he might faint. He steadied himself on the bannister rail. Rutherford was at the bottom of the stairs with a walking stick clamped into the back of the mouth of the dog and holding tight at the animal's collar.

Erlich walked past him out through the front door into the howling night.

That it was his last night in his own country had not at all disturbed him.

He had taken Bissett back to his train, his arm hugging his shoulders. Bissett had slurred his thanks. He had stood by the train's window until it had gathered speed, and he had seen that Bissett's eyes had followed him as far as it was possible to see him. He had gone back to the room in the Great Western Hotel, and he had taken a glass of mineral water with the men from the Embassy, and they had made their plans for the following day. They couldn't do without him, Colt thought, but it was obviously as much as they could tolerate, having to work with him. His association with the Colonel bewildered them even as it discomfited them.

The house was dark when he came back. He had gone up the stairs to his room as quietly as when he had climbed the stairs in Bissett's house, and he did not think he had wakened the couple and their baby.

It was his last night in England, and he had not cared to think that thought. He had tried to free himself from the thought of his mother and her bedroom that had become a sickroom, and from the thought of his father and the long, cold days of his vigil, and from the thought of Fran and her freedom and her love and her big dog and her snaring wires. Colt had torn the thoughts from his mind because they were a danger to him.

His country was his mother and his father and his Fran, but he had turned his back on them. It would have weakened him if he had told Fran that he was hers, that he would come back, by Christ, some time, to his Fran. Might have told her, but he would have to have told himself first and he couldn't sap himself with such a thought.

Colt slept. The hard outline of the Ruger pistol under his pillow did not trouble his sleep.

At daybreak, the Swede drove the fast straight road that cut across the rich land between the great waterways of the Euphrates and the Tigris. Behind him was modern Iraq, the Atomic Energy Commission headquarters at Tuwaithah and the sprawl of the al-Qaqa military industrial complex further south near al-Hillah where the rocket fuel was manufactured that would launch the Condor intermediate-range missile. And behind him was the ancient site of Babylon, where a thousand Sudanese labourers had worked all weathers for three years to recreate the citadel of Nebuchadnezzar.

It was an hour's run, the journey to Baghdad.

He saw the first giant-sized portraits of the smiling Chairman of the Revolutionary Command Council, and the streets were choked by the early traffic. His routine was that he went first to the coffee shop of the Ishtar Sheraton, to leave his car there for the kids to clean before he walked across the Jumhuriyah Bridge. He ignored his usual route into the city, along Fourteenth July Street. He turned left onto Imam Musa, into the slow crawl amongst the lorries and the cars that pushed towards Al Kadhim Street, and the new Post Office.

He waved his identity card at the Ministry policeman, he was gestured on.

Bissett drove through the Falcon Gate at the normal time, the same cars around him that were there every morning. It was what they had said to him, a normal day, his last day.

But already he was the stranger. He drove down Third Avenue, seeing F and B areas as a stranger would, and the great grey box building that housed the laser equipment and then the four high-rise chimneys and then the bulk of the A area and then the colossus that was A90.

He no longer belonged.

Today he did not care whether A90 would come into service two years late or three years late. It did not matter to him whether the fourth Trident submarine were cancelled, whether the new cruise-launched missile to replace the WE-177 bomb ever reached development and manufacture.

He saw the H3 building as a stranger would have seen it. It was no longer his place of work, no longer his second home.

If it had not been for the confidence he felt in the young man, then he would never have dared, he told himself, to come back, to play this last act, as a normal day. He showed his identity card again. He carried his raincoat and his brief-case, with his sandwiches and his thermos, into H3. He smiled at Carol, he nodded to Wayne, he acknowledged the chiming greetings of the Clerical Assistants. Basil came in behind him, shivering from the cold, peeling the bicycle clips from his ankles. Basil had never spoken up for him, and Basil's word could have turned the scale for his promotion. Carol and the Clerical Assistants had only ever paid him token respect. Wayne sneered at him. He was a stranger to them all, he had been for years.

'Ah, Frederick . . .'

'Yes, Reuben?'

Boll, all bustling self-importance, came into the outer office. 'Tomorrow, listen, very boring, but will you attend the SPSO/ SPEO meeting?'

'I don't . . .'

'No problem, Frederick, they won't eat you. I'll have gone and Basil's much too busy. Just go and take a note, see they don't decide anything stupid. It's in A45/3, at nine-fifteen. You can do that for me?'

'Of course.'

'Good man.'

Of course he would agree to attend but the Senior Principal Scientific Officers and the Senior Principal Engineering Officers would have to manage without him because he would be in Baghdad.

'Excellent, glad I caught you . . . Goodbye, everybody.'

'Goodbye,' Bissett said, and he shook Boll's hand. 'Send us a postcard.'

He went to his room.

It was to be a normal day, just that. He switched on his terminal and gave the screen time to warm. Just another day, the stranger's last day.

It was the time that Sara liked least at home.

It was the time after he had gone to work, and she was back from dropping the boys at school. The beds needed making, the boys' washing was on their bedroom floor, the breakfast things were still on the table. She made a mug of instant. She sat at the kitchen table. She had the radio playing a phone-in.

Drunk again, that's what he had been, and practically midnight when he had come home. She had been awake, of course, because she had reached the stage when she had wondered how much longer before she phoned the police, or started to ring round the hospitals. He had said that he had been late at work – she knew by now, surely, that he couldn't bring papers out – and that he had stopped off in the bar at Boundary Hall. But, he never worked late, and he never went to Boundary Hall, and the first and last time when he had drunk too much had been at Debbie's party when he had been in the corner, all evening, with the young man in jeans.

It was the morning that she should have been at Debbie's. Her head was bent in her confusion, and the beds went unmade and the washing undone, and the plates were still in the sink. She had come upstairs, broken off from getting the boys' lunches ready, and he had been in their bedroom still. She had stood in the door, and he hadn't known she was behind him. She had watched as he put into a suitcase the suit that he had taken to

284

New Mexico, the nearest thing he had to a summer suit. She had seen him open the second to bottom drawer of his chest and take out his summer shirts, and put these in the case, and the case back on top of the wardrobe.

The confusion boiled in her head, that Frederick should seem suddenly to have snapped, after the business with the police, the pressure, obviously, of his work, weeks of not hardly talking to her at all, now this odd business of taking the boys to school, taking them swimming, playing games with them. Was he saying goodbye? It was as if he had been standing in the door – just as she was this morning – watching her on Debbie's bed with Justin. It couldn't be so, but she felt weak with the sense of having destroyed her home, maybe even driven Frederick out of his wits, certainly put the happiness of her children at risk by that one massive lapse, that great tumbling fall from grace. It was not enough. Not lapse enough. She craved a longer, more clarifying fall. Not enough, Justin, not by any means enough, and yet Frederick was on the point of abandoning her. Well, by heavens, he wasn't going without a word. He wasn't going to creep out without an explanation. She would wait until the weekend. She would wait no longer. She stirred herself to the routine of her day, her normal day.

As he walked up the wide steps he saw none of them. His right hand was on the tape spool in his jacket pocket. His left hand was in his trouser pocket, fingering the key to the post-restante box.

It was the start of the day's business in the new Post Office. Noisy queues, shoving and pushing, had already formed. There were Egyptians thronging at the counters to send the registered mail to Cairo and Alexandria and Ismailia with the small amounts of foreign currency permitted. There were Kuwaitis in line for use of the international telephone cubicles. There were Sudanese shouting for the telegram forms. There were the men who stood by the walls and who watched.

The Swede never went directly to the box. He followed a procedure given him by his Control. He must always join the longest queue first. He should join the queue, shuffle forward, gradually turn this way and that, he should see everybody in the cavernous hall of the Post Office. He should never hurry when he came to deliver and to receive from the post-restante box.

He always played the game to himself that the Chairman of the Revolutionary Command Council was Sven . . . Each of the techno-mercenaries at Tuwaithah had their own name for the Chairman of Revolutionary Command Council. He was Gunther, he was Pierre, he was Giancarlo . . . They lived in a world whose every wall had ears, where servants were never trusted. They could talk openly of Gunther and Pierre and Giancarlo and Sven. It was the Swede's little joke to himself, that Sven had a new set of teeth.

The portrait poster was above the benches that were set the length of the wall opposite the post-restante boxes. The Chairman wore the heavily decorated uniform of a paratrooper and round his head was a *quaffiya*. His smile would have brightened a dark night. Sven's new dentures . . . There were two men sitting under the poster, and he saw that their eyes never left the post-restante boxes. The Swede's hope died a little. He stayed in the queue and he studied again every wall and corner of the interior of the Post Office. It was ten minutes before he was sure. There were four more men, other than the two men who sat on the bench under Sven's broad smile, whose attention was fixed upon the post-restante boxes.

He was the only Westerner so far as he could see. He was tall, he was blond, he was pale-skinned. It was impossible that he had not been noticed. He had seen the men who watched the post-restante boxes, he could not know how many men watched him.

The sane thing to have done would have been to bend to his shoelace, retie it, put the tape on the floor, kick it away amongst the sandalled feet, then to walk out. But the tape was too precious to him . . .

He made a gesture of impatience, he looked long and hard at his watch, he shrugged. He spun on his heel.

He tried to stop himself from running. The fear surged in him. When he was close to the wide door of the new Post Office, he saw a man reach into his jacket pocket and take out a personal radio. Then he ran.

The bright sunshine, the white concrete dust of the unfinished pavement, blinded him when he came to the bottom of the steps outside. Fear pulsed inside him.

His eyes cleared, he blinked hard. He saw the two cars on the far side of Al Kadhim Street, and there were men in each car. He ran.

The bungalow that had been home for the two Italians driven from Tuwaithah by an unexploded letter bomb was vacant.

Under the direction of the housing manager, a workforce of women was brought that day to the bungalow. It was cleaned, it was scrubbed and it was polished. The rugs were taken outside and beaten. The kitchen was washed from ceiling to floor. New linen was put on the bed in the main bedroom. Fresh flowers were arranged in vases. In the refrigerator were put a dozen cans of beer and two bottles of French white wine and food and cartons of milk.

The Baghdad flight, it was announced, was delayed indefinitely for operational reasons.

A few of the passengers, the foreigners, the ones not already checked in and through to the duty-free lounges, vented their anger at the Iraqi Airlines desk. They were the minority. The majority accepted the situation and the free meal vouchers without complaint.

He was in the heart of the ancient round city. He ran, in fear of his life, in the narrow and dark-shadowed streets.

He had seen them last when he had stopped, panting, in the shelter of a black awning, and he had seen them quartering,

287

searching, and a car drawing up at a crossing, disgorging others to join the hunt fifty, perhaps sixty yards back down the alleyway.

The alley he was in was not wide enough for a car and down the middle of it ran a sewer carrying grey-blue slime. There were narrow and obscure openings, their steel shutters lifted, where melons and limes and tomatoes were sold, where the metalworkers plied their trade, where iced lemon juice was poured into dull dirty glasses. These he passed, sometimes running, sometimes where the press of people was too thick walking briskly, his head down, as if on some anxious errand. Overhead, filtering the sunlight from the blond gold of his hair, were lines of hanging washing. This was the quarter of the poor, the crippled and the bereaved of the war, those ignored now by the regime. No voice was raised to point him out to the dark-suited men of the Department of Public Security. The Swede was a fugitive. He would not be helped and he would not be hindered.

It began to settle in the Swede's mind that even if he discarded the tape he could not ever return to Tuwaithah. He had been watched too long in the Post Office. He would be recognized. Even if he could reach his car, he would be trapped at a roadblock. The gathering fear seemed to tug at his legs. The Swede stopped at a stall, bought a black woollen hat and an old khaki greatcoat. He paid for them three times what he would have if he had stopped to barter. He pulled the hat hard over his ears and shrugged into the coat as he left the labyrinthine alleys of the ancient round city. He prayed to his northern, foreign God for the preservation of his life and the safety of his tape.

It was as he crossed in front of the Central Railway Station forecourt that he saw the man with the personal radio that he had seen in the Post Office. He saw him and turned briskly away. Too late. He had been recognized in his khaki greatcoat and his black cap. The man started towards him and then seemed to think better of it. The Swede could hear him shouting into his radio as he ducked into the crowd and began running as soon as he turned the first corner.

*   *   *

288

Bissett could imagine it, his situation in three months, six months, when he would be desperate for access to his computer terminal in H3/2. But he did not consider taking any material with him. He would take with him only what he could carry in his head.

For his first week there he would sit alone and write out every small item from his memory. Maybe it would take him two or three weeks. When he had cleared his memory, then he would be free to set up his research unit and to plan the administration of his department.

All morning he funnelled his screen across past papers, past calculations, past reports.

And then he had concentrated on what they liked in H area to call the 'physics of the extreme'. Workings and statistics and figures tumbling up in front of his eyes. The heart core of a warhead detonation, reactions at 100,000,000° Centigrade, pressures of 20,000,000 atmospheres. Work from the lasers, studies from the 'Viper' fast-pulse reactor that could produce peak power of 20,000 megawatts . . . So much for him to learn again, so little time before the end of his last day. It was like examination revision, which he had done so well at Leeds. Working quietly, methodically, at speed, he could nevertheless reflect that it would be peculiar to communicate his work to a stranger. It wasn't a question of morality, just that it would be peculiar. But then he had never worked anywhere except at the Establishment, had never had strangers as colleagues, never since he had joined.

He consigned to memory the charts, as much as he could, that dictated beryllium weights, how the tritium material could be melded in minute particles into the molten shape of ochre-coloured plutonium cores, the thickness of the highly enriched uranium that formed the concentric circle around the pluto-nium inside the quality gold crust.

There was a knock at his door.

He felt the frozen stampede of guilt. He swivelled to face the door.

Carol, hugging a plastic bucket to her waist. 'Sorry to disturb you, Dr Bissett. You remember the electrician who had the accident on the A90 site, poor love, there's a collection for him.'

He reached into his trouser pocket.

'He's paralysed, Dr Bissett.'

He abandoned his trouser pocket. He had four ten pound notes in his wallet, no five pound notes. He took a ten pound note and dropped it into the bucket, amongst the pound coins and the fifty pence pieces. 'Oh, that's lovely, Dr Bissett, that's really nice of you. So sorry to have disturbed you. Thanks ever so much.' He saw the way that Carol eyed him, like he'd cracked her image of him. It would be all round H3 that Dr Bissett had put ten pounds in her bucket.

He came out of the lavatory, in the early afternoon, not looking where he was going, struggling to retain the figures, graph shapes, calculation analyses, swimming in his mind, and walked straight into Basil.

They grabbed at each other. Bissett's hands had hold of the weathered old sinew of Basil's arms below the short sleeves of his shirt. Typical of Basil, late November and dressed as he would have been in June. They made their apologies. Bissett wanted to be away, but Basil would have none of it.

'Your paper, very good. Reuben showed it me. I thought it was first class.'

Bissett blushed. 'Thanks.'

'And you may as well know that I have written to the Security Officer to tell him that, in my opinion, you were treated outrageously over that business with the files. I have asked that my letter, my assessment of you, should go on your file.'

His voice was a whisper. 'That's kind of you, Basil. Thank you very much.'

'Absolutely nothing, Frederick.'

He broke away. He went back to his office. He closed the door behind him. The stranger in the brotherhood. He bent once more to the last hours at his screen. Just a normal day, his last.

*   *   *

The Swede saw the flag fluttering high above the rich foliage of the trees, and at the same instant he heard the shriek of the siren. There was a wide road for him to cross to get to the gates. There was a car thrashing forward through the traffic towards him.

There were guards in front of the gates, local militia.

He would not have thought that he could run further, faster.

He thought the siren was to warn the guards.

The Swede stumbled out into the road. The traffic parted for him. He had in his sights only the gate, and piercing his ears was the rant of the closing siren. Lead legs, empty lungs, darting crazily through the buses and vans and cars. And then he jerked to his left to avoid a cyclist and the cyclist hit him and he fell. Because he fell, crashing knees and hands and chest onto the road, the Peugot with the siren missed him. From the road, from the hot tarmacadam, he had looked up, the split moment, and he had seen the face of the driver career past him before the car skidded into the cyclist.

He heard a scream and the brake squeal. He pushed himself up. He ran again.

He staggered off the road, across the wide footpath.

There was the shouting behind him. He saw the gaping curiosity, the bewilderment, on the faces of the militia men at the gate. One militia man tried half-heartedly to block him with his rifle barrel.

He ran on. He ran through the gate. Behind him now the siren and the shouting. He ran up the driveway. He ran through the wide doorway that was the entrance to the principal building of the British Embassy.

He no longer heard the shouting, he no longer heard the siren. He lay on the floor in front of the reception desk, and a voice said, 'Good afternoon, sir, how can I be of help to you?'

He jerked up from his bed. Rutherford was in the doorway, and he carried his handset telephone, and it looked to Erlich as if Rutherford's world had fallen in.

Rutherford said, 'They pulled us out.'

'I don't have to ask why . . . ?'

'His father's raised Curzon Street and burned senior ears.'

Erlich said bitterly, 'Your people have one hell of an idea of consistent thinking.'

'I can't argue with that.'

'Are they reared on milk and rice? Haven't they balls when the going's tough?'

'My orders are crystal clear. Get back to my desk and bring you with me. It's probably not worth saying . . . I'm sorry.'

He might as well have gone to Mombasa. He didn't think that he would see Jo again, and it had been for nothing, his virtuous stuff about duty. What did she think? That he could drop everything and head for the African sunshine? He might as well leave tonight before they threw the book at him. Probably Ruane had a transcript of Major Tuck's observations on his desk even now, with an acid memo from Mr Barker about the great astonishment of Her Majesty's Government that Mr Erlich should be armed with a Smith and Wesson rather than the regulation-issue kitchen knife.

'We should have checked the car.'

'We should have stayed in the office and moved paper round, what every other bastard does.'

Erlich said, 'If he'd been there, I'd have shot him.'

'Can you be ready to leave in ten minutes?'

'I'll be ready.'

They came in turn to see the Swede in a small room in the heart of the Embassy building. There were no windows and the walls were reinforced, soundproofed. He had drunk five glasses of fresh orange juice.

The first to see him had been the Information Attaché, who swept up all the loose strands of the Embassy's work, and he had gone away to deliver his report. There was a military policeman outside the door. The military policeman, on the Diplomatic List, was the Ambassador's driver, and he carried a Browning automatic pistol in a shoulder holster under his blazer jacket.

After the Information Attaché, the Swede was interviewed briefly by the Assistant Military Attaché, and then again left alone. From the Ambassador's first-floor windows, the deployment of militia and plain-clothes men from the Department of Public Security was clearly visible.

Next in line was the Chargé, the Ambassador's deputy. The Swede was not to know that while he sat with the Chargé a telephone call had been received from the Foreign Ministry demanding the immediate expulsion from the protection of diplomatic premises of a dangerous foreign criminal. The Chargé left him, and the military policeman gave him some English newspapers and offered him the choice of tea or coffee. There was some difficulty with the supply of fresh oranges. The Swede gratefully accepted tea. Sometimes he heard muffled talk in the corridor outside, but it was too distorted for him to understand.

The fourth man who came was different.

He was athletically thin. He had the old-fashioned razored moustache trim on his upper lip, and he wore rumpled jeans and a loose knit cardigan and a check shirt without a tie. The fourth man was what he had waited for. The Swede stood.

'You don't need my name, and I don't need yours,' the Station Officer said. 'Best you come with me, my office is quiet, and there's a tape recorder.'

'Good night, Carol.' She looked up. Her console was already under its plastic sheet, and she was filing.

'Good night, Dr Bissett . . . and thanks for the ten pounds, that was great . . . are you coming in first in the morning, or going straight to that meeting?'

'Er, I'll decide tomorrow. Good night, then.'

He had left his office as he had always left it. He had left behind the photograph of Sara and the photograph of Adam and Frank. He carried in his briefcase only his empty sandwich box and his empty vacuum flask.

He drove away from H area.

He passed Basil, pedalling into the wind along Third Avenue.

He passed the towering outline of the building that was A90.

He passed Wayne, waiting at the bus stop for the transport to the main gate and the coach park, and he remembered that he had heard Wayne say that his Mini had gearbox trouble.

He passed the signposts to the A area, the plutonium factory, where in the morning there was to be a meeting in A45/3 of Senior Principal Scientific Officers and Senior Principal Engineering Officers. He passed Carol's husband, the lathe operator, hurrying towards the canteen area and the bar where he would have managed three pints before his better half dragged him out and home. He passed the molehill mounds that were the testing and manufacturing areas for the chemists who worked with explosives.

Bissett came to the Falcon Gate. He showed his identity card, and was waved through. He braked at the junction with the Burghfield Common to Kingsclere road. He waited for the traffic to allow him to enter the flow . . . and further on turned left in Mulfords Hill.

The end of a normal day.

The tape recorder was switched off.

For a few moments, in silence, the Station Officer continued his scrawled longhand précis of what he had heard.

'Thank you . . . Perhaps you wouldn't mind just waiting in here for a little while . . . oh, and don't go near the windows.'

He let himself out of his office. He told the military policeman that no one, not even the Ambassador, was to go through that door without his permission. He waited long enough to see the military policeman draw his automatic pistol from his shoulder holster and hold it behind his buttocks.

The Station Officer walked swiftly down the corridor, down the stairs, down into the basement to the Embassy's communications area.

*   *   *

'You're not serious . . . ?'

'It's my chance.'

'You can't possibly expect me to take you seriously.'

'Can't you just once listen . . . ?'

It had started downstairs. Bissett had begun it in the kitchen. He had followed Sara into the kitchen, left the children in front of the television, and he had put his arms round Sara's waist as she had been stirring the soup on the hob, and he had told her. Too late to wonder if there might have been a better time. It could have been after the party at those awful friends of hers, or when he had first gone to London, or after the meeting in Strat-field Mortimer, or last night. Could have been any of them, but it hadn't been, it had been in the kitchen with the digital clock throwing up the numbers, telling him that the minutes were rushing away from them.

It had started in the kitchen. It had gone on through the hall-way, where the boys could hear her, and up the stairs, and into their bedroom.

She could have listened to him.

She could have been quiet at least, and supportive.

She could have let him finish his explanation.

Too much to ask for . . .

'Even by your standards it is pretty *fucking* stupid.'

'The boys will hear you . . .'

'Don't you involve my boys.'

'They're my sons, too, Sara.'

'They won't want to know you. Nobody'll want to know you, you silly little man . . .'

She had been his wife for twelve years. They didn't row, they didn't argue. When there was friction between them, then each in their own way sulked and withdrew inside a barricaded shell. Never voices raised, because the children would hear. She had never abused him like this before, never.

'I have the opportunity to better myself. I am going to head a department. It's the equivalent, really, of a chair at a major university.'

'Oh, I get it.' She laughed out loud. There was her shrill laughter beating around his ears. 'It's your vanity . . .'

'It's for you, don't you see that? It's for you and our children.'

'Count us out, it's *your* ego trip, you go on your bloody own.'

He tried to touch her. She recoiled.

'There will be a lovely house for you, a good school for the boys . . .'

'God, are you dim . . . What am I? I am the wife of a traitor. What are the boys? They are the children of a traitor . . . Have you the least understanding of what you have done?'

He bridled at her. 'Waste of my time, trying to get support from you.'

'Support for what? For giving away this country's secrets . . . If you've any sense, any, you'll just walk away from it.'

'No.'

'For the love of anything sensible.'

'I'm committed.'

'Committed, to whom? Why not to me, to the boys?'

'To Colt.'

'Christ . . . who the fuck is Colt?'

'You met him, at the party you took me to . . .'

He saw her reaction. As if the contempt went from her. As if the passion had left her.

'. . . Who you left me talking to. Where were you . . . ?'

'I was . . .'

'Where were you?'

'I went . . .'

'Where were you?'

'Our host was laying me, like you never did. So it felt bloody fucking good.'

It was as if he had not heard her. His voice was a whisper. 'I'm flying to Baghdad this evening. Everything I have done is for you. I am going to be collected in thirty-five minutes. Everything has been for you and for the boys. We can make a new life, a happy and prosperous life for our family. We owe them nothing here . . .'

'At the very least, you owe them loyalty.'

He shouted. He felt the tear in his throat from the scream of his voice. 'Who ever showed me loyalty? None of them there gave loyalty to me . . . Sara, when did you show me loyalty?'

'Frederick, stop this insanity at once!'

'I'm going.'

'Without any of us.'

'You're not there every day. You're not sneered at by Reuben Boll, patronized by Basil Curtis. You're not passed over. You're not humiliated.'

'Without any of us, Frederick. Make up your mind.'

'Please, please . . .'

'Are you going?'

He did not know how to touch her, how to win her. 'I'll send you money . . . Yes.'

She went to the wardrobe. She opened the wardrobe door. She threw his suits, his jackets, his trousers, his ties, onto the floor at his feet. She lifted the suitcase from the top of the wardrobe and hurled it onto his clothes. She went to the chest of drawers. She opened each of the drawers and threw his socks, shirts, vests, underpants, handkerchiefs, pullovers. All onto the heap, all burying the suitcase.

'When you go out of our lives . . .'

'Sara, please, it is only for you.'

She said, 'When you go out of our lives, don't *ever* try to come back.'

Alone in their bedroom he packed his suitcase, and he waited for the ring at the front-door bell.

His briefcase was on his chair, and his carefully furled umbrella was on the desk, and he was just putting on his coat. Martins winced at the ring of his telephone.

'It's Mid-East Desk. Meeting, please, soonest.'

The Sniper said, 'It's not actually convenient. I was just on my way home.'

'Sorry about that, but there's a storm blowing . . . soonest, please. Main meeting room.'

*   *   *

Hobbes knocked once and came fast into Dickie Barker's office.

'Apologies, Mr Barker, it's Mid-East Desk at Century. They would like you down there . . .'

'I've got far more important . . .'

'The car will be at the front for you in one minute. I gather it's Frederick Bissett.'

16

The boys were still in the sitting room and the television was still on. Sara stood with her back to the door and she had said that she would fight to prevent him getting in, yes, even to say goodbye to his boys. He had never once in their marriage lifted a hand against Sara.

The bell rang. From where he was in the kitchen he could see past her. He could see the shape of Colt through the misted glass of the front door.

He lifted his suitcase. He had taken only the clothes that he thought were his best. The remainder lay scattered on the floor of the bedroom. Books would have been too cumbersome. He could order all the books he needed. He had taken the ribbon-tied packet of his parents' letters, he had taken her photograph and the photograph of the boys that had been on his chest of drawers.

He carried the suitcase towards her. There was only the sound of the television from behind the door that she guarded. He thought the boys would be cowering together on the settee, too frightened by all that they had overheard to move or to call out. Sara's face was turned away from him. She was white-faced, and the muscles at her throat were taut. He saw that her fists were tensed. He would not have dared to try to fight his way past her. He wondered how she had been, how she had looked, when she was on the bed with Debbie Pink's husband. 'No, no . . .'

'Please, Sara, please . . .'

'Get out of our lives.'

'I'll write to you.'

'They'll go straight into the bin.'

No, no, just what she had said to taunt him. No, no, not true.

'It's only for you, Sara.'

'Get out.'

It was where the fight died in him. He was still carrying the suitcase, weighed down by it. It was the moment when he wavered. He could turn round. He could go upstairs with the suitcase and he could unpack it. He could put the photographs back on the chest beside the bed. He could come down the stairs and he could hold Sara and he could go into the sitting room and he could hug his boys. The moment when the doubt bit at him . . .

The bell rang again.

She went forward. She never looked at him. She opened the door.

'Good evening, Mrs Bissett. Good evening, Dr Bissett.'

He saw the face of Colt. Colt smiled. He thought that he would have followed Colt to Hell.

Colt said, 'We should be on the move, Dr Bissett.'

He went out through the front door.

He turned.

Sara looked through him, as if he wasn't there. There was the sound of the television. He strained for the voices of his children, and he did not hear them.

'I'll write.'

She closed the door in his face.

There was the scrape of the bolt being pushed across.

Colt said, 'Let me take your suitcase, Dr Bissett.'

Hobbes was in exalted company.

The Deputy Director General, second man at Century House, was at the head of the table. To his right were his own men, Head of Mid-East Desk, Head of Israel Desk, Head of Syria/Jordan/Iraq Desk. To the left of the Deputy Director General were Dickie Barker, with Hobbes behind him, and a Chief Inspector from Special Branch.

It had come out of the blue, which was why they were all

talking to each other, none of them listening. It had come out of the wide blue yonder, and stunned them.

Twice, the Deputy Director General had attempted to get the meeting to order. Hobbes saw that the Head of Israel Desk, nice-looking youngster, was obviously under pressure, and disliking hearing anything to do with the Head of Syria/Jordan/Iraq Desk, Percy Martins.

The Deputy Director General rapped the table with his metal spectacle case. Hit the table, so it would need a French polisher, until he'd closed down the talk.

'Order, please, quiet, *please.*'

And he achieved what he wished, at the expense of a dented moonscape on the table's surface.

'What I was saying . . .'

'Don't, Percy.'

'I'll be heard, this is an Israeli source, and the Israeli effort is always to stir confusion . . .'

'You've said that twice, thank you, Percy, that's enough. Gentlemen, please, order and quiet. We have very little time, certainly not another minute to waste . . . A compromised Israeli agent has beached himself at our Embassy in Baghdad. Iraq is either extremely discomfited or putting on a remarkably good likeness. The Embassy is besieged, APCs, machine guns trained on every door and window. The local evaluation is that the agent is straight, that the tape he's handed over is genuine. Voices on the tape are the Director of Atomic Energy Commission at Tuwaithah and an unidentified Colonel of Intelligence. The tape tells us, in unmistakable terms – we have the transcript, here it is, it says – "He's coming. It is confirmed. Dr Bissett is coming tomorrow night. We will hold a plane, if necessary; he will be on the flight from London tomorrow night." What is our response to be? Gentlemen?'

'I repeat,' Martins said. 'Anything with the Israeli tag on it you treat with extreme caution.'

The Head of Israel Desk said, 'If it's a matter of evaluating intelligence that comes courtesy of Tel Aviv or courtesy of Baghdad, then . . .'

'Right now Baghdad happens to be, if you didn't know it, of extreme importance to us.'

The Deputy Director General snapped. 'Will you kindly stop bickering, Percy, and, gentlemen, your responses, *please.*'

'I am only trying to prevent us falling flat on our faces.'

'Percy, *shut up.*'

Pretty encouraging, Hobbes thought. The men way above his lowly level were bigger fools than the doorman at Curzon Street.

'Hold the Iraqi flight out, indefinitely,' the Chief Inspector from Special Branch said.

Martins shook his head, as if he were with children. 'Oh dear me, no. Diplomatic repercussions would be incalculable.'

'No need for that, I think,' said the Head of Israel Desk. 'Just take Bissett before he boards. Lift him quietly at the airport, before he checks in. Who will be the wiser?'

Martins said, 'Oh, super. Bissett will be the one wearing the tracksuit marked FRED. BISSETT. No one will have the least difficulty recognizing him, but just in case he's forgotten to bring his tracksuit, we have his photograph I expect, and his description? I'll tell you what, though, you park even two or three reasonably intelligent plain-clothes men on the Iraq Airlines desk, you'll frighten him off. You'll lose him. That's assuming he hasn't gone abroad already disguised as an air hostess. And where are you going to look for him then, eh?'

The Chief Inspector shrugged. 'Someone could be brought up from Aldermaston . . . ?'

Martins grimaced. 'Thursday evening, you must be joking. They've all gone home. Have we reached the Security Officer? Have we a list of Bissett's colleagues, their home addresses? Have we cars standing by to run them to Heathrow? Has Frederick Bissett's home been checked? Has it? This plane that is supposedly delayed, do we know its provisional departure time? I think, Deputy Director General, we need some answers, to these and a number of other questions, before we can settle our best course of action.'

Head of Israel Desk said, 'Mr Martins will be able to help us with the Iraqi Embassy staff who will no doubt be at Heathrow. It will be instructive to know which of them has been dealing with Bissett.'

Hobbes felt the jab of Barker's elbow into his ribcage. He didn't need to be told. Hobbes ducked away, into the outer office.

The Security Officer at Atomic Weapons Establishment . . .

Personnel at Atomic Weapons Establishment . . .

The Security Officer's home at Silchester . . .

Bissett's home . . .

Newbury exchange Supervisor . . .

British Airport Authority . . .

If he was ever sacked, he would do a bomb in telesales, top the bonus bill.

He went back inside. He could see it as clear as daylight.

It was Martins now who waved his hand for quiet, gestured to Hobbes to speak.

Hobbes said, 'The Security Officer at AWE left his office an hour ago, not expected back, the Night Duty Security Officer has been there only seven weeks and has never set eyes on Bissett. Bissett works at H3 building. Personnel is not sufficiently manned to provide a list of Bissett's immediate colleagues until the morning. At his home, the Security Officer's wife says her husband is at a committee meeting of the Reading Modelling Society. I have somebody looking into that, but I'm not confident we'll have a number within the time at our disposal. The exchange says that Bissett's receiver has been taken off the hook. Heathrow says the Iraqi Airlines flight has filed for permission to take off an hour and a half from now.'

'Well done . . .' Martins leaned back in his chair. 'That would tell me that they are expecting Bissett at the airport in three quarters of an hour, give or take ten minutes, and we will have no one there who has an idea what he looks like . . . Or are we suggesting that we should tannoy him?'

'Excuse me . . .'

'Yes, Mr Hobbes?'

'One of my people interviewed Bissett this week.'

'Come again?'

'We were called in by the Security Officer and we interviewed him.'

'I think we should hear about this, don't you, Deputy Director-General? Yes? Pray, Mr Hobbes, enlighten us.' Martins had leaned forward. A big man, intimidating. The force of his gaze was on Hobbes.

'Bissett was stopped at the Main Gate; taking files out; we have been running some checks . . .'

'I'm sorry. This side of the table, we're all sorry. The Security Service goes down to AWE, checks out a man, and now we're told . . .'

Hobbes saw Barker's face spin at him. God, the hatred.

Hobbes said, 'The enquiry is not completed.'

'It would be in – how do you say? – in an ongoing situation, is that it, Mr Hobbes?' The fat at Martins's chin wobbled in silent mirth, the eyes of the Chief Inspector searched the ceiling.

'The man who interviewed him, he should be on his way back into London right now. He'll be on the motorway coming in from the west. I can divert him.'

Martins clapped his hands. 'Done. Finished. Thank you, Mr Hobbes. Plain-clothes at Heathrow, all in mufti. Spot him, pull him out. No fuss, no bother, no incident . . . if that suits Mr Barker?'

Barker nodded. The Deputy Director General, relief writ large on his features, dragged his papers together. 'Thank you gentlemen. Thank you, Percy . . . a decisive contribution.'

'Experience, that's all that counts. I've said it before, Deputy Director General, but I do think some of the younger people would profit from a spell in the field.'

Nobody at the table caught the Sniper's eye, none of them could bear to.

* * *

'Rutherford . . . ?'

'Hello, Rutherford speaking.'

'It's Hobbes.'

'Yes.'

'This is not secure, right?'

'Correct.'

Rutherford had the portable telephone to his ear, but Erlich could hear what was said at the other end.

'Where are you?'

'On the M3, approaching Junction 2, that's the M25.'

'How long to Heathrow?'

'Traffic's heavy, I don't know . . . could be fifteen minutes, might be more.'

'Make it fifteen. Like there's no tomorrow. And there may not be.'

'What's the problem?'

'Your friend from Berkshire? Are you with me?'

'Don't tell me. The top man has rung the boss and complained about my manners.'

'Not the top man, you halfwit. The chappie with the briefcase . . .'

'*He* complained? Jesus . . .'

'*Listen*, you bloody fool. Don't say anything, just put your foot on the floor and listen. He's going walkabout, going out on that flight tonight . . .'

'What flight?'

'Nebuchadnezzar's place, got it?'

'No, I haven't got it. I went to a school, not a seminary.'

'Baghdad,' Erlich said softly.

'OK I got it,' said Rutherford.

'You're the only one that I can get there in time who knows what he looks like. Terminal Three. State airline desk. Got it? Due to check in any time from now. Should be one or two friendly faces dotted about. Just don't let go of the man with the briefcase until help arrives. You still got the handcuffs?'

'My American buddy used them on a nursing sister last night,

305

but I managed to get them back. He's wearing them now. They're rather fetching. I'm on the M25 now. How many people with the briefcase?'

'No means of knowing. But I don't think he'll be expecting you. Try and do this one right. How's the traffic?'

'It's moving. The whole world is going at about sixty-five. If this keeps up, we'll be there in ten, twelve minutes.'

'Fine. Good luck. And Rutherford, one last thing: all of this is out of bounds to your American friend.'

'He won't like that one bit . . .'

'Correction,' said Erlich, 'he *doesn't* like it one bit, but he doesn't give a fuck one way or the other.'

'What's that?' Hobbes said.

'It's Erlich,' Rutherford said. 'He says he'll do exactly what he's told and won't ask any questions.'

'Good enough. Time for you to put both hands on the wheel. 'Bye.'

Rutherford was pushing the Astra bumper to bumper with a BMW 7 series. White knuckles on the wheel, he cursed the BMW and a Granada that didn't want to pull over out of the way of a toy car. They knifed the traffic lanes, came across out of the fast lane to a cacophony of horns behind them.

'So? What's the hurry?' Erlich said.

'I'm going to trust you,' Rutherford said, 'because I may need you. When I was away these last few days, I was checking out a man at our Atomic Weapons place. He'd been caught trying to take some paperwork home. Obviously, I should have bunged him in the slammer, but I gave him the benefit of the doubt, at least until the Colt business was over and done with, and fuck me if the conniving little prick isn't booked onto a flight to Baghdad. He's due at the airport any minute.'

'How can I help?'

'I'm wondering. The chief problem at the airport is traffic wardens. The most useful thing you could do would be to hand-cuff the first two traffic wardens you see to the wheel. That should keep it pinned down for a while, and there's no prospect of your doing it with charm. On the other hand – *will you get the fuck out of my way? Jesus!*' Rutherford carved his way out of the traffic streams, off the roundabout onto the airport boundary road. Erlich was thinking that at least it took his mind off Jo in Mombasa, or pretty Penny Rutherford. Another five minutes of this and he wasn't going to see either of them again. One more American official murdered by an Englishman. He shut his eyes and the vision of the marmoreal Harry Lawrence in the mortuary lodged in his mind.

'No. I'd like you with me,' Rutherford grinned. 'There's bound to be an escort, probably armed. If they can't get the runner onto the plane, they'll try and spirit him away. I'll nail the man. You put your delicate paws on all his luggage and beat off all comers. Try and exercise a little British discretion. My people wouldn't want any sort of *fuss*. Understood?'

'Got you.'

Erlich had not seen Rutherford with the blood pulsing before. He thought he liked what he saw.

The lights of the new Babylon, the high-rise concrete apartment blocks, the huge modern hotels, the status symbols of the new regime, danced off the eddying current of the great, slow-moving Tigris and backlit the ancient domes of the mosques and the timeless narrow outlines of the minarets in the ancient city.

The area around the Embassy and its ten acres of gardens had been sealed. The armoured personnel carriers were in shadow, half hidden under the low foliage of the evergreen trees. Those who lived nearby had retreated behind their gates. The Military Attaché estimated that there were a minimum of two hundred troops surrounding the compound. The locally employed staff had been sent home, and told not to return until the matter, the difficulty, had been sorted out. The French had been advised, with regret, that the British Embassy could not be represented at their reception that evening.

The Ambassador met the Colonel at the front door.

'No, sir, in view of the intolerable situation around this mission, you will not come one step further.'

'You are harbouring, Excellency, a criminal.'

'Am I?'

'An enemy of the State.'

'And what is his name?'

The Ambassador could see the Colonel hesitate and wondered what orders the man had given to the half-dozen heavily armed soldiers who flanked him. Probably just to look as dangerous and nasty as possible but not to shoot anyone. This show of force was as hollow as it was menacing. But that this plausible thug was agitated was not in doubt. Angry, but for the moment, stymied.

'Well, come on, what's the name of this enemy of the State?'

'He ran in here.'

'Who did? People run in and out of here the whole time.'

'You know who came.'

'How can I identify this criminal if you do not even know his name?'

'You take a risk with me . . .'

'Kindly remember where you are, my good fellow. You are not in the Abu Ghraib gaol now, you are outside Her Britannic Majesty's legation. Come back in the morning, with a name, with a charge sheet to tell me what crimes have been committed by this anonymous felon, and perhaps we can talk again.'

He stared into the eyes of the Colonel. He thought of the agent of the Mossad, prostrate with exhaustion, pretty much at the end of his tether, closeted with his Station Officer, and he remembered all that he had read and been told of espionage agents who had been abused into confession and strangled from the gallows.

He stared at the Colonel and saw the eyes of a killer, the eyes of a torturer.

He said easily, 'And if you come back tomorrow with a clear idea of what you are looking for, and the proper documents, of course, you will be so good as to leave your thugs outside the Embassy's grounds. Good night to you.'

He walked back inside. He heard the door close behind him. He heard the bolts pushed to. He saw the merciless smile of his Military Attaché, formerly commanding officer of the 2nd Battalion, the Parachute Regiment. He did not trust himself at that moment to walk steadily up the stairs, in full view of his staff, to compose his next signals to London.

It was not original, but it was heartfelt. 'God, what a bloody awful country,' he said. 'Could someone get me a gin and tonic?'

On the last part of the journey to the airport, Bissett had been quiet. Colt supposed that he would be thinking of what he had left behind in Lilac Gardens, the woman who wouldn't kiss him goodbye, the kids he hadn't even mentioned tonight.

Colt talked to him because he felt sorry for the man.

As he swung the car off the main road and into the airport's feeder lanes, he said, 'Heh, Dr Bissett, will you know me when you're there, when you're the big shot?'

'God, Colt, how could you? 'Course I'll remember you . . .'

'No, no. You'll be in a big car, you'll have a driver. You won't want to know a scruff-bum like me.'

It was meant lightly. It was just talk, just Colt trying to lift the man.

But in Bissett's answer there was an urgent, passionate sincerity.

'I'll always know you, Colt, for what you've done for me. I am going to tell them that they owe my being there to you. I will make certain that you are properly rewarded . . .'

'You'll be in your posh compound, Dr Bissett. You'll have taken off.'

'Whatever you need, I'll get for you.'

'I don't need anything.'

'Whatever, a car, a house of your own, anything . . .'

Colt drove into the long-term car park. He meandered towards a free space. The roar of aircraft engines spilled into the car.

'Everybody has to want *something*.'

'Not me, Dr Bissett.'

'Possessions, what you have, what's important to you.'

'I own nothing . . .'

'Nothing?'

'. . . only myself.'

Colt smiled, like it wasn't important. Of course, it would be important to Bissett because he had walked out on his job, and his oath, and his country, and his wife and boys, for $175,000 per annum. But that wasn't Colt's problem, never had been, and he wasn't about to make it his problem now. He reached across Bissett and opened the glove compartment, and took out the Ruger. He saw that Bissett gaped.

'What's that . . . ?'

'It's a close-quarters handgun, Dr Bissett.'

'What for, for heaven's sake?'

'For our protection, yours and mine.'

'But I didn't know . . .'

Colt climbed out of the car. He locked his door. He watched as Bissett locked the passenger door. He had the Ruger in the plastic bag. He would palm the bag to Namir or Faud at the check-in desk.

He took Bissett's suitcase, and his own grip, and he led the way towards the stop where the buses for the terminals pulled in.

'I'm sorry, Major Tuck. The whole village will be sorry.'

He wanted her out of the room. He wanted to be alone with his wife, the last time. The District Nurse had slipped her fingers over the sunken eyes. At long last, it was over.

She was at the door. She said that she would go down to the kitchen and make a pot of tea. The wind beat around the rafter beams, surged under the eaves of the roof.

'Colt . . . ?'

'Gone, clear of them, but he was here when she needed him.'

'That's something to be thankful for, Major.'

'We can be more thankful that he's gone.'

There had been the shots in the night. Obviously not for Colt, otherwise that American wouldn't have come back. The District Nurse had told him that old Brennie's dog had been killed, didn't know where nor how.

She left him alone in the quiet of the room. He heard her going down the staircase.

He yearned for his son. But Colt was gone, and he could only pray, as he knelt by his wife's bedside, holding her hand, through his tears, for the boy's safety.

As they hurtled out of the tunnel under the runway into the airport, Rutherford said, 'Once more into the breach, old thing, and this time, as you heard the man say, let's do it right.' Outside Terminal Three, they pulled into a space vacated by a taxi and jumped out.

'We'll walk, Bill. When we get inside, we may even saunter. You look so like a policeman you had better stay a pace or two behind. We don't want to attract attention. Look up, will you?'

'I'll catch up. And James – good luck.'

He was thinking of Frederick Bissett. He walked towards the doors of the terminal. He was thinking of the hunted and frightened little man who had sat across the room from him, Bissett of H area, and he remembered the explosion of emotion. Wife trouble, eh?

Erlich was at his shoulder.

He went inside.

He saw Namir fifty paces away through the shifting mêlée of travellers on the concourse. He saw Namir stop and turn and look around him and over the sea of heads, as if he was searching for the familiar face.

Bissett was right against him, as if he were frightened of being left behind.

Colt said, 'Our friends are here, Dr Bissett, all in place.'

*　　*　　*

311

Erlich walked behind Rutherford, edging their way through queues of passengers and their luggage. There was a pier of airline stands between them and the Iraqi Airlines desk.

Rutherford was looking to his right. Rutherford was looking so goddam hard that he walked right into an Asian who must have had everything he owned piled on a baggage trolley. Man and trolley rocked and stayed upright. He'd never seen it, because he was looking right . . . Erlich looked right. A taller man, back to them, fair hair cut short. A shorter man facing them, dark curly hair, heavy spectacles, and looking like he was scared shitless of flying. Two men, tall and short, would have been Arabic. The two Arabic men seemed to be reassuring him.

He heard Rutherford say, 'That's him, the little one with the black hair and glasses. See the minders? Watch my back, will you?'

Rutherford going forward.

Passengers, airline people, cleaners, parting a way for him. Rutherford starting to charge, Erlich jogging to stay with him.

Rutherford shouted, 'Dr Bissett . . .'

Didn't have to shout. What had he shouted for? Just had to keep walking . . .

'Stand where you are, Dr Bissett . . .'

It was then he saw Colt. He saw what the kid in the Kifisia suburb had described, and what the police photograph had shown, and what Hannah Worthington had said she had seen. He saw Colt.

The shorter guy, curly hair and heavy spectacles, he'd frozen. The two Arabs, they'd melted. One yell, one warning shout and they were gone.

Colt was bigger than he had expected him to be. More solid in his shoulders, and more presence than he had thought of him as having. He saw a tanned and open face with the anger starting to work on it, the killer of Harry Lawrence. Words in his head, flywheel fast. The shorter guy, dark curly hair and heavy spectacles, was reaching for Colt, as if that was his only salvation, and Colt had his fist in a plastic bag. And people walking round them and wheeling trolleys past them, and kissing goodbye. Erlich saw Colt's gun, saw it snaking out, coming up. Lethal Assault in fucking Progress. He saw a .22 calibre pistol with silencer.

He had seen Colt . . .

Rutherford going forward. Colt going left. Colt taking the shorter guy with him.

He had the revolver out of his hip holster.

Safety off. Isosceles stance. Isosceles stance and Turret One, because Colt was coming across his aim, and dragging the guy with him.

Deep in his lungs, hard down in his gut, Erlich yelled.

'Freeze, FBI, freeze.'

Pandemonium around him. Men and women and children throwing themselves at the shined floor of the concourse.

The gun was coming up, Colt's gun. Colt had five paces to the pier. Colt would have gained the cover of the pier if he hadn't been dragging and heaving on the arm of the man with the dark curly hair.

And Rutherford was charging for the guy, like there wasn't a gun. And Rutherford was . . .

Erlich fired.

And Rutherford was going . . .

Erlich fired.

And Rutherford was going down onto the concourse . . .

Erlich fired.

Rutherford was on his face on the shined flooring . . . Couldn't see Colt, couldn't see the guy with the dark curly hair. Could only see the corner of the pier and the cringing people.

He had fired three shots, like they had taught him. He heard nothing, and they had lectured him that his ears, in Condition Black, would be dead to the screaming and bawling around him. He could see the mouths of the people, prised open for screaming, shouting.

He saw the heave of Rutherford's shoulders, and then the stillness.

He saw the first trickle, blood, slip from Rutherford's mouth.

17

It was strange ground for Colt. He had been through the airport, right, but as a passenger. He had never reconnoitred Heathrow. He gave way to his instinct.

He stampeded out through the electronic glass doors, forcing Bissett in front of him.

He had learned many times the lesson of flight. Distance was critical. The first minute of flight was vital, the first five minutes were more vital, the first thirty minutes were the most vital, and the key was distance.

Into the first minute . . . Following his instinct and praying for luck. He had no plan. He came out of the glass doors and into the cold night air. If the American was there, then the other one must have been there too. And if those two were there, then there must have been others, and chances were, they were armed as well. Christ, they'd been blown all ends up. Anyway, they must all have been shattered by the accident. And who was it, the man who was shot, who had been shouting for Bissett? As he heaved Bissett along, across the taxi lane, there was a double-decker bus cruising past the terminal. He ran round the front of the bus, clinging to Bissett's elbow, and the Ruger was already gouging in the small of his back, tucked safe in the belt of his trousers. He jumped for the open platform at the tail of the bus, and he levered the dead weight of Bissett after him, his feet scrabbling on the tarmac. The man was ash-pale. There would have been a conductor on the bus, must have been upstairs taking money. There were eyes on them. Colt smiled, like he and his friend were just happy to have caught the bus. The bus turned away from the terminal and headed for the tunnel. There was his luck. He had his hand under Bissett's armpit, because he thought that if he let go his grip the man might spill down into the aisle of the bus.

Into the first five minutes, into the gaudy orange light of the tunnel. At the roundabout at the end of the tunnel, as they emerged, Colt saw the first police cars, the first blue revolving lights, and the first sirens, bullocking into the traffic heading into the tunnel and towards the terminals. Colt saw that the bus swung up the hill, going left. Distance was what counted. Past the fire station . . . He saw, out through the grimed windows of the bus, the lines of the cars in the long-term parks. The conductor was halfway down the steps to the upper deck of the bus. They were in traffic themselves, dawdling at perhaps ten miles an hour. Colt was on the tail platform. He didn't tell Bissett. If he had told Bissett then the man might have hung on to something. He had hold of Bissett's arm again, and he jumped, and he took Bissett with him. Colt was on his feet, and Bissett was sprawled, half on the pavement and half in the road, and there was a squeal as the car following the bus braked to miss them. They ran what would have been close to 150 yards, and all the time they ran Bissett was failing. They went into the long-term park.

Into the first thirty minutes . . . The car started. Colt had Bissett in the passenger seat. He told Bissett to take off his coat, shove it under the seat, and to help Colt get out of his own jacket, and put that too under the seat. He screamed the car towards the exit. Colt took a hand off the wheel and snatched Bissett's spectacles from his face. He paid off the attendant. He muttered something about leaving his passport at home, that was how he explained his coming out with only eighteen minutes on his ticket. There were more blue lights and sirens on the perimeter road, and a police van passed them, going up the wrong side, and then swerved at the airport exit filter to go half across the road. It was six, seven, minutes since they had crashed out of the terminal. Colt was calm. They would have had descriptions, clothes and hair and spectacles. Nothing he could do about the hair, and he had done something about the coat colours and something about Bissett's glasses. He saw the faces of the two young policemen who had been in the blocking van, and they didn't seem to know what they were at, and the one had his ear cocked to his radio on the collar of his tunic. Another minute, another ninety seconds, and they might not have made it out. He was waved through.

He didn't speak.

He wriggled in his seat, he moved his hip so that he could get the pistol clear of his belt, and he laid it on his lap. He heard the deep and sharp panting of Bissett's breath, like the man was in crisis.

Colt was hammering for the motorway.

If Erlich had gone faster, straight off, then he might have made it through before the block was set on the east side perimeter road, close to Cargo.

He had not gone fast. Rutherford was dead. Christ Almighty. Dead before he could reach him, and hold his wrist, his head. Oh no, oh Jesus . . . !

What he remembered of the terminal, coming out of the concourse, hitting the night air, with the big red bus pulling away in front of him, was that sound had slipped back to his ears. He had heard a woman screaming, and he had realized that he still held the Smith and Wesson in his hand, and he had heard the placid voice of the announcer over the speakers. There had been a woman screaming, and he had holstered the revolver, and the announcer had been giving the final call, last call, for passengers on Gulf Airlines to Bahrain and Dubai. He could remember that . . . He had shot a colleague, and they were calling for the passengers for the flight to Bahrain and Dubai.

He might have been delayed more, but he showed the uniformed officers his FBII/D. They wouldn't have gotten round yet to worrying about Bill Erlich. Their airwaves would have been full of Colt's description, and what Bissett was wearing . . . but he wasn't ready for thinking yet, because of the great sickness in his stomach and the numbness in his mind.

316

He was William David Erlich, born May 7th, 1958, son of Gerry Erlich and Marianne (Erlich) Mason, Special Agent of the Federal Bureau of Investigation, and he could not think straighter than a bent dime because he had shot James Rutherford dead, and he had left him. So little of it that he could remember, the shooting. The blurred and fast-moving shape of Colt, 'Freeze,' he remembered his roar and the lumbering outline of Rutherford . . .

He had shot pretty Penny Rutherford's man. He knew where he had to go.

What Hobbes saw first was the slack line of the white tape.

He elbowed his way through the quiet and staring crowds. He flashed his card, he bent under the tape. They had not even covered the body. He was careful to avoid the three cartridge cases on the concourse floor. A dozen long strides from the body was a suitcase and a grip bag.

He asked what had happened.

He was told. There were two Branch men who had seen it all and had the crack of emotion in their voices.

The taller Branch man said, 'It was really difficult, it was so quick. We didn't know what we were looking for until your man yelled out. There was a fair-haired man, mid-twenties. He had a smaller man with him, glasses and raincoat. They were with two Arabs . . .'

The other Branch man said, 'They were close to the check-in on the delayed Iraqi flight. They train you for this, it's nothing like the training when it happens . . .'

'Oh, God . . .' the taller Branch man mouthed.

'Spit it out,' Hobbes demanded.

'We had a photograph, about two weeks back. Iraqi link. English . . .'

'Oh, Christ,' the shorter Branch man seemed to crumple. 'There's an all airport and all port watch.'

Venom in Hobbes's voice. 'Just go back to bloody sleep. He's Colin Olivier Louis Tuck.'

Hobbes walked away from them. The equation was sharp in his mind. Colt was with the Iraqis, Bissett was with the Iraqis, Colt was with Bissett. And wasn't life simple, when the light shone on it?

Hobbes spoke fast over his personal radio. He repeated himself, three, four times, so that at Curzon Street there was no possibility of a further mistake. Colt was the name he gave over and over again, and the flat statement that he would strangle those responsible, himself and with his own hands, if every airport and every ferry port in Great Britain did not have the photograph of Colt out on the Emigration Desk.

He went back to the Branch men.

Hobbes gave the taller of them the name of Dan Ruane and his office number.

'I want him here. I want him here immediately . . . God, what a shambles.'

He was told what was in place, where the blocks had been set. He was told it was twenty-nine minutes since the shooting. He was shown where the fair-haired man with the pistol, Colt, had fled, taking Bissett with him, through the concourse door. He was told that the American had followed him out, gone after them.

He stood a few paces from the body. He could hear Barker's 'We all get what we want, a good result' ringing in his ears. He wondered who Barker would send to break it to Rutherford's wife. There was a wife, because her photograph was in Rutherford's office. It would be a bastard of a job, telling the wife that probably no one from D Branch had met.

Hobbes knew precious little about firearms, but he matched the torn hole in the collar of Rutherford's jacket, and the two more holes in the centre of the back of the jacket, with the three cartridge cases that he had seen. It was what bloody well happened, wasn't it, when some bastard American was allowed to pretend he was on a backstreet in Chicago, and not in a crowded terminal at Heathrow.

*   *   *

318

It couldn't have been a nightmare from which he now awoke. No nightmare, because the crash of the firing was still in his ears, and the fleeting vision of the crouched marksman was still in his mind, and there was the tear in the knee of his trousers where he had fallen from the bus. Each time his fingers went back to the frayed edge of the material, to the bleeding, grazed knee, he knew, more certainly, that it was not a nightmare from which he could awake. They were off the motorway . . . He pieced it together in his memory, which was worse than a nightmare. Colt was talking with two of the men who had greeted him, who had both on each occasion been in the hotel at Paddington. Then he was ignored. There was some anxiety, something about the delay on the flight. And then his own name shouted. A man running towards him, and shouting his name. Colt's gun up, and Colt dragging him. The sight of the marksman going to the crouch with the handgun held out in front of his face. The other man shouting his name and running between them and the marksman, and the battering of the gun. He thought he had seen the running man fall. They had shot their own man . . .

Colt had brought the car off the motorway. They were past Crowthorne, past Bramshill. Close to Stratfield Saye where he and Sara had twice taken the boys to walk round the Wellington estate. Close to Stratfield Mortimer, where he had met Colt in the pub car park. He felt through the tear at the knee of his trousers, and his fingers were sticky from his own blood.

'Are you all right, Colt . . . ?'

'I'm in great shape.'

'What happened, Colt . . . ?'

He heard the hoarse, dry laugh. 'We got stuffed.'

'Who were they?'

'One was the Security Service, he got in the way of the one from the FBI, the one who yelled. They were waiting for us, Dr Bissett. That flight wasn't going anywhere because they knew we were travelling. You got me? We were set up.'

'No, not by me.'

'Not by you.'

'You don't think I betrayed it?'

'You didn't know the flight we were going on, you didn't know anything.'

He saw the young man's face. There was no panic, apparently no fear. Colt drove faster than he would have attempted on the smaller roads they now took.

'Are we together, Colt?'

'Have you a better idea, Dr Bissett?'

'Where are we going?'

The same dry-throat laugh of Colt. They were through Mattingley and Rotherwick, village roads, going south and west.

The car jolted through a pothole. It was the moment he remembered. The man who had been in the outer office of H3, sitting beside Carol's desk. The man who had come to see him. The man younger than himself . . . He remembered Rutherford, the man who had brought the stench of fear into his room, into H3/2.

'Colt, I *cannot* go back.'

'You go back, Dr Bissett, and it's to gaol till you die.'

He heard the reed whine of his own voice. 'Are you frightened, Colt?'

'When I have my back to the wall, when I have nowhere to run to, then I'll be frightened. Not before.'

Bissett shuddered. He had seen the crouched stance of a marksman. He had seen a gun aimed at him. It was worse than a nightmare because he could not go back, could not wake. He could go only where Colt ran.

His fingers played in the tear at the knee of his trousers, which was the stark living nightmare of his world.

'You take a rifle to a man like that,' Martins said. 'You give it to a professional. What you do not do is put such a matter into the hands of a bungling amateur.'

He rolled the brandy in the glass. He had helped himself twice while they had waited for Barker's return. The Deputy Director General nodded agreement.

Barker said, 'A rifle, no doubt a sniper's rifle, is your only policy, Percy. Can we put the old trophies back in mothballs, where they belong, and see if we can retrieve this appalling situation? I take it that that's what we are here to do. And just let me remind you: it's a situation brought about by your friends the Iraqis.'

There was a tired smile on Martins's face. He was the man who had sent a sniper beyond reach and beyond help into the Beqa'a Valley. His authority seemed unassailable.

Barker would have been back in Curzon Street not more than ten minutes before he had heard the news from Heathrow and Hobbes's report, been turned around, spun like a top, sent back to Century House.

Martins said, 'When the report goes to the Prime Minister, as most assuredly it will, I will be remarkably happy that it is beyond my remit to explain how the only firepower directed against a known terrorist, in a crowded and public place, was in the hands of a rather junior American, along for the ride.'

'A terrorist in the pay of your friends.'

'Please, gentlemen, please.'

'My advice, DDG, we maintain strictest silence on this matter. It may be fashionable in some circles to represent the Iraqis as just the refuse of the Middle East, but thankfully, we do not conduct our affairs on the say-so of Amnesty International. They have a stable regime in a turbulent area . . .'

Barker snarled, 'They send a murderer onto our streets, they suborn one of our nuclear scientists; they lay siege to our embassy in Baghdad – and all you want to do is to send them a basket of flowers. They are dangerous, these people. They are thieves and muggers on the grand scale. Unless a line is drawn and they are stopped on that line, they have the potential of causing catastrophe.'

'A pretty speech but hollow. In other words, they do what quite a lot of people do. Frankly, Dickie, I'd have expected a little more sophistication from someone in your position. Nevertheless, I want their gunman dealt with, and I want our scientist returned, and I want the siege on our embassy lifted, and I want a blanket over the whole wretched matter.'

'Well, we agree on that at least, and now, if you will excuse me, I have business to do, and I have a young widow to visit.' Barker pushed back his chair.

'You also have an American to find, before he does any more damage . . .' Martins drank deeply. 'Well, that's it then, DDG, and I'm glad you agree with me that this is a matter for the Prime Minister's desk . . .'

'I had to come, to tell you . . .'

Erlich stood in the hallway of the small house.

'. . . it was my gun, and I shot him . . .'

The door to the street was open behind him.

'. . . I had the target in the sights. I just didn't see him . . .'

Penny Rutherford stood in front of him. She would have been changing flowers in the sitting room when he had rung the bell. She was still holding the flowers, chrysanthemums, and they were dead.

'. . . he wouldn't have known anything, I promise you, no pain . . .'

She turned away from him. She walked the length of the hallway, and into the kitchen. He watched as she put the flowers into the garbage. He watched her, down the length of the little house that was her home.

'. . . I'll never forgive myself, Penny, I'm just so sorry.'

She turned and her voice was the clear-cut wind streaming from the storm's eye.

'All your crap about dedication, all your bloody *duty*, and what am I left with? You stupid, silly little man. He was mine, God, what else did I have? Go away, go away from me. Go back to your bloody kindergarten, where you came from, go back to your bloody guns and toys. Go somewhere where you can't hurt good people. Get *out*, I don't want you here. I don't want your *apologies*, for God's sake. Just *go*.'

He closed the door behind him.

Erlich drove away fast. There was only one place now he could head for.

Dan Ruane stood in the middle of the concourse. There were high white sheet-screens around the shooting scene. Rutherford's body was still there, but covered by a blanket. There was the fast flash of the photographer's bulb, Scene of Crime completing their work. The suitcase and the grip bag were now open. The clothes were being lifted out, checked, noted, piled. There were chalk circles round the three spent cartridge cases.

'We lost a brave and able young man because your cowboy didn't know what the hell he was doing . . .'

'Crap.'

'. . . and because he couldn't face the music, he ran.'

'You won't like it, Hobbes, but you're going to get them, home truths, stuffed up your gullet. The failure was yours. You moved nowhere on this. Every break you had, every lead, came from Bill Erlich. You sit in your goddam ivory towers, you think you matter in the world, whatever world. Erlich came here expecting action, expecting a good scene, and he got himself pissed on. Your resources are pathetic. Your work rate is pathetic. Your commitment, beside Bill Erlich's, well, it's laughable.'

The photographer with the flash camera on the tripod was watching him. The two detectives on their knees and taking the clothes from the suitcase and the grip bag were listening to him. The policeman with the chalk mess on his fingers eyed him. And Dan Ruane, the big man, didn't give a damn who listened.

Hobbes stood his ground. 'He ran away . . .'

'Say that again, and I'll put your teeth at the back of your throat.'

Hobbes stood his full height. 'Grow up, Ruane. This isn't the Wild West. Just tell me where you think he's gone.'

It might just be, just, that Erlich had one more chance, not more than one more chance. And it might just be, just, that if Erlich didn't take that chance then Dan Ruane would be on the flight out with him. One more chance, and that was stretching it, that was all Erlich had.

'He'll have gone where he reckons Colt's gone . . . Have you a better idea where he should have gone?'

'We have very little time, Dr Bissett.'

'Yes.'

'What we have going for us, and it's not a lot, is that with everything else that's queuing up, they take time to get their act in place.'

'Yes.'

'What I reckon is that the ferries are our best chance. You with me?'

'Which ferries?'

'Weymouth, Bridport down south, boat across to France. One of the night sailings. They'll take time to get their act in place, that's our best hope.'

'If you say so, Colt.'

They were past Salisbury. Colt drove into the lay-by beside the darkened windows of the shop. The village was called Bishopstone. It was a small place, tucked away from the great world in vast tracts of farmland. He had followed the side roads, as far as was possible, through the villages. He was safe among the villages and on the high-hedged lanes, because that was the country he knew. Bishopstone and Heathrow, they were not of the same world.

'We have to decide where we go from here,' Colt said.

'You make the decision.'

There was a quiet grimace on Colt's face. 'It's rather awkward . . . They'll give it back to you, of course, but I don't have enough money for the ferry tickets. Will you lend me what we need?'

'I've just small change.'

'You haven't . . . ?'

'I left my cheque book at home, for Sara . . . I doubt I've five pounds . . .'

'Jesus . . .'

Colt heard the cringe in Bissett's voice. 'I left my cheque card, too. I didn't think I'd need English money in Baghdad.'

Colt's eyes never left the road.

He drove on. Wild and lovely and lonely country, on from Bishopstone, and once he braked hard and threw Bissett forward, and he missed the big sow badger that treated the road as its own. At Broad Chalke, he found a telephone box that was not vandalized. He took coins from his pocket. He parked under trees, away from the lights near the telephone box and the bus stop.

She was out in the scullery, working to a hurricane lamp because the electricity had never been run into the damp stone extension of the kitchen.

The telephone rang.

Fran was good at it and old Vic, down at the pub, would take all the plucked pheasants she could bring to him.

She came out of the scullery, and the breast feathers were spilling off her arms and her chest, through the kitchen and through the small room where old Brennie grunted before the closed fire. The cottage was bitter quiet without Rocco's snore, without the jangle of his collar chain. She never knew whether it was real, him sleeping through the telephone's ringing. He said it was the war, the trench slits, sleeping in them and all, under the artillery at Monte Cassino.

She heard his voice. 'Thought you were gone, Colt.'

He said that he was in deep trouble.

'They going to get you, Colt?'

He said that a man had been shot, likely killed, because they were trying to get to him.

'What you wanting from me?'

He said that the boys would have money, Billy and Zap, Charlie and Kev, Dazzer and Zack, Johnny. He said that without money he was gone, and she should try old Vic. He said that he needed five hundred.

'I can't get that sort of money, Colt, not quick.'

He said that if he did not have the money, then he was gone. He said that he would be there in an hour, in the village, for the money. And they'd get it back, he'd see to that.

'They been here for you, Colt. You shouldn't be coming. They shot Rocco in the Top Spinney and they went into your house, Colt. They went into your mother's room with guns.'

He asked, were they in the village now.

'I been in all evening, I don't know whether they're back on Top Spinney.'

'One hour, and I'm sorry as hell about Rocco . . .' he said.

'Colt, you wouldn't have known, your mother died this evening.'

She heard in the telephone the sharp gasp of breath, and the purring when the line was cut.

Namir and Faud were seen arriving back at the Embassy. The time of their arrival was noted, they were photographed. The building was under observation by the Watchers from B Branch. All calls into and out of the Embassy were intercepted. The urgent summons for the Military Attaché to return to his office was picked up. A telex marked MOST URGENT – IMMEDIATE ACTION was sent to Government Communications Headquarters calling for exceptionally thorough monitoring of all frequencies used by the Embassy for transmissions to Baghdad. The first transmission from the Embassy was sent twenty-two minutes after the return of the Military Attaché.

In London there were no troops, no machine guns, no armoured personnel carriers, but the Iraqi Embassy was as effectively sealed as the British Embassy in Baghdad. B Branch Watchers were peeled off duty outside the Soviet Embassy, and the Syrian Embassy, away from the mosque that attracted the fundamentalist fringe in Holland Park, away from the Kilburn and Cricklewood pubs where the songs of Irish rebellion were sung. The Watchers gathered on the street corners near the building, and they sat in cars that were hazed with cigarette smoke. The building was surrounded, and a telephone call ensured that Faud's car, with one wheel on a double yellow line, was clamped.

It was not possible at that early stage in the operation to crack the code the Iraqis were using, but the volume of the radio traffic grew to an abnormally high level.

'We were betrayed.'

The Director had come from his dinner table. He had waved the Colonel to a seat, but the Colonel had preferred to stand, sensing that Dr Tariq had not understood what he had said.

'We were betrayed in London.'

'What . . . ? And Bissett . . . ?'

'They knew. It appears they would not have allowed our flight to leave. There was a shooting in the airport, at our airline's desk. There were security men there, waiting for Bissett.'

'He was shot? It is incredible.'

'It seems not. My information is that one of their policemen was the casualty. We have to assume that Bissett was arrested.'

'Betrayed . . .' It was as a bell that tolled in the Director's mind, the chime of disaster. He was the man responsible for Tuwaithah. He had the plutonium; he had the *yellow-cake* from which the highly enriched uranium could be produced; he had the hot cell boxes; he had the engineering expertise; he had the technicians; he had the chemists. He lacked so little. He had given undertakings to the Chairman of the Revolutionary Command Council. Dr Tariq felt the cold of the night around him.

'From within,' the Colonel said. 'It was why I telephoned you. It was simple deduction. The leakage had to be from inside. There was a European we chased. I needed to know who, today, was absent from his work, and the description of your man who was missing. My mistake was to have rushed to his safe haven before I telephoned you.'

The Colonel spoke of the tall, gangling scientist, with the pallor of northern Europe, with long fair hair. The man who had taken refuge in the British Embassy.

327

The Swede had been the guest of the Director at dinner, and he had brought back delicacies from Stockholm for the Director's table.

It was Dr Tariq himself, a quarter of an hour later, who found the rifle microphone stowed inside the tubular metal walking stick. He held the rifle microphone in his shaking hand. He looked into the face of the Colonel. He saw the mirror of his own fear. They were both no more than servants of a regime that ruled by the noose and the *accident* and the bullet from close quarters in the nape of the neck.

The act that Colt feared was remorselessly put into place. The description and photograph of Frederick Bissett were sent to every commercial airport in the country. The same were despatched to every ferry port. With the photograph and description went the order that if any official slipped their detail to the media then retribution would be savage. There was no wish to boast that a Senior Scientific Officer of the Atomic Weapons Establishment had been lost. Firearms were drawn from police armouries by selected and trained officers. And the last thing Dickie Barker did before he left to offer his condolences to the widow of James Rutherford was to order the despatch of a team of Special Branch marksmen and detectives trained in covert surveillance to Wiltshire, to liaise there with his man, Hobbes.

There were six of them in the house, and Sara had seen that two of them wore holsters strapped to their chests underneath their jackets. She had seen the guns in the holsters when they had reached up to push aside the narrow hatch into the roof space. They had begun the search without waiting for the Security Officer.

She was not asked whether she agreed, she was told that it would be better that the boys go to a neighbour's house, and she was told that would happen as soon as a woman police constable was available. It was quite systematic, the way in which they had begun to pull the house, her home, apart. When the woman police constable had arrived, let in by a detective because she was no longer mistress of 4, Lilac Gardens, she was asked which of her neighbours should have the boys. She pointed next door, not to little Vicky. She pointed to the plumber's house.

She could not protest when her boys were ushered out of her kitchen by the woman police constable. They were white-faced when they went, and she thought they were too much in shock to have cried. And the boys who were ten years old and eight years old held each other's hand, and the woman police constable had her cool uniformed arm round the younger, smaller, shoulder as she took them through the front door.

She felt the shame. She knew the awful, sick depths of despair.

Within a minute, two minutes, of the children being taken from her, the Security Officer had arrived. He had introduced himself and then clumped away up the stairs to assess the state of the search. Now he was back, now he crowded into her kitchen.

God, Frederick Bissett, you bastard . . . Her husband. Her choice.

Sara reached towards her kettle. She looked at the Security Officer. He nodded. She was permitted to make herself a pot of tea. While the kettle boiled, while she took her milk out of the fridge and a mug from the cupboard, he busied himself with the file that he had brought. She made her pot of tea. She poured a mug of tea for herself, and stirred in the milk. She didn't ask the Security Officer if he wanted tea, didn't offer it to him. Behind his glasses she saw the sharp bright blinking from small eyes. She saw that he wore old corduroy trousers, and that the buttons of his cardigan were tight on his gut. It seemed to matter to him not at all that she had not offered him a cup of tea.

Frederick Bissett, her husband, had brought this creature into her house.

She sipped at the tea. From upstairs she could hear the clatter of drawers being pulled out, and she could hear the whine of the vinyl being lifted from its adhesive, and she could hear the scream as the floorboards were prised up. It was her house, and it was being torn apart. Sometimes she heard laughter. It was just a job of work to them.

She sat with her mug of tea and her shame and her despair.

'Now then, Mrs Bissett, can we get on?'

His elbows were out over the kitchen table. He overwhelmed the chair on which Frederick usually sat. If he had come through the door at that moment, her husband, into her home that was being wrecked, she might have taken a kitchen knife to him.

'When did you first know, Mrs Bissett, that your husband was a traitor?'

But, he was her husband . . .

'Come on now, Mrs Bissett, I don't wish to be unpleasant, but my inescapable duty now is to minimize the damage your husband can do to this country. I need answers, and I need them quickly. It would be very nice, Mrs Bissett, if we could sit down in your lounge, make some small talk, and eventually ease round to the business of my visit. But that's not possible. I am in charge of security at AWE and from the point of view of the national interest, that is the most sensitive base in Britain. So I don't have time to mess around. Believe me, I get no pleasure seeing what is happening to you and your children and your home, but I will have answers, and fast.'

He was her husband, and she had chosen him, for better and for worse . . .

'How long has Dr Bissett been in the pay of the Iraqi Government?'

She had told him that he owed them loyalty. She looked into the slug's face across the table.

'Mrs Bissett, if you do not cooperate then it will come a great deal harder for you, and a great deal harder for your children.'

He had said that what he did was for her, and for their boys, whatever anybody would say . . .

'Where is he?'

'I don't have to answer questions, Mrs Bissett.'

There was her brittle and frightened laugh. 'Don't you know where he is?'

'That's other people's work, to find him. My work is to close down the damage he has done to AWE . . . You're an educated woman, Mrs Bissett, I don't need to spell out to you how intolerably unstable a world it could be if people like the Iraqis can *buy* their way into the nuclear club . . . What did he take with him?'

'I have nothing to say to you.'

'Did he take papers with him?'

'I have nothing to say.'

'It's the worst sort of traitor, Mrs Bissett, your greedy little rat.'

'Nothing.'

The eyes of the Security Officer were beaded at her. 'I suppose that he thought he had a grievance, was that it? There are 5000 people working at the Establishment. Life is not roses for all of them, for some of them, life is damned hard. They soldier on, they don't believe there is an alternative, they weather their problems. Your husband is unique in the history of the Establishment, not for having a sense of grievance, nor for finding life hard. He is unique in that, the greedy little rat, he took foreign gold, and he betrayed every trust that had been put in him.'

She shook her head, she had nothing to say.

She thought that her life was destroyed. She thought that her children would struggle into manhood before they could shrug off the disgrace brought to them by their father. She heard a floorboard above them, in the bathroom, splinter and break. She heard a cackle of laughter.

She scraped her chair round, she faced the door. She thought of the man at Debbie's party who had been called Colt. Her back was to the Security Officer. She thought of the eyes of Colt, blue and cold. She thought of the man who had taken her husband from her.

The voice behind her intoned, 'You are making life harder for yourself, Mrs Bissett.'

She turned and spat, 'What did *you* do for him? What did *any of you* do for him, ever? When he cried for help, which of you answered?'

She would not say another word. She would sit through the rest of the evening while her home around her reverberated with the search.

It was for her that he had done it, that is what her husband had said, for her and for their boys.

She would sit for the whole of the rest of the evening not hearing the questions of the Security Officer, not listening to the breaking of her home, and she would stare out of the window in the kitchen door into the blackness of the night.

He had taken a position in the shadow under the old kitchen-garden wall, very near to where he had crossed it with James so few hours ago. There was an owl calling in the oak beyond the wall, and before it had settled onto a perch close to the ivy drape of the main trunk, he had seen the white silent wing flap as it had swooped close to him. He had cowered from the bird, but now the bird with the haunting call was his company. Erlich who was hidden by the wall of a kitchen garden and the silver-white owl on the perch above him, watched the Manor House together. It was good to have the owl there. He thought that when the owl went, flew away in fear, then he would know that Colt had come back to the Manor House. There was a light on the stairs. He could see no other light in the house, and he had seen no movement. For comfort, and because his spirits were so low, he said to himself:

> All of the night was quite barred out except
> An owl's cry, a most melancholy cry
>
> Shaken out long and clear upon the hill,
> No merry note, nor cause of merriment,
> But one telling me plain what I escaped
> And others could not, that night, as in I went.

And salted was my food, and my repose
Salted and sobered, too, by the bird's voice
Speaking for all who lay under the stars,
Soldiers and poor, unable to rejoice.

And the verses were short comfort. His mind turned, was driven to those whom he had destroyed by that ambition to climb the success ladder. James Rutherford was dead and pretty Penny Rutherford was bereaved. And he would have lost the respect, so important to him, of Dan Ruane.

Snap out of it, Bill. Stop whining and get the job done.

It was, to Bissett, madness.

He thought they were all yobs in the pub, louts, all of them except for the old man who was little better than a tramp, and except for the girl. It was quite ridiculous to have gone into the pub.

Colt stood with his back to the open fire, and the old man with the rough torn trousers and the winter overcoat held together at the waist with baling twine was sitting. All the rest were standing, and the pub bar was alive with their talk, country accents, and their obscenities and their excitement and their laughter. It was the court of King Colt. He stood in front of the fire, a pint glass in his hand, the handle of the Ruger pistol bulging from his belt and the fat shape of the silencer tautening his trousers below his hip. Sheer madness.

The girl was pretty. He noticed that. He did not often think that a girl was pretty. But there was something extravagant and untamed about this girl, and the rich red of her hair was thrown back long on her shoulders, and he could see bloodstains with the dirt on her fingers, and there were down feathers hooked to the thread of her sweater, and her boots scattered mud on the flagstone floor. She had kissed Colt when they came in and held his body and squeezed herself against him. He watched the girl . . . The girl was moving among them, and each in turn, with the play-acting of reluctance, was adding to the rolled wad of banknotes in her bloodstained, dirt-stained hands.

Of course, they needed the money. The money was vital to them. The money was for their ferry tickets, but Colt had said in the car that their time was short. They should have taken the money in the car park, not switched off the engine, taken the money and gone, made for the coast. She had been round all of the men . . . how was it possible that these yobs and louts had so much money in their hip pockets? And the old man who looked like a tramp took £10 notes out of a tobacco tin and put them in the girl's hands. Bissett watched her as she went to the bar, and he heard the bell as the till sprung open, and the man behind the bar gave her more.

She passed the money to Colt. They were all applauding, all of the yobs and louts. This was their hero. In the land of the blind, the one-eyed . . . None of them looked at him as he stood beside the door. He had refused a drink. He coughed. He thought that by coughing he could hurry Colt.

Colt looked at him, and there was the raffish, reckless smile. Colt thrust the wad of money into his trouser pocket. He came to Bissett.

'It's your business, Colt, I know, but we've lost an awful amount of time.'

Colt said, 'Won't be much longer. I'm sorry, Dr Bissett, just a little bit longer . . .'

'We don't have any more time to waste.'

'A few minutes only.'

'What on earth for . . . ?'

A terrible sadness pinched Colt's face. 'To go home.'

The heavy oak plank door of the back bar whined open.

18

The village constable stepped into the back bar of the pub.

Because he lived in the next village along, he was not seen in this community as often as he would have liked. Once a fortnight, at least that, he committed himself to spending an evening, whatever the weather, just walking through the village. It was nearly half past nine when he came into the back bar of the pub . . . He had been away from his car for an hour now. His car was parked, and locked securely, beside the football pitch and the play swings. He was quite unaware of the increasingly anxious radio traffic beamed from Warminster towards that car. And, on the back seat of the car was his personal radio, gone down that morning, crossed wires or something broken in its innards, and ready to be taken to the Warminster stores in the morning for replacing.

Desmond nodded to old Vic, a good publican who kept a good house, a proper village pub. He thought old Vic didn't look well.

Being away from his car for an hour had been breaking pretty basic rules because he was out of radio contact all that time. He had called in on Mrs Williams to check that the new wire window-guards were ready to be erected on the shop next week, and he had knocked on the solicitor's door to remind him that his shotgun licence needed renewing, and as was his custom, he had stood for fifteen minutes against the trunk of one of the big beech trees at the end of the Manor House drive until he had felt a sense of shame at prying on the world of the bereaved. He had been on his way back to his car when he had passed the pub car park and seen that two vehicles there had their lights still on.

The noise died around him. The talk, the chat, fled the back bar. OK, OK, so the local Law had wandered in, but it wasn't the first time and it wouldn't be the last. There was no call for them to be reacting like he was Inland Revenue . . . and old Vic looked fit to drop behind the bar counter.

'Evening, Vic, a Cortina and a Nova out there, lights on. The time you close this place up, they'll be dead in the batteries . . .'

Old Vic had his mouth hanging open. The jukebox was playing.

'. . . Know whose they are?'

He turned.

He smiled affably. They were scattered around the back bar and they all stared at him. He knew them all . . . old Brennie, Poaching, convictions going back forty-eight years, last time done under the Armed Trespass Act of 1968 . . . Fran, nothing ever proved, should have been, and would be . . . Billy and Zap both for Receiving and Handling lead off a church roof in Frome . . . Zack, Larceny and Aggravated Assault, gone inside for it . . . Kev, once breathalysed for an eighteen-month ban, twice in court for Driving without Insurance, fined . . . Johnny, still on probation for Vandalism, smashing up the bus shelter . . . He knew them all, and he smiled warmly to each in turn. Normally, every other time that he came into the pub, his ritual visits, he took a bit of banter. Coexistence, wasn't it? He was local, they were local. Normally, there was banter that didn't go way over. Desmond didn't mind the banter . . . Not a bloody sound in the back bar of the pub to mix with the God-awful noise of the jukebox. Old Brennie looking at his flies, Fran at the smoke-stained ceiling, Billy and Zap in their beer and caught in mid-sentence, Zack in his fag packet, Kev rooted with the handful of coins he was going to feed into the jukebox, Johnny blushing because he was the youngest and the one who always ended with the rap. He saw the feathers on Fran's jersey. He didn't care, bigger game around than pheasants off the estate, and she'd only be making seventy-five pence a bird off old Vic, and that was plucked.

He knew them all. They were the flotsam of the village and

336

they were the strength of the village, they were the heart of it . . . He saw the young man.

He saw the young man, and then behind the young man he saw the stooping figure with the heavy-frame spectacles and the curled black hair receding and the sports jacket that was a half size too small. He saw the young man.

The young man gazed back into his face. Every last one of them other than the young man seemed to cower away from him, even Fran who was wild was back on her heels. Not the young man.

He saw the tan. He saw the short-cut fair hair. He saw the eyes that were bright with anger at him. There was no fear in that face. He had seen the photograph.

They had shown it him the first day that he had been assigned to the posting in the village up the lanes. It had been a good photograph.

He saw the metalled handle of the pistol bulging out from the young man's belt.

He looked into the face of Colt.

The jukebox died.

The silence suffocated the back bar of the pub.

He knew it was Colt.

Desmond had been to the Ashford Police Training College. At Ashford they taught a young constable how to look after himself if he were trying to break up a fight outside a pub at closing time, how to intervene in a domestic row, how to tackle a fleeing thief. He had been good on unarmed combat. Not firearms, though, they didn't teach firearms. Guns were for the zombie men who guarded the Northern Ireland politicians who had their gentry farms in the county, and for the squads that were detailed to protect the Royals when they came to open a new annexe in the hospitals of the local market towns. He knew sweet nothing about confronting an armed man. He was into the back bar, halfway across it towards the bar counter. Couldn't just turn, not on his bloody heel, like nothing had happened, and walk out. At the Police Training College they had said that if guns were involved then there were no heroes required, whistle up on the radio and get scarce till the professionals arrived. He had no radio. He could not turn back for the door. He saw the hand of Colt on his hip and close to the handle of the pistol.

No, he wasn't a hero . . . It was his instinct for survival.

He was a vertigo man on the clifftop.

He lunged.

If he had not tried to prise the truncheon from his slim hip pocket as he went forward . . .

If he had watched both hands and not the pistol handle in Colt's belt . . .

He was launched when he knew that the heel of Colt's hand . . . not the pistol, not the bullet . . . was the threat.

Razor fast, the heel of the hand, rising at his throat.

There was the ripple of shock through Colt's wrist and the length of his forearm. The heel of his hand took the centre point of the police constable's neck. And the policeman went down. He did not stagger or topple, he went down like a dropped sack of potatoes.

There was the gasp, in unison, all around Colt.

It was not what he had wanted to do. He had not wanted to shoot the American who was stumbling in confusion across the path of the fusillade aimed at a man who wrote vitriol from abroad against the Chairman of the Revolutionary Command Council. Nor had he wanted to break the bones and the faces of two army deserters coming in desperation to a campsite to steal a jeep. Nor had he wanted to throttle the life from the gross bum-boy who had tried to roll a backpacker sleeping rough alongside the road to Fremantle. He stood rock still, and his weight was forward on the balls of his feet as if the police constable still offered a threat to him.

They all stared at him.

He looked into the faces of old Vic and his Fran, and old Brennie, and of Billy and Zap, and Zack, and Kev and Johnny.

He saw their fear, and he saw the terror that collapsed the face of Dr Bissett who backed away to the far corner of the back bar.

The words came . . .

'Christ, you screwed it now.'

'No call for that.'

'What you done that for?'

'We live here, Colt . . .'

He stood his ground. He was the one who never panicked. He was the one who would never be taken. He stood straight and tall and the police constable was prone at his feet. He saw the shoulders of the police constable heave up as the spasm muscles tried to find breath for the lungs down the passage of the damaged windpipe. He was 200 yards from his home. Running, like he could run because he was fit, he could have gone to the front door of his home, the Manor House, in a half of a minute.

He heard the creak of the door behind him . . . Zap gone.

Had he come to the village for money? Had he come home to see his father the one last time, and to see his mother who was dead for the one last time? There was the movement to his right flank. Pathetic bastards. The dross of the village, gone nowhere, met nobody, seen nothing . . . Kev sneaking through the door.

Bissett whimpered, like a dog waiting to be kicked, he thought, in the far corner of the bar.

From Warminster they had little call to come to the village. The village was a backwater. The convoy of police cars, four of them, and nine policemen had been delayed in the yard at the back of the Warminster police station for more than thirty-five minutes while the numbers were made up, and while the Duty Inspector fumed at the failure of Communications to raise the local man. They came into the village. Their orders were to seal the one road running through the village at each end, and to maintain a discreet watch on the Manor House, and to do nothing if they saw the bastard because he had had a handgun at Heathrow and because the firearms unit was being helicoptered from London.

They saw the police car parked beside the goalposts of the football pitch. The lead car stopped. The Sergeant was still examining the car when there was the thud of the footfall of the two running youths.

'Heh, you, stop there. You seen Desmond?'

Kev stammered, 'Be in the pub . . . in there . . .'

Oh, was he, by Christ . . . The Sergeant grimaced . . . A bloody earful coming young Master Desmond's way, using his work transport to get out on the piss, with his wife saying over the telephone that he was gone on patrol. In the pub, by Christ.

'Thank you, son.'

Zap stuttered, 'Don't be going in there . . . he's a gonner in there . . . Get in there he'll bloody kill you, like him . . .'

'All right, young 'un, who's been killed?'

'Your copper,' Kev said.

'Who by?'

'By Colt,' Zap said.

The Sergeant, middle-aged and heavy, ran for his car and his radio.

He stood above the police constable.

Again the slither of feet on the flags of the back bar and the heave of the door of the back bar. Billy and Zack gone.

He wanted to go to his father. He wanted to sit beside the bed in which he had last seen his mother. He wanted to flop on the bed in the room that had been his. The room was the shrine to his youth. His father had told him that, after the raid by the Regional Crime Squad, after the room had been searched by armed detectives, his mother had gone into the room and restored it just as it had been when they had first sent him away to the boarding school at the coast near Seaton in Dorset . . .

'Please, Colt, hurry . . .'

Bissett coming across the back bar towards him.

'. . . We have to go.'

'Shut up.'

'To the ferry . . .'

340

'Shut up, damn you.'

'I was just trying to say . . .'

Bissett's hand pulling at his arm. Colt dragged the fingers off his sleeve.

'Don't touch me, don't ever cling to me.'

Old Brennie was on his feet, and nodding gravely towards old Vic behind the bar counter, the way he always nodded when he had supped up his beer and it was time to walk home, and he'd stop halfway down the road, like he always did, and empty his bladder into the privet hedge at the front of the comprehensive schoolteacher's garden.

There was the bleat of Bissett's voice in his ear. 'Why don't we go . . . ?'

Because going was for ever. Going now was never to return. All the months in Oz, all the weeks on the big laden tanker, all the long days of the training in Baghdad and the long nights in the Haifa Street Housing Project were bearable only because there was the certainty that one month, one week, one day and one night he would return to the village and the love of his father and his mother. When he went this time, he was gone for ever, he was never to return.

'OK, OK,' Colt said.

He saw that Fran squatted now on the floor and that she stared into the half-obscured face of the police constable. He would finish his drink. They would remember him in the back bar of the village pub for ever and a day because he had finished his drink and then he had gone out into the night, never to return. He lifted the glass. Three gulps and he would finish the glass, just as he would have finished the glass in three gulps if the police constable had not walked in to warn of Zack's car and Johnny's car with the lights left on in the car park.

Colt grinned. 'Cheers, Dr Bissett.'

The Duty Inspector at Warminster gave his order. The pub was to be surrounded. All possible light was to be thrown from headlights and flash lamps at the front and rear and sides of the pub.

341

The blue lamps on the roofs of the police vehicles were to be switched on.

Over the radio link, he told his Sergeant, 'Just keep them bottled up there, George. The heavy crowd's close to you now. Just keep them bottled, pray God they don't do a runner.'

There was the racing of vehicle wheels across the loose gravel of the car park, the crunch of the brakes, the beam of light cutting through the thin curtains of the back bar. And the white light was mixed with the flash of the blue, penetrating.

Colt choked on the last swill of his glass.

The light was over Bissett's face, white and blue, dappled like sunshine and cloud.

His glass slammed down onto the table. He drew the Ruger from his belt and the foresight caught at the waist of his trousers and there was the rip of the material . . . He would never be taken . . . and Bissett cowered away from him.

Fran said, 'You shouldn't have done it, you didn't need to hurt him . . .'

She had her hand, rough and callused and worn and the hand that he loved, cupped under the head of the policeman. She had turned his body over as if she believed that were the way to help him to breathe.

He felt the clammy damp of a prison cell.

One more, one more for the road, and when he looked to the bar counter he saw that old Vic had gone. He had the gun in his hand and he advanced across the bar towards Bissett, and Bissett shrank from him.

He saw it go. Erlich saw the first flutter beats of the ghost flight. It was gone without sound. There was a scudding moment of moonlight, enough to catch at the wide wingspan of the owl. There was the silence of the flight, then the sharp warning cry of the bird, and it was gone.

He heard the movement of the cars down at the other end of the road through the village, and when he stood to his full height

342

he could see, slashed by the winter trees, the lights that were white and blue.

He came from his hiding place. He walked across the Manor House's lawn and onto the drive to the road.

Ahead of him was the facade of the pub, bathed in warm lights. He walked forward. This was his war. Colt was his.

He saw the policemen crouched down behind the opened doors of their cars, and far away in the night he heard the clatter of a helicopter.

He walked to the Sergeant.

'My name's Erlich, Federal Bureau of Investigation.'

'Oh yes. Heard about you from young Desmond. Young lad just told me . . .'

'You have him in there? Colt?'

'Right now I do. If he doesn't do a runner . . .'

'You got firearms?'

'On the way.'

'What you got to stop him running?'

'There's nine of us.'

'Where is he?'

'Back bar, through the side entrance, it's where he was last.'

Erlich pulled the Smith and Wesson from the holster at his belt. The Sergeant didn't seem to want to argue. Erlich thought the Sergeant was bright, wasn't going to fuss that a Fed was on his territory, and armed. Round the corner of the building, into the glare of the light came the girl and a youth with a shaven head and tattoo work over his arms and they carried the slumped weight of a policeman. Erlich remembered him, and he remembered his cup of tea on the best china and homemade cakes. And he remembered the girl and the way that she had stared her hatred into the torch beam when she had come to take away her dead dog.

He walked forward and the headlights threw his shadow huge against the front stonework of the pub. He could hear, mingled with the wind, the closing thump of the helicopter's rotors.

Colt was his.

* * *

The military policeman locked the door behind him.

The Station Officer carried the tray into his office.

The Swede was crouched on the low camp bed that had been made up for him, and there was a second bed against the far wall from the door. The Station Officer put the tray down on his desk. He took out from his pocket, where it was awkward, his PPK pistol and laid it on the desk alongside the tray of sandwiches with the bottle of champagne.

'Will you surrender me?'

'Give you up? Good God, no.'

'Did Bissett get onto the flight?'

'He was blocked.'

'Thank God.'

'It's what you risked your life for . . . The champagne comes with warm wishes from your friends in Tel Aviv.'

The Swede started to eat, and when he drank he coughed and then giggled his appreciation.

He watched.

With fast and controlled movements, Colt had the pistol cleared and the magazine out and there was the dead metal rattle of the mechanism firing, and then Colt had checked each round before feeding it into the stick magazine.

Bissett watched.

They were going to break out. He did not have to be told. They were going to run at the cordon of white and blue light, they were going to sprint for the dark shadow line beyond the brilliance of the perimeter that was strung around the pub. He heard, muffled by the thickness of the old stone walls of the building, a distant pulse of growing sound.

All the time he was watching the sharp and more confident hand movements of Colt.

He thought of his father and mother, of the small terraced home in the small streets of Leeds. He thought of their letters, abandoned in his suitcase at the airport. They would not have understood. He had told them so little from the time that he had first taken his appointment at the Establishment. His father and his mother were against the Bomb, they all were in that street. He had won for them no pride for working as a government scientist. He might as well have been a deputy manager at an amusement arcade, or running a local Radio Rentals . . . Yes, he thought they would despise him now, his mother and his father. He would never go home to greet his father on the day that his mother died. They would not have understood. It was not his fault . . . He had outgrown them. They were no longer a part of his life . . .

He watched.

Colt had finished with the pistol, and now he crouched and undid the knots at both his trainer shoes, and he had retired the laces.

It was not possible that Colt could not hear the coming thunder sound breaking through the windows of the back bar, permeating the stone walls.

'It'll be all right, Colt . . .'

'Why not?'

'We're going together?'

'Of course.'

'Do you think we can do it?'

'No problem.'

There was sick fear in Bissett's stomach. They would run at the lights. He would let Colt hold him by the wrist and he would cling to Colt's sleeve, and they would run.

'What's that noise?'

Colt said, like it didn't matter, 'I'm just going upstairs. I want a better view of the ground. You shouldn't worry, Dr Bissett. It's a helicopter, they'll be bringing in their heavy mob, I expect . . . nothing to worry on, Dr Bissett.'

'I'm sorry about your mother, Colt, really sorry.'

'I'll be a minute, then it's running time.'

He heard the shuffle ripple of Colt's feet, and he was gone onto the narrow and twisted staircase that led out from behind the bar counter.

And the silence in Bissett's ears was broken by the drumbeat of the helicopter banking on its flight path over the village.

He heard the helicopter put down.

Erlich thought it sounded, from its power, a big transporter. They would be getting their act together at last. Armed men, and the big guys from London. He thought that they would not have room in their plan for Bill Erlich, number three from Rome, wanted for questioning in connection with the death of James Rutherford. He was in the porchway to the back bar. He had the Smith and Wesson in his hand. Held beside his ear.

The helicopter had cut its rotors.

He strained to hear the sound of voices, Colt's voice. He listened for the sound of movement.

Bill Erlich readied himself for the charge through the closed heavy door.

He was the law-enforcement man. He was small-town America's hero. He was the Mid-West glamour kid. He was the Special Agent, the hero, the good kid, and he had come to get the scum face, the dirtbag, who had dared to stand against Old fucking Uncle fucking Sam. Ride on, Bill Erlich, Special Agent, hero, good kid. He was the guy who rode off into the setting sun, he was the joker that they loved to patronize in their rocking chairs on the verandah behind the white picket fencing. Heh, Bill, how's it going ... ? Going OK, don't you know. Going good, just have to get into this goddam museum pile, move around a bit, find the mother. Got to shoot, kill, bury the mother. Got to line up then for the thanks of the great fat smug ranks of the bastards, so that they can say 'thank you', and light up the barbecue, and unpack the camper trailer, and turn their backs on what their taxes pay for. And who cared ... ? Did any bastard care on the east side, getting their cocktails in before the Beltway home? Any bastard on the west coast, just back from lunch, care? Did they hell ... He was FBI, he was armed, he was going to shoot a guy who had killed an American

346

government servant. It was what a good government and a grateful people paid Bill Erlich to do, to get on with. Did they care? Did they, hell . . .

He was breathing hard, like he had been taught to, like through the heavy stained door to the back bar was Condition Black . . . Holy God . . .

The wind and the first shower of rain funnelled up the road through the village, caught at the legs and backs of those who watched.

The group grew. The solicitor stood with his eldest son under a tilted golf club umbrella. The bank manager was there, with his pyjama trouser bottoms peeping from underneath the waterproof leggings. The Home Farm tenant was there, rubicund and overweight and chewing a cube of cheese and with his dog, Rocco's sire, at his heel. Old Vic and his wife were there, and he had a quarter bottle of rum in his hip pocket.

In the centre of the road, as far forward as they were allowed to stand, were Billy and Zap, Kev, Zack, Charlie, and Johnny with his arm hard round Fran's shoulder.

In their clusters they waited.

The solicitor said that if ever there was a boy born to be hanged it was Colin Tuck, God rest his mother, and his son who was Colt's exact contemporary, who had secretly admired him and who had yearned for Fran for years, said nothing. The District Nurse, who had just joined them, said that it was the blessing of God that Louise Tuck had not lived to witness this final humiliation. And she thought that when it was over she would go to the Manor House and break the news to him, and make him one last pot of tea. The bank manager said that he had heard at Rotary that Colt was wanted for terrorism now and that prison would be too good for him. The Home Farm tenant said that he had always known the kid to be a wrong 'un, stood out a mile since he had got himself involved with those Animal Liberation bastards. Old Vic said he'd miss him, didn't mind who knew it, and his wife said that she had never known anything but politeness from Colt. Zack said, and he laughed but sure as hell it wasn't funny to him, that he'd be kissing goodbye, and the rest of them, to what they had raised in the pub. Kev said, bright-eyed in excitement, that Colt had the gun, and that Colt would take them with him. Fran cried and buried her cheek in Johnny's chest.

All of them, waiting for the action, waiting for it to end, stood among the puddles and the tractor mud. They watched what Colt brought to their village, his village.

In a blur of movement the shrouded figures ran to take their positions round the building and the outhouses and garages at the back. Heavy movements because they were weighed down with their bulletproof vests and ammunition pouches and radios and the battery-driven power lamps and the image intensifiers on the barrels of their rifles.

Hobbes tried to scrape the helicopter sound from his ears. He hadn't got a bloody coat, and he had walked across the football pitch from the helicopter and already his London shoes squelched. He was told that an American, an FBI agent, had been allowed forward because he was the only one on site with a handgun.

'Where forward, Sergeant? The back door?' In a sickening instant Hobbes could see how this nightmare would end.

'Commander,' he yelled.

'Right beside you, Mr Hobbes,' said a calm voice. 'We've seen him, and we know where he is. Do you want him out of there?'

'What's he doing, for Christ's sake?'

'He looks as though he's counting to a hundred before he goes through the back door.'

'Well . . . My God Almighty would certainly say that he's earned the privilege, going in first. Your cat's paw, eh, Commander? Just don't have him shot by one of ours. Or the boffin, for heaven's sake. Got that?'

'Yes, Mr Hobbes.'

*   *   *

He thought that Colt should have been back.

All the time he watched the staircase. It must have been three, four minutes since he had last heard Colt's step from the ceiling above the back bar.

He did what Colt had done. He untied the laces of his shoes and he retied them tight, strained the cord and then tied a double knot. They would be running across fields, couldn't have his shoes sucked off in the mud, not if he were running and needing to keep up with Colt.

It was the third time that he had undone his laces and retied them, reknotted them.

They should have been, if they had taken off from the airport when he had been told they would take off, somewhere over the Eastern Mediterranean, somewhere over Greece, or over Cyprus. They should have been beyond recall, sharing a drink and a meal with Colt in the safety of the aeroplane. He was tired, so tired . . . The dragging on of the day that had started with breakfast in Lilac Gardens, and with the drive up Mount Pleasant and Mulfords Hill, and with the check at the Falcon Gate, and with the examination of his I/D at the H3 barrier. So tired . . . He thought of the hours he had spent in front of his screen, working, concentrating. So tired . . . and he heard again Basil's muttered and embarrassed praise of his paper, and the cheerfulness of Boll's departure. So tired . . . and there was a meeting in the morning of Senior Principal Scientific Officers and Senior Principal Engineering Officers at which he was expected. It was all madness, and sharp through the exhaustion of his mind was the shouting of his name in the airport, the clatter of gunfire, the collapse of a man in pursuit.

So tired, and so scared by the running away. But they had still the chance of the ferry.

He watched the staircase behind the bar counter. He looked for the reckless and vivid smile of Colt.

He was ready, ready to run with Colt.

*   *   *

'Mrs Bissett, until we can resolve our differences, you won't get to bed, I won't move out of your house, and you don't get your children back.'

'I have nothing to say.'

The Security Officer settled again on the kitchen chair. The house was quiet. There were only two policemen left in the house with them, and they were sprawled out in the sitting room. The search was over. She knew they had found nothing, because as the ripping and tearing went on she had heard the bad temper replace their earlier laughter and chat. She had not heard them attempt to repair what they had broken.

She stared out through the window. She had not turned when the telephone had rung, nor when the Security Officer had been called out of the kitchen, nor when he had come back and the chair had groaned under his weight.

'Mrs Bissett, please listen to me very carefully. Your husband was being escorted from the country by a man wanted for murder in Athens, London and Australia. He was intercepted. This young man . . .'

She muttered the name, the name was Colt.

'. . . is armed. He is dangerous and unstable. We have to fear for your husband's safety. They are together at the moment in a public house in Wiltshire. They are ringed by armed police. There is a distinct possibility that the young man will reject all sensible courses of action, that he will try to break out. He is armed, so he may open fire on police officers, and the armed officers may be forced to return fire . . .'

She shuddered.

'. . . and then Frederick would be in the gravest danger. It is a small thing to ask of you, but it could save his life.'

She thought of him going out into the dusk, going through her front door, stumbling after Colt, the humiliation of her rejection.

'. . . We can put you in direct contact with the police there . . .'

'No.'

'So that you speak to Frederick, and urge him to surrender . . .'

'No.'

'We want him out of there, Mrs Bissett, away from the potential crossfire.'

'I said, no.'

She stared at the window set in the kitchen door, at the raindrops dancing on it like a curtain in the wind.

The Security Officer said, 'With a bitch like you for a wife, it's no wonder the poor devil wanted out.'

His hand was on the door latch.

He had the Smith and Wesson tight in his hand, barrel against his ear.

Past Flight or Fight, way beyond that.

Erlich would fight . . .

As he raised the latch he heard the first shimmer of the grating of the metal pieces.

No more caution.

His hip barged into the unfastened door.

The light spilled into his face, and he was moving.

Erlich came into the back bar, and he cannoned off a table, glasses flying, smashing, and he tripped on a chair, and he stumbled, and all the time he was in motion. It was Condition Black. He saw the table peel away towards the fireplace, and the chair career towards the bar counter. He saw the line of upended bottles with optics on their necks, the mounted fox's head with its teeth bared, and the half-finished glasses on the other tables and the ashtrays full. All the time moving until he reached the solid protection of the jukebox. He was crouched down. He was at Isosceles stance, and he pivoted his upper body behind the aiming position of his revolver in Turret One.

He saw the man from the airport on his knees, dark curly hair, his eyeline caught him, thick-rimmed heavy spectacles, dismissed him. He quartered the back bar . . . No sign of Colt . . . Shit . . . The adrenaline draining from him. All the push, drive, impetus of belting his way into the back bar, safety off, index finger inside the trigger guard, and he did not find Colt.

351

He yelled, 'Where is Colt?'

The man seemed frozen in the position of tying his shoe-laces.

He was met by the empty, terrified stare of the man, and the silence trimmed his shout.

He gazed down at the man over the V-sight and foresight of the revolver, and he could see that there was the increasing shake of his locked fists. Keyed up to go in, and he had lost the brilliance of surprise and his nerves caught at him and the barrel cavorted in the grip of his hands.

'Where the fuck is he?'

He saw the man's head turn. He saw the man look back towards the counter, and beyond the counter was the gape of the open door that led to the staircase and darkness. He could see the first steps of the staircase. The man's head swung back, as if he knew he had been caught out.

Erlich eased himself up from behind the cover of the juke-box. He was panting . . . One thing to open the door and charge into the back bar, another thing to go walkabout up a staircase into darkness . . . He rocked again on his feet. His decision. Quantico teaching said that an agent should never, alone, follow a man up a staircase, and never, ever, into an unlit staircase.

He was on the line, he was alone.

'Good God,' Basil Curtis was bemused. 'You quite astonish me.'

The Security Officer invited himself into the bed-sitting room. There was a strong smell of cat. He looked around him. More books than he had ever seen in such a room, three walls of them, from floor to ceiling and piles of them elsewhere. And a cat litter-tray in one corner. Quite extraordinary to the Security Officer that Curtis, famously the best brain at AWE, paid more, certainly, than anyone else there, should choose to live in a single man's quarters in the Boundary Hall accommodation.

'He was going to Iraq, it's cut and dried.'

He saw that Curtis had covered, with the newspaper he had been reading in bed, a half-written letter on his desk. The cat emerged from the wardrobe and observed the Security Officer with distaste. Curtis stood in his striped flannel pyjamas, holding a mug of cocoa.

'I wouldn't have believed it . . . but, of course, I didn't know him well.'

He could see a pink hot-water bottle peeping from under the back-turned bedclothes.

The Security Officer said, 'I am beginning to understand why Bissett ran.'

'I think that we should allow events to run their course, away from view. I don't want anything public, Mr Barker. I only want a message sent in private to that regime of blood. My advice, go home, get a solid night's sleep.'

'Very good, Prime Minister.'

'Good night, Mr Barker.'

Too old and too tired to wrestle through the night with the new world of the Rutherfords and the Erlichs, the Colts and the Frederick Bissetts. He would have one more word with Hobbes at the Pig and Whistle to let him know that both he and the Prime Minister required a total blanket over the outcome, tell him to push the goggling bystanders back another 200 yards, confiscate any cameras etc. etc. As to the outcome, it scarcely troubled him to consider it. There was not a lot he could do to influence the outcome now. These sieges had a habit of going on for half a day, minimum. Hobbes could, by God, earn a spur here after his craven performance at Century. Yes, he would go to bed and be ready to pick up the pieces in the morning. With Tuck's boy and the lunatic Erlich in the frame, there would, by God, be pieces.

Later, he would leave through the basement tunnel, he would walk out via the doors of the Cabinet Office. He would wait on the wide Whitehall pavement for a cruising taxi. And he would wonder if Penny Rutherford slept, whether she had taken the pill that the Curzon Street doctor would have left her. And he would wonder – if Erlich got the better of Tuck's boy – if he could persuade Ruane to send him away, right away, before Rutherford's funeral.

He could walk out through the back door and put his gun back in his holster, and he could tell the guys from the Special Weapons unit that there was no way Bill Erlich was going to do the right thing by his friend if it meant climbing a staircase into darkness.

His decision.

He could shift his ass up the stairs and search till he found the bastard, and hit down each door, and belt open each cupboard, and kick over each bed, until he found the mother.

He wasn't as good as when he had come in. It was going away from him, ebbing with each of the slow seconds as the time slipped by him. His eyes had never left the staircase. All the time he had expected to see the barrel that was the integral silencer and the fast-coming bulky shape of Colt behind it.

He started to move. The man was in front of him.

There was the raised hatch that cut off the barman's place from his customers. His route would be through the hatch and behind the counter and onto the bottom step of the staircase.

All the time watching the opening to the staircase . . .

He heard the crash of the breaking glass.

Erlich half swivelled.

The man had stood, and he had a glass in his hand with the drinking rim broken, and the man stood across Erlich's path and the broken glass was his weapon.

'Put that down.'

'You're not going up.'

'Get out of my way.'

'Not going up.'

The sound of their voices . . . Erlich thought Colt would be at the top of the staircase. It was goddam crazy. Why not send him a message Western Union, Federal Express . . .

354

'You'd better move, buddy, or you're going to get yourself hurt.'

The man held his ground. Erlich hardly saw the broken drinking end of the glass. Eyes on the staircase. The staircase was Colt. Colt was danger. Danger was not a nutcake with a broken glass, like he was high on smack or hash. Danger was Colt, sober and cold. He took a pace forward.

He saw, from the corner of his eye, that the glass was aimed at his face.

Erlich tried to sound calm. 'Stand back.'

The glass was held at arm's stretch. The broken end was a foot from his face.

'He's my friend.'

'I don't even know who you are.'

'I am Colt's friend.'

He saw the veins in the man's throat, and he saw the tremble in the wrist that held the glass. This was the man he had seen at the airport. Then he had been a craven passenger of Colt's. He was a man with no pedigree of violence, who just once and only once had wound himself to the point of no return.

'He's a psychopath, your friend. A killer, do you understand that?'

The glass was in front of Erlich's face.

'He gave me a chance, no one else did.'

'You're not my quarrel, buddy, so put that thing down and if you know what's good for you, you'll walk right through the back door with your hands in the air.'

Erlich went forward. The glass rose towards his eyes.

'No one else,' the man screamed.

He felt the judder of pain at his cheek and his chin.

Erlich fired.

He saw the man pitch away from him. He could not remember the name that Rutherford had shouted at the airport. He heard nothing. He saw the glass fall and break apart. He heard nothing . . . He saw the blood dribble on the floor and the blood splattered on the wall and over a glass case with a pair of stuffed pheasants.

*   *   *

The rain fell hard about him. It ran on his face. The rain and the wind that drove it and the cloud mist were his freedom.

It was his joy when he had felt the sting of the rain as he had first pushed up the skylight window. The happiness had been with him all along the roof gulley, and after he had dropped down beside the old water barrel. He had rejoiced to be free as he had crawled flat on his stomach along the rows of cabbages and between the stems of the laurel bushes that made the overgrown edge between the outbuildings and the open field.

In the moment that he reached the tree line of the Top Spinney he heard the clatter of two shots.

He did not pause.

His freedom was the night around him.

EPILOGUE

It was only when all the other passengers had gone and he was left with the cabin crew that the three men came on board. They shook his hand.

It was the day before Christmas. There was a carol playing over the loudspeakers in Arrivals, and he saw through the tinted glass that there was a sleet storm blowing in from the west and towards London.

He had no luggage. He wore the same clothes in which he had fled into the haven of the Embassy, and he carried only an overcoat that the Station Officer had said he would certainly need even if he was only in London for ten minutes. It was too small for him but it would be a keepsake. They took him to a VIP lounge, and they poured him a drink.

The man called Percy Martins was saying, '. . . No morality at all, I don't think he understood the meaning of right or wrong, but most certainly blessed by a totally destructive charm – completely undermined Bissett, I gather. The problem was his father, a war hero, a maverick soldier operating behind enemy lines. Colt tried to emulate him, but never succeeded.

'We're not entirely sorry that we missed him, not at my level anyway. They had dogs out at first light, but there was nothing for them to follow, the rain did for the scent. Frankly, when he does turn up again it's going to be headaches all round, but his trail's cold right now.

'It's what took so long to negotiate your release. Didn't catch on straight away because it cost us a week or so to break the code they were using. Baghdad didn't believe Colt was not captured. Wanted him back in exchange for you. Although the

London end never had the nerve to propose it. They even sent a chap disguised as a florist to quiz the locals. We put *him* in the bag, I'm happy to say. Seems that the man running Colt was the Colonel whose voice you recorded at Tuwaithah, same Colonel who kicked up a fuss on the Embassy doorstep. The voices match exactly. He wasn't going to let you go without that he got his Colt in return, but wiser heads prevailed – I have some good friends in quite high places – and anyway the ubiquitous Colonel has fallen from grace. No longer on the letterhead.

'Anyway, you're safely out and we've a trade mission going in next week, so all's well that ends well. Cheers.'

The Swede saw the youngest of the three men check his watch, and nod. The Swede drained his glass. Martins clasped him by the hand.

Two of them took him on, and Martins stayed in the lounge.

He strode, long stepping paces, between the two men. He was happy to walk. For the last five weeks he had been allowed only one daily circuit of the Embassy compound, after dark always and with the military policeman tracking him. He was glad to start to work off the stiffness in his knees.

They moved across the concourse, threading their way between queues of holidaymakers.

Hobbes said, 'It's all luck in this business, or lack of it. It was Bissett's luck that he found himself up against an FBI agent called Erlich. Erlich's mission in life was to hunt down this Colt.

'Wild horses weren't going to stop him. He shot at Colt in a terminal as crowded as this one is, and killed a young man in my department. He practically tore the pub apart looking for Colt when he had finished off Bissett. I saw Erlich off when he went, back to his base in Rome. Couldn't help feeling sorry for him. Be a waste if he quit. He's a very thorough policeman. He'd found a cigar butt of Colt's in Athens at the scene of crime where Colt shot the joker from the Agency, and he went through Colt's home in Wiltshire like a terrier till he found a matching butt in a dustbin. DNA test proved it from the saliva, good enough for a court of law. Here or in the States. And it will come to that, in my view. It may be convenient in some quarters that Colt disappeared, but with his Colonel gone in Baghdad he has no bolt-hole. He'll turn up sooner or later and Erlich will be waiting for him. I'll be waiting for him and every policeman in Britain too, but the conviction will be down to Erlich.'

Only one of them went with the Swede through the side doors that bypassed the emigration formalities.

They went past the armed police, and the dogs, and the El A1 security teams.

They were allocated seats immediately behind the forward place that was already occupied by the sky marshal.

Tork said, 'You'll be wanting to know about Bissett. It's only what I heard today from "Sniper" Martins – miserable bastard, isn't he? – between the time my flight came in and you landed. The conclusion seems to be that Bissett was just another unhappy little man who was offered the moon and was daft enough to reach for it. He was actually prepared to go and work for the Iraqis because his bank manager was nagging him, and his supervisor was bullying him. It was as pathetic as that. The very last thing he did in his whole life was probably the only thing that he did that deserved admiration. Poor old Bissett, standing up for the man he thought was his friend, and getting himself shot for it. Saved us a deal of bother. We wouldn't have *wanted* to prosecute, and there wasn't much evidence that could have been brought against him if we had.

'The general opinion at Atomic Weapons is that Bissett really had very little to offer the Iraqis. It was all a bit of a confidence trick. You know what it is, the people who do the recruiting always talk up their client. I think that when they found out what they'd got, there would have been some pretty unhappy gentlemen at Tuwaithah.

'The story put out was that he had got himself involved with a lunatic fringe outfit called the Animal Liberation Front and that rather than face the shame of exposure he took his own life.

'We were quite good about it to his family. We cooked up some story about a promotion having just been agreed, so his

359

widow gets a better pension, and more importantly she doesn't holler her mouth off. She's left the district already and the house is up for sale.

'It's the old story, it never happened. There was no Colt, there was no Bill Erlich, there was no Frederick Bissett . . .'

The aircraft cabin was filling.

There was the frantic stampede of passengers along the aisle of the aircraft. For the life of him Tork could not understand why it was that grown men and women, all with their own seats, needed to behave as if there were one last place at the back of a Moscow bread queue. Noise all around them, shouting dinning in their ears.

Tork said, 'You'll be working at Dimona, I suppose. We're just a little way back from the seafront in Tel Aviv. Do stay in touch, this is my card . . .

'The sadness of it is that what you do, I do, may only *delay* the work at Tuwaithah and Mount Karochooq. It's a dangerous world, and I doubt that we have made it less dangerous for more than a few months. What my masters and your masters will do with those few months, God knows. My guess is that my masters will wake up to the threat when it's too late, to the terrifying reality of a nuclear capability in Iraq. But then, that's the sort of people they are . . .'

The engines were on, gathering power.

The Swede slept.

THE OUTSIDERS

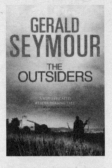

'Once again demonstrating his ability to probe the moral murki-
ness of the spy trade and create an absorbingly diverse ensemble,
Seymour crafts a sophisticated, reader-teasing tale.'
The Sunday Times

MI5 officer Winnie Monks has never forgotten the death of a young
agent on her team at the hands of a former Russian Army Major-
turned-gangster. Ten years later, she hears the Major is travelling to a
Spanish villa and she asks permission to send in a surveillance unit.

There is an empty property next door, perfect to spy from –
and as a base for Winnie's darker, less official plans.

But this villa isn't deserted: the owners have invited a young
British couple to 'house sit' while they are away.

Jonno and Posie think they are embarking on a carefree holiday in the sun.
But, when the Secret Service arrives in paradise, *everything* changes.

'Those [Seymour] sends off into dangerous territory are, in fact,
his readers. With each book, we enter a dangerous universe, and
are totally involved with utterly plausible characters, faced with
moral choices that are rarely straightforward.'
Independent

HODDER

A DENIABLE DEATH

AN EPIC NOVEL OF HIGH COURAGE AND LOW CUNNING, OF LIFE AND DEATH IN THE MORAL MAZE OF THE POST-9/11 WORLD.

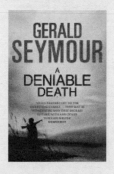

'Gerald Seymour is the grand-master of the contemporary thriller and A DENIABLE DEATH is his greatest work yet. Gripping, revealing and meticulously researched, this is a page-turning masterpiece that will literally leave you breathless.'
Major Chris Hunter, bestselling author of *Extreme Risk*

YOU WATCH. YOU WAIT. THE HOURS SLIDE SLOWLY PAST.

A WHOLE DAY. THEN TWO.

YOU LIE UNDER A MERCILESS SUN IN A MOSQUITO-INFESTED MARSH.

YOU CAN'T MOVE, LEAVE, OR RELAX.

YOUR MUSCLES ACHE FROM CLENCHING TIGHT FOR SO LONG.

IF YOU ARE DISCOVERED, YOU WILL BE TORTURED THEN KILLED.

AND HER MAJESTY'S GOVERNMENT WILL DENY ALL KNOWLEDGE OF YOU.

'Great storytelling . . . you just have to read this novel . . . absolutely gripping'
Eurocrime

HODDER

THE DEALER AND THE DEAD

THE ARMS DEALER BETRAYED THEM.
THE SURVIVORS WANT REVENGE.

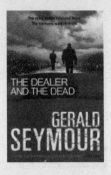

'*The Dealer and the Dead* is Seymour firing on all cylinders
and his rivals need, once again, to look to their laurels'
Independent

In a moonlit field near the Serbian border, Croatian villagers waited for an arms shipment that would never come. They
will never forget that night, or the slaughter that followed.

Eighteen years later, a body is discovered in a field, and with it the identity of
the arms dealer who betrayed them. Now the villagers can plot their revenge.

For Harvey Gillott, it was all a long time ago. But now the
hand of the past is reaching out across Europe, to Harvey's house in leafy England. And it's holding a gun . . .

'The final scenes are brilliantly orchestrated . . . Without doubt, *The Dealer
and the Dead* is one of the finest thrillers to be published so far this year'
Yorkshire Evening Post

HODDER

THE COLLABORATOR

CORRUPTION. BETRAYAL. REVENGE.

'A dense, intensely satisfying thriller from one of the modern
masters of the craft, Seymour's latest novel will remind the world
just how phenomenally accomplished a thriller writer he is.'
Daily Mail

Eddie Deacon has a new girlfriend. She's beautiful, clever and Italian.

And then she disappears.

What Eddie doesn't know is that Immacolata Borelli is the daughter of a
merciless Naples gangster. She can no longer live with her conscience and
has decided to collaborate with the police to bring down her own family.

But the Borellis will not lose their empire without a fight. They will
use or destroy anything and anyone to prevent her from talking.

Including Eddie.

'Tight writing and meticulous research . . . Seymour paints the
streets of Naples and their dark denizens with an artist's brush
that lingers equally on the grime, the glitter and the blood'
The Times

HODDER

In the best books, the ending often comes as a shock.
Not just because of that one last twist in the tale,
but because you have been so absorbed in their world,
that coming back to the harsh light of reality is a jolt.

If that describes you now, then perhaps you should track down
some new leads, and find new suspense in other worlds.

Join us at www.hodder.co.uk, or follow us on
Twitter @hodderbooks, and you can tap in to a
community of fellow thrill-seekers.

Whether you want to find out more about this book,
or a particular author, watch trailers and interviews, have
the chance to win early limited editions, or simply browse
our expert readers' selection of the very best books,
we think you'll find what you're looking for.

And if you don't, that's the place to tell us what's missing.

We love what we do, and we'd love you to be part of it.

www.hodder.co.uk